..., near..
...arming ...mmer. has won the RT Reviewers'
Choice Best ...ward, is a Top Pick author and has been
nominated for numerous awards. Now living her dream, she
resides with her patient husband, one amazing daughter (the
other remarkable daughter is off chasing her own dreams)
and two spoiled cats. She'd love to hear from you via her
website, www.jenniferfaye.com.

Michelle Douglas has been writing for Mills & Boon since
2007 and believes she has the best job in the world. She lives
in a leafy suburb of Newcastle, on Australia's east coast,
with her own romantic hero, a house full of dust and books,
and an eclectic collection of '60s and '70s vinyl. She loves
to hear from readers and can be contacted via her website:
www.michelle-douglas.com.

Susan Meier is the author of over fifty books for Mills & Boon. *The Tycoon's Secret Daughter* was a RITA® Award finalist and *Nanny for the Millionaire's Twins* won the Book Buyers' Best award and was a finalist in the National Readers' Choice awards. She is married and has three children. One of eleven children herself, she loves to write about the complexity of families and totally believes in the power of love.

Award-winning author **Jennifer Faye** pens fun, heart-warming romances. Jennifer has won the RT Reviewers' Choice Best Book Award, the CataRomance Reviewers' Choice Award, been a finalist for the prestigious RITA® Award, and has been nominated for numerous other awards. She lives with her very own hero, two spoilt cats and three dogs. When she's not writing Jennifer enjoys reading, baking and taking long walks. Jennifer loves to hear from readers—you can reach her via her website: www.jenniferfaye.com

Michelle Douglas has been writing for Mills & Boon since 2007, and believes she has the best job in the world. She lives in a leafy suburb of Newcastle, Australia, with her own romantic hero and a house full of dust and books. When she's not writing Michelle loves to read, cook and garden. You can contact her via her website: www.michelle-douglas.com

First Published in Great Britain 2018
by Mills & Boon, an imprint of HarperCollins*Publishers*
1 London Bridge Street, London, SE1 9GF

UNDER THE TUSCAN SUN... © 2018 Harlequin Books S. A.

A Bride For The Italian Boss © 2015 Harlequin Books S.A.
Return Of The Italian Tycoon © 2015 Harlequin Books S.A.
Reunited By A Baby Secret © 2015 Harlequin Books S.A.

Special thanks and acknowledgement are given to Susan Meier, Jennifer Faye and Michelle Douglas for their contributions to *The Vineyards of Calanetti* series

ISBN: 978-0-263-26702-0

05-0318

Under the Tuscan Sun...

SUSAN MEIER

JENNIFER FAYE

MICHELLE DOUGLAS

MILLS & BOON

A BRIDE FOR THE
ITALIAN BOSS

SUSAN MEIER

I want to thank the lovely editors at Mills & Boon
for creating such a great continuity!

Everyone involved LOVED this idea. Thank you!

CHAPTER ONE

ITALY HAD TO BE the most beautiful place in the world.

Daniella Tate glanced around in awe at the cobblestone streets and blue skies of Florence. She'd taken a train here, but now had to board a bus for the village of Monte Calanetti.

After purchasing her ticket, she strolled to a wooden bench. But as she sat, she noticed a woman a few rows over, with white-blond hair and a slim build. The woman stared out into space; the faraway look in her eyes triggered Daniella's empathy. Having grown up a foster child, she knew what it felt like to be alone, sometimes scared, usually confused. And she saw all three of those emotions in the woman's pretty blue eyes.

An announcement for boarding the next bus came over the public address system. An older woman sitting beside the blonde rose and slid her fingers around the bag sitting at her feet. The pretty blonde rose, too.

"Excuse me. That's my bag."

The older woman spoke in angry, rapid-fire Italian and the blonde, speaking American English, said, "I'm sorry. I don't understand a word of what you're saying."

But the older woman clutched the bag to her and very clearly told the American that it was her carry-on.

Daniella bounced from her seat and scurried over. She faced the American. "I speak Italian, perhaps I can help?"

Then she turned to the older woman. In flawless Italian, she asked if she was sure the black bag was hers, because there was a similar bag on the floor on the other side.

The older woman flushed with embarrassment. She apologetically gave the bag to the American, grabbed her carry-on and scampered off to catch her bus.

The pretty blonde sighed with relief and turned her blue eyes to Daniella. "Thank you."

"No problem. When you responded in English it wasn't a great leap to assume you didn't speak the language."

The woman's eyes clouded. "I don't."

"Do you have a friend coming to meet you?"

"No."

Dani winced. "Then I hope you have a good English-to-Italian dictionary."

The American pointed to a small listening device. "I've downloaded the 'best' language system." She smiled slightly. "It promises I'll be fluent in five weeks."

Dani laughed. "It could be a long five weeks." She smiled and offered her hand. "I'm Daniella, by the way."

The pretty American hesitated, but finally shook Daniella's hand and said, "Louisa."

"It's my first trip to Italy. I've been teaching English in Rome, but my foster mother was from Tuscany. I'm going to use this final month of my trip to find her home."

Louisa tilted her head. "Your foster mother?"

Dani winced. "Sorry. I'm oversharing."

Louisa smiled.

"It's just that I'm so excited to be here. I've always wanted to visit Italy." She didn't mention that her long-time boyfriend had proposed the day before she left for her teaching post in Rome. That truly would be oversharing, but also she hadn't known what to make of Paul's request to marry him. Had he proposed before her trip to tie her to him? Or had they hit the place in their relationship where marriage really was the next step? Were they ready? Was marriage right for them?

Too many questions came with his offer of marriage. So she hadn't accepted. She'd told him she would answer him when she returned from Italy. She'd planned this February side trip to be a nice, uncomplicated space of time before she settled down to life as a teacher in the New York City school system. Paul had ruined it with a proposal she should have eagerly accepted, but had stumbled over. So her best option was not to think about it until she had to.

Next month.

"I extended my trip so I could have some time to bum around. See the village my foster mother came from, and hopefully meet her family."

To Daniella's surprise, Louisa laughed. "That sounds like fun."

The understanding in Louisa's voice caused Danielle to brighten again, thinking they had something in common. "So you're a tourist, too?"

"No."

Dani frowned. Louisa's tone in that one simple word suddenly made her feel as if she'd crossed a line. "I'm sorry. I don't mean to pry."

Louisa sighed. "It's okay. I'm just a bit nervous. You were kind to come to my rescue. I don't mean to be such a ninny. I'm on my way to Monte Calanetti."

Daniella's mouth fell open. "So am I."

The announcement that their bus was boarding came over the loudspeaker. Danielle faced the gate. Louisa did, too.

Dani smiled. "Looks like we're off."

"Yes." Louisa's mysterious smile formed again.

They boarded the bus and Daniella chose a spot in the middle, believing that was the best place to see the sights on the drive to the quaint village. After tucking her backpack away, she took her seat.

To her surprise, Louisa paused beside her. "Do you mind if I sit with you?"

Daniella happily said, "Of course, I don't mind! That would be great."

But as Louisa sat, Daniella took note again that something seemed off about her. Everything Louisa did had a sense of hesitancy about it. Everything she said seemed incomplete.

"So you have a month before you go home?"

"All of February." Daniella took a deep breath. "And I intend to enjoy every minute of it. Even if I do have to find work."

"Work?"

"A waitressing job. Or maybe part-time shop clerk. That kind of thing. New York is a very expensive place to live. I don't want to blow every cent I made teaching on a vacation. I'll need that money when I get back home. So I intend to earn my spending money while I see the sights."

As the bus eased out of the station, Louisa said, "That's smart."

Dani sat up, not wanting to miss anything. Louisa laughed. "Your foster mother should have come with you."

Pain squeezed Daniella's heart. Just when she thought she was adjusted to her loss, the reality would swoop in and remind her that the sweet, loving woman who'd saved her was gone. She swallowed hard. "She passed a few months ago. She left me the money for my plane ticket to Italy in her will."

Louisa's beautiful face blossomed with sympathy. "I'm so sorry. That was careless of me."

Daniella shook her head. "No. You had no way of knowing."

Louisa studied her. "So you have no set plans? No schedule of things you want to see and do? No places you've already scouted out to potentially get a job?"

"No schedule. I want to wing it. I've done a bit of research about Rosa's family and I know the language. So I think I'll be okay."

Louisa laughed. "Better off than I'll be since I don't know the language." She held up her listening device. "At least not for another five weeks."

The bus made several slow turns, getting them out of the station and onto the street.

Taking a final look at Florence, Dani breathed, "Isn't this whole country gorgeous?" Even in winter with barren trees, the scene was idyllic. Blue skies. Rolling hills.

"Yes." Louisa bit her lip, then hesitantly said, "I'm here because I inherited something, too."

"Really?"

"Yes." She paused, studied Daniella's face as if assessing if she could trust her before continuing, "A villa."

"Oh, my God! A *villa*!"

Louisa glanced away. "I know. It's pretty amazing. The place is called Palazzo di Comparino."

"Do you have pictures?"

"Yes." She pulled out a picture of a tall, graceful house. Rich green vines grew in rows in the background beneath a blue sky.

It was everything Dani could do not to gape in awe. "It's beautiful."

Louisa laughed. "Yes. But so far I haven't seen anything in Italy that isn't gorgeous." She winced. "I hate to admit it, but I'm excited."

"I'd be beyond excited."

"I'm told Monte Calanetti developed around Palazzo Chianti because of the vineyard which is part of the villa I inherited. Back then, they would have needed lots of help picking grapes, making the wine. Those people are the ancestors of the people who live there now."

"That is so cool."

"Yes, except I know nothing about running a vineyard."

Daniella batted a hand. "With the internet these days, you can learn anything."

Louisa sucked in a breath. "I hope so."

Daniella laid her hand on Louisa's in a show of encouragement. "You'll be fine."

Louise's face formed another of her enigmatic smiles and Daniella's sixth sense perked up again. Louisa appeared to want to be happy, but behind her smile was something...

Louisa brought her gaze back to Daniella's. "You know, I could probably use a little help when I get there."

"Help?"

"I don't think I'm just going to move into a villa without somebody coming to question me."

"Ah."

"And I'm going to be at a loss if they're speaking Italian."

Dani winced. "Especially if it's the sheriff."

Louisa laughed. "I don't even know if they have sheriffs here. My letter is in English, but the officials are probably Italian. It could turn out to be a mess. So, I'd be happy to put you up for a while." She caught Dani's gaze. "Even all four weeks you're looking for your foster mom's relatives—if you'd be my translator."

Overwhelmed by the generous offer, Daniella said, "That would be fantastic. But I wouldn't want to put you out."

"You'll certainly earn your keep if somebody comes to check my story."

Daniella grinned. "I'd be staying in a villa."

Louisa laughed. "I *own* a villa."

"Okay, then. I'd be happy to be your translator while I'm here."

"Thank you."

Glad for the friendship forming between them, Daniella engaged Louisa in conversation as miles of hills and blue, blue sky rolled past them. Then suddenly a walled village appeared to the right. The bus turned in.

Aged, but well-maintained stucco, brick and stone buildings greeted them. Cobblestone streets were filled with
happy, chatting people. Through the large front windows
of the establishments, Dani could see the coffee drinkers
or diners inside while outdoor dining areas sat empty because of the chilly temperatures.

The center circle of the town came into view. The bus
made the wide turn but Dani suddenly saw a sign that read
Palazzo di Comparino. The old, worn wood planks had a
thick black line painted through them as if to cancel out
the offer of vineyard tours.

Daniella grabbed Louisa's arm and pointed out the window. "Look!"

"Oh, my gosh!" Louisa jumped out of her seat and
yelled, "Stop!"

Daniella rose, too. She said, *"Fermi qui, per favore."*

It took a minute for the bus driver to hear and finally
halt the bus. After gathering their belongings, Louisa and
Daniella faced the lane that led to Louisa's villa. Because
Dani had only a backpack and Louisa had two suitcases and
a carry-on bag, Daniella said, "Let me take your suitcase."

Louisa smiled. "Having you around is turning out to
be very handy."

Daniella laughed as they walked down the long lane that
took them to the villa. The pale brown brick house soon became visible. The closer they got, the bigger it seemed to be.

Louisa reverently whispered, "Holy cow."

Daniella licked her suddenly dry lips. "It's huge."

The main house sprawled before them. Several stories
tall, and long and deep, like a house with suites not bedrooms, Louisa's new home could only be described as a
mansion.

They silently walked up the stone path to the front door.
When they reached it, Louisa pulled out a key and manipu-
lated the lock. As the door opened, the stale, musty scent
of a building that had been locked up for years assaulted

them. Dust and cobwebs covered the crystal chandelier in the huge marble-floored foyer as well as the paintings on the walls and the curved stairway.

Daniella cautiously stepped inside. "Is your family royalty?"

Louisa gazed around in awe. "I didn't think so."

"Meaning they could be?"

"I don't know." Louisa turned to the right and walked into a sitting room. Again, dust covered everything. A teacup sat on a table by a dusty chair. Passing through that room, they entered another that appeared to be a library or study. From there, they found a dining room.

Watermarks on the ceiling spoke of damage from a second-floor bathroom or maybe even the roof. The kitchen was old and in need of remodeling. The first-floor bathrooms were outdated, as was every bathroom in the suites upstairs.

After only getting as far as the second floor, Louisa turned to Daniella with tears in her eyes. "I'm so sorry. I didn't realize the house would be in such disrepair. From the picture, it looked perfect. If you want to get a hotel room in town, I'll understand."

"Are you kidding?" Daniella rolled Louisa's big suitcase to a stop and walked into the incredibly dusty, cobweb-covered bedroom. She spun around and faced Louisa. "I love it. With a dust rag, some cleanser for the bathroom and a window washing, this room will be perfect."

Louisa hesitantly followed Daniella into the bedroom. "You're an optimist."

Daniella laughed. "I didn't say you wouldn't need to call a contractor about a few things. But we can clean our rooms and the kitchen."

Raffaele Mancini stared at Gino Scarpetti, a tall, stiff man, who worked as the maître d' for Mancini's, Rafe's very exclusive, upscale, Michelin-starred restaurant located in the heart of wine country.

Mancini's had been carefully crafted to charm customers. The stone and wood walls of the renovated farmhouse gave the place the feel of days long gone. Shutters on the windows blocked the light of the evening sun, but also added to the Old World charisma. Rows of bottles of Merlot and Chianti reminded diners that this area was the home of the best vineyards, the finest wines.

Gino ripped off the Mancini's name tag pinned to his white shirt. "You, sir, are now without a maître d'."

A hush fell over the dining room. Even the usual clink and clatter of silverware and the tinkle of good crystal wineglasses halted.

Gino slapped the name tag into Rafe's hand. Before Rafe could comment or argue, the man was out the door.

Someone began to clap. Then another person. And another. Within seconds the sophisticated Tuscany restaurant dining room filled with the sounds of applause and laughter.

Laughter!

They were enjoying his misery!

He looked at the line of customers forming beside the podium just inside the door, then the chattering diners laughing about his temper and his inability to keep good help. He tossed his hands in the air before he marched back to the big ultramodern stainless-steel restaurant kitchen.

"You!"

He pointed at the thin boy who'd begun apprenticing at Mancini's the week before. "Take off your smock and get to the maître d' stand. You are seating people."

The boy's brown eyes grew round with fear. "I…I…"

Rafe raised a brow. "You can't take names and seat customers?"

"I can…"

"But you don't want to." Rafe didn't have to say anything beyond that. He didn't need to say, "If you can't obey orders, you're fired." He didn't need to remind anyone in *his* kitchen that he was boss or that anyone working in the restaurant needed to be able to do *anything* that needed to be done to assure the absolute best dining experience for the customers. Everyone knew he was not a chef to be trifled with.

Except right now, in the dining room, they were laughing at him.

The boy whipped off his smock, threw it to a laundry bin and headed out to the dining room.

Seeing the white-smocked staff gaping at him, Rafe shook his head. "Get to work!"

Knives instantly rose. The clatter of chopping and the sizzle of sautéing filled the kitchen.

He sucked in a breath. Not only was his restaurant plagued by troubles, but now it seemed the diners had no sympathy.

"You shouldn't have fired Gino." Emory Danoto, Rafe's sous-chef, spoke as he worked. Short and bald with a happy face and nearly as much talent as Rafe in the kitchen, Emory was also Rafe's mentor.

Rafe glanced around, inspecting the food prep, pretending he was fine. Damn it. He *was* fine. He did not want a frightened rabbit working for him. Not even outside the kitchen. And the response of the diners? That was a fluke. Somebody apparently believed it was funny to see a world-renowned chef tortured by incompetents.

"I didn't fire Gino. He quit."

Emory cast him a condemning look. "You yelled at him."

Rafe yelled, "I yell at everybody." Then he calmed himself and shook his head. "I am the chef. I *am* Mancini's."

"And you must be obeyed."

"Don't make me sound like a prima donna. I am doing what's best for the restaurant."

"Well, Mr. I'm-Doing-What's-Best-for-the-Restaurant, have you forgotten about our upcoming visit from the Michelin people?"

"A rumor."

Emory sniffed a laugh. "Since when have we ever ignored a rumor that we were to be visited? Your star rating could be in jeopardy. You're the one who says chefs who ignore rumors get caught with their pants down. If we want to keep our stars, we have to be ready for this visit."

Rafe stifled a sigh. Emory was right, of course. His trusted friend only reminded him of what he already knew. Having located his business in the countryside, instead of in town, he'd made it even more exclusive. But that also meant he didn't get street traffic. He needed word of mouth. He needed every diner to recommend him to their friends. He needed to be in travel brochures. To be a stop for tour buses. To be recommended by travel agents. He couldn't lose a star.

The lunch crowd left. Day quickly became night. Before Rafe could draw a steady breath the restaurant filled again. Wasn't that the way of it when everything was falling apart around you? With work to be done, there was no time to think things through. When the last patron finally departed and the staff dispersed after the kitchen cleaning, Rafe walked behind the shiny wood bar, pulled a bottle of whiskey from the shelf, along with a glass, and slid onto a tall, black, wrought iron stool.

Hearing the sound of the door opening, he yelled, "We're closed." Then grimaced. Was he trying to get a reputation for being grouchy rather than exacting?

"Good thing I'm not a customer, then."

He swiveled around at the sound of his friend Nico Amatucci's voice.

Tall, dark-haired Nico glanced at the whiskey bottle, then sat on a stool beside Rafe. "Is there a reason you're drinking alone?"

Rafe rose, got another glass and set it on the bar. He poured whiskey into the glass and slid it to Nico. "I'm not drinking alone."

"But you were going to."

"I lost my maître d'."

Nico raised his glass in salute and drank the shot. "You're surprised?"

"I'm an artist."

"You're a pain in the ass."

"That, too." He sighed. "But I don't want to be. I just want things done correctly. I'll spread the word tomorrow that I'm looking for someone. Not a big deal." He made the statement casually, but deep down he knew he was wrong. It was a big deal. "Oh, who am I kidding? I don't have the week or two it'll take to collect résumés and interview people. I need somebody tomorrow."

Nico raised his glass to toast. "Then, you, my friend, are in trouble."

Didn't Rafe know it.

CHAPTER TWO

THE NEXT MORNING, Daniella and Louisa found a tin of tea and some frozen waffles in a freezer. "We're so lucky no one had the electricity shut off."

"Not lucky. The place runs off a generator. We turn it on in winter to keep the pipes from freezing."

Daniella and Louisa gasped and spun around at the male voice behind them.

A handsome dark-haired man stood in the kitchen doorway, frowning at them. Though he appeared to be Italian, he spoke flawless English. "I'm going to have to ask you to leave. I'll let you finish your breakfast, but this is private property."

Louisa's chin lifted. "I know it's private property. I'm Louisa Harrison. I inherited this villa."

The man's dark eyes narrowed. "I don't suppose you have proof of that?"

"Actually, I do. A letter from my solicitor." She straightened her shoulders. "I think the better question is, who are you?"

"I'm Nico Amatucci." He pointed behind him. "I live next door. I've been watching over this place." He smiled thinly. "I'd like to see the letter from your solicitor. Or—" he pulled out his cell phone "—should I call the police?"

Louisa brushed her hands down her blue jeans to remove the dust they'd collected when she and Daniella had searched for tea. "No need."

Not wanting any part of the discussion, Daniella began preparing the tea.

"And who are you?"

She shrugged. "Just a friend of Louisa's."

He sniffed as if he didn't believe her. Not accustomed to being under such scrutiny, Daniella focused all her attention on getting water into the teapot.

Louisa returned with the letter. When Nico reached for it, she held it back. "Not so fast. I'll need the key you used to get in."

He held Louisa's gaze. Even from across the room, Daniella felt the heat of it.

"Only if your papers check out." His frosty smile could have frozen water. "Palazzo di Comparino has been empty for years. Yet, suddenly here you are."

"With a letter," she said, handing it to Nico.

He didn't release her gaze as he took the letter from her hands, and then he scanned it and peered at Louisa again. "Welcome to Palazzo di Comparino."

Daniella let out her pent-up breath.

Louisa held his gaze. "Just like that? How do you know I didn't fake this letter?"

Giving the paper back to her, he said, "First, I knew the name of the solicitor handling the estate. Second, there are a couple of details in the letter that an outsider wouldn't know. You're legit."

Though Daniella would have loved to have known the details, Louisa didn't even seem slightly curious. She tucked the sheet of paper into her jeans pocket.

Nico handed his key to Louisa as he glanced around the kitchen. "Being empty so long, the place is in disrepair. So if there's anything I can do to help—"

Louisa cut him off with a curt "I'm fine."

Nico's eyes narrowed. Daniella didn't know if he was

unaccustomed to his offers of assistance being ignored, or if something else was happening here, but the kitchen became awkwardly quiet.

When Daniella's teapot whistled, her heart jumped. Always polite, she asked, "Can I get anyone tea?"

Watching Louisa warily, Nico said, "I'd love a cup."

Drat. He was staying. Darn the sense of etiquette her foster mother had drilled into her.

"I'll make some later," Louisa said as she turned and walked out of the kitchen, presumably to put the letter and the key away.

As the door swung closed behind her, Nico said, "She's a friendly one."

Daniella winced. She'd like to point out to Mr. Nico Amatucci that he'd been a tad rude when he'd demanded to see the letter from the solicitor, but she held her tongue. This argument wasn't any of her business. She had enough troubles of her own.

"Have you known Ms. Harrison long?"

"We just met. I saw someone mistakenly take her bag and helped because Louisa doesn't speak Italian. Then we were on the same bus."

"Oh, so you hit the jackpot when you could find someone to stay with."

Daniella's eyes widened. The man was insufferable. "I'm not taking advantage of her! I just finished a teaching job in Rome. Louisa needs an interpreter for a few weeks." She put her shoulders back. "And today I intend to go into town to look for temporary work to finance a few weeks of sightseeing."

He took the cup of tea from her hands. "What kind of work?"

His softened voice took some of the wind out of her sails. She shrugged. "Anything really. Temp jobs are temp jobs."

"Would you be willing to be a hostess at a restaurant?"

Confused, she said, "Sure."

"I have a friend who needs someone to fill in while he hires a permanent replacement for a maître d' who just quit."

Her feelings for the mysterious Nico warmed a bit. Maybe he wasn't so bad after all? "Sounds perfect."

"Do you have a pen?"

She nodded, pulling one from her purse.

He scribbled down the address on a business card he took from his pocket. "Go here. Don't call. Just go at lunchtime and tell Rafe that Nico sent you." He nodded at the card he'd handed to her. "Show him that and he'll know you're not lying."

He set his tea on the table. "Tell Ms. Harrison I said goodbye."

With that, he left.

Glad he was gone, Daniella glanced at the card in her hands. How could a guy who'd so easily helped her have such a difficult time getting along with Louisa?

She blew her breath out on a long sigh. She supposed it didn't matter. Eventually they'd become friends. They were neighbors after all.

Daniella finished her tea, but Louisa never returned to the kitchen. Excited to tell Louisa of her job prospect, Dani searched the downstairs for her, but didn't find her.

The night before they'd tidied two bedrooms enough that they could sleep in them, so she climbed the stairs and headed for the room Louisa had chosen. She found her new friend wrestling with some bedding.

"What are you doing?"

"I saw a washer and dryer. I thought I'd wash the bedclothes so our rooms really will be habitable tonight."

She raced to help Louisa with the huge comforter. "Our rooms were fine. We don't need these comforters, and the sheets had been protected from the dust by the comforters so they were clean. Besides, these won't fit in a typical washer."

Louisa dropped the comforter. "I know." Her face fell in dismay. "I just need to do something to make the place more livable." Her gaze met Daniella's. "There's dust and clutter...and watermarks that mean some of the bathrooms and maybe even the roof need to be repaired." She sat on the bed. "What am I going to do?"

Dani sat beside her. "We're going to take things one step at a time." She tucked Nico's business card into her pocket. "This morning, we'll clean the kitchen and finish our bedrooms. Tomorrow, we'll pick a room and clean it, and every day after that we'll just keep cleaning one room at a time."

"What about the roof?"

"We'll hope it doesn't rain?"

Louisa laughed. "I'm serious."

"Well, I have a chance for a job at a restaurant."

"You do?"

She smiled. "Yes. Nico knows someone who needs a hostess."

"Oh."

She ignored the dislike in her friend's voice. "What better way to find a good contractor than by chitchatting with the locals?"

Louisa smiled and shook her head. "If anybody can chitchat her way into finding a good contractor, it's you."

"Which is also going to make me a good hostess."

"What time's your appointment?"

"Lunchtime." She winced. "From the address on this card, I think we're going to have to hope there's a car in that big, fancy garage out back."

Standing behind the podium in the entry to Mancini's, Rafe struggled with the urge to throw his hands in the air and storm off. On his left, two American couples spoke broken, ill-attempted Italian in an effort to make reservations for that night. In front of him, a businessman demanded to be seated immediately. To his right, a couple kissed. And behind them, what seemed to be a sea of diners groused and grumbled as he tried to figure out a computer system with a seating chart superimposed with reservations.

How could no one in his kitchen staff be familiar with this computer software?

"Everybody just give me a minute!"

He hit a button and the screen disappeared. After a second of shock, he cursed. He expected the crowd to groan. Instead they laughed. *Laughed. Again, laughter!*

How was it that everybody seemed to be happy that he was suffering? These people—customers—were the people he loved, the people he worked so hard to please. How could they laugh at him?

He tried to get the screen to reappear, but it stayed dark.

"Excuse me. Excuse me. Excuse me."

He glanced up to see an American, clearly forgetting she was in Italy because she spoke English as she made her way through the crowd. Cut in an angled, modern style, her pretty blond hair stopped at her chin. Her blue eyes were determined. The buttons of her black coat had been left open, revealing jeans and pale blue sweater.

When she reached the podium, she didn't even look at Rafe. She addressed the gathered crowd.

"Ladies and gentlemen," she said in flawless Italian. "Give me two minutes and everyone will be seated."

His eyebrows rose. She was a cheeky little thing.

When she finally faced him, her blue eyes locked on his. Rich with color and bright with enthusiasm, they didn't merely display her confidence, they caused his heart to give a little bounce.

She smiled and stuck out her hand. "Daniella Tate. Your friend Nico sent me." When he didn't take her hand, her smile drooped as she tucked a strand of yellow hair behind her ear. But her face brightened again. She rifled in her jeans pocket, pulled out a business card and offered it to him. "See?"

He glanced at Nico's card. "So he believes you are right to be my hostess?"

"Temporarily." She winced. "I just finished a teaching position in Rome. For the next four weeks I'm sightseeing, but I'm trying to supplement my extended stay with a temp job. I think he thinks we can help each other—at least while you interview candidates."

The sweet, melodious tone of her voice caused something warm and soft to thrum through Rafe, something he'd never felt before—undoubtedly relief that his friend had solved his problem.

"I see."

"Hey, buddy, come on. We're hungry! If you're not going to seat us we'll go somewhere else."

Not waiting for him to reply, Daniella nudged Rafe out of the way, stooped down to find a tablet on the maître d' stand shelf and faced the dining area. She quickly drew squares and circles representing all the tables and wrote the number of chairs around each one. She put an X over the tables that were taken.

Had he thought she was cheeky? Apparently that was just the tip of the iceberg.

She faced the Americans. "How many in your party?"

"Four. We want reservations for tonight."

"Time?"

"Seven."

Flipping the tablet page, she wrote their name and the time on the next piece of paper. As the Americans walked out, she said, "Next?"

Awestruck at her audacity, Rafe almost yelled.

Almost.

He could easily give her the boot, but he needed a hostess. He had a growing suspicion about the customers laughing when he lost his temper, as if he was becoming some sort of sideshow. He didn't want his temper to be the reason people came to his restaurant. He wanted his food, the fantastic aromas, the succulent tastes, to be the draw. Wouldn't he be a fool to toss her out?

The businessman pushed his way over to her. "I have an appointment in an hour. I need to be served first."

Daniella Tate smiled at Rafe as if asking permission to seat the businessman, and his brain emptied. She really was as pretty as she was cheeky. Luckily, she took his blank stare as approval. She turned to the businessman and said, "Of course, we'll seat you."

She led the man to the back of the dining room, to a table for two, seated him with a smile and returned to the podium.

Forget about how cheeky she was. Forget about his brain that stalled when he looked at her. She was a very good hostess.

Rafe cleared his throat. "Talk to the waitresses and find out whose turn it is before you seat anyone else." He cleared his throat again. "They have a system."

She smiled at him. "Sure."

His heart did something funny in his chest, forcing his gaze to her pretty blue eyes again. Warmth whooshed through him.

Confused, he turned and marched away. With so much at stake in his restaurant, including, it seemed, his reputation, his funny feelings for an employee were irrelevant. Nothing. Whatever trickled through his bloodstream, it had to be more annoyance than attraction. After all, recommendation from Nico or not, she'd sort of walked in and taken over his restaurant.

Dani stared after the chef as he left. She wasn't expecting someone so young...or so gorgeous. At least six feet tall, with wavy brown hair so long he had it tied off his face and gray eyes, the guy could be a celebrity chef on television back home. Just looking at him had caused her breathing to stutter. She actually felt a rush of heat careen through her veins. He was *that* good-looking.

But it was also clear that he was in over his head without a maître d'. As she'd stood in the back of the long line to get into the restaurant, her good old-fashioned American common sense had kicked in, and she'd simply done what needed to be done: pushed her way to the front, grabbed some menus and seated customers. And he'd hired her.

Behind her someone said, "You'd better keep your hair behind your ears. He'll yell about it being in your face and potentially in his food once he gets over being happy you're here."

She turned to see one of the waitresses. Dressed in black trousers and a white blouse, she looked slim and professional.

"*That* was happy?"

Her pretty black ponytail bobbed as she nodded. "*Sì*. That was happy."

"Well, I'm going to hate seeing him upset."

"Prepare yourself for it. Because he gets upset every day. Several times a day. That's why Gino quit. I'm Allegra, by the way. The other two waitresses are Zola and Giovanna. And the chef is Chef Mancini. Everyone calls him Chef Rafe."

"He said you have a system of how you want people seated?"

Allegra took Daniella's seating chart and drew two lines dividing the tables into three sections. "Those are our stations. You seat one person in mine, one person in Zola's and one person in Gio's, then start all over again."

Daniella smiled. "Easy-peasy."

"*Scusi?*"

"That means 'no problem.'"

"Ah. *Sì*." Allegra smiled and walked away. Daniella took two more menus and seated another couple.

The lunchtime crowd that had assembled at the door of

Mancini's settled quickly. Dani easily found a rhythm of dividing the customers up between the three waitresses. Zola and Gio introduced themselves, and she actually had a good time being hostess of the restaurant that looked like an Old World farmhouse and smelled like pure heaven. The aromas of onions and garlic, sweet peppers and spicy meats rolled through the air, making her confident she could talk up the food and promise diners a wonderful meal, even without having tasted it.

During the lull after lunch, Zola and Gio went home. The dining room grew quiet. Not sure if she should stay or leave, since Allegra remained to be available for the occasional tourist who ambled in, Daniella stayed, too.

In between customers, she helped clear and reset tables, checked silverware to make sure it sparkled, arranged chairs so that everything in the dining room was picture-perfect.

But soon even the stragglers stopped. Daniella stood by the podium, her elbow leaning against it, her chin on her closed fist, wondering what Louisa was doing.

"Why are you still here?"

The sound of Rafe's voice sent a surge of electricity through her.

She turned with a gasp. Her voice wobbled when she said, "I thought you'd need me for dinner."

"You were supposed to go home for the break. Or are you sneakily trying to get paid for hours you really don't work?"

Her eyes widened. Anger punched through her. What the hell was wrong with this guy? She'd done him a favor and he was questioning her motives?

Without thinking, she stormed over to him. Putting herself in his personal space, she looked up and caught his gaze. "And how was I supposed to know that, since you didn't tell me?"

She expected him to back down. At the very least to realize his mistake. Instead, he scoffed. "It's common sense."

"Well, in America—"

He cut her off with a harsh laugh. "You Americans.
Think you know everything. But you're not in America
now. You are in Italy." He pointed a finger at her nose.
"You will do what I say."

"Well, I'll be happy to do what you say as soon as you
say something!"

Allegra stopped dropping silverware onto linen-cov-
ered tables. The empty, quiet restaurant grew stone-cold
silent. Time seemed to crawl to a stop. The vein in Rafe's
temple pulsed.

Dani's body tingled. Every employee in the world knew
it wasn't wise to yell at the boss, but, technically, she wasn't
yelling. She was standing up to him. As a foster child, she'd
had to learn how to protect herself, when to stay quiet and
when to demand her rights. If she let him push her around
now, he'd push her around the entire month she worked
for him.

He threw his hands in the air, pivoted away from her
and headed to the kitchen. "Go the hell home and come
back for dinner."

Daniella blew out the breath she'd been holding. Her
heart pounded so hard it hurt, but the tingling in her blood
became a surge of power. He might not have said the words,
but she'd won that little battle of wills.

Still, she felt odd that their communication had come
down to a sort of yelling match and knew she had to get
the heck out of there.

She grabbed her purse and headed for the old green car
she and Louisa had found in the garage.

Ten minutes later, she was back in the kitchen of Palazzo di Comparino.

Though Louisa had sympathetically made her a cup of
tea, she laughed when Daniella told her the story.

"It's not funny," Dani insisted, but her lips rose into a smile when she thought about how she must have looked standing up to the big bad chef everybody seemed to be afraid of. She wouldn't tell her new friend that standing up to him had put fire in her blood and made her heart gallop like a prize stallion. She didn't know what that was all about, but she did know part of it, at least, stemmed from how good-looking he was.

"Okay. It was a little funny. But I like this job. It would be great to keep it for the four weeks I'm here. But he didn't tell me what time I was supposed to go back. So we're probably going to get into another fight."

"Or you could just go back at six. If he yells that you're late, calmly remind him that he didn't give you the time you were to return. Make it his fault."

"It is his fault."

Louisa beamed. "Exactly. If you don't stand up to him now, you'll either lose the job or spend the weeks you work for him under his thumb. You have to do this."

Dani sighed. "That's what I thought."

Taking Louisa's advice, she returned to the restaurant at six. A very small crowd had built by the maître d' podium, and when she entered, she noticed that most of the tables weren't filled. Rafe shoved a stack of menus at her and walked away.

She shook her head, but smiled at the next customers in line. He might have left without a word, but he hadn't engaged her in a fight and it appeared she still had her job.

Maybe the answer to this was to just stay out of his way?

The evening went smoothly. Again, the wonderful scents that filled the air prompted her to talk up the food, the waitstaff and the wine.

After an hour or so, Rafe called her into the kitchen. Absolutely positive he had nothing to yell at her about, she straightened her shoulders and walked into the stainless-steel room and over to the stove where he stood.

"You wanted to see me?"

He presented a fork filled with pasta to her. "This is my signature ravioli. I hear you talking about my dishes, so I want you to taste so you can honestly tell customers it is the best food you have ever eaten."

She swallowed back a laugh at his confidence, but when her lips wrapped around the fork and the flavor of the sweet sauce exploded on her tongue, she pulled the ravioli off the fork and into her mouth with a groan. "Oh, my God."

"It is perfect, *si*?"

"You're right. It is probably the best food I've ever eaten."

Emory, the short, bald sous-chef, scrambled over. "Try this." He raised a fork full of meat to her lips.

She took the bite and again, she groaned. "What is that?"

"Beef *brasato*."

"Oh, my God, that's good."

A younger chef suddenly appeared before her with a spoon of soup. "Minestrone," he said, holding the spoon out to her.

She drank the soup and closed her eyes to savor. "You guys are the best cooks in the world."

Everyone in the kitchen stopped. The room fell silent.

But Emory laughed. "Chef Rafe is *one* of the best chefs in the world. These are his recipes."

She turned and smiled at Rafe. "You're amazing."

She'd meant his cooking was amazing. His recipes were amazing. Or maybe the way he could get the best out of his staff was amazing. But saying the words while looking into his silver-gray eyes, the simple sentence took on a totally different meaning.

The room grew quiet again. She felt her face reddening. Rafe held her gaze for a good twenty seconds before he finally pointed at the door. "Go tell that to customers."

She walked out of the kitchen, licking the remains of the fantastic food off her lips as she headed for the podium.

With the exception of that crazy little minute of eye contact, tasting the food had been fun. She loved how proud the entire kitchen staff seemed to be of the delicious dishes they prepared. And she saw the respect they had for their boss. Chef Rafe. Clearly a very talented man.

With two groups waiting to be seated, she grabbed menus and walked the first couple to a table. "Right this way."

"Any specialties tonight?"

She faced the man and woman behind her, saying, "I can honestly recommend the chef's signature ravioli." With the taste of the food still on her tongue, she smiled. "And the minestrone soup is to die for. But if you're in the mood for beef, there's a beef *brasato* that you'll never forget."

She said the words casually, but sampling the food had had the oddest effect on her. Suddenly she felt part of it. She didn't merely feel like a good hostess who could recommend the delicious dishes because she'd tasted them. She got an overwhelming sense that she was meant to be here. The feeling of destiny was so strong it nearly overwhelmed her. But she drew in a quiet breath, smiled at the couple and seated them.

Sense of destiny? That was almost funny. Children who grew up in foster care gave up on destiny early, and contented themselves with a sense of worth, confidence. It was better to educate yourself to be employable than to dally in daydreams.

As the night went on, Rafe and his staff continued to give her bites and tastes of the dishes they prepared. As she became familiar with the items on the menu, she tempted guests to try things. But she also listened to stories of the sights the tourists had seen that day, and soothed the egos of those who spoke broken Italian by telling stories of teaching English as a second language in Rome.

And the feeling that she was meant to be there grew, until her heart swelled with it.

* * *

Rafe watched her from the kitchen door. Behind him, Emory laughed. "She's pretty, right?"

Rafe faced him, concerned that his friend had seen their thirty seconds of eye contact over the ravioli and recognized that Rafe was having trouble seeing Daniella Tate as an employee because she was so beautiful. When she'd called him amazing, he'd struggled to keep his gaze off her lips, but that didn't stop the urge to kiss her. It blossomed to life in his chest and clutched the air going into and out of his lungs, making them stutter. He'd needed all of those thirty seconds to get ahold of himself.

But Emory's round face wore his usual smile. Nothing out of the ordinary. No light of recognition in his eyes. Rafe's unexpected reactions hadn't been noticed.

Rafe turned back to the crack between the doors again. "She's chatty."

"You did tell her to talk up the food." Emory sidled up to the slim opening. "Besides, the customers seem to love her."

"Bah!" He spun away from the door. "We don't need for customers to love her. They come here for the food."

Emory shrugged. "Maybe. But we're both aware Mancini's was getting to be a little more well-known for your temper than for its meals. A little attention from a pretty girl talking up *your* dishes might just cure your reputation problem. Put the food back in the spotlight instead of your temper."

"I still think she talks too much."

Emory shook his head. "Suit yourself."

Rafe crossed his arms on his chest. He would suit himself. He was *famous* for suiting himself. That was how he'd gotten to be a great chef. By learning and testing until he created great meals. And he wanted the focus on those meals.

The first chance he got, he intended to have a talk with Daniella Tate.

CHAPTER THREE

AT THE END of the night, when the prep tables were spotless, the kitchen staff raced out the back door. Rafe ambled into the dining room as the waitresses headed for the front door, Daniella in their ranks.

Stopping behind the bar, he called, "No. No. You...Daniella. You and I need to talk."

Her steps faltered and she paused. Eventually, she turned around. "Sure. Great."

Allegra and Gio tossed looks of sympathy at her as the door closed softly behind them.

Her shoulders straightened and she walked over to him. "What is it?"

"You are chatty."

She burst out laughing. "I know." As comfortable as an old friend, she slid onto a bar stool across from him. "Got myself into a lot of trouble in school for that."

"Then you will not be offended if I ask you to project a more professional demeanor with the customers?"

"Heck, no. I'm not offended. I think you're crazy for telling me not to be friendly. But I'm not offended."

Heat surged through Rafe's blood, the way it had when she'd nibbled the ravioli from his fork and called him amazing. But this time he was prepared for it. He didn't know what it was about this woman that got him going, why their arguments fired his blood and their pleasant encounters made him want to kiss her, but he did know he had to control it.

He pulled a bottle of wine from the rack beneath the bar and poured two glasses. Handing one of the glasses to her, he asked, "Do you think it's funny to argue with your boss?"

"I'm not arguing with you. I'm giving you my opinion."

He stayed behind the bar, across from her so he could see her face, her expressive blue eyes. "Ah. So, now I understand. You believe you have a right to an opinion."

She took a sip of the wine. "Maybe not a right. But it's kind of hard not to have an opinion."

He leaned against the smooth wooden surface between them, unintentionally getting closer, then finding that he liked it there because he could smell the hint of her perfume or shampoo. "Perhaps. But a smart employee learns to stifle them."

"As you said, I'm chatty."

"Do it anyway."

She sucked in a breath, pulling back slightly as if trying to put space between them. "Okay."

He laughed. "Okay? My chatty hostess is just saying okay?"

"It's your restaurant."

He saluted her with his wineglass. "At least we agree on something."

But when she set her glass on the bar, slid off the stool and headed for the door, his heart sank.

He shook his head, grabbed the open bottle of wine and went in the other direction, walking toward the kitchen where he would check the next day's menu. It was silly, foolish to be disappointed she was leaving. Not only did he barely know the woman, but he wasn't in the market for a girlfriend. His instincts might be thinking of things like kissing, but he hadn't dated in four years. He had affairs and one-night stands. And a smart employer didn't have a one-night stand with an employee. Unless he wanted trouble. And he did not.

He'd already had one relationship that had almost destroyed his dream. He'd fallen so hard for Kamila Troccoli that when she wasn't able to handle the demands of his schedule, he'd pared it back. Desperate to keep her, he'd refused plum apprenticeships, basically giving up his goal of being a master chef and owning a chain of restaurants.

But she'd left him anyway. After a year of building his life around her, he'd awakened one morning to find she'd simply gone. It had taken four weeks before he could go back to work, but his broken heart hadn't healed until he'd realized relationships were for other men. He had a dream that a romance had nearly stolen from him. A wise man didn't forget hard lessons, or throw them away because of a pretty girl.

Almost at the kitchen door, he stopped. "And, Daniella?"

She faced him.

"No jeans tomorrow. Black trousers and a white shirt."

Daniella raced to her car, her heart thumping in her chest. Having Rafe lean across the bar, so close to her, had been the oddest thing. Her blood pressure had risen. Her breathing had gone funny. And damned if she didn't want to run her fingers through his wavy hair. Unbound, it had fallen to his shoulders, giving him the look of a sexy pirate.

The desire to touch him had been so strong, she would have agreed to anything to be able to get away from him so she could sort this out.

And just when she'd thought she was free, he'd said her name. *Daniella.* The way it had rolled off his tongue had been so sexy, she'd shuddered.

Calling herself every kind of crazy, she got into Louisa's old car and headed home. A mile up the country road, she pulled through the opening in the stone wall that allowed entry to Monte Calanetti. Driving along the cobblestone street, lit only by streetlights, she marveled at the way her heart warmed at the quaint small town. She'd never felt so at peace as she did in Italy, and she couldn't wait to meet her foster mother's relatives. Positive they'd make a connection, she could see herself coming to Italy every year to visit them.

She followed the curve around the statue in the town square before she made the turn onto the lane for Palazzo di Comparino. She knew Louisa saw only decay and damage when she looked at the crumbling villa, but in her mind's eye Dani could see it as it was in its glory days. Vines heavy with grapes. The compound filled with happy employees. The owner, a proud man.

A lot like Rafe.

She squeezed her eyes shut when the familiar warmth whooshed through her at just the thought of his name. What was it about that guy that got to her? Sure, he was sexy. Really sexy. But she'd met sexy men before. Why did this one affect her like this?

Louisa was asleep, so she didn't have anyone to talk with about her strange feelings. But the next morning over tea, she told Louisa everything that had happened at the restaurant, especially her unwanted urge to touch Rafe when he leaned across the bar and was so close to her, and Louisa—again—laughed.

"This is Italy. Why are you so surprised you're feeling everything a hundred times more passionately?"

Dani's eyes narrowed. Remembering her thoughts about Monte Calanetti, the way she loved the quaint cobblestone streets, the statue fountain in the middle of the square, the happy, bustling people, she realized she did feel everything more powerfully in Italy.

"Do you think that's all it is?"

"Oh, sweetie, this is the land of passion. It's in the air. The water. Something. As long as you recognize what it is, you'll be fine."

"I hope so." She rose from the table. "I also hope there's a thrift shop in town. I have to find black trousers and a white blouse. Rafe doesn't like my jeans."

Louisa laughed as she, too, rose from the table. "I'll bet he likes your jeans just fine."

Daniella frowned.

Louisa slid her arm across her shoulder. "Your butt looks amazing in jeans."

"What does that have to do with anything?"

Louisa gave her a confused look, then shook her head. "Did you ever stop to think that maybe you're *both* reacting extremely to each other. That it's not just you feeling everything, and that's why it's so hard to ignore?"

"You think he's attracted to me?"

"Maybe. Dani, you're pretty and sexy." She laughed. "And Italian men like blondes."

Daniella frowned. "Oh, boy. That just makes things worse."

"Or more fun."

"No! I have a fiancé. Well, not a fiancé. My boyfriend asked me to marry him right before I left."

"You have a boyfriend?"

She winced. "Yeah."

"And he proposed right before you left?"

"Yes."

Louisa sighed. "I guess that rules out an affair with your sexy Italian boss."

Daniella's eyes widened. "I can't have an affair!"

"I know." Louisa laughed. "Come on. Let's go upstairs and see what's in my suitcases. I have to unpack anyway. I'm sure I have black pants and a white shirt."

"Okay."

Glad the subject had changed, Daniella walked with Louisa through the massive downstairs to the masterpiece stairway.

Louisa lovingly caressed the old, worn banister. "I feel

like this should be my first project. Sort of like a symbol that I intend to bring this place back to life."

"Other people might give the kitchen or bathrooms a priority."

Louisa shook her head. "The foyer is the first thing everyone sees when they walk in. I want people to know I'm committed and I'm staying."

"I get it."

It took ten minutes to find the black pants and white shirt in Louisa's suitcase, but Dani remained with Louisa another hour to sort through her clothes and hang them in the closet.

When it was time to leave, she said goodbye to Louisa and headed to the restaurant for the lunch crowd. She stashed her purse on the little shelf of the podium and waited for someone to unlock the door to customers so she could begin seating everyone.

Rafe himself came out. As he walked to the door, his gaze skimmed over her. Pinpricks of awareness rained down on her. Louisa's suggestion that he was attracted to her tiptoed into her brain. What would it be like to have this sexy, passionate man attracted to her?

She shook her head. What the heck was she thinking? He was only looking at her to make sure she had dressed appropriately. He was *not* attracted to her. Good grief. All they ever did was snipe at each other. That was not attraction.

Although, standing up to him did warm her blood...

After opening the door, Rafe strode away without even saying good morning, proving, at least to Dani, that he wasn't attracted to her. As she seated her first customers, he walked to the windows at the back of the old farmhouse and opened the wooden shutters, revealing the picturesque countryside.

The odd feeling of destiny brought Daniella up short again. This time she told herself it was simply an acknowledgment that the day was beautiful, the view perfect. There was no such thing as someone "belonging" somewhere. There was only hard work and planning.

An hour into the lunch shift, a customer called her over and asked to speak with the chef. Fear shuddered through her.

"Rafe?"

The older man nodded. "If he's the chef, yes."

She couldn't even picture the scene if she called Rafe out and this man, a sweet old man with gray hair, blue eyes and a cute little dimple, complained about the food. So she smiled. "Maybe I can help you?"

"Perhaps. But I would like to speak with the chef."

Officially out of options, she smiled and said, "Absolutely."

She turned to find Rafe only a few steps away, his eyes narrowed, his lips thin.

She made her smile as big as she could. "Chef Rafe..." She motioned him over. When he reached her, she politely said, "This gentleman would like to speak with you."

The dining room suddenly grew quiet. It seemed that everyone, including Daniella, held their breath.

Rafe addressed the man. "Yes? What can I do for you? I'm always happy to hear from my customers."

His voice wasn't just calm. It was warm. Dani took a step back. She'd expected him to bark. Instead, he was charming and receptive.

"This is the best ravioli I've ever eaten." The customer smiled broadly. "I wanted to convey my compliments to the chef personally."

Rafe put his hands together as if praying and bowed slightly. *"Grazie."*

"How did you come to pick such a lovely place for a restaurant?"

"The views mostly," Rafe said, smiling, and Dani stared at him. Those crazy feelings rolled through her again.

When it came to his customers he was humble, genuine. And very, very likable.

He turned to her and nodded toward the door. "Customers, Daniella?"

"Yes! Of course!" She pivoted and hurried away to seat the people at the door, her heart thrumming, her nerve endings shimmering. Telling herself she was simply responding to the happy way he chatted with a customer, glad he hadn't yelled at the poor man and glad everything was going so well, she refused to even consider that her appreciation of his good looks was tipping over into a genuine attraction.

She was so busy she didn't hear the rest of Rafe's conversation with the older couple. When they left, Rafe returned to the kitchen and Daniella went about her work. People arrived, she seated them, the staff served them and Rafe milled about the dining room, talking with customers. They gushed over the scene visible through the back windows. And he laughed.

He *laughed*. And the warmth of his love for his customers filled her. But that still didn't mean she was attracted to him. She appreciated him, yes. Respected him? Absolutely. But even though he was gorgeous, she refused to be attracted to him. Except maybe physically…the man *was* gorgeous. And having a boyfriend didn't mean she couldn't *notice* good-looking men… Did it?

When the lunch crowd emptied, and Gio and Zola left, Daniella turned to help Allegra tidy the dining room, but Rafe caught her arm. "Not so fast."

The touch of his hand on her biceps sent electricity straight to her heart. Which speeded up and sent a whoosh of heat through her blood.

Darn it. She *was* attracted to him.

But physically. Just physically.

She turned slowly.

Bright with anger, his gaze bored into her. "What in the hell did you think you were doing?"

With electricity careening through her, she pulled in a shaky breath. "When?"

"When the customer asked to speak with me!" He threw his hands in the air. "Did you think I did not see? I see everything! I heard that man ask to speak with me and heard you suggest that he talk to you."

She sucked in a breath to steady herself. "I was trying to head off a disaster."

"A disaster? He wanted to compliment the chef and you tried to dissuade him. Did you want the compliment for yourself?"

She gasped. "No! I was worried he was going to complain about the food." She took a step closer, now every bit as angry as he was. He was so concerned about his own agenda, he couldn't even tell when somebody was trying to save his sorry butt. "And that you'd scream at him and the whole dining room would hear."

He matched the step she took. "Oh, really? You saw how I spoke to him. I love my customers."

She held her ground. Her gaze narrowed on him. Her heart raced. "Yeah, well I know that now, but I didn't know it when he asked to speak with you."

"You overstepped your boundaries." He took another step, and put them so close her whole body felt energized—

Oh, no.

Now she knew what was going on. She didn't just think Rafe was handsome. She wasn't just *physically* attracted to him. She was completely attracted to him. And she wasn't yelling at him because she was defending herself. She was yelling because it was how he communicated with her. Because he was a stubborn, passionate man, was this how she flirted with him?

Not at all happy with these feelings, she stepped away

from him. Softening her voice, she said, "It won't happen again."

He laughed. "What? You suddenly back down?"

She peered over at him. Why hadn't he simply said, "Thank you," and walked away? That's what he usually did.

Unless Louisa was right and he was attracted to her, too?

The mere thought made her breathless. She sneaked a peek at him—he was distinguished looking with his long hair tied back and his white smock still crisp and clean after hours of work. The memory of his laughter with the customer fluttered through her, stealing her breath again. He was a handsome man, very, very good at what he did and dedicated to his customers. He could have his pick of women. And he was attracted to her?

Preposterous. She didn't for a second believe it, but she was definitely attracted to him. And she was going to have to watch her step.

She cleared her throat. "Unless you want me to hang out until the dinner crowd, I'll be going home now."

He shook his head. "Do not overstep your boundaries again."

She licked her suddenly dry lips. "Oh, believe me, I'll be very, very careful from here on out."

Rafe watched her walk away. His racing heart had stilled. The fire in his blood had fizzled. Disappointment rattled through him. He shook his head and walked back into the kitchen.

"Done yelling at Daniella?"

Rafe scowled at Emory. "She oversteps her place."

"She's trying to keep the peace. To keep the customers happy. And, in case you haven't noticed, they are happy. Today they were particularly happy."

He sniffed in disdain. "I opened the dining room to the view from the back windows."

Emory laughed. "Seriously? You're going with that?"

"All right! So customers like her."

"And no one seems to be hanging around hoping you'll lose your temper."

He scowled.

"She did exactly what we needed to have done. She shifted the temperament in the dining room. Customers are enjoying your food. You should be thrilled to have her around."

Rafe turned away with a "Bah." But deep down inside he *was* thrilled to have her around.

And maybe that wasn't as much of a good thing as Emory thought it was. Because the whole time he was yelling at her, he could also picture himself kissing her.

Worse, the part of him that usually toed the line wasn't behaving. That part kept reminding him she was temporary. She might be an employee, but she wasn't staying forever. He *could* have an affair with this beautiful, passionate woman and not have to worry about repercussions because in a few weeks, she'd be gone. No scene. No broken heart. No expectations. They could have a delicious affair.

CHAPTER FOUR

DANIELLA RETURNED HOME that night exhausted. Louisa hadn't waited up for her, but from the open cabinet doors and trash bags sitting by the door, it was apparent she'd begun cleaning the kitchen.

She dragged herself up the stairs, showered and crawled into bed, refusing to think about the possibility that Rafe might be attracted to her. Not only did she have a marriage proposal waiting at home, but, seriously? Her with Rafe? Mr. Unstable with the former foster child who needed stability? That was insanity.

She woke early the next morning and, after breakfast, she and Louisa loaded outdated food from the pantry into even more trash bags.

Wiping sweat from her brow, Louisa shook her head at the bag of garbage she'd just hauled to the growing pile by the door. "We don't even know what day to set out the trash."

Busy sweeping the now-empty pantry, Dani said, "You could always ask Nico."

Louisa rolled her eyes. "I'm not tromping over to his villa to ask about trash."

"You could call him. I have his card." She frowned. "Or Rafe has his card. I could ask for it back tonight."

"No, thanks. I'll figure this out."

"Or maybe I could ask the girls at the restaurant? Given

that we're so close to Monte Calanetti, one of them probably lives in the village. She'll know what day the trash
truck comes by."

Louisa brightened. "Yes. Thank you. That would be
great."

But Dani frowned as she swept the last of the dirt onto
her dustpan. Louisa's refusal to have anything to do with
Nico had gone from unusual to impractical. Still, it wasn't
her place to say anything.

She dressed for work in the dark trousers and white shirt
Rafe required and drove to the restaurant. Walking in, she
noticed that two of the chefs were different, and two of the
chefs she was accustomed to seeing weren't there. The
same was true in the dining room. Allegra was nowhere
to be seen and in her place was a tall, slim waitress named
Mila, short for Milana, who told Daniella it was simply
Allegra's day off and probably the chefs', too.

"Did you think they'd been fired?" Mila asked with a
laugh.

Dani shrugged. "With our boss, you never know."

Mila laughed again. "Only Chef Rafe works twelve
hours a day, seven days a week."

"I guess I should ask for a schedule, then."

She turned toward the kitchen but Mila stopped her. "Do
yourself a favor and ask Emory about it."

Thinking that sounded like good advice, she nodded and
walked into the kitchen. Emory stood at a stainless-steel
prep table in the back of the huge, noisy, delicious-smelling
room. Grateful that Rafe wasn't anywhere in sight, she approached the sous-chef.

"*Cara!*" he said, opening his arms. "What can I do for
you?"

"I was wondering if there was a schedule."

The short, bald man smiled. "Schedule?"

"I'm never really sure when I'm supposed to come in."

"A maître d' works all shifts."

At the sound of Rafe's voice behind her, she winced, sucked in a breath and faced him. "I can't work seven days a week, twelve hours a day. I want this month to do some sightseeing. Otherwise, I could have just gone back to New York City."

He smiled and said, "Ah."

And Daniella's heart about tripped over itself in her chest. He had the most beautiful, sexy smile she had ever seen. Directed at her, it stole her breath, weakened her knees, scared her silly.

"You are correct. Emory will create a schedule."

Surprised at how easy that had been, and not about to hang around when his smile was bringing out feelings she knew were all wrong, she scampered out of the kitchen. Within minutes, Rafe came into the dining room to open Mancini's doors. As he passed her, he smiled at her again.

When he disappeared behind the kitchen doors, she blew out her breath and collapsed against the podium. What was he doing smiling at her? Dear God, was Louisa right? Was he interested in her?

She paused. No. Rafe was too business oriented to be attracted to an employee. This wasn't about attraction. It was about her finally finding her footing with him. He hadn't argued about getting her a schedule. He'd smiled because they were beginning to get along as employer and employee.

Guests began arriving and she went to work. There were enough customers that the restaurant felt busy, but not nearly as busy as they were for dinner. She seated an American couple and walked away but even before she reached the podium, they waved her back.

She smiled. "Having trouble with the Italian?"

The short dark-haired man laughed. "My wife teaches Italian at university. We actually visit every other year. Though this is our first time at Mancini's."

"Well, a very special welcome to you, then. What can I help you with?"

He winced. "Actually, we were kind of hoping to just have soup or a salad, but all you have is a full menu."

"Yes. The chef loves his drama."

The man's wife reached over and touched his arm. "I am sort of hungry for this delicious-sounding spaghetti. Maybe we can eat our big meal now and eat light at dinner."

Her husband laughed. "Fine by me."

Dani waved Gio over to take their orders, but a few minutes later, she had a similar conversation with a group of tourists who had reservations that night at a restaurant in Florence. They'd stopped at Mancini's looking for something light, but Rafe's menu only offered full-course meals.

With the lunchtime crowd thinned and two of the three waitresses gone until dinner, Dani stared at the kitchen door. If she and Rafe really had established a proper working relationship, shouldn't she tell him what customers told her?

Of course, she should. She shouldn't be afraid. She should be a good employee.

She headed for the kitchen. "May I speak with you, Chef Rafe?"

His silver-gray eyes met hers. "Yes?"

She swallowed. It was just plain impossible not to be attracted to this guy. "It's... I... Do you want to hear the things the customers tell me?"

Leaning against his prep table behind him, holding her gaze, he said, "Yes. I always want the opinions of customers."

She drank in a long breath. The soft, seductive tone of his voice, the way he wouldn't release her gaze, all reminded her of Louisa's contention that he was attracted to her. The prospect tied her tongue until she reminded herself that they were at work. And he was dedicated to his diners. In this kitchen, that was all that mattered.

"Okay. Today, I spoke with a couple from the US and a group of tourists, both of whom only wanted soup or salad for lunch."

"We serve soup and salad."

"As part of a meal."

"So they should eat a meal."

"That was actually their point. They didn't want a whole meal. Just soup and salad."

Rafe turned to Emory, his hands raised in question as if he didn't understand what she was saying.

She tried again. "Look. You want people to come in for both lunch and dinner but you only offer dinners on the menu. Who wants a five-course meal for lunch?"

The silver shimmer in Rafe's eyes disappeared and he gaped at her. "Any Italian."

"All right." So much for thinking he was attracted to her. The tone of his voice was now definitely all business and when it came to his business, he was clearly on a different page than she was. But this time she knew she was right. "Maybe Italians do like to eat that way. But half your patrons are tourists. If they want a big meal, they'll come at dinnertime. If they just want to experience the joy that is Mancini's, they'll be here for lunch. And they'll probably only want a salad. Or maybe a burger."

"A burger?" He whispered the word as if it were blasphemy.

"Sure. If they like it, they'll be back for dinner."

The kitchen suddenly got very quiet. Every chef in the room and both busboys had turned to face her.

Rafe quietly said, "This is Italy. Tourists want to experience the culture."

"Yes. You are correct. They do want to experience the culture. But that's only part of why tourists are here. Most tourists don't eat two huge meals a day. It couldn't hurt to put simple salads on the lunch menu, just in case a tourist or two doesn't want to eat five courses."

His gray eyes flared. When he spoke, it was slowly, deliberately. "Miss Daniella, you are a tourist playing hostess. I am a world-renowned chef."

This time the softness of his voice wasn't seductive. It was insulting and her defenses rose. "I know. But I'm the one in the dining room, talking with your customers—"

His eyes narrowed with anger and she stepped back, suddenly wondering what the hell she was doing. He was her boss. As he'd said, a world-renowned chef. Yet here she was questioning him. She couldn't seem to turn off the self-defense mechanisms she'd developed to protect herself in middle school when she was constantly teased about not having a home or questioned because her classmates thought being a foster kid meant she was stupid.

She sucked in a long, shaky breath. "I'm sorry. I don't know why I pushed."

He gave her a nod that more or less dismissed her and she raced out of the kitchen. But two minutes later a customer asked to speak with Rafe. Considering this her opportunity to be respectful to him, so hopefully they could both forget about their soup and salad disagreement, she walked into the kitchen.

But she didn't see Rafe.

She turned to a busboy. "Excuse me. Where's Chef Rafe?"

The young kid pointed at a closed door. "In the office with Emory."

She smiled. "Thanks."

She headed for the door. Just when she would have pushed it open, she heard Emory's voice.

"I'm not entirely sure why you argue with her."

"*I* argue with *her*? I was nothing but nice to that girl and she comes into my kitchen and tells me I don't know my own business."

Dani winced, realizing they were talking about her.

Emory said, "We need her."

And Rafe quickly countered with, "You are wrong. Had Nico not sent her, we would have hired someone else by now. Instead, because Nico told her I was desperate, we're stuck with a woman who thinks we need her, and thinks that gives her the right to make suggestions. Not only do we not need her, but I do not want her here—"

The rest of what Rafe said was lost on Dani as she backed away from the door.

Rafe saying that she wasn't wanted rolled through her, bringing up more of those memories from middle school before she'd found a permanent foster home with Rosa. The feeling of not being wanted, not having a home, rose in her as if she were still that teenage girl who'd been rejected so many times that her scars burrowed the whole way to her soul.

Tears welled in her eyes. But she fought them, telling herself he was right. She shouldn't argue with him. But seriously, this time she'd thought she was giving a valuable suggestion. And she'd stopped when she realized she'd pushed too far.

She just couldn't seem to get her bearings with this guy. And maybe it was time to realize this really wasn't the job for her and leave.

She pivoted away from the door, raced out of the kitchen and over to Gio. "Um, the guy on table three would like to talk with Rafe. Would you mind getting him?"

Gio studied her face, undoubtedly saw the tears shimmering on her eyelids and smiled kindly. "Sure."

Dani walked to the podium, intending to get her purse and her coat to leave, but a customer walked in.

Rafe shook his head as Emory left the office with a laugh. He'd needed to vent and Emory had listened for a few minutes, then he'd shut Rafe down. And that was good. He'd been annoyed that Dani challenged him in front of his staff. But venting to Emory was infinitely better than firing her.

Especially since they did need her. He hadn't even started interviewing for her replacement yet.

He walked into the kitchen at the same time that Gio did. "Chef Rafe, there's a customer who would like to speak with you."

He turned to the sink, rinsed his hands and grabbed his towel, before he motioned for Gio to lead him to the customer.

Stepping into the dining room, he didn't see Dani anywhere, but before he could take that thought any further, he was beside a happy customer who wanted to compliment him on his food.

He listened to the man, scanning the dining room for his hostess. When she finally walked into the dining room from the long hall that led to the restrooms, he sighed with relief. He accepted the praise of his customer, smiled and returned to his work.

An hour later, Dani came into the kitchen. "Chef Mancini, there's a customer who would like to speak with you."

Her voice was soft, meek. She'd also called him Chef Mancini, not Chef Rafe, but he didn't question it. A more businesslike demeanor between them was not a bad thing. Particularly considering that he'd actually wanted to have an affair with her and had been thinking about that all damned day—until they'd gotten into that argument about soup and salad.

Which was why the smile he gave her was nothing but professional. "It would be my pleasure."

He expected her to say, "Thank you." Instead, she nodded, turned and left the kitchen without him.

He rinsed his hands, dried them and headed out to the dining room. She waited by a table in the back. When she saw him she motioned for him to come to the table.

As he walked up, she smiled at the customers. She said, "This is Chef Mancini." Then she strode away.

He happily chatted with the customer for ten minutes, but his gaze continually found Daniella. She hadn't waited for him in the kitchen, hadn't looked at him when he came to the table—had only introduced him and left. Her usually sunny smile had been replaced by a stiff lift of her lips. Her bright blue eyes weren't filled with joy. They were dull. Lifeless.

A professional manner was one thing. But she seemed to be…hurt.

He analyzed their soup-and-salad conversation and couldn't find anything different about that little spat than any of their disagreements—except that he'd been smiling at her when she walked in, thinking about kissing her. Then they'd argued and he'd realized what a terrible idea kissing her was, and that had shoved even the thought of an affair out of his head.

But that was good. He should not want to get involved with an employee. No matter how pretty.

When the restaurant cleared at closing time, he left, too. He drove to his condo, showered and put on jeans and a cable-knit sweater. He hadn't been anywhere but Mancini's in weeks. Not since Christmas. And maybe that was why he was having these odd thoughts about his hostess? Maybe it was time to get out with people again? Maybe find a woman?

He shrugged into his black wool coat, took his private elevator to the building lobby and stepped outside.

His family lived in Florence, but he loved little Monte Calanetti. Rich with character and charm, the stone-and-stucco buildings on the main street housed shops run by open, friendly people. That was part of why he'd located Mancini's just outside of town. Tourists loved Monte Calanetti for its connections to the past, especially the vineyard of Palazzo di Comparino, which unfortunately had closed. But tourists still came, waiting for the day the vineyard would reopen.

Rafe's boots clicked on the cobblestone. The chill of the February night seeped into his bones. He put up the collar of his coat, trying to ward off the cold. It didn't help. When he reached Pia's Tavern, he stopped.

Inside it would be warm from a fire in the stone fireplace in the back. He could almost taste the beer from the tap. He turned and pushed open the door.

Because it was a weekday, the place was nearly empty. The television above the shelves of whiskey, gin and rum entertained the two locals sitting at the short shiny wood bar. The old squat bartender leaned against a cooler beside the four beer taps. Flames danced in the stone fireplace and warmed the small, hometown bar. As his eyes adjusted to the low lights, Rafe saw a pretty blonde girl sitting alone at a table in the back.

Dani.

He didn't know whether to shake his head or turn around and walk out. Still, when her blue eyes met his, he saw sadness that sent the heat of guilt lancing though him.

Before he could really think it through, he walked over to her table and sat across from her.

"Great. Just what every girl wants. To sit and have a drink with the boss who yells at her all day."

He frowned. "Is that why you grew so quiet today? Because I yelled at you? I didn't yell. I just didn't take your suggestion. And that is my right. I am your boss."

She sucked in a breath and reached for her beer. "Yes, I know."

"You've always known that. You ignore it, but you've always known. So this time, why are you so upset?"

She didn't reply. Instead, she reached for her coat and purse as if she intended to go. He caught her arm and stopped her.

Her gaze dropped to his hand, then met his.

Confused, he held her blue, blue eyes, as his fingers slid against her soft pink skin. The idea of having an affair with her popped into his head again. They were both incredibly passionate people and they'd probably set his bedroom on fire, if they could stop arguing long enough to kiss.

"Please. If I did something wrong, tell me—"

An unexpected memory shot through him. He hadn't cared what a woman thought since Kamila. The reminder of how he'd nearly given up his dream for her froze the rest of what he wanted to say on his tongue and forced him back to business mode.

"If you are gruff with customers I need to know why."

"I'm not gruff with customers." Her voice came out wispy and smoky.

"So it's just me, then?"

"Every time I try to be nice to you, you argue with me."

He laughed. "When did you try to be nice to me?"

"That suggestion about lunch wasn't a bad one. And I came to you politely—"

"And I listened until you wouldn't quit arguing. Then I had to stop you."

"Yes. But after that you told Emory I wasn't needed." She sniffed a laugh. "I heard you telling him you didn't even want me around."

His eyes narrowed on her face. "I tell Emory things like that all the time. I vent. It's how I get rid of stress."

"Maybe you should stop that."

He laughed, glad his feisty Dani was returning. "And maybe you should stop listening at the door?"

She shook her head and shrugged out of his hold. "I wasn't listening. You were talking loud enough that I could easily hear you through the door."

She rose to leave again. This time he had no intention of stopping her, but a wave of guilt sluiced through him. Her face was still sad. Her blue eyes dull. All because of his attempt to blow off steam.

She only got three steps before he said, "Wait! You are right. I shouldn't have said you weren't wanted. I rant to

Emory all the time. But usually no one hears me. So it doesn't matter."

She stopped but didn't return to her seat. Standing in the glow of the fireplace, she said, "If that's an apology, it's not a very good one."

No. He supposed it wasn't. But nobody ever took his rants so seriously. "Why did it upset you so much to hear you weren't wanted?"

She said nothing.

He rose and walked over to her. When she wouldn't look at him, he lifted her chin until her gaze met his. "There is a story there."

"Of course there's a story there."

He waited for her to explain, but she said nothing. The vision of her walking sadly around the restaurant filled his brain. He'd insulted hundreds of employees before, trying to get them to work harder, smarter, but from the look in her eyes he could see this was personal.

"Can you tell me?"

She shrugged away again. "So you can laugh at me?"

"I will not laugh!" He sighed, softened his voice. "Actually, I'm hoping that if you tell me it will keep me from hitting that nerve again."

"Really?"

"I'm not an idiot. I don't insult people to be cruel. When I vent to Emory it means nothing. When I yell at my employees I'm trying to get the best out of them. With you, everything's a bit different." He tossed his hands. He wouldn't tell her that part of the problem was his attraction. Especially since he went back and forth about pursuing it. Maybe if he'd just decide to take romance off the table, become her friend, things between them would get better? "It might be because you're American not European. Whatever the case, I'd like to at least know that I won't insult you again."

The bartender walked over. He gruffly threw a beer

throwaway comment about her not being wanted made his heart hurt.

"I'm sorry."

She sipped her wine. "And right about now, I'm feeling pretty stupid. You're a grouch. A perfectionist who yells at everyone. I should have realized you were venting." She met his gaze. "I'm the one who should be sorry."

"You do realize you just called me a grouch."

She took another sip of her wine. "And a perfectionist." She caught his gaze again. "See? You don't get offended."

He laughed.

She smiled.

Longing filled Rafe. For years he'd satisfied himself with one-night stands, but she made him yearn for the connection he'd had only once before. With her he wasn't Chef Rafe. She didn't treat him like a boss. She didn't talk to him like a boss...

Maybe because she had these feelings, too?

He sucked in a breath, met her gaze. "Tell me more."

"About my life?"

"About anything."

She set down her wineglass as little pinpricks of awareness sprung up on her arms.

She hadn't realized how much she'd longed for his apology until he'd made it. But now that he was asking to hear about her life, everything inside her stilled. How much to tell? How much to hold back? Why did he want to know? And why did she ache to tell him?

He offered his hand again and she glanced into his face. The lines and planes of his chin and cheeks made him classically handsome. His sexy unbound hair brought out urges in her she hadn't ever felt. She'd love to run her fingers through it while kissing him. Love to know what it would feel like to have his hair tumble to his face while they made love.

She stopped her thoughts. She had an almost fiancé at home, and Rafe wasn't the most sympathetic man in the world. He was bold and gruff, and he accepted no less than total honesty.

But maybe that's what appealed to her? She didn't want sympathy. She just wanted to talk to someone. To really be heard. To be understood.

"I had a good childhood," he said, breaking the awkward silence, again nudging his hand toward her.

She didn't take his hand, so he used it to inch her wine closer. She picked it up again.

"Even as a boy, I was fascinated by cooking."

She laughed, wondering why the hell she was tempting fate by sitting here with him when she should leave. She might not be engaged but she was close enough. And though she'd love to kiss Rafe, to run her fingers through that wild hair, Paul was stability. And she needed stability.

"My parents were initially put off, but because I also played soccer and roughhoused with my younger brother, they weren't worried."

She laughed again. He'd stopped trying to take her hand. And he really did seem to want to talk. "You make your childhood sound wonderful."

He winced. "Not intentionally."

"You don't have to worry about offending me. I don't get jealous of others' good lives. Once Rosa took me in, I had a good life."

"How old were you?"

"Sixteen."

"She was brave."

"Speaking from experience?"

"Let's just say I had a wild streak."

Looking at his hair, which curled haphazardly and made his gray eyes appear shiny and mysterious, Dani didn't doubt he had lots of women who'd helped his wild streak along.

Still, she ignored the potential to tease, to flirt, and said, "Rosa really was brave. I wasn't so much of a handful because I got into trouble, but because I was lost."

"You seem a little lost now, too."

Drat. She hadn't told him any of this for sympathy. She was just trying to keep the conversation innocent. "Seriously. You're not going to feel sorry for me, are you?"

"Not even a little bit. If you're lost now, it's your own doing. Something you need to fix yourself."

"That's exactly what I believe!"

He toasted. "To us. Two just slightly off-kilter people who make our own way."

She clinked her glass to his before taking another sip of wine. They finished their drinks in silence, which began to feel uncomfortable. If she were free, she probably would be flirting right now. But she wasn't.

Grabbing her jacket and purse, she rose from her seat. "I guess I should get going."

He rose, too. "I'll walk you to your car."

Her heart kicked against her ribs. The vision of a goodnight kiss formed in her brain. The knowledge that she'd be a cheat almost choked her. "There's no reason."

"I know. I know. It's a very peaceful little town. No reason to worry." He smiled. "Still, I've never let a woman walk to her car alone after dark."

Because that made sense, she said, "Okay." Side by side they ambled up the sidewalk to the old, battered green car Louisa had lent her.

When they reached it, she turned to him with a smile. "Thank you for listening to me. I actually feel better."

"Thank you for talking to me. Though I don't mind a little turmoil in the restaurant, I don't want real trouble."

She smiled up at him, caught the gaze of his pretty gray eyes, and felt a connection that warmed her. She didn't often tell anyone the story of her life, but he had really listened. Genuinely cared.

"So you're saying yelling is your way of creating the kind of chaos you want?"

"You make me sound like a control freak."

"You are."

He laughed. "I know."

They gazed into each other's eyes long enough for Dani's heart to begin to thrum. Knowing they were now crossing a line, she tried to pull away, but couldn't. Just when she was about to give one last shot at breaking their contact, he bent his head and kissed her.

Heat swooshed through her on a wave of surprise. Her hands slid up his arms, feeling the strength of him, and met at the back of his neck, where rich, thick hair tickled her knuckles. When he coaxed open her mouth, the taste of wine greeted her, along with a thrill so strong it spiraled through her like a tornado. The urge to press herself against him trembled through her. She'd never felt anything so powerful, so wanton. She stepped closer, enjoying sensations so intense they stole her breath.

His hands trailed from her shoulders, down her back to her bottom and that's when everything became real. What was she doing kissing someone when she had a marriage proposal waiting for her in New York?

CHAPTER FIVE

NOTHING IN RAFE'S life had prepared him for the feeling of his lips against Dani's. He told himself it was absurd for an experienced man to think one kiss different from another, but even as that thought floated to him, her lips moved, shifted, and need burst through him. She wasn't a weak woman, his Dani. She was strong, vital, and she kissed like a woman starving for the touch of a man. The kind of touch he longed to give her. And the affair was back on the table.

Suddenly, Dani jumped back, away from him. "You can't kiss me."

The wildness in her eyes mirrored the roar of need careening through him. The dew of her mouth was sprinkled on his lips. His heart pounded out an unexpected tattoo, and desire spilled through his blood.

He smiled, crossed his arms on his chest and leaned against the old car. "I think I just did."

"The point is you shouldn't kiss me."

"Because we work together?" He glanced to the right. "Bah! You Americans and your puritanical rules."

"Oh, you hate rules? What about commitments? I'm engaged!"

That stopped the need tumbling through him. That stopped the sweet swell of desire. That made him angry that she'd led him on, and feel stupid that he hadn't even suspected that a woman as pretty and cheerful as his Dani would have someone special waiting at home.

"I see."

She took three steps back, moving herself away from her own transportation. "I didn't mean to lead you on." She groaned and took another step back. "I didn't think I *was* leading you on. We were talking like friends."

He shoved off the car. "We were."

"So why'd you kiss me?"

He shrugged, as if totally unaffected, though a witch's brew of emotions careered through him like a runaway roller coaster. "It felt right." Everything about her felt right, which only annoyed him more.

She took another step away from him. "Well, it was wrong."

"If you don't stop your retreat, you're going to end up back in the tavern."

She sucked in a breath.

He opened her car door. "Get in. Go home. We're fine. I don't want you skittering around like some frightened mouse tomorrow. Let's just pretend that little kiss never happened."

He waited, holding open the door for her until he realized she wouldn't go anywhere near her car while he stood beside it. Anger punched up again. Still, keeping control, he moved away.

She sighed with relief and slid into her car.

He calmly started the walk to his condo, but when he got inside the private elevator he punched the closed door, not sure if he was angry with himself for kissing her or angry, *really angry*, that she was engaged. Taken.

He told himself not to care. Were they to have an affair, it would have been short because she was leaving, returning to America.

And even if she wasn't, even if they'd been perfect for

each other, he didn't do relationships. He knew their cost.
He knew he couldn't pay it.

When the elevator doors opened again, he stepped out
and tossed his keys on a convenient table in the foyer of his
totally remodeled condo on the top floor of one of Monte
Calanetti's most beautiful pale stone buildings. The quiet
closed in on him, but he ignored it. Sometimes the price a
man paid for success was his soul. He put everything he
had into his meals, his restaurant, his success. He'd almost
let one woman steal his dream—he wouldn't be so foolish
as to even entertain the thought a second time.

The next day he worked his magic in the kitchen, confident
his attraction to Dani had died with the words *I'm engaged.*
He didn't stand around on pins and needles awaiting her
arrival. He didn't think about her walking into the kitchen.
He refused to wonder whether she'd be happy or angry. Or
ponder the way he'd like to treat her to a full-course meal,
watch the light in her eyes while she enjoyed the food he'd
prepare especially for her...

Damn it.

What was he doing thinking about a woman who was
engaged?

He walked through the dining room, checking on the
tables, opening the shutters on the big windows to reveal
the striking view, not at all concerned that she was late,
except for how it would impact his restaurant. So when the
sound of her bubbly laugher entered the dining room, and
his heart stopped, he almost cursed.

Probably not seeing him in the back of the dining room,
she teased with Allegra and Gio, a clear sign that the kiss
hadn't affected her as much as it had affected him. He remembered the way she'd spoken to him the night before.
One minute she was sad, confiding, the next she would say
something like, "You should stop that." Putting him in his

place. Telling him what to do. And he wondered, really, who had confided in whom the night before?

Walking to the kitchen, he ran his hand along the back of his neck. Had he really told her about his family? Not that it was any great secret, but his practice was to remain aloof. Yet, somehow, wanting to comfort her had bridged that divide and he'd talked about things he normally kept out of relationships with women.

As he approached a prep table, Emory waved a sheet of paper at him. "I've created the schedule for Daniella. I'm giving her two days off. Monday and Tuesday. Two days together, so she can sightsee."

His heart stuttered a bit, but he forced his brain to focus on work. "And just who will seat people on Monday and Tuesday?"

"Allegra has been asking for more hours. I think she'll be fine in the position as a stand-in until, as Daniella suggested, we hire two people to seat customers."

He ignored the comment about Daniella. "Allegra is willing to give up her tips?"

"She's happy with the hourly wage I suggested."

"Great. Fine. Wonderful. Maybe you should deal with staff from now on."

Emory laughed. "This was a one-time thing. A favor to Daniella. I'm a chef, too. I might play second to you, but I'm not a business manager. In fact, you're the one who's going to take this to Dani."

Ignoring the thump of his heart at having to talk to her, Rafe snatched the schedule sheet out of Emory's hands and walked out of the kitchen, into the dining room.

His gaze searched out Dani and when he found her, their eyes met. They'd shared a conversation. They'd shared a kiss. But she belonged to someone else. Any connection he felt to her stopped now.

He broke the eye contact and headed for Allegra.

"Emory tells me you're interested in earning some extra money and you're willing to be Dani's fill-in."

Her eyes brightened. *"Sì."*

"Excellent. You will come in Monday and Tuesday for Dani, then." He felt Dani's gaze burning into him, felt his face redden with color like a schoolboy in the same room with his crush. Ridiculous.

He sucked in a breath, pasted a professional smile on his face and walked over to Dani. He handed the sheet of paper to her. "You wanted a schedule. Here is your schedule."

Her blue eyes rose slowly to meet his. She said, "Thanks."

The blood in his veins slowed to a crawl. The noise in the dining room disappeared. Every nuance of their kiss flooded his memory. Along with profound disappointment that their first kiss would be their last.

He fought the urge to squeeze his eyes shut. Why was he thinking these things about a woman who was taken? All he'd wanted was an affair! Now that he knew they couldn't have one, he should just move on.

"You wanted time off. I am granting you time off."

He turned and walked away, satisfied that he sounded like his normal self. Because he was his normal self. No kiss…no *woman* would change him.

Lunch service began. Within minutes, he was caught up in the business of supervising meal prep. As course after course was served, an unexpected thought came to Rafe. An acknowledgment of something Dani had said. He didn't eat a multicourse lunch. He liked soup and salad. Was Dani right?

Dani worked her shift, struggling to ward off the tightness in her chest every time Rafe came out of the kitchen. Memories of his kiss flooded her. But the moment of pure pleasure had been darkened by the realization that she had a proposal at home…yet she'd kissed another man. And it had been a great kiss. The kind of kiss a woman loses herself in. The kind of kiss that could have swept her off her feet if she wasn't already committed.

She went home in between lunch and dinner and joined Louisa on a walk through the house as she mentally charted everything that needed to be repaired. The overwhelmed villa owner wasn't quite ready to do an actual list. It was as if Louisa needed to get her bearings or begin acclimating to the reality of the property she owned before she could do anything more than clean.

At five, Dani put on the black trousers and white blouse again and returned to the restaurant. The time went more smoothly than the lunch session, mostly because Rafe was too busy to come into the dining room, except when a customer specifically asked to speak with him. When she walked into the kitchen to get him, she kept their exchanges businesslike, and he complied, not straying into more personal chitchat. So when he asked for time with her at the end of the night again, she shivered.

She didn't think he intended to fire her. He'd just given her a schedule. He also wouldn't kiss her again. He seemed to respect the fact that there was another man in the picture, even if she had sort of stretched the truth about being *engaged*. But that was for both of their benefits. She had a proposal waiting. Her life was confusing enough already. There was no point muddying the waters with a fling. No point in leading Rafe on.

She had no idea why he wanted to talk to her, but she decided to be calm about it.

When he walked out of the kitchen, he indicated that she should sit at the bar, while he grabbed a bottle of wine.

After a sip, she smiled. "I like this one."

"So you are a fan of Chianti."

She looked at the wine in the glass, watched how the light wove through it. "I don't know if I'm a fan. But it's good." She took a quiet breath and glanced over at him. "You wanted to talk with me?"

"Today, I saw what you meant about lunch being too much food for some diners."

She turned on her seat, his reply easing her mind enough that she could be comfortable with him. "Really?"

"Yes. We should have a lunch menu. We should offer the customary meals diners expect in Italy, but we should also accommodate those who want smaller lunches."

"So I made a suggestion that you're going to use?"

He caught her gaze. "You're not a stupid woman, Dani. You know that. Otherwise, you wouldn't be so bold in your comments about the restaurant."

She grinned. "I am educated."

He shook his head. "And you have instincts." He picked up his wineglass. "I'd like you to work with me on the few selections we'll add."

Her heart sped up. "Really?"

"Yes. It was your suggestion. I believe you should have some say in the menu."

That made her laugh.

"And what is funny about that?" His voice dripped with incredulity, as if he had no idea how to follow her sometimes. His hazy gray eyes narrowed in annoyance.

She sipped her wine, delaying her answer to torment him. He was always so in control that he was cute when he was baffled. And it was fun to see him try to wrangle himself around it.

Finally she said, "You're not the big, bad wolf you want everybody to believe."

His eyes narrowed a little more as he ran his thumb along his chin. His face was perfect. Sharp angles, clean lines, accented by silvery eyes and dark, dark hair that gave him a dramatic, almost mysterious look.

"I don't mind suggestions to make the business better. Ask Emory. He's had a lot more say than you would think."

She smiled, not sure why he so desperately wanted to cling to his bossy image. "I still say you're not so bad."

* * *

Rafe's blood heated. The urge to flirt with Dani, and then seduce her, roiled like the sea before a storm. He genuinely believed she was too innocent to realize he could take her comments about his work demeanor as flirting, and shift the conversation into something personal. But he also knew they couldn't work together if she continued to be so free with him.

"Be careful what you say, little Dani, and how you take our conversations. Because I am bad. I am not the gentleman you might be accustomed to. Though I respect your engagement, if you don't, I'll take that as permission to do whatever I want. You can't have a fiancé at home and free rein to flirt here."

Her eyes widened. But he didn't give her a chance to comment. He grabbed the pad and pencil he'd brought to the bar and said, "So what should we add to this lunch menu you want?"

She licked her lips, took a slow breath as if shifting her thoughts to the task at hand and said, "Antipasto and minestrone soup. That's obvious. But you could add a garden salad, club sandwich, turkey sandwich and hamburgers." She slowly met his gaze. "That way you're serving a need without going overboard."

With the exception of the hamburger, which made him wince, he agreed. "I can put my own spin on all of these, use the ingredients we already have on hand, redo the menu tonight and we'll be ready to go tomorrow."

She gaped at him. "Tomorrow? Wow."

He rose. "This is my business, Dani. If a suggestion is good, there is no point waiting forever. I get things done. Go home. I will see you tomorrow."

She walked to the door, and he headed for the kitchen where he could watch her leave from the window above the sink, making sure nothing happened to her. No matter how hard he tried to stop it, disappointment rose up in

him. At the very least, it would have been nice to finish a
glass of wine with her.

But he couldn't.

Dani ran to her car, her blood simmering, her nerve endings
taut. They might have had a normal conversation about his
menu. She might have even left him believing she was okay
with everything he'd said and they were back to normal.
But she couldn't forget his declaration that he was bad. It
should have scared her silly. Instead, it tempted her. She'd
never been attracted to a man who was clearly all wrong
for her, a man with whom she couldn't have a future. Everything she did was geared toward security. Everything
about him spelled danger.

So why was he so tempting?

Walking into the kitchen of Louisa's run-down villa,
she found her friend sitting at the table with a cup of tea.

Louisa smiled as she entered. "Can I get you a cup?"

She squeezed her eyes shut. "I don't know."

Louisa rose. "What's wrong? You're shaking."

She dropped to one of the chairs at the round table. "Rafe
and I had a little chat after everyone was gone."

"Did he fire you?"

"I think I might have welcomed that."

Louisa laughed. "You need a cup of tea." She walked to
the cupboard, retrieved the tin she'd bought in the village,
along with enough groceries for the two of them, and ran
water into the kettle. "So what did he say?"

"He told me to be careful where I took our conversations."

"Are you insulting him again?"

"He danced around it a bit, but he thinks I'm flirting
with him."

Eyes wide, Louisa turned from the stove. "Are you?"

Dani pressed her lips together before she met Louisa's
gaze. "Not intentionally. You know I have a fiancé."

"Sounds like you're going to have to change the way you act around Rafe, then. Treat him the way he wants to be treated, like a boss you respect. Mingle with the wait-staff. Enjoy your job. But stay away from him."

The next day, Rafe stacked twenty-five black leather folders containing the new menus on the podium for Dani to distribute when she seated customers.

An hour later, she entered the kitchen, carrying them. Her smile as radiant as the noonday sun, she said, "These look great."

Rafe nodded, moving away from her, reminding himself that she was engaged to another man. "As I told you last night, this is a business. Good ideas are always welcome."

Emory peeked around Rafe. "And, please, if you have any more ideas, don't hesitate to offer them."

Rafe said, "Bah," and walked away. But he saw his old, bald friend wink at Dani as if they were two conspirators. At first, he was comforted that Emory had also succumbed to Dani's charms, but he knew that was incorrect. Emory liked Dani as a person. While Rafe wanted to sleep with her. But as long as he reminded himself his desires were wrong, he could control them.

Customer response to the lunch menu was astounding. Dani took no credit for the new offerings and referred comments and compliments to him. Still, she was in the spotlight everywhere he went. Customers loved her. The waitstaff deferred to her. Her smile lit the dining room. Her laughter floated on the air. And he was glad when she said goodbye at the end of the day, if only so he could get some peace.

Monday morning, he arrived at the restaurant and breathed in the scent of the business he called home. Today would be a good day because Dani was off. For two glorious days he would not have to watch his words, watch where his eyes went or control hormones he didn't understand. Plus, her having two days off was a great way to transition his thoughts away from her as a person and to her as an employee.

And who knew? Maybe Allegra would work so well as a hostess that he could actually cut Dani's hours even more. Not in self-preservation over his unwanted attraction, but because this was a business. He was the boss. And the atmosphere of the restaurant would go back to normal.

As Emory supervised the kitchen, Rafe interviewed two older gentlemen for Dani's job. Neither was suitable, but he comforted himself with the knowledge that this was only his first attempt at finding her replacement. He had other interviews scheduled for that afternoon and the next day. He *would* replace her.

Allegra arrived on time to open for lunch. Because they were enjoying an unexpected warm spell, he opened the windows and let the breeze spill in. The scents of rich Tuscan foods drifted from the kitchen. And just as Rafe expected, suddenly, all became right with the world.

Until an hour later when he heard a clang and a clatter from the dining room. He set down his knife and stormed out. Gio had dropped a tray of food when Allegra had knocked into her.

"What is this?" he asked, his hands raised in confusion. "You navigate around each other every day. Now, today, you didn't see her?"

Allegra stooped to help Gio pick up the broken dishes. "I'm sorry. It's just nerves. I was turned away, talking to the customer and didn't watch where I was going."

"Bah! Nerves. Get your head on straight!"

Allegra nodded quickly and Rafe returned to the kitchen. He summoned the two busboys to the dining room to clean up the mess and everything went back to normal.

Except customers didn't take to Allegra. She was sweet, but she wasn't fun. She wasn't chatty. A lifelong resident, she didn't see Italy through the eyes of someone who loved it with the passion and intensity of a newcomer as Dani did.

One customer even asked for her. Rafe smiled and said she had a day off. The customer asked for the next shift she'd be working so he could return and tell her of his trip to Venice.

"She'll be back on Wednesday," Rafe said. He tried to pretend he didn't feel the little rise in his heart at the thought of her return, but he'd felt it. After only a few hours, he missed her.

CHAPTER SIX

AND SHE MISSED HIM.

The scribbled notes of things she remembered her foster mother telling her about her Italian relatives hadn't helped her to find them. But Dani discovered stepping stones to people who knew people who knew people who would ultimately get her to the ones she wanted.

Several times she found herself wondering how Rafe would handle the situation. Would he ask for help? What would he say? And she realized she missed him. She didn't mind his barking. He'd shown her a kinder side. She remembered the conversation in which he'd told her about his family. She loved that he'd taken her suggestion about a lunch menu. But most of all, she replayed that kiss over and over and over in her head, worried because she couldn't even remember her first kiss with Paul.

Steady, stable Paul hadn't ever kissed her like Rafe had. Ever. But he had qualities Rafe didn't have. Stability being number one. He was an accountant at a bank, for God's sake. A man did not get any more stable than that. She'd already had a life of confusion and adventure of a sort, when she was plucked from one foster home and dropped in another. She didn't want confusion or danger or adventure. She wanted stability.

That night when she called Paul, he immediately asked

when she was returning. Her heart lifted a bit hearing that. "I hate talking on the phone."

It was the most romantic thing he'd ever said to her. Until he added, "I'd rather just wait until you get home to talk."

"Oh."

"Now, don't get pouty. You know you have a tendency to talk too much."

She *was* chatty.

"Anyway, I'm at work. I've got to go."

"Oh. Okay."

"Call me from your apartment when you get home."

She frowned. Home? Did he not want to talk to her for an entire month? "Aren't you going to pick me up at the airport?"

"Maybe, but you'll probably be getting in at rush hour or something. Taking a taxi would be easier, wouldn't it? We'll see how the time works out."

"I guess that makes sense."

"Good. Gotta run."

Even as she disconnected the call, she thought of Rafe. She couldn't see him telling his almost fiancée to call when she arrived at her apartment after nearly seven months without seeing each other. He'd race to the airport, grab her in baggage claim and kiss her senseless.

Her breath vanished when she pictured the scene, and she squeezed her eyes shut. She really could not think like that. She absolutely couldn't start comparing Paul and Rafe. Especially not when it came to passion. Poor sensible Paul would always suffer by comparison.

Plus, her feelings for Rafe were connected to the rush of pleasure she got from finding a place in his restaurant, being more than useful, offering ideas a renowned chef had implemented. For a former foster child, having somebody give her a sense of worth and value was like gold.

And that's all it was. Attraction to his good looks and

appreciation that he recognized and told her she was doing a good job.

She did not want him.

Really.

She needed somebody like Paul.

Though she knew that was true, it didn't sit right. She couldn't stop thinking about the way he didn't want to pick her up at the airport, how he'd barely had two minutes to talk to her and how he'd told her not to call again.

She tried to read, tried to chat with Louisa about the house, but in the end, she knew she needed to get herself out of the house or she'd make herself crazy.

She told Louisa she was going for a drive and headed into town.

Antsy, unable to focus, and afraid he was going to royally screw something up and disappoint a customer, Rafe turned Mancini's over to Emory.

"It's not like you to leave so early."

"It's already eight o'clock." Rafe shrugged into his black wool coat. "Maybe too many back-to-back days have made me tired."

Emory smiled. "Ah, so maybe like Dani, you need a day off?"

Buttoning his coat, he ignored the dig and walked to the back door. "I'll see you tomorrow."

But as he was driving through town, he saw the ugly green car Dani drove sitting at the tavern again. The last time she'd been there had been the day he'd inadvertently insulted her. She didn't seem like the type to frequent taverns, so what if she was upset again?

His heart gave a kick and he whipped his SUV into a parking place, raced across the quiet street and entered the tavern to find her at the same table she'd been at before.

He walked over. She glanced up.

Hungrier for the sight of her than was wise, he held her

gaze as he slid onto the chair across from her. "So this is how you spend your precious time off."

She shook her head. "Don't start."

He hadn't meant to be argumentative. In fact that was part of their problem. There was no middle with them. They either argued or lusted after each other. Given that he was her boss and she was engaged, both were wrong.

The bartender ambled over. He set a coaster in front of Rafe with a sigh. "You want another bottle of that fancy wine?"

Rafe shook his head and named one of the beers on tap before he pointed to Dani's glass. "And another of whatever she's having."

As the bartender walked away, she said, "You don't have to buy me a beer."

"I'm being friendly because I think we need to find some kind of balance." He was tired of arguing, but he also couldn't go on thinking about her all the time. The best way to handle both would be to classify their relationship as a friendship. Tonight, he could get some questions answered, get to know her and see that she was just like everybody else. Not somebody special. Then they could both go back to normal.

"Balance?"

He shrugged. Leaning back, he anchored his arm across the empty chair beside him. "We're either confiding like people who want to become lovers, or we fight."

She turned her beer glass nervously. "That's true."

"So, we drink a beer together. We talk about inconsequential things, and Wednesday when you return to Mancini's, no one snipes."

She laughed.

He smiled. "What did you do today?"

"I went to the town where my foster mother's relatives lived."

His beer arrived. Waiting for her to elaborate, he took

a sip. Then another. When she didn't say anything else, he asked, "So did you find them?"

"Not yet. But I will."

Her smooth skin virtually glowed. Her blue eyes met his. Interest and longing swam through him. He ignored both in favor of what now seemed to be a good mission. Becoming friends. Finding a middle ground where they weren't fighting or lusting, but a place where they could coexist.

"What did you do today?"

"Today I created a lasagna that should have made customers die from pleasure."

She laughed. "Exaggerate much?"

He pointed a finger at her. "It's not an exaggeration. It's confidence."

"Ah."

"You don't like confidence?"

She studied his face. "Maybe it's more that I don't trust it."

"What's to trust? I love to cook, to make people happy, to surprise them with something wonderful. But I didn't just open a door to my kitchen and say, come eat this. I went to school. I did apprenticeships. My confidence is in my teachers' ability to take me to the next level as much as it is in my ability to learn, and then do."

Her head tilted. "So it's not all about you."

He laughed, shook his head. "Where do you get these ideas?"

"You're kind of arrogant."

He batted his hand. "Arrogant? Confident? Who cares as long as the end result is good?"

"I guess…"

"I know." He took another sip of beer, watching as she slid her first drink—which he assumed was warm—aside and reached for the second glass he'd bought for her. "Not much of a drinker?"

"No."

"So what are you?"

She laughed. "Is this how you become friends with someone?"

"Conversation is how everyone becomes friends."

"I thought it was shared experience."

"We don't have time for shared experience. If we want to become friends by Wednesday we need to take shortcuts."

She inclined her head as if agreeing.

He waited. When she said nothing, he reframed his question. "So you are happy teaching?"

"I'm a good teacher."

"But you are not happy?"

"I'm just not sure people are supposed to be happy."

He blinked. That was the very last thing he'd expected to hear from his bubbly hostess. "Seriously?"

She met his gaze. "Yeah. I think we're meant to be content. I think we're meant to find a spot and fill it. But happy? That's reserved for big events or holidays."

For thirty seconds, he wished she were staying in Italy. He wished he had time enough to show her the sights, teach her the basics of cooking, make her laugh, show her what happiness was. But that wasn't the mission. The mission was to get to know her just enough that they would stop arguing.

"This from my happy, upbeat hostess?"

She met his gaze again. "I thought we weren't going to talk about work."

"We're talking about you, not work."

She picked up her beer glass. "Maybe this isn't the best time to talk about me."

Which only filled him with a thousand questions. When she was at Mancini's she was usually joyful. After a day off, she was as sad as the day he'd hurt her feelings? It made no sense…unless he believed that she loved working in his restaurant enough that it filled her with joy.

That made his pulse jump, made his mind race with thoughts he wasn't supposed to have. So he rose.

"Okay. Talking is done. We'll try shared experience." He pointed behind her. "We'll play darts."

Clearly glad they'd no longer be talking, she laughed. "Good."

"So you play darts at home in New York?"

She rose and followed him to the board hung on a back wall. They passed the quiet pool table, and he pulled some darts from the corkboard beside the dartboard.

"No, I don't play darts."

"Great. So we play for money?"

She laughed again. "No! We'll play for fun."

He sighed as if put out. "Too bad."

But as they played, she began to talk about her search for her foster mother's family. Her voice relaxed. Her smile returned. And Rafe was suddenly glad he'd found her. Not for his mission to make her his friend. But because she was alone. And in spite of her contention that people weren't supposed to be happy, her normal state was happy. He'd seen that every day at the restaurant. But something had made her sad tonight.

Reminded of the way he had made her sad by saying she wasn't needed, he redoubled his efforts to make her smile.

It was easy for Dani to dismiss the significance of Rafe finding her in the bar. They lived in a small town. He didn't have a whole hell of a lot of choices for places to stop after work. So she wouldn't let her crazy brain tell her it was sweet that he'd found her. She'd call it what it was. Lack of options.

Playing darts with her, Rafe was kind and polite, but not sexy. At least not deliberately sexy. There were some things a really handsome man couldn't control. So she didn't think he was coming on to her when he swaggered over to pull the darts from the board after he threw them. She didn't coaster on the table, even though Dani and Rafe stood by the fireplace. "What'll it be?"

Rafe tugged Dani's hand. "Come. We'll get a nice Merlot. And talk."

She slid her hand out of his, but she did return to her seat. He named the wine he wanted from the bartender, and with a raise of his bushy brows, the bartender scrambled off to get it. When he returned with the bottle and two glasses, Rafe shooed him away, saying he'd pour.

Dani frowned. "No time for breathing?"

He chuckled. "Ah. So she thinks she knows wine?"

Her head lowered. "I don't."

His eyes narrowed as he studied her. The sad demeanor was back. The broken woman. "And all this rolls together with why I insulted you when I said you weren't wanted?"

She sighed. "Sort of. I don't know how to explain this so you'll understand, but the people I'm looking for aren't my relatives."

He smiled. "They're people who owe you money?"

She laughed. The first genuine laugh in hours and the tight ball of tension in Rafe's gut unwound.

"They are the family of the woman who was my foster mother."

"Foster mother?"

"I was taken from my mother when I was three. I don't remember her. In America, when a child has no home, he or she is placed with a family who has agreed to raise her." She sucked in a breath and took the wineglass he offered her. "Foster parents aren't required to keep you forever. So if something happens, they can give you back."

She tried to calmly give the explanation but the slight wobble of her voice when she said "give you back" caused the knot of tension to reform in Rafe's stomach. He imagined a little blue-eyed, blonde girl bouncing from home to home, hugging a scraggly brown teddy bear, and his

CHAPTER SEVEN

WHEN DANI ENTERED the restaurant on Wednesday ten minutes before the start of her shift, Rafe stood by the bar, near the kitchen. As if he'd sensed her arrival, he turned. Their gazes caught. Dani's heart about pounded its way out of her chest. She reminded herself that though they'd spent an enjoyable evening together playing darts at the tavern, for him it had been about becoming friends. He hadn't made any passes at her—though he'd had plenty of chances—and he'd made a very good argument for why being friends was a wise move for them.

Still, when he walked toward her, her heart leaped. But he passed the podium to unlock the front door. As he turned to return to the kitchen, he said, "Good morning."

She cleared her throat, hoping to rid it of the fluttery feeling floating through her at being in the same room with him. Especially since they were supposed to be friends now. Nothing more. "Good morning."

"How did your search go for your foster mother's relatives yesterday?"

She shook her head. "Still haven't found them, but I got lots of information from people who had been their neighbors. Most believe they moved to Rome."

"Rome?" He shook his head. "No kidding."

"Their former neighbors said something about one of

their kids getting a job there and the whole family wanting to stay together."

"Nice. Family should stay together."

"I agree."

She turned to the podium. He walked to the kitchen. But she couldn't help thinking that while Paul hadn't said a word about her quest for Rosa's family, Rafe had immediately asked. Like someone who cared about her versus someone who didn't.

She squeezed her eyes shut and told herself not to think like that. They were *friends. Only friends.*

But all day, she was acutely aware of him. Anytime she retrieved him to escort him to a table, she felt him all around her. Her skin tingled. Everything inside her turned soft and feminine.

At the end of the night, the waitstaff and kitchen help disappeared like rats on a sinking ship. Rafe ambled to the bar, pulled a bottle of wine from the rack behind it.

The Chianti. The wine he'd ordered for them at the tavern.

Her heart trembled. She'd told him she liked that wine.

Was he asking her to stay now? To share another bottle of the wine she'd said she liked?

Longing filled her and she paused by the podium. When he didn't even look in her direction, she shuffled a bit, hoping the movement would cause him to see her and invite her to stay.

He kept his gaze on a piece of paper sitting on the bar in front of him. Still, she noticed a second glass by the bottle. He had poured wine in one glass but the other was empty—yet available.

She bit her lip. Was that glass an accident? An oversight? Or was that glass her invitation?

She didn't know. And things were going so well between

them professionally that she didn't want to make a mistake that took them back to an uncomfortable place.

Still, they'd decided to be friends. Wouldn't a friend want another friend to share a glass of wine at the end of the night?

She drew in a slow breath. She had one final way to get him to notice her and potentially invite her to sit with him. If he didn't take this hint, then she would leave.

Slowly, cautiously, she called, "Good night."

He looked over. He hesitated a second, but only a second, before he said, "Good night."

Disappointment stopped her breathing. Nonetheless, she smiled and headed for the door. She walked to Louisa's beat-up old car, got in, slid the key in the ignition...

And lowered her head to the steering wheel.

She wanted to talk to him. She wanted to tell him about the countryside she'd seen as she looked for Rosa's relatives. She longed to tell him about the meals she'd eaten. She yearned to ask him how the restaurant had been the two days she was gone. She needed to get not just the cursory answers he'd given her but the real in-depth stuff. Like a friend.

But she also couldn't lie to herself. She wanted that crazy feeling he inspired in her. Lust or love, hormones or genuine attraction, she had missed that feeling. She'd missed *him*. No matter how much she told herself she just wanted to be his friend, it was a lie.

A light tapping on her window had her head snapping up.

Rafe.

She quickly lowered the window to see what he wanted. "Are you okay?"

Her heart swelled, then shrank and swelled again. Everything he did confused her. Everything she felt around him confused her even more.

"Are you ill?"

She shook her head.

Damn it. She squeezed her eyes shut and decided to just go with the truth. "I saw you with the wine and thought I should have joined you." She caught the gaze of his smoky-gray eyes. "You said we were going to be friends. And I was hoping you sitting at the bar with a bottle of wine was an invitation."

He stepped back. She'd never particularly thought of a chef's uniform as being sexy, but he'd taken off the jacket, revealing a white T-shirt that outlined muscles and a flat stomach. Undoubtedly hot from working in the kitchen, he didn't seem bothered by the cold night air.

"I always have a glass of wine at the end of the night."

So, her instincts had been wrong. If she'd just started her car and driven off, she wouldn't be embarrassed right now. "Okay. Good."

He glanced down into the car at her. "But I wouldn't have minded company."

Embarrassment began to slide away, only to be replaced by the damnable confusion. "Oh."

"I simply don't steal women who belong to other men."

"It wouldn't be stealing if we were talking about work, becoming friends like you said we should."

"That night was a one-time thing. A way to get to know each other so we could stop aggravating each other."

"So we're really not friends?"

He laughed and glanced away at the beautiful starlit sky. "We're now friendly enough to work together. Men only try to become 'real' friends so that they can ultimately become lovers."

The way he said *lovers* sent a wave of yearning skittering along her nerve endings. It suddenly became difficult to breathe.

He caught her gaze again. "I've warned you before to be careful with me, Dani. I'm not a man who often walks away from what he wants."

"Wow. You are one honest guy."

He laughed. "Usually I wouldn't care. I'd muscle my way into your life and take what I wanted. But you're different. You're innocent."

"I sort of liked being different until you added the part about me being innocent."

"You are."

"Well, yeah. Sort of." She tossed her hands in exasperation, the confusion and longing getting the better of her. "But you make it sound like a disease."

"It's not. It's actually a quality men look for in a woman they want to keep."

Her heart fluttered again. "Oh?"

"Don't get excited about that. I'm not the kind of guy who commits. I like short-term relationships because I don't like complications. I'm attracted to you, yes, but I also know myself. My commitment to the restaurant comes before any woman." He forced her gaze to his again. "This thing I feel for you is wrong. So as much as I wanted you to take the hint tonight and share a bottle of wine with me, I also hoped you wouldn't. I don't want to hurt you."

"We could always talk about the restaurant."

"About how you were missed? How a customer actually asked for you?"

She laughed. "See? That's all great stuff. Neutral stuff."

"I suppose you also wouldn't be opposed to hearing that Emory thinks that after the success of your lunch menu, we should encourage you to make suggestions."

Pride flooded her. "Well, I'll do my best to think of new things."

He glanced at the stars again. Their conversation had run its course. He stood in the cold. She sat in a car that could be warm if she'd started the darn thing. But the air between them was anything but cool, and she suddenly realized they were kidding themselves if they believed they could be just friends.

He looked down and smiled slightly. "Good night, Dani."

He didn't wait for her to say good-night. He walked away.

She sat there for a few seconds, tingling, sort of breathless, but knowing he was right. They couldn't be friends and they couldn't have a fling. She *was* innocent and he would hurt her. And though technically she'd stretched the truth about being engaged, it was saving her heartbreak.

After starting her car, she pulled out, watching in the rearview mirror as he revved the engine of his big SUV and followed her to Monte Calanetti.

Though Dani dressed in her usual black trousers and white blouse the next morning, she took extra care when she ironed them, making them crisper, their creases sharper, so she looked more professional when she arrived at the restaurant.

Rafe spoke sparingly. It wasn't long before she realized that unless she had a new idea to discuss, they wouldn't interact beyond his thank-you when she introduced him to a customer who wanted to compliment the chef.

She understood. Running into each other at the tavern the first time and talking out their disagreement, then playing darts the second, had made them friendly enough that they no longer sniped. But having minimal contact with her was how he would ignore their attraction. They weren't right for each other and, older, wiser, he was sparing them both. But that didn't really stop her attraction to him.

To keep herself from thinking about Rafe on Friday, she studied the customer seating, the china and silverware, the interactions of the waitresses with the customers, but didn't come up with an improvement good enough to suggest to him.

A thrill ran through her at the knowledge that he took her ideas so seriously. Here she was, an educated but simple girl from Brooklyn, being taken seriously by a lauded European chef.

The sense of destiny filled her again, along with Rafe's comment about happiness. This time her thoughts made her gasp. What if this feeling of rightness wasn't about Rafe or Italy? What if this sense of being where she belonged was actually telling her the truth about her career choice? She loved teaching, but it didn't make her feel she belonged the way being a part of this restaurant did. And maybe this sense of destiny was simply trying to point her in the direction of a new career when she returned to the United States?

The thought relieved her. Life was so much simpler when the sense of destiny was something normal, like an instinct for the restaurant business, rather than longing for her boss—a guy she shouldn't even be flirting with when she had a marriage proposal waiting for her at home.

Emory came to the podium and interrupted her thoughts. "These are the employee phone numbers. Gio called off sick for tonight's shift. I'd like you to call in a replacement."

She glanced up at him. "Who should I call?"

He smiled. "Your choice. Being out here all the time, you know who works better with whom."

After calling Zola, she walked back to the kitchen to return the list.

Emory shook his head. "This is your responsibility now. A new job for you, while you're here, to make my life a little easier."

She smiled. "Okay."

Without looking at her, Rafe said, "We'd also like you to begin assigning tasks to the busboys. After you say goodbye to a guest, we'd like you to come in and get the busboys. That will free up the waitresses a bit."

The feeling of destiny swelled in her again. The new tasks felt like a promotion, and there wasn't a person in the world who didn't like being promoted.

When Rafe refused to look at her, she winked at Emory. "Okay."

Walking back to the dining room, she fought the feeling that her destiny, her gift, was for this particular restaurant. Especially since, when returning to New York, she'd start at the bottom of any dining establishment she chose to work, and that would be a problem since she'd only make minimum wage. At Mancini's, she only needed to earn extra cash. In New York, would a job as a hostess support her?

The next day, Lazare, one of the busboys, called her "Miss Daniella." The shift from Dani to Miss Daniella caught on in the kitchen and the show of respect had Daniella's shoulders straightening with confidence. When she brought Rafe out for a compliment from a customer, even he said, "Thank you, Miss Daniella," and her heart about popped out of her chest with pride.

That brought her back to the suspicion that her sense of destiny wasn't for the restaurant business, but for *this* restaurant and these people. If she actually got a job at a restaurant in New York, she couldn't expect the staff there to treat her this well.

Realizing all her good fortune would stop when she left Mancini's, her feeling of the "destiny" of belonging in the restaurant business fizzled. She would go home to a tiny apartment, a man whose marriage proposal had scared her and a teaching position that suddenly felt boring.

"Miss Daniella," Gio said as she approached the podium later that night. "The gentleman at table two would like to speak to the chef."

She said it calmly, but there was an undercurrent in her voice, as if subtly telling Daniella that this was a problem situation, not a compliment.

She smiled and said, "Thank you, Gio. I'll handle it."

She walked over to the table.

The short, stout man didn't wait for Dani to speak. He immediately said, "My manicotti was dry and tasteless."

Daniella inclined her head in acknowledgment of his comment. "I'm sorry. I'm not sure what happened. I'll tell the kitchen staff."

"I want to talk to the chef."

His loud, obnoxious voice carried to the tables around him. Daniella peeked behind her at the kitchen door, then glanced at the man again. The restaurant had finally freed itself of people curious about Rafe's temper. The seats had filled with customers eager to taste his food. She would not let his reputation be ruined by a beady-eyed little man who probably wanted a free dinner.

"We're extremely busy tonight," she told the gentleman as she looped her fingers around his biceps and gently urged him to stand. "So rather than a chat with the chef, what if I comp your dinner?"

His eyes widened, then returned to normal, as if he couldn't believe he was getting what he wanted so easily. "You'll pay my tab?"

She smiled. "The whole meal." A quick glance at the table told her that would probably be the entire day's wage, but it would be worth it to avoid a scene.

"I'd like dessert."

"We'll get it for you to go." She nodded to Gio, who quickly put two slices of cake into a take-out container and within seconds the man and his companion were gone.

Rafe watched from the sliver of a crack he created when he pushed open the kitchen door a notch. He couldn't hear what Dani said, but he could see her calm demeanor, her smiles, the gentle but effective way she removed the customer from Rafe's dining room without the other patrons being any the wiser.

He laughed and Emory walked over.

"What's funny?"

"Dani just kicked somebody out."

Emory's eyes widened. "We had a scene?"

"That's the beauty of it. Even though he started off yelling, she got him out without causing even a ripple of trouble. I'll bet the people at the adjoining tables weren't even aware of what was happening beyond his initial grousing."

"She is worth her weight in gold."

Rafe pondered that. "Gio made the choice to get her rather than come to me."

Emory said, "She trusts Dani."

He walked away, leaving Rafe with that simple but loaded thought.

At the end of the night, the waitstaff quickly finished their cleanup and began leaving before the kitchen staff. Rafe glanced at the bar, thought about a glass of wine and decided against it. Instead, he walked to the podium as Dani collected her purse.

He waited for the waitresses on duty to leave before he faced Dani.

"You did very well tonight."

"Thank you."

"I saw you get rid of the irate customer."

She winced. "I had to offer to pay for his meal."

"I'll take care of that."

Her gaze met his, tripping the weird feeling in his chest again.

"Really?"

"Yes." He sucked in a breath, reminding himself he didn't want the emotions she inspired in him. He wanted a good hostess. He didn't want a fling with another man's woman.

"I trust your judgment. If not charging for his food avoided a scene, I'm happy to absorb the cost."

"Thanks."

He glanced away, then looked back at her. "Your duties just keep growing."

"Is this your subtle way of telling me I overstepped?"

He shook his head. "You take work that Emory and I would have to do. Things we truly do not have time for."

"Which is good?"

"Yes. Very good." He gazed into her pretty blue eyes and fought the desire to kiss her that crept up before he could stop it. His restaurant was becoming exactly what he'd envisioned because of her. Because she knew how to direct diners' attention and mood. It was as if they were partners in his venture and though the businessman in him desperately fought his feelings for her, the passionate part of him wanted to lift her off the ground, swing her around and kiss her ardently.

But that was wrong for so many reasons that he got angry with himself for even considering it.

"I was thinking tonight that a differentiation between you and the waitresses would be good. It would be a show of authority."

"You want me to wear a hat?"

He laughed. Was it any wonder he was so drawn to her? No one could so easily catch him off guard. Make him laugh. Make him wish for a life that included a little more fun.

"I want you to wear something other than the dark trousers and white blouses the waitresses wear. Your choice," he said when her face turned down with a puzzled frown. "A dress. A suit. Anything that makes you look like you're in charge."

Her gaze rose to meet his. "In charge?"

"Of the dining room." He laughed lightly. "You still have a few weeks before I give you my job."

She laughed, too.

But when her laughter died, they were left gazing into each other's eyes. The mood shifted from happy and businesslike to something he couldn't define or describe. The click of connection he always felt with her filled him. It think he was trying to entice her when he laughed at her poor attempts at hitting the board. And she absolutely made nothing of it when he stood behind her, took her arm and showed her the motion she needed to make to get the dart going in the right direction.

Even though she could smell him, feel the heat of his body as he brushed up against her back, and feel the vibrations of his warm whisper as he pulled her arm back and demonstrated how to aim, she knew he meant nothing by any of it. He just wanted to be friends.

When their third beer was gone and the hour had gotten late, she smiled at him. "Thank you. That was fun."

His silver eyes became serious. "You were happy?"

She shook her head at his dog-with-a-bone attitude. "Sort of. Yes. It was a happy experience."

He sniffed and walked back to their table to retrieve his coat. "Everyone is made to be happy."

She didn't believe that. Though she liked her life and genuinely liked people, she didn't believe her days were supposed to be one long party. But she knew it was best not to argue. She joined him at their table and slipped into her coat.

"I'll walk you to your car."

She shook her head. "No." Their gazes caught. "I'm fine."

He dipped his head in a quick nod, agreeing, and she walked out into the cold night. Back into the world where her stable fiancé wouldn't even pick her up at the airport.

was hot and sweet, but pointless, leaving an emptiness in the pit of his stomach.

He said, "Good night, Dani," and walked away, into the kitchen and directly to the window over the sink. A minute later, he watched her amble across the parking lot to her car, start it and drive off, making sure she had no trouble.

Then he locked the restaurant and headed to his SUV.

He might forever remember the joy in her blue eyes when he told her that he wanted her to look like the person of authority in the dining room.

But as he climbed into his vehicle, his smile faded. Here he was making her happy, giving her promotions, authority, and just when he should have been able to kiss her to celebrate, he'd had to pull back...because she was taken.

Was he crazy to keep her on, to continually promote her, to need her for his business when it was clear that there was no chance of a relationship between them?

Was he being a sucker?

Was she using him?

Bah! What the hell was he doing? Thinking about things that didn't matter? The woman was leaving in a few weeks. And that was the real reason he should worry about depending on her. Soon she would be gone. So why were he and Emory leaning on her?

Glad he had more maître d' interviews scheduled for the following Monday, he started his car and roared out of the parking lot. He would use what he had learned about Dani's duties for his new maître d'. But he wouldn't give her any more authority.

And he absolutely would stop all thoughts about wanting to swing her around, kiss her and enjoy their success. It was not "their" success. It was his.

It was also her choice to have no part in it.

Sunday morning, Dani arrived at the restaurant in a slim cream-colored dress. She had curled her hair and pinned it in a bundle on top of her head. When Rafe saw her his jaw fell.

She looked regal, sophisticated. Perfect as the face of his business.

Emory whistled. "My goodness."

Rafe's breath stuttered into his lungs. He reminded himself of his thoughts from the night before. She was leaving. She wanted no part in his long-term success. He and Emory were depending on her too much for someone who had no plans to stay.

But most of all, leaving was her choice.

She didn't want him or his business in her life. She was here only for some money so she could find the relatives of her foster mother.

The waitresses tittered over how great she looked. Emory walked to the podium, took her hands and kissed both of her cheeks. The busboys blushed every time she was near.

She handled it with a cool grace that spoke of dignity and sophistication. Exactly what he wanted as the face of Mancini's. As if she'd read his mind.

Laughing with Allegra, she said, "I feel like I'm playing dress up. These are Louisa's clothes. I don't own anything so pretty."

Allegra sighed with appreciation. "Well, they're perfect for you and your new position."

She laughed again. "Rafe and Emory only promoted me because I have time on my hands in between customers. While you guys are hustling, I'm sort of looking around, figuring things out." She leaned in closer. "Besides, the extra authority doesn't come with more money."

As Allegra laughed, Rafe realized that was true. Unless Dani was a power junkie, she wasn't getting anything out of her new position except more work.

So why did she look so joyful in a position she'd be leaving in a few weeks?

Sunday lunch was busier than normal. Customers came in, ate, chatted with Dani and left happy.

Which relieved Rafe and also caused him to internally scold himself for distrusting her. He didn't know why she'd taken such an interest in his restaurant, but he should be glad she had.

She didn't leave for the space between the last lunch customer and the first dinner customer because the phone never stopped ringing.

Again, Rafe relaxed a bit. She had good instincts. Now that his restaurant was catching on, there were more dinner reservations. She stayed to take them. She was a good, smart employee. Any mistrust he had toward her had to be residual bad feelings over not being able to pursue her when he so desperately wanted to. His fault. Not hers.

In fact, part of him believed he should apologize. Or maybe not apologize. Since she couldn't see inside his brain and know the crazy thoughts he'd been thinking, a compliment would work better.

He walked out of the kitchen to the podium and smiled when he saw she was on the phone. Their reservations for that night would probably be their best ever.

"So we're talking about a hundred people."

Rafe's eyebrows rose. A hundred people? He certainly hoped that wasn't a single reservation for that night. Yes, there was a private room in which he could probably seat a hundred, but because that room was rarely used, those tables and chairs needed to be wiped down. Extra linens would have to be ordered from their vendor. Not to mention enough food. He needed advance warning to serve a hundred people over their normal customer rate.

He calmed himself. She didn't know that the room hadn't been used in months and would need a good dusting. Or about the linens. Or the extra food. Once he told her, they could discuss the limits on reservations.

When she finally replaced the receiver on the phone, her blue eyes glowed.

Need rose inside him. Once again he fought the unwanted urge to share the joy of success with her. No matter how he sliced it, she was a big part of building his clientele. And rather than worry about her leaving, a smart businessman would be working to entice her to stay. To make *his* business *her* career, and Italy her new home.

Romantic notions quickly replaced his business concerns. If she made Italy her home, she might just leave her fiancé in America, and he could—

Realizing he wasn't just getting ahead of himself, he was going in the wrong direction, he forced himself to be professional. "It sounds like you got us a huge reservation."

"Better."

He frowned. "Better? How does something get better than a hundred guests for dinner?"

She grinned. "By catering a wedding! They don't even need our dishes and utensils. The venue is providing that. All they want is food. And for you that's easy."

Rafe blinked. "What?"

"Okay, it's like this. A customer came in yesterday. The dinner they chose was what his wife wanted to be served for their daughter's wedding at the end of the month. When they ate your meal, they knew they wanted you to cook food for their daughter's wedding. The bride's dad called, I took down the info," she said, handing him a little slip. "And now we have a new arm of your business."

Anything romantic he felt for Dani shrank back against the rising tide of red-hot anger.

"I am not a caterer."

He controlled his voice, didn't yell, didn't pounce. But he saw recognition come to Dani's eyes. She might have only worked with him almost two weeks, but she knew him.

Her fingers fluttered to her throat. "I thought you'd be pleased."

"I have a business plan. I have Michelin stars to protect. I will not send my food out into the world for God knows who to do God knows what with it."

She swallowed. "You could go to the wedding—"

"And leave the restaurant?"

She sucked in a breath.

"Call them back and tell them you checked with me and we can't deliver."

"But...I..." She swallowed again. "They needed a commitment. Today. I gave our word."

He gaped at her. "You promised something without asking me?" It was the cardinal sin. The unforgivable sin. Promising something that hadn't been approved because she'd never consulted the boss. Every employee knew that. She hadn't merely overstepped. She'd gone that one step too far.

Her voice was a mere whisper when she said, "Yes."

Anger mixed with incredulity at her presumptuousness, and he didn't hesitate. With his dream in danger, he didn't even have to think about it. "You're fired."

CHAPTER EIGHT

"Leave now."

Dani's breaths came in quick, shallow puffs. No one wanted to be fired. But right at that moment she wasn't concerned about her loss. Her real upset came from failing Rafe. She'd thought he'd be happy with the added exposure. Instead, she'd totally misinterpreted the situation. Contrary to her success in the dining room, she wasn't a chef. She didn't know a chef's concerns. She had no real restaurant experience.

Still, she had instincts—

Didn't she?

"I'll fix this."

He turned away. "This isn't about fixing the problem. This is about you truly overstepping this time. I don't know if it's because we've had personal conversations or because to this point all of your ideas have been good. But no one, absolutely no one, makes such an important decision without my input. You are fired."

He walked into the kitchen without looking back. Dani could have followed him, maybe even should have followed him, but the way he walked away hurt so much she couldn't move. She could barely breathe. Not because she'd angered him over a mistake, but because he was so cool. So distant. So deliberate and so sure that he wanted her gone. As if their evenings at the tavern hadn't happened, as if all those stolen moments—that kiss—had meant nothing, he was tossing her out of his life.

Tears stung her eyes. The pain that gripped her hurt like a physical ache.

But common sense weaved its way into her thoughts. Why was she taking this personally? She didn't love him. She barely knew him. She had a fiancé—almost. A guy who might not be romantic, but who was certainly stable. She'd be going home in a little over two weeks. There could be nothing between her and Rafe. He was passion wrapped in electricity. Moody. Talented. Sweet but intense. Too sexy for his own good—or hers. And they weren't supposed to be attracted to each other, but they were.

Staying at Mancini's had been like tempting fate. Teasing both of them with something they couldn't have. Making them tense, and him moody. Hot one minute and cold the next.

So maybe it really was time to go?

She slammed the stack of menus into their shelf of the podium, grabbed her purse and raced out.

When she arrived at the villa, Louisa was on a ladder, staring at the watermarks as if she could divine how they got there.

"What are you doing home?"

Dani yanked the pins holding up her short curls and let them fall to her chin, as she kicked off Louisa's high, high heels.

"I was fired."

Louisa climbed off the ladder. "What?" She shook her head. "He told you to dress like the authority in the dining room and you were gorgeous. How could he not like how you looked?"

"Oh, I think he liked how I looked." Dani sucked in a breath, fully aware now that that was the problem. They were playing with fire. They liked each other. But neither of them wanted to. And she was done with it.

"Come to Rome with me."

"You're not going to try to get your job back?"

"It just all fell into place in my head. Rafe and I are attracted, but my boyfriend asked me to marry him. Though I didn't accept, I can't really be flirting with another guy. So Rafe—"

Louisa drew in a quick breath. "You know, I wasn't going to mention this because it's not my business, but now that you brought it up... Don't you think it's kind of telling that you hopped on a plane to Italy rather than accept your boyfriend's proposal?"

"I already had this trip scheduled."

"Do you love this guy?"

Dani hesitated, thinking of her last conversation with Paul and how he'd ordered her not to call him anymore. The real kicker wasn't his demand. It was that it hadn't affected her. She didn't miss their short, irrelevant conversations. In six months, she hadn't really missed *him*.

Oh, God. That was the thing her easy, intense attraction to Rafe was really pointing out. Her relationship to Paul might provide a measure of security, but she didn't love him.

She fell to a kitchen chair.

"Oh, sweetie. If you didn't jump up and down for joy when this guy proposed, and you find yourself attracted to another man, you do not want to accept that proposal."

Dani slumped even further in her seat. "I know."

"You should go back to Mancini's and tell Rafe that."

She shook her head fiercely. "No. *No!* He's way too much for me. Too intense. Too *everything*. He has me working twelve-hour days when I'm supposed to be on holiday finding my foster mother's relatives, enjoying some time with them before I go home."

"You're leaving me?"

Dani raised her eyes to meet Louisa's. "You've always known I was only here for a month. I have just over two weeks left. I need to start looking for the Felice family now." She smiled hopefully because she suddenly, fervently didn't want to be alone, didn't want the thoughts about Rafe that would undoubtedly haunt her now that she knew she couldn't accept Paul's proposal. "Come with me."

"To Rome?"

"You need a break from studying everything that's wrong with the villa. I have to pay for a room anyway. We can share it. Then we can come back and I'll still have time to help you catalog everything that needs to be fixed."

Louisa's face saddened. "And then you'll catch a plane and be gone for good."

Dani rose. "Not for good." She caught Louisa's hands. "We're friends. You'll stay with me when you have to come back to the States. I'll visit you here in Italy."

Louisa laughed. "I really could use a break from staring at so many things that need repairing and trying to figure out how I'm going to get it all done."

"So it's set. Let's pack now and go."

Within an hour, they were at the bus station. With Mancini's and Rafe off the list of conversation topics, they chit-chatted about the scenery that passed by as their bus made its way to Rome. Watching Louisa take it all in, as if trying to memorize the country in which she now owned property, a weird sense enveloped Dani. It was clear that everything was new, unique to Louisa. But it all seemed familiar to Dani, as if she knew the trees and grass and chilly February hills, and when she returned to the US she would miss them.

Which was preposterous. She was a New York girl. She needed the opportunities a big city provided. She'd never lived in the country. So why did every tree, every landmark, every winding road seem to fill a need inside her?

The feeling followed her to Rome. To the alleyways between the quaint buildings. To the sidewalk cafés and bistros. To the Colosseum, museums and fountains she took Louisa to see.

And suddenly the feeling named itself. *Home.* What she felt on every country road, at every landmark, gazing at every blue, blue sky and grassy hill was the sense that she was home.

She squeezed her eyes shut. She told herself she wasn't home. She was merely familiar with Italy now because she'd lived in Rome for months. Though that made her feel better for a few minutes, eventually she realized that being familiar with Rome didn't explain why she'd felt she belonged at Mancini's.

She shoved that thought away. She did not belong at Mancini's.

The next day, Dani and Louisa found Rosa's family and were invited to supper. The five-course meal began, reminding her of Rafe, of his big, elaborate dinners, the waitresses who were becoming her friends, the customers who loved her.The weepy sense that she had lost her home filled her. Rightly or wrongly, she'd become attached to Mancini's, but Rafe had fired her.

She had lost the place where she felt strong and smart and capable. The place where she was making friends who felt like family. The place where she—no matter how unwise—was falling for a guy who made her breath stutter and her knees weak.

Because the guy she felt so much for had fired her.

Her brave facade fell away and she excused herself. In the bathroom, she slid down the wall and let herself cry. She'd never been so confused in her life.

"Rafe, there's a customer who'd like to talk to you."

Rafe set down his knife and walked to Mila, who stood in front of the door that led to the dining room. "Great, let's go."

Pleased to be getting a compliment, he reached around

Mila and pushed open the door for her. Since Dani had gone, compliments had been fewer and farther between. He needed the boost.

Mila paused by a table with two twentysomething American girls. Wearing thick sweaters and tight jeans, they couldn't hide their tiny figures. Or their ages. Too old for college and too young to have amassed their own fortunes, they appeared to be the daughters of wealthy men, in Europe, spending their daddies' money. Undoubtedly, they'd heard of him. Bored and perhaps interested in playing with a celebrity chef, they might be looking for some fun. If he handled this right, one of them could be sharing Chianti with him that night.

Ignoring the tweak of a reminder of sharing that wine with Dani, her favorite, he smiled broadly. "What can I do for you ladies?"

"Your ravioli sucked."

That certainly was not what he'd expected.

He bowed slightly, having learned a thing or two from his former hostess. He ignored the sadness that shot through him at even the thought of her, and said, "Allow me to cover your bill."

"Cover our bill?" The tiny blonde lifted a ravioli with her fork and let it plop to her plate. "You should pay us for enduring even a bite of this drivel."

The dough of that ravioli had serenaded his palms as he worked it. The sweet sauce had kissed his tongue. The problem wasn't his food but the palates of the diners.

Still, remembering Dani, he held his temper as he gently reached down and took the biceps of the blonde. "My apologies." He subtly guided her toward the door. The woman was totally cooperative until they got to the podium, and then she squirmed as if he was hurting her, and made a hideous face. Her friend snapped a picture with her phone.

"Get it on Instagram!" the blonde said as they raced out the door. "Rafe Mancini sinks to new lows!"

Furious, Rafe ran after them, but they jumped into their car and peeled out of his parking lot before he could catch them.

After a few well-aimed curses, he counted to forty. Great. Just when he thought rumors of his temper had died, two spoiled little girls were about to resurrect them.

He returned to the quiet dining room. Taking another page from Dani's book, he said, "I'm sorry for the disturbance. Everyone, please, enjoy your meals."

A few diners glanced down. One woman winced. A couple or two pretended to be deep in conversation, as if trying to avoid his misery.

With a weak smile, he walked into the kitchen, over to his workstation and picked up a knife.

Emory scrambled over and whispered, "You're going to have to find her."

Facing the wall, so no one could see, Rafe squeezed his eyes shut. He didn't have to ask who *her* was. The shifts Daniella had been gone had been awful. This was their first encounter with someone trying to lure out his temper, but there had been other problems. Squabbles among the waitresses. Seating mishaps. Lost reservations.

"Things are going wrong, falling through the cracks," Emory continued.

"This is my restaurant. I will find and fix mistakes."

"No. If there's anything Dani taught us, it's that you're a chef. You are a businessman, yes. But you are not the guy who should be in the dining room. You are the guy who should be trotted out for compliments. You are the special chef made more special by the fact that you must be enticed out to the dining room."

He laughed, recognizing he liked the sound of that because he did like to feel special. Or maybe he liked feeling that his food was special.

"Did you ever stop to think that you don't have a temper with the customers or the staff when Dani's around?"

He didn't even try to deny it. With the exception of being on edge because of his attraction to her, his temperament had improved considerably. "Yes."

Emory chuckled as if surprised by his easy acquiescence. "Because she does the tasks that you aren't made to do, which frees you up to do the things you like to do. So, let's just bring her back."

Missing Dani was about so, so much more than Emory knew. Not just a loss of menial tasks but a comfort level. It was as if she brought sunshine into the room. Into his life. But she was engaged.

"Why should I go after her?" Rafe finally faced Emory. "She is returning to America in two weeks."

"Maybe we can persuade her to stay?"

He sniffed a laugh. Leaning down so that only Emory would hear, he said, "She has a fiancé in New York."

Emory's features twisted into a scowl. "And she's in Italy? For months? Without him? Doesn't sound like much of a fiancé to me."

That brought Rafe up short. There was no way in hell he'd let the woman he loved stay alone in Italy for *months*. Especially not if the woman he loved was Daniella.

He didn't tell Emory that. His reasoning was mixed up in feelings that he wasn't supposed to have. He'd gone the route of a relationship once. He'd given up apprenticeships to please Kamila. Which meant he'd given up his dream for her. And still they hadn't made it.

But he'd learned a lesson. Relationships only put the future of his restaurants at stake, so he satisfied himself with one-night stands.

Dani would not be a one-night stand.

But Mancini's really wasn't fine without her.

And Mancini's was his dream. He needed Daniella at his restaurant way too much to break his own rule about relationships. And that was the real bottom line. Getting involved with her would risk his dream as much as Kamila had. He needed her as an employee and he needed to put everything else out of his mind.

Emory caught Rafe's arm. "Maybe there is an opportunity here. If she's truly unhappy, especially with her fiancé, you might be able to convince her Mancini's should be her new career."

That was exactly what Rafe intended to do.

"But you can't have that discussion over the phone. You need to go to Palazzo di Comparino tomorrow. Talk to her personally. Make your case. Offer her money."

"Okay. I'll be out tomorrow morning, maybe all day if I need the time. You handle things while I'm gone."

Emory grinned. "That's my boy."

At the crack of dawn the next morning, Louisa woke Dani and said she was ready to take the bus back to Monte Calanetti. She was happy to have met Dani's foster mom's relatives, but she was nervous, antsy about Palazzo di Comparino. It was time to go back.

After grabbing coffee at a nearby bistro, Dani walked her friend to the bus station, then spent the day with her foster mother's family. By late afternoon, she left, also restless. Like Louisa, she'd loved meeting the Felice family, but they weren't *her* family. Her family was the little group of restaurant workers at Mancini's.

Saddened, she began the walk back to her hotel. A block before she reached it, she passed the bistro again. Though the day was crisp, it was sunny. Warm in the rays that poured down on a little table near the sidewalk, she sat.

She ordered coffee, telling herself it wasn't odd that she felt a connection to the staff at Mancini's. They were nice people. Personable. Passionate. Of course, she felt as if they were family. She'd mothered the waitresses, babied the customers and fallen for Emory like a favorite uncle.

But she'd never see any of them again. She'd been fired

from Mancini's. Rafe hated her. She wouldn't go home happy, satisfied to have met Rosa's relatives, because the connection she'd made had been to a totally different set of people. She would board her plane depressed. Saddened. Returning to a man who didn't even want to pick her up at the airport. A man whose marriage proposal she was going to have to refuse.

A street vendor caught her arm and handed her a red rose.

Surprised, she looked at him, then the rose, then back at him again. "*Grazie*... I think."

He grinned. "It's not from me. It's from that gentleman over there." He pointed behind him.

Dani's eyes widened when she saw Rafe leaning against a lamppost. Wearing jeans, a tight T-shirt and the waist-length black wool coat that he'd worn to the tavern, he looked sexy. But also alone. Very alone. The way she felt in the pit of her stomach when she thought about going back to New York.

Her gaze fell to the rose. Red. For passion. But with someone like Rafe who was a bundle of passion about his restaurant, about his food, about his customers, the color choice could mean anything.

Carrying the rose, she got up from her seat and walked over to him. "How did you find me?"

"Would you believe I guessed where you were?"

"That would have to be a very lucky guess."

He sighed. "I talked to your roommate, Louisa, this afternoon. She told me where you were staying, and I drove to Rome. Walking to your hotel, I saw you here, having coffee."

He glanced away. "Look, can we talk?" He shoved his hands tightly into the side pockets of his coat and returned his gaze to hers. "We've missed you."

"We?"

She almost cursed herself for the question. But she

needed to hear him say it so she'd know she wasn't crazy, getting feelings for a guy who found it so easy to fire her.

"*I've* missed you." He sighed. "Two trust-fund babies faked me out the other night. They insulted my food and when they couldn't get a rise out of me, they made it look like I was tossing one out on her ear to get a picture for Instagram."

She couldn't help it. She laughed. "Instagram?"

"It's the bane of my existence."

"But you hadn't lost your temper?"

He shook his head and glanced away. "No. I hadn't." He looked back at her. "I remembered some things you'd done." He smiled. "I learned."

Her heart picked up at the knowledge that he'd learned from her, and the thrill that he was here, that he'd missed her. "You're not a bad guy."

His face twisted around a smile he clearly tried to hide. "According to Emory, I'm just an overworked guy. And interviewing for a new maître d' isn't helping. Especially when no one I talk to fits. It's why I need you. You're the first person to take over the dining room well enough that I don't worry."

She counted to ten, breathlessly waiting for him to expand on that. When he didn't, she said, "And that's all it is?"

"I know you want there to be something romantic between us. But there are things that separate us. Not just your fiancé, but my temperament. Really? Could you see yourself happy with me? Or when you look at me, do you see a man who takes what he wants and walks away? Because that's the man I really am. I put my restaurant first. I have no time for a relationship."

Her heart wept at what he said. But her sensible self, the lonely foster child who didn't trust the wash of feelings that raced through her every time she got within two feet of him, understood. He was a gorgeous man, born for the limelight, looking to make a name for himself. She was a foster kid, looking for a home. Peace. Quiet. Security. They might be physically attracted, but, emotionally, they were totally wrong for each other. No matter how drawn she was to him, she knew the truth as well as he did.

"You can't commit?"

He shook his head. "My commitment is to Mancini's. To my career. My reputation. I want to be one of Europe's famed chefs. Mancini's is my stepping stone. I do not have time for what other men want. A woman on their arm. Fancy parties. Marriage. To me those are irrelevant. All I want is success. So I would hurt you. And I don't want to hurt you."

"Which makes anything between us just business?"

"Just business."

Her job at Mancini's had awakened feelings in Dani she'd never experienced. Self-worth. A sense of place. An unshakable belief that she belonged there. And the click of connection that made her feel she had a home. Something deep inside her needed Mancini's. But she wouldn't go back only to be fired again.

"And you need me?"

He rolled his eyes. "You Americans. Why must you be showered with accolades?"

Oh, he did love to be gruff.

She slid her hand into the crook of his elbow and pointed to her table at the bistro. "I don't need accolades. I need acknowledgment of my place at Mancini's…and my coffee. I'm freezing."

He pulled his arm away from her hand and wrapped it around her shoulders. She knew he meant it only as a gesture between friends, but she felt his warmth seep through to her. Longing tugged at her heart. A fierce yearning that clung and wouldn't let go.

"You should wear a heavier coat."

His voice was soft, intimate, sending the feeling of rightness through her again.

"It was warm when I came here."

"And now it is cold. So from here on I will make sure you wear a bigger coat." He paused. His head tilted. "Maybe you need me, too?"

She did. But not in the way he thought. She wanted him to love her. Really love her. But to be the man of her dreams, he would have to be different. To be warm and loving. To want her—

And he might. Today. But he'd warned her that anything he felt for her was temporary. He couldn't commit. He didn't want to commit. And unless she wanted to get her heart broken, she had to really hear what he was saying. If she was going to get the opportunity to go back to the first place in her life that felt like home, Mancini's, and the first people who genuinely felt like family, his staff, then a romance between them had to be out of the question.

"I need Mancini's. I like it there. I like the people."

"Ah. So we agree."

"I guess. All I know for sure is that I don't want to go back to New York yet."

He laughed. They reached her table and he pulled out her chair for her. "That doesn't speak well of your fiancé."

Hauling in a breath, she sat, but she said nothing. Her stretching of the truth to Rafe about Paul being her fiancé sat in her stomach like a brick. Still, even though she knew she was going to reject his marriage proposal, it protected her and Rafe. Rafe wouldn't go after another man's woman. Not even for a fling. And he was right. If they had a fling, she would be crushed when he moved on.

One of his eyebrows rose, as he waited for her reply.

She decided they needed her stretched truth. But she couldn't out-and-out lie. "All right. Paul is not the perfect guy."

"I'm not trying to ruin your relationship. I simply believe you should think all of this through. You have a place here in Italy. Mancini's needs you. I would like for you to stay in Italy and work for me permanently, and if you decide to, then maybe your fiancé should be coming here."

She laughed. Really? Paul move to Italy because of her? He wouldn't even drive to the airport for her.

Still, she didn't want Paul in the discussion of her returning to Mancini's. She'd already decided to refuse his proposal. If she stayed in Italy, it had to be for her reasons.

"I think we're getting ahead of ourselves. I have a few weeks before I have to make any decisions."

"Two weeks and two days."

"Yes."

He caught her hands. Kissed the knuckles. "So stay. Stay with me, Daniella. Be the face of Mancini's."

Her heart kicked against her ribs. The way he said "Stay with me, Daniella" froze her lungs, heated her blood. She glanced at the red rose sitting on the table, reminded herself it didn't mean anything but a way to break the ice when he found her. He wasn't asking her to stay for any reason other than her abilities in his restaurant. And she shouldn't want to stay for any reason other than the job. If she could prove herself in the next two weeks, she wouldn't be boarding a plane depressed. She wouldn't be boarding a plane at all. She'd be helping to run a thriving business. Her entire life would change.

She pulled her hands away. "I can't accept Louisa's hospitality forever. I need to be able to support myself. Hostessing doesn't pay much."

He growled.

She laughed. He was so strong and so handsome and so perfect that when he let his guard down and was himself, his real self, with her, everything inside her filled with crazy joy. And maybe if she just focused on making him her friend, a friend she could keep forever, working for him could be fun.

"I can't pay a hostess an exorbitant salary."

"So give me a title to justify the money."

He sighed. "A title?"

"Sure, something like general manager should warrant a raise big enough that I can afford my own place."

His eyes widened. "General manager?"

"Come on, Rafe. Let's get to the bottom line here. If things work out when we return to Mancini's, I'm going to be taking on a huge chunk of your work. I'm also going to be relocating to another *country*. You'll need to make it worth my while."

He shook his head. "Dear God, you are bossy."

"But I'm right."

He sighed. "Fine. But if you're getting that title, you will earn it."

She inclined her head. "Seems fair."

"You'll learn to order supplies, check deliveries, do the job of managing things Emory and I don't have time for."

"Makes perfect sense."

He sighed. His eyes narrowed. "Anything else?"

She laughed. "One more thing." Her laughter became a silly giggle when he scowled at her. "A ride back to Louisa's."

He rolled his eyes. "Yes. I will drive you back to Louisa's. If you wish, I will even help you find an apartment."

Leaving the rose, she stood and pushed away from the table. "You keep getting ahead of things. We have two weeks for me to figure out if staying at Mancini's is right for me." She turned to head back to the hotel to check out, but spun to face him again. "Were I you, I'd be on my best behavior."

The next morning, she called Paul. If staying in Italy was the rest of her life, the *real* rest of her life, she had to make things right.

"Do you know what time it is?"

She could hear the sleep in his voice and winced. "Yes. Sorry. But I wanted to catch you before work."

"That's fine."

She squeezed her eyes shut as she gathered her courage. It seemed so wrong to break up with someone over the phone and, yet, they'd barely spoken to each other in six months. This was the right thing to do.

"Look, Paul, I'm sorry to tell you this over the phone, but I can't accept your marriage proposal."

"What?"

She could almost picture him sitting up in bed, her bad news bringing him fully awake.

"I'm actually thinking of not coming back to New York at all, but staying in Italy."

"What? What about your job?"

"I have a new job."

"Where?"

"At a restaurant."

"So you're leaving teaching to be a waitress?"

"A hostess."

"Oh, there's a real step up."

"Actually, I'm general manager," she said, glad she'd talked Rafe into the title. She couldn't blame Paul for being confused or angry, and knew he deserved an honest explanation.

"And I love Italy. I feel like I belong here." She sucked in a breath. "We've barely talked in six months. I'm going to make a wild guess that you haven't even missed me. I think we were only together because it was convenient."

Another man's silence might have been interpreted as misery. Knowing Paul the way she did, she recognized it as more or less a confirmation that she was right.

"I'm sorry not to accept your proposal, but I'm very happy."

After a second, he said, "Okay, then. I'm glad."

The breath blew back into her lungs. "Really?"

"Yeah. I did think we'd make a good married couple,

but I knew when you didn't say yes immediately that you might have second thoughts."

"I'm sorry."

"Don't be sorry. This is just the way life works sometimes."

And that was her pragmatic Paul. His lack of emotion might have made her feel secure at one time, but now she knew she needed more.

They talked another minute and Dani disconnected the call, feeling as if a weight had been taken from her shoulders, only to have it quickly replaced by another one. She'd had to be fair to Paul, but now the only defense she'd have against Rafe's charms would be her own discipline and common sense.

She hoped that was enough.

CHAPTER NINE

HER RETURN TO the restaurant was as joyous as a celebration. Emory grinned. The waitresses fawned over her. The busboys grew red faced. The chefs breathed a sigh of relief.

Annoyance worked its way through Rafe. Not that he didn't want his staff to adore her. He did. That was why she was back. The problem was he couldn't stop reliving their meeting in Rome. He'd said everything that he'd wanted to say. That he'd missed her. That he wanted her back. But he'd kept it all in the context of business. He'd missed her help. He wanted her to become the face of Mancini's. He didn't want anything romantic with her because he didn't want to hurt her. He'd been all business. And it had worked.

But with her return playing out around him, his heart rumbled at the injustice. He hadn't lied when he said he didn't want her back for himself, that he didn't want something romantic between them. His fierce protection of Mancini's wouldn't let him get involved with an employee he needed. But here at the restaurant, with her looking so pretty, helping make his dream a reality, he just wanted to kiss her.

He reminded himself that she had a fiancé—

A fiancé she admitted was not the perfect guy.

Bah! That fiancé was supposed to be the key weapon in his arsenal of ways to keep himself away from her. Her admission that he wasn't perfect, even the fact that she was considering staying in Italy, called her whole engagement into question. And caused all his feelings for her to surface and swell.

She swept into the kitchen. Wearing a blue dress that highlighted her blue eyes and accented a figure so lush she was absolutely edible, she glided over to Emory. He took her hands and kissed the back of both.

"You look better than anything on the menu."

Rafe sucked in a breath, controlling the unwanted ripple of longing.

Dani unexpectedly stepped toward Emory, put her arms around him and hugged him. Emory closed his eyes as if to savor it, a smile lifted his lips.

Rafe's yearning intensified, but with it came a tidal wave of jealousy. He lowered his knife on an unsuspecting stalk of celery, chopping it with unnecessary force.

Dani faced him. "Why don't you give me the key and I'll open the front door for the lunch crowd?"

He rolled his gaze toward her slowly. Even as the businessman inside him cheered her return, the jealous man who was filled with need wondered if he wasn't trying to drive himself insane.

"Emory, give her your key."

The sous-chef instantly fished his key ring out of his pocket and dislodged the key for Mancini's. "Gladly."

"Don't be so joyful." He glanced at Dani again, at the soft yellow hair framing her face, her happy blue eyes. "Have a key made for yourself this afternoon and return Emory's to him."

She smiled. "Will do, boss."

She walked out of the kitchen, her high heels clicking on the tile floor, her bottom swaying with every step, all eyes of the kitchen staff watching her go.

Jealousy spewed through him. "Back to work!" he yelped, and everybody scrambled.

Emory sauntered over. "Something is wrong?"

He chopped the celery. "Everything is fine."

The sous-chef glanced at the door Dani had just walked through. "She's very happy to be back."

Rafe refused to answer that.

Emory turned to him again. "So did you talk her into staying? Is her fiancé joining her here? What's going on?"

Rafe chopped the celery. "I don't know."

"You don't know if she's staying?"

"She said her final two weeks here would be something like a trial run for her."

"Then we must be incredibly good to her."

"I gave her a raise, a title. If she doesn't like those, then we should be glad if she goes home to her *fiancé*." He all but spat the word *fiancé*, getting angrier by the moment, as he gave Dani everything she wanted but was denied everything he wanted.

Emory said, "I still say something is up with this fiancé of hers. If she didn't tell him she's considering staying in Italy, then there's trouble in paradise. If she did, and he isn't on the next flight to Florence, then I question his sanity."

Rafe laughed.

"Seriously, Rafe, has she talked to you about him? I just don't get an engaged vibe from her."

"Are you saying she's lying?"

Emory inclined his head. "I don't think she's lying as much as I think her fiancé might be a real dud, and her engagement as flat as a crepe."

Rafe said only, "Humph," but once again her statement that her fiancé wasn't the perfect guy rolled through his head.

"I only mention this because I think it works in our favor."

"How so?"

"If she's not really in love, if her fiancé doesn't really love her, we have the power of Italy on our side."

"To?"

"To coax her to stay. To seduce her away from a guy who doesn't deserve her."

Rafe chopped the celery. His dreams were filled with scenarios where he seduced Daniella. Except he had a feeling that kind of seducing wasn't what Emory meant.

"Somehow or another we have to be so good to her that she realizes what she has in New York isn't what she wants."

Sulking, Rafe scraped the celery into a bowl. Why did he have to be the one doing all the wooing? *He* was a catch. He wanted her eyelashes to flutter when he walked by and her eyes to warm with interest. He had some pride, too.

Emory shook his head. "Okay. Be stubborn. But you'll be sorry if some pasty office dweller from New York descends on us and scoops her back to America."

Rafe all but growled in frustration at the picture that formed in his head. Especially since she had said her fiancé wasn't perfect. Shouldn't a woman in love swoon for the man she's promised to marry?

Yes. Yes. She should.

Yet, here she was, considering staying. Not bringing her fiancé into the equation.

And he suddenly saw what Emory was saying.

She wasn't happy with her fiancé. She was searching for something. She'd gone to Rome looking for her foster mother's relatives—family! What Dani had been looking for in Rome was family! That was why she was getting so close to the staff at Mancini's.

Still, something was missing.

He tapped his index fingers against his lips, thinking, and when the answer came to him he smiled and turned to Emory. "I will need time off tomorrow."

Emory's face fell. "You're taking another day?"

"Just lunch. And Daniella will be out for lunch, too."

Emory caught his gaze. "Really?"

"Yes. Don't go thinking this is about funny business.

I'm taking her apartment hunting. Dani is a woman looking for a family. She thinks she's found it with us. But Mancini's isn't a home. It's a place of business. Once I help her get a house, somewhere to put down roots, it will all fall into place for her."

Rafe's first free minute, he called the real estate agent who'd sold him his penthouse. She told him she had some suitable listings in Monte Calanetti and he set up three appointments for Daniella.

When the lunch crowd cleared, he walked into the empty, quiet dining room.

Dani smiled as he approached. "You're not going to yell at me for not going home and costing you two hours' wages are you?"

"You are management now. I expect you here every hour the restaurant is open."

"Except my days off."

He groaned. "Except your days off. If you feel comfortable not being here two days every week, I am fine with it. But if something goes wrong, you will answer for it."

She laughed. "Whatever. I've been coaching Allegra. She'll be much better from here on out. No more catastrophes while I'm gone."

"Great. I've lined up three appointments for us tomorrow."

She turned from the podium. "With vendors?"

"With my friend who is a real estate agent."

"I told you we shouldn't get ahead of ourselves."

"Our market is tight. You must be on top of things to get a good place."

"I haven't—"

He interrupted her. "You haven't decided you're staying. I get that. But if you choose to stay, I don't want you panicking. Getting ahead of a problem is how a smart businessperson staves off disaster."

"Yeah, I know."

"Good. Tomorrow morning, Emory will take over lunch prep while you and I apartment hunt. We can be back for dinner."

Sun poured in through the huge window of the kitchen of the first unit Maria Salvetti showed Rafe and Dani the next morning. Unfortunately, cold air flowed in through the cracks between the window and the wall.

Dani eased her eyes away from the unwanted ventilation and watched as Rafe walked across a worn hardwood floor, his motorcycle boots clicking along, his jeans outlining an absolutely perfect behind and his black leather jacket, collar flipped up, giving him the look of a dangerous rebel.

For the second time that morning, she told herself she was grateful he'd been honest with her about his inability to commit. She didn't know a woman who wouldn't fall victim to his steel-gray eyes and his muscled body. She had to be strong. And her decision to stay at Mancini's had to be made for all the right reasons.

She faced Maria. "I'd have to fix this myself?"

"*Sì*. It is for sale. It is not a rental."

She turned to Rafe. "I wouldn't have time to work twelve-hour days and be my own general contractor."

"You could hire someone."

She winced as she ran her hand along the crack between the wall and window. "Oh, yeah? Just how big is my raise going to be?"

"Big enough."

She shook her head. "I still don't like it."

She also didn't like the second condo. She did have warm, fuzzy feelings for the old farmhouse a few miles away from the village, but that needed more work than the first condo she'd seen.

Maria's smile dipped a notch every time Dani rejected a prospective home. She'd tried to explain that she wasn't even sure she was staying in Italy, but Maria kept plugging along.

After Dani rejected the final option, Maria shook Rafe's hand, then Dani's and said, "I'll check our listings again and get back to you."

She slid into her car and Dani sighed, glad to be rid of her. Not that Maria wasn't nice, but with her decision about staying in Italy up in the air, looking for somewhere to live seemed premature. "Sorry."

"Don't apologize quite yet." He pulled his cell phone from his jacket and dialed a number. "Carlo, this is Rafe. Could you have a key for the empty condo at the front desk? *Grazie.*" He slipped his phone into his jacket again.

She frowned at him. "You have a place to show me?"

He headed for his SUV, motioning for her to follow him. "Actually, I thought Maria would have taken you to his apartment first. It's a newly renovated condo in my building."

She stopped walking. "*Your* building?" She might be smart enough to realize she and Rafe were a bad bet, but all along she'd acknowledged that their spending too much time together was tempting fate. Now he wanted them to live in the same building?

"After Emory, you are my most valued employee. A huge part of Mancini's success. We need to be available for each other. Plus, there would be two floors between us. It's not like we'd even run into each other."

She still hesitated. "Your building's that big?"

"No. I value my privacy that much." He sighed. "Seriously. Just come with me to see the place and you will understand."

Dani glanced around as she entered the renovated old building, Rafe behind her. Black-and-white block tiles were accented by red sofas and chairs in a lounge area of the lobby. The desk for the doorman sat discreetly in a corner.

Leaning over her shoulder, Rafe said, "My home is the penthouse."

His warm breath tickled her ear and desire poured through her. She almost turned and yelled at him for flirting with her. Instead, she squelched the feeling. He probably wasn't flirting with her. This was just who he was. Gorgeous. Sinfully sexy. And naturally flirtatious. If she really intended to stay in Italy and work for him, she had to get accustomed to him. As she'd realized after she'd spoken to Paul, she would need discipline and common sense to keep her sanity.

He pointed at the side-by-side elevators. "I don't use those, and you can't use them to get to my apartment."

His breath tiptoed to her neck and trickled down her spine. Still, she kept her expression neutral when she turned and put them face-to-face, so close she could see the little flecks of silver in his eyes.

Just as her reactions couldn't matter, how he looked—his sexy face, his smoky eyes—also had to be irrelevant. If she didn't put all this into perspective now, this temptation could rule her life. Or ruin her life.

She gave him her most professional smile. "And I'd be a few floors away?"

"Not just a few floors, but also a locked elevator."

Dangling the apartment key, he motioned for her to enter the elevator when it arrived. They rode up in silence. He unlocked the door to the available unit and she gasped.

"Oh, my God." She spun to face him. "I can afford this?"

He laughed. "Yes."

From the look of the lobby, she'd expected the apartment to be ultramodern. The kind of place she would have killed to have in New York. Black-and-white. Sharp, but sterile. Something cool and sophisticated for her and distant Paul.

But warm beiges and yellows covered these walls. The

kitchen area was cozy, with a granite-topped breakfast bar where she could put three stools.

She saw it filled with people. Louisa. Coworkers from Mancini's. And neighbors she'd meet who could become like a family.

She caught that thought before it could take root. Something about Italy always caused her to see things through rose-colored glasses, and if she didn't stop, she was going to end up making this choice before she knew for certain that she could work with Rafe as a friend or a business associate, and forget about trying for anything more.

She turned to Rafe again. "Don't make me want something I can't have."

"I already told you that you can afford it."

"I know."

"So why do you think you can't have it?"

It was exactly what she'd dreamed of as a child, but she couldn't let herself fall in love with it. Or let Rafe see just how drawn she was to this place. If he knew her weakness, he'd easily lure her into staying before she was sure it was the right thing to do.

She pointed at the kitchen, which managed to look cozy even with sleek stainless-steel appliances, dark cabinets and shiny surfaces. "It's awfully modern."

"So you want to go back to the farmhouse with the holes in the wall?"

"No." She turned away again, though she lovingly ran her hand along the granite countertop, imagining herself rolling out dough to make cut-out cookies. She'd paint them with sugary frosting and serve them to friends at Christmas. "I want a homey kitchen that smells like heaven."

"You have that at Mancini's."

"I want a big fat sofa with a matching chair that feels like it swallows you up when you sit in it."

"You can buy whatever furniture you want."

"I want to turn my thermostat down to fifty-eight at night so I can snuggle under thick covers."

He stared at her as if she were crazy. "And you can do that here."

"Maybe."

"Undoubtedly." He sighed. "You have an idealized vision of home."

"Most foster kids do."

He leaned his shoulder against the wall near the kitchen. His smoky eyes filled with curiosity. She wasn't surprised when he said, "You've never really told me about your life. You mentioned getting shuffled from foster home to foster home, but you never explained how you got into foster care in the first place."

She shrugged. Every time she thought about being six years old, or eight years old, or ten years old—shifted every few months to the house of a stranger, trying unsuccessfully to mingle with the other kids—a flash of rejection froze her heart. She was an adult before she'd realized no one had rejected her, per se. Each child was only protecting himself. They'd all been hurt. They were all afraid. Not connecting was how they coped.

Nonetheless, the memories of crying herself to sleep and longing for something better still guided her. It was why she believed she could keep her distance from Rafe. Common sense and a longing for stability directed her decisions. Along with a brutal truth. The world was a difficult place. She knew that because she'd lived it.

"There's not much to tell. My mom was a drug addict."

He winced.

"There's no sense sugarcoating it."

"Of course there is. Everyone sugarcoats his or her past. It's how we deal."

She turned to him again, surprised by the observation. She'd always believed living in truth kept her sane. He seemed to believe exactly the opposite.

"Yeah. What did you sugarcoat?"

"I tell you that I'm not a good bet as a romantic partner."

She sniffed a laugh.

"What I should have said is that I'm a real bastard."

She laughed again. "Seriously, Rafe. I got the message the first time. You want nothing romantic between us."

"Mancini's needs you and I am not on speaking terms with any woman I've ever dated. So I keep you for Mancini's."

She looked around at the apartment, unable to stop the warm feeling that flooded her when he said he would keep her. Still, he didn't mean it the way her heart took it. So, remembering to use her common sense, she focused her attention on the apartment, envisioning it decorated to her taste. The picture that formed had her wrestling with the urge to tell him to get his landlord on the line so she could make an offer—then she realized something amazing.

"You knew I'd love this."

He had the good graces to look sheepish. "I assumed you would."

"No assuming about it, you *knew*."

"All right, I knew you would love it."

She walked over to him, as the strangest thought formed in her head. Maybe it wouldn't take a genius to realize the way to entice a former foster child would be with a home. But no one had ever wanted her around enough to figure that out.

"How did you know?"

He shrugged. His strong shoulders lifted the black leather of his jacket and ruffled the curls of his long, dark hair. "It didn't take much to realize that you'd probably lost your sense of home when your foster mother died."

She caught his gaze. "So?"

"So, I think you came to Italy hoping to find it with her relatives."

"They're nice people."

"Yes, but you didn't feel a connection to Rosa's nice relatives. Yet, you keep coming back to Mancini's, because you did connect with us."

Her heart stuttered. Even her almost fiancé hadn't understood why she so desperately wanted to find Rosa's family. But Rafe, a guy who had known her a little over two weeks, a guy she'd had a slim few personal conversations with, had seen it.

He'd also hit the nail on the head about Mancini's. She felt they were her family. The only thing she didn't have here in Italy was an actual, physical home.

And he'd found her one.

He cared about her enough to want to please her, to satisfy needs she kept close to her heart.

Afraid of the direction of her thoughts, she turned away and walked into the master bedroom. Seeing the huge space, her eyebrows rose. "Wow. Nice."

Rafe was right behind her. "Are you changing the subject on me?"

She pivoted and faced him. He seemed genuinely clueless about what he was doing. Not just giving her everything she wanted, but caring about her. He was getting to know her—the real her—in a way no one else in her life ever had. And the urge to fall into his arms, confess her fears, her hopes, her longings, was so strong, she had to walk away from him. If she fell into his arms now, she'd never come out. Especially if he comforted her. God help her if he whispered anything romantic.

"I think we need to change the subject."

"Why?"

She walked over to him again. For fifty cents, she'd answer him. She'd put her arms around his neck and tell him he was falling for her. The things he did—searching her out in Rome, making her general manager, helping her find a home—those weren't things a boss did. No matter how much he believed he needed her as an employee, he also had feelings for her.

But he didn't see it.

And she didn't trust it. He'd said he was a bastard? What if he really was? What if he liked her now, but didn't tomorrow?

"Because I'm afraid. Every time I put down roots, it fails." She said the words slowly, clearly, so there'd be no misunderstanding. Rafe was a smart guy. If she stayed in Italy, shared the joy of making Mancini's successful, no matter how strong she was, how much discipline she had, how much common sense she used, there was a chance she'd fall in love with him.

And then what?

Would she hang around his restaurant desperate for crumbs of affection from a guy who slept with her, then moved on?

That would be an epic fail. The very thought made her ill.

Because she couldn't tell him that, she stuck with the safe areas. The things they could discuss.

"For as good as I am at Mancini's, I can see us having a blowout fight and you firing me again. And for as much as I like the waitstaff, I can see them getting new jobs and moving on. This decision comes with risks for me. I know enough not to pretend things will be perfect. But I have to have at least a little security."

"You and your security. Maybe to hell with security and focus on a little bit of happiness."

Oh, she would love to focus on being happy. Touring Italy with him, stolen kisses, nights of passion. But he'd told her that wasn't in the cards and she believed him. Somehow she had to stop herself from getting those kinds of thoughts every time he said something that fell out of business mode and tipped over into the personal. That would be the only way she could stay at Mancini's.

When she didn't answer, he sighed. "I don't think it's an accident you found Mancini's."

"Of course not. Nico sent me."

"I am not talking about Nico. I'm talking about destiny."

She laughed lightly and walked away from him. It was almost funny the way he used the words and phrases of a lover to lure her to a job. It was no wonder her thoughts always went in the wrong direction. He took her there. Thank God she had ahold of herself enough to see his words for what they were. A very passionate man trying to get his own way. To fight for her sanity, she would always have to stand up to him.

"Foster kids don't get destinies. We get the knowledge that we need to educate ourselves so we can have security. If you really want me to stay, let me come to the decision for the right reasons. Because if I stay, you are not getting rid of me. I will make Mancini's my home." She caught his gaze. "Are you prepared for that?"

CHAPTER TEN

WAS HE PREPARED for that?

What the hell kind of question was that for her to ask?

He caught her arm when she turned to walk away. "Of course, I'm prepared for that! Good God, woman, I drove to Rome to bring you back."

She shook her head with an enigmatic laugh. "Okay. Just don't say I didn't warn you."

He rolled his eyes heavenward. Women. Who could figure them out? "I am warned." He motioned to the door. "Come. I'll drive you back to Louisa's."

But by the time they reached Louisa's villa and he drove back to his condo to change for work, her strange statement had rattled around in his head and made him crazy. Was he prepared for her staying? Idiocy. He'd all but made her a partner in his business. He *wanted* her to stay.

He changed his clothes and headed to Mancini's. Walking into the kitchen, he tried to shove her words out of his head but they wouldn't go—until he found the staff in unexpectedly good spirits. Then his focus fell to their silly grins.

"What's going on?"

Emory turned from the prep table. "Have you seen today's issue of *Tuscany Review*?"

In all the confusion over Daniella, he'd forgotten that today was the day the tourist magazine came out. He snatched it from Emory's hands.

"Page twenty-nine."

He flicked through the pages, getting to the one he wanted, and there was a picture of Dani. So many tourists had snapped pictures that someone from the magazine could have come in and taken this one without anyone in the restaurant paying any mind.

He read the headline. "Mancini's gets a fresh start."

"Read the whole article. It's fantastic."

As he began to skim the words, Emory said, "There's mention of the new hostess being pretty and personable."

Rafe inclined his head. "She is both."

"And mention of your food without mention of your temper."

His gaze jerked up to Emory. "No kidding."

"No kidding. It's as if your temper didn't exist."

He pressed the magazine to his chest. "Thank God I went to Rome and brought her back."

Daniella pushed open the door. Dressed in a sheath the color of ripe apricots, she smiled as she walked toward Rafe and Emory. "I heard something about a magazine."

Rafe silently handed it to her.

She glanced down and laughed. "Well, look at me."

"Yes. Look at you." He wanted to pull her close and hug her, but he crossed his arms on his chest. The very fact that he wanted to hug her was proof he needed to keep his distance. Even forgetting about the fiancé she had back home, she needed security enough that he wouldn't tempt her away from finding it. Her staying had to be about Mancini's and her desire for a place, a home. He had to make sure she got what she wanted out of this deal—without breaking her heart. Because if he broke her heart, she'd leave. And everything they'd accomplished up to now would have been for nothing.

"You realize that even if every chef and busboy cycles out, and every waitress quits after university, Emory and I will always be here."

Emory grinned at Daniella. Rafe nudged him. "Stop behaving like one of the Three Stooges. This is serious for her."

She looked up from the magazine with a smile for Rafe. "Yes. I know you will always be here." Her smile grew. "Did you ever stop to think that maybe that's part of the problem?"

With that she walked out of the kitchen and Rafe shook his head.

"She talks in riddles." But deep down he knew what was happening. He'd told her they'd never become lovers. She had feelings for him. Hell, he had feelings for her, but he intended to fight them. He'd told her anything between them was wrong, so she had to be sure she could work with him knowing there'd never be anything between them.

And maybe that's what she meant about being prepared.

Lately, it seemed he was fighting his feelings as much as she was fighting hers.

Two nights later, as the dinner service began to slow down, Rafe stepped out into the dining room to see his friend Nico walking into Mancini's. Nico's eyes lit when he saw Dani standing at the podium.

"Look at you!" He took her hand and gave her a little twirl to let her show off another pretty blue dress that hugged her figure.

Jealousy rippled through Rafe, but he squelched it. He put her needs ahead of his because that served Mancini's needs. It was a litany he repeated at least four times a day. After her comment about him being part of the reason her decision was so difficult, he'd known he had to get himself in line or lose her.

As he walked out of the kitchen, he heard Nico say, "Rafe tells me you're working out marvelously."

She smiled sheepishly. "I can't imagine anyone not loving working here."

Rafe sucked in a happy breath. She loved working at Mancini's. He knew that, of course, but it was good to hear her say it. It felt normal to hear her say it. As if she knew she belonged here. Clearly, keeping his distance the past two days had worked. Mancini's was warm and happy. The way he'd always envisioned it.

"We don't have reservations," Nico said when Dani glanced at the computer screen.

She smiled. "No worries. The night's winding down. We have plenty of space."

Seeing him approach, Nico said, "And here's the chef now."

"Nico!" Rafe grabbed him and gave him a bear hug. "What brings you here?"

"I saw your ravioli on Instagram and decided I had to try it."

"Bah! Damned trust-fund babies. I should—" He stopped suddenly. Half-hidden behind Nico was Marianna Amatucci, Nico's sister, who'd been traveling for the past year. Short with wild curly hair and honey skin, she was the picture of a natural Italian beauty.

"Marianna!" He nudged Nico out of the way and hugged her, too, lifting her up to swing her around. Rafe hadn't even seen her to say hello in months. Having her here put another piece of normalcy back in his life.

She giggled when he plopped her to the floor again.

"Daniella," he said, one hand around Marianna's waist, the other clasped on Nico's shoulder. "These are my friends. Nico and his baby sister, Marianna. They get the best table in the house."

She smiled her understanding, grabbed two menus and led Nico and Marianna into the dining room. "This way."

Rafe stopped her. "Not *there*. I want them by my kitchen." He took the menus from her hands. "I want to spoil them."

Nico chuckled and caught Dani's gaze. "What he really means is use us for guinea pigs."

She laughed, her gaze meeting Nico's and her cheeks turning pink.

An unexpected thought exploded in Rafe's brain. He'd told Dani he wanted nothing romantic between them. Her fiancé was a dud. Nico was a good-looking man. And Dani was a beautiful, personable woman. If she stayed, at some point, Dani and Nico could become lovers.

His gut tightened.

Still, shouldn't he be glad if Nico was interested in Daniella and that interest caused her to stay?

Of course he should. What he wanted from Daniella was a face for his business. If Nico could help get her to stay, then Rafe should help him woo her.

"You are lucky the night is nearly over," Rafe said as he pulled out Marianna's chair. He handed the menus to them both.

Smiling warmly at Nico, Dani said, "Can I take your drink orders?"

Nico put his elbow on the table and his chin on his fist as he contemplated Daniella, as if she were a puzzle he was trying to figure out.

Thinking of Dani and Nico together was one thing. Seeing his friend's eyes on her was quite another. The horrible black syrup of jealously poured through Rafe's veins like hot wax.

Unable to endure it, he waved Daniella away. "Go. I will take his drink order. You're needed at the door. The night isn't quite over yet."

She gave Nico one last smile and headed to her post.

Happier with her away from Nico, Rafe listened to his friend's wine choice.

Marianna said, "Just water for me."

Rafe gaped at her. "You need wine."

She shook her head. "I need water."

Rafe's jaw dropped. "You cannot be an Italian and refuse wine with dinner."

Nico waved a hand. "It's not a big deal. She's been weird ever since she came home. Just bring her the water."

Rafe called Allegra over so she could get Nico's wine from the bar and Marianna's water. All the while, Dani walked customers from the podium, past Nico, who would watch her amble by.

Rafe sucked in a breath, not understanding the feelings rumbling through him. He wanted Daniella to stay. Nico might give her a reason to do just that. He could not romance her himself. Yet he couldn't bear to have his friend even look at her?

"Give me ten minutes and I will make you the happiest man alive."

Nico laughed, his eyes on Daniella. "I sincerely doubt you can do that with food."

Jealousy sputtered through Rafe again. "Get your mind out of the gutter and off my hostess!"

Nico's eyes narrowed. "Why? Are you staking a claim?"

Rafe's chest froze and he couldn't speak. But Marianna shook her head. "Men. Does it always have to be about sex with you?"

Nico laughed.

Rafe spun away, rushing into the kitchen, angry with Nico but angrier with himself. He should celebrate Nico potentially being a reason for Daniella to stay. Instead, he was filled with blistering-hot rage. Toward his friend. It was insane.

To make up for his unwanted anger, he put together the best meals he'd ever created. Unfortunately, it didn't take ten minutes. It took forty.

Allegra took out antipasto and soups while he worked. When he returned to the dining room, there were no more people at the door. All customers had been seated. Tables that emptied weren't being refilled. Anticipating going home, the busboys cheerfully cleared away dishes.

And Dani sat with Nico and Marianna.

Forcing himself to be friendly—happy—Rafe set the plates of food in front of Nico and his sister.

Marianna said, "Oh, that smells heavenly."

Nico nodded. "Impressive, Rafe."

Dani inhaled deeply. "Mmm…"

Nico grinned, scooped up some pasta and offered it to Dani. "Would you like a bite?"

"Oh, I'd love a bite!"

Nico smiled.

Unwanted jealousy and an odd proprietary instinct rushed through Rafe. Before Daniella could take the bite Nico offered, Rafe grabbed the back of her chair and yanked her away from the table.

"I want her to eat that meal later tonight."

Nico laughed. "Really? What is this? A special occasion?"

Rafe knew Nico meant that as a joke, but he suddenly felt like an idiot as if Nico had caught his jealousy. He straightened to his full six-foot height. "Not a special occasion, part of the process. She's eaten bits of food to get our flavor, but tonight I had planned on treating her to an entire dinner."

Dani turned around on her chair to catch his gaze. "Really?"

Oh, Lord.

Something soft and earthy trembled through him, replacing his jealousy and feelings of being caught, as if they had never existed. Trapped in the gaze of her blue eyes, he quietly said, "Yes."

She rose, putting them face-to-face. "A private dinner?"

He shrugged, but everything male inside him shimmered. After days of only working together, being on his best behavior, he couldn't deny how badly he wanted time alone with her. He didn't want Nico to woo her. *He* wanted to woo her.

"Yes. A private dinner."

She smiled.

His breath froze. She was happy to be alone with him? He'd warned her...yet she still wanted to be alone with him? And what of her fiancé?

He pivoted and returned to the kitchen, not sure what he was doing. But as he worked, he slowed his pace. He rejected ravioli, spaghetti Bolognese. Both were too simple. Too common—

If he was going to feed her an entire meal, it would be his best. Pride the likes of which he'd never felt before rose in him. Only the best for his Dani.

He stopped, his finger poised above a pot, ready to sprinkle a pinch of salt.

His Dani?

He squeezed his eyes shut. Dear God. This wasn't just an attraction. He was head over heels crazy for her.

Dani alternated between standing nervously by the podium and sitting with Nico and Marianna.

The dining room had all but emptied, yet she couldn't seem to settle. Her fluttery stomach had her wondering if she'd even be able to eat what Rafe prepared for her.

A private dinner.

She had no idea what it meant, but when he emerged from the kitchen and walked to Nico's table, her breath stalled. He'd removed his smock and stood before the Amatuccis in dark trousers and a white T-shirt that outlined his taut stomach. Tight cotton sleeves rimmed impressive biceps and Dani saw a tattoo she'd never noticed before.

"I trust you enjoyed your dinners."

Nico blotted his mouth with a napkin, then said, "Rafe, you truly are gifted."

Rafe bowed graciously.

"And, Marianna." When Rafe turned to see her half-eaten meal, he frowned. "Why you not eat?"

She smiled slightly. "You give everyone enough to feed an army. Half was plenty."

"You'll take the rest home?"

She nodded and Rafe motioned for Allegra to get her plate and put her food in a take-out container.

Rafe chatted with Nico, calmly, much more calmly than Dani felt, but the second Allegra returned with the take-out container, Marianna jumped from her seat.

"I need to get home. I don't know what's wrong with me tonight, but I'm exhausted."

Nico rose, too. "It is late. Dinner was something of an afterthought. I promised Marianna I'd get her back at a decent hour. But I knew you'd want to see her after her year away, Rafe."

Rafe kissed her hand. "Absolutely. I'm just sorry she's too tired for us to catch up."

Dani frowned. Nico's little sister didn't look tired. She looked pale. Biting her lower lip, Dani realized she'd only known one other person who'd looked that way—

Rafe waved her over. "Say good-night to Nico and his sister."

Keeping her observations to herself, Dani smiled. "Good night, Marianna."

Marianna returned her smile. "I'm sure we'll be seeing more of you since Nico loves Rafe's food."

Nico laughed, took both her hands and kissed them. "Good night, Daniella. Tell your roomie I said hello."

Daniella's face reddened. Louisa had been the topic of most of Nico's questions when she'd sat with him and his sister, but there was no way in hell she'd tell Louisa Nico had mentioned her. Still, she smiled. Every time she talked to Nico, she liked him more. Which only made Louisa's dislike all the more curious.

"Good night, Nico."

After helping Marianna with her coat, Rafe walked his friends to their car. Dani busied herself helping the waitresses finish dining room cleanup. She didn't see Rafe return, but when a half hour went by, she assumed he'd come in through the back door to the kitchen.

Of course, he could be talking to beautiful Marianna. She might be with her brother, but that brother was a friend of Rafe's. And Nico had said he wanted to bring Marianna to Mancini's because he knew Rafe would want to see her. They probably had all kinds of stories to reminisce about. Marianna might be too young to have been his first kiss, his first love, but she was an adult now. A beautiful woman.

Realizing how possible it was that Rafe might be interested in Marianna, Dani swayed, but she quickly calmed herself. If she decided to stay, watching him with other women would be part of her life. She had to get used to this. She had to get accustomed to seeing him flirt, seeing beautiful women like Marianna look at him with interest.

She tossed a chair to the table with a little more force than was necessary.

Gio frowned. "Are you okay?"

She smiled. "Yes. Perfect."

"If you're not okay, Allegra and I can finish."

"I'm fine." She forced her smile to grow bigger. "Just eager to be done for the night."

As they finished the dining room, Rafe walked out of the kitchen to the bar. He got a bottle of wine and two glasses. As their private dinner became a reality, Dani's stomach tightened.

She squeezed her eyes shut, scolding herself. The dinner might be private for no other reason than the restaurant would be closed. Rafe probably didn't want to be alone with her as much as he wanted her to eat a meal, as hostess, so she could get the real experience of dining at Mancini's.

The waitresses left. The kitchen light went out, indicating Emory and his staff had gone.

Only she and Rafe remained.

He faced her, pointed at a chair. "Sit."

Okay. That was about as far from romantic as a man could get. This "private" dinner wasn't about the two of them having time together. It was about a chef who wanted his hostess to know his food.

She walked over, noticing again how his tight T-shirt accented a strong chest and his neat-as-a-pin trousers gave him a professional look. But as she got closer, Louisa's high, high heels clicking on the tile floor, she saw his gaze skim the apricot dress. His eyes warmed with interest. His lips lifted into a slow smile.

And her stomach fell to the floor. *This* was why she'd never quite been able to talk herself out of her attraction to him. He was every bit as attracted to her. He might try to hide it. He might fight it tooth and nail. But he liked her as more than an employee.

She reached the chair. He pulled it out, offering the seat to her.

As she sat, her back met his hands still on the chair. Rivers of tingles flowed from the spot where they touched. Her breath shuddered in and stuttered out. Nerves filled her.

He stepped away. "We're skipping soup and salad, since it's late." All business, he sat on the chair next to hers. He lifted the metal cover first from her plate, then his own. "I present beef *brasato* with pappardelle and mint."

When the scent hit her, her mouth watered. All thoughts of attraction fled as her stomach rumbled greedily. She closed her eyes and savored the aroma.

"You like?"

Unable to help herself, she caught his gaze. "I'm amazed."

"Wait till you taste."

He smiled encouragingly. She picked up her fork, filled it with pasta and slid it into her mouth. Knowing he'd made this just for her, the ritual seemed very decadent, very sensual. Their eyes met as flavor exploded on her tongue.

"Oh, God."

He grinned. "Is good?"

"You know you don't even have to ask."

He sat back with a laugh. "I was top of my class. I trained both in Europe and the United States so I could ascertain the key to satisfying both palates." He smiled slowly. "I am a master."

She sliced off a bit of the beef. It was so good she had to hold back a groan. "No argument here."

"Wait till you taste my tiramisu."

"No salad but you made dessert?"

He leaned in, studied her. "Are you watching your weight?"

She shook her head. "No."

"Then prepare to be taken to a world of decadence."

She laughed, expecting him to pick up his fork and eat his own meal. Instead, he stayed perfectly still, his warm eyes on her.

"You like it when people go bananas over your food."

"Of course."

But that wasn't why he was studying her. There was a huge difference between pride in one's work and curiosity about an attraction and she knew that curiosity when she saw it.

She put down her fork, caught in his gaze, the moment. "What are we really doing here, Rafe?"

He shook his head. "I'm not sure."

"You aren't staring at me like someone who wants to make sure I like his food."

"You are beautiful."

Her heart shivered. Her eyes clung to his. She wanted him to have said that because he liked her, because he was ready to do something about it. But a romance between them would be a disaster. She'd be hurt. She'd have to leave Monte Calanetti. She could not take anything he said romantically.

Forking another bite of food, she casually said, "Beauty doesn't pay the rent."

His voice a mere whisper, he said, "Why do you tease me?"

Her face fell. "I don't tease you!"

"Of course, you do. Every day you dress more beautifully, but you don't talk to me."

"I'm smart enough to stay away when a guy warns me off."

"Yet you tell me I must be prepared for you to stay."

"Because you..." *Like me.* She almost said it. But his admitting he liked her would be nothing but trouble. He might like her in the moment, but he wouldn't like her forever. It was stupid to even have that discussion.

She steered them away from it. "Because if I stay, no more firing me. You're getting me permanently."

"You keep saying that as if I should be afraid." He slid his arm to the back of her chair. His fingers rose to toy with the blunt line of her chin-length hair. "But your staying is not a bad thing."

The wash of awareness roaring through her disagreed. If she fell in love with him, her staying would be a very bad thing. His touching her did not help matters. With his fingers brushing her hair, tickling her nape, she couldn't move...could barely breathe.

His hand shifted from her hairline and wrapped around the back of her neck so he could pull her closer. She told herself to resist. To be smart. But something in his eyes wouldn't let her. As she drew nearer, he leaned in. Their gazes held until his lips met hers, then her eyelids dropped. Her breathing stopped.

Warm and sweet, his lips brushed her, and she knew why she hadn't resisted. She so rarely got what she wanted in life that when tempted she couldn't say no. It might be wrong to want him, but she did.

His hand slid from her neck to her back, twisting her to

sit sideways on her chair. Her arms lifted slowly, her hands hesitantly went to his shoulders. Then he deepened the kiss and her mind went blank.

It wasn't so much the physical sensations that robbed her of thought but the fact that he kissed her. He finally, finally kissed her the way he had the night he'd walked her to her car.

When he thought she was free.

When he wanted there to be something between them.

The kiss went on and on. Her senses combined to create a flood of need so strong that something unexpected suddenly became clear. She was already in love with Rafe. She didn't have to worry that someday she might fall in love. Innocent and needy as she was, she had genuinely fallen in love—

And he was nowhere near in love with her.

He was strong and stubborn, set in his ways. He said he didn't do relationships. He said he didn't have time. He'd told her he hurt women. And if he hurt her, she'd never be able to work for him.

Did she want to risk this job for a fling?

To risk her new friends?

Did she want to be hurt?

Hadn't she been hurt, rejected enough in her life already?

She jerked away from him.

He pulled away slowly and ran his hand across his forehead. "Oh, my God. I am so sorry."

"Sorry?" She was steeped in desire sprinkled with a healthy dose of fear, so his apology didn't quite penetrate.

"I told you before. I do not steal other men's women."

"Oh." She squeezed her eyes shut. Paul was such a done deal for her that she'd taken him out of the equation. But Rafe didn't know that. For a second she debated keeping up the charade, if only to protect herself. But they had hit the point where that wasn't fair. She couldn't let Rafe go on thinking he was romancing another man's woman. Especially not when she had been such a willing participant.

She sucked in a breath, caught his gaze and quietly said, "I'm not engaged."

Rafe sat up in his chair. "What?"

She felt her cheeks redden. "I'm not engaged."

His face twisted with incredulity. "You *lied*?"

"No." She bounced from her seat and paced away. "Not really. My boyfriend had asked me to marry him. I told him I needed time to think about it. I was leaving for Italy anyway—"

He interrupted her as if confused. "So your boyfriend asked you to marry him and you ran away?"

She swallowed. "No. I inherited the money for a plane ticket to come here to find Rosa's relatives and I immediately tacked extra time onto my teaching tour. All that had been done before Paul proposed."

"So his proposal was a stopgap measure."

She frowned. "Excuse me?"

"Not able to keep you from going to Italy, he tied you to himself enough that you would feel guilty if you got involved with another man while you were away." He caught her gaze. "But it didn't work, did it?"

She closed her eyes. "No."

"It shouldn't have worked. It was a ploy. And you shouldn't feel guilty about anything that happened while you were here since you're really not engaged."

"Well, it doesn't matter anyway. I called him after we returned from Rome and officially rejected his proposal."

"You told him no?"

She nodded. "And told him I might be staying in Italy." She sucked in a breath. "He wished me luck."

Rafe sat back in his chair. "And so you are free." He combed his fingers through his hair. Laughed slightly.

The laugh kind of scared her. She'd taken away the one barrier she knew would protect her. All she had now to keep her from acting on her love for him was her willpower. Which she'd just proven wasn't very strong.

"I should go."

His gaze slowly met hers. "You haven't finished eating."

His soulful eyes held hers and her stomach jumped. Everything about him called to her on some level. He listened when she talked, appreciated her work at his restaurant... was blisteringly attracted to her.

What the hell would have happened if she hadn't broken that kiss? What would happen if she stayed, finished her meal, let them have more private time? With Paul gone as protection, would he seduce her? And if she resisted... what would she say? Another lie? *I don't like you? I'm not interested? I don't want to be hurt?*

The last wasn't a lie. And it would work. But she didn't want to say it. She didn't want to hear him tell her one more time that he couldn't commit. She didn't want this night to end on a rejection.

"I want to go home."

His eyes on her, he rose slowly. "Let's go, then. I will clean up in the morning."

Finally breaking eye contact, she walked to the front of Mancini's to get her coat. Her legs shook. Her breaths hurt. Not because she knew she was probably escaping making love, but because he really was going to hurt her one day.

CHAPTER ELEVEN

THE NEXT MORNING, Rafe was in the dining room when Dani used her key to unlock the front door and enter Mancini's. Around him, the waitresses and busboys busily set up tables. The wonderful aromas of his cooking filled the air. But when she walked in, Dani brought the real life to the restaurant. Dressed in a red sweater with a black skirt and knee-high boots, she was just the right combination of sexy and sweet.

And she'd rejected him the night before.

Even though she'd broken up with her man in America.

Without saying good morning, without as much as meeting her gaze, he turned on his heel and walked into the kitchen to the prep tables where he inspected the handiwork of two chefs.

He waved his hand over the rolled-out dough for a batch of ravioli. "This is good."

He tasted some sauce, inclined his head, indicating it was acceptable and headed for his workstation.

Emory scrambled over behind him. "Is Daniella here?"

"Yes." But even before Rafe could finish the thought, she pushed open the swinging doors to the kitchen and entered. She strolled to his prep table, cool and nonchalant as if nothing had happened between them.

But lots had happened between them. He'd kissed her. And she'd told him she didn't have a fiancé. Then she'd run. Rejecting him.

"Good morning."

He forced his gaze to hers. His eyes held hers for a beat before he said, "Good morning."

Emory caught her hands. "Did you enjoy your dinner?"

She laughed. "It was excellent." She met Rafe's gaze again. "Our chef is extraordinary."

His heart punched against his ribs. How could a man not take that as a compliment? She hadn't just eaten his food the night before. She'd returned his kiss with as much passion and fervor as he'd put into it.

Emory glowed. "This we know. And we count on you to make sure every customer knows."

"Oh, believe me. I've always been able to talk up the food from the bites you've given me. But eating an entire serving has seared the taste of perfection in my brain."

Emory grinned. "Great!"

"I think our real problem will be that I'll start stealing more bites and end up fat as a barrel."

Emory laughed but Rafe looked away, remembering his question from the night before. *Are you watching your weight?* One memory took him back to the scene, the mood, the moment. How nervous she'd seemed. How she'd jumped when his hand had brushed her back. How her jitters had disappeared while they were kissing and didn't return until they'd stopped.

Because she had to tell him about her fiancé.

She wasn't engaged.

She *had* responded to him.

Emory laughed. "Occupational hazard."

Her gaze ambled to Rafe's again. All they'd had the night before was a taste of what could be between them. Yes, he knew he'd warned her off. But she'd still kissed him. He'd given her plenty of time to move away, but she'd stayed. Knowing his terms—that he didn't want a relationship—she'd accepted his kiss.

With their gazes locked, she couldn't deny it. He could see the heat in her blue eyes.

"From here on out, when we create a new dish or perfect an old one," Emory continued, oblivious to the nonverbal conversation she and Rafe were having, "you will sample."

"I want her to have more than a sample."

The words sprang from him without any thought. But he wouldn't take them back. He no longer *wanted* an affair with her. He now *longed* for it, yearned for it in the depths of his being. And they were adults. They weren't kids. Love affairs were part of life. She might get hurt, or because they were both lovers and coworkers, she might actually understand him. His life. His time constraints. His passion for his dream—

She might be the perfect lover.

The truth of that rippled through him. It might not be smart to gamble with losing her, but he didn't think he'd lose her. In fact, he suddenly, passionately believed a long-term affair was the answer to their attraction.

"And I know more than a sample would be bad for me." She shifted her gaze to Emory before smiling and walking out of the kitchen.

Rafe shook his head and went back to his cooking. He had no idea if she was talking about his food or the subtle suggestion of an affair he'd made, but if she thought that little statement of hers was a deterrent, she was sadly mistaken.

Never in his life had he walked away from something he really wanted and this would not be an exception. Especially since he finally saw how perfect their situation could be.

Dani walked out of the kitchen and pressed her hand to her jumpy stomach. Those silver-gray eyes could get more across in one steamy look than most men could in foreplay.

To bolster her confidence, which had flagged again, she

reminded herself of her final thoughts as she'd fallen asleep the night before. Rafe was a mercurial man. Hot one minute. Cold the next. And for all she knew, he could seduce her one day and dump her the next. She needed security. Mancini's could be that security. She would not risk that for an affair. No matter how sexy his eyes were when he said it. How deep his voice.

She walked to the podium. Two couples awaited. She escorted them to a table. As the day wore on, customer after customer chatted with her about their tours or, if they were locals, their homes and families. The waitstaff laughed and joked with each other. The flow of people coming in and going out, eating, serving, clearing tables surrounded her, reminded her that *this* was why she wanted to stay in Italy, at Mancini's. Not for a man, a romance, but for a life. The kind of interesting, fun, exciting life she'd never thought she'd get.

She wanted this much more than she wanted a fling that ended in a broken heart and took away the job she loved.

At the end of the night, Emory came out with the white pay envelopes. He passed them around and smiled when he gave one to Dani. "This will be better than last time."

"So my raise is in here?"

"Yes." He nodded once and strode away.

Dani tucked the envelope into her skirt pocket and helped the waitresses with cleanup. When they were done, she grabbed her coat, not wanting to tempt fate by being the only remaining employee when Rafe came out of the kitchen.

She walked to her car, aware that Rafe's estimation of her worth sat by her hip, half afraid to open it. He had to value her enough to pay her well or she couldn't stay. She would not leave the security of her teaching job and an apartment she could afford, just to be scraping by in a foreign country, no matter how much she loved the area, its people and especially her job.

After driving the car into a space in Louisa's huge garage, Dani entered the house through the kitchen.

Louisa sat at the table, enjoying her usual cup of tea before bedtime. "How did it go? Was he nice? Was he romantic? Or did he ignore you?"

Dani slipped off her coat. "He hinted that we should have an affair."

"That's not good."

"Don't worry. I'm not letting him change the rules he made in Rome. He said that for us to work together there could be nothing between us." She sucked in a breath. "So he can't suddenly decide it's okay for us to have an affair."

Louisa studied her. "I think you're smart to keep it that way, but are you sure it's what you want?"

"Yes. Today customers reminded me of why I love this job. Between lunch and dinner, I worked with Emory to organize the schedule for ordering supplies and streamline it. He showed me a lot of the behind-the-scenes jobs it takes to make Mancini's work. Every new thing I see about running a restaurant seems second nature to me."

"And?"

"And, as I've thought all along, I have instincts for the business. This could be more than a job for me. It could be a real career. If Rafe wants to risk that by making a pass at me, I think I have the reasoning set in my head to tell him no."

Louisa's questioning expression turned into a look of joy. "So you're staying?"

"Actually—" she waved the envelope "—it all depends on what's in here. If my salary doesn't pay me enough for my own house or condo, plus food and spending money, I can't stay."

Louisa crossed her fingers for luck. "Here's hoping."

Dani shook her head. "You know, you're so good to me I want to stay just for our friendship."

Louise groaned. "Open the darned thing already!"

She sliced a knife across the top of the envelope. When she saw the amount of her deposit, she sat on the chair across from Louisa. "Oh, my God."

Louisa winced. "That bad?"

"It's about twice what I expected." She took a breath. "What's he doing?"

Louisa laughed. "Trying to keep you?"

"The amount is so high that it's actually insulting." She rose from her seat, grabbed her coat and headed for the door. "Half this check would have been sufficient to keep me. This amount? It's—offensive." Almost as if he was paying her to sleep with him. She couldn't bring herself to say the words to Louisa. But how coincidental was it that he'd dropped hints that he wanted to have an affair, then paid her more money than she was worth?

The insult of it vibrated through her. The nerve of that man!

"Where are you going?"

"To toss this back in his face."

Yanking open the kitchen door, she bounded out into the cold, cold garage. She jumped into the old car and headed back to Monte Calanetti, parking on a side street near the building where Rafe had shown her the almost-perfect condo.

But as she strode into the lobby, she remembered she needed a key to get into the elevator that would take her to the penthouse. Hoping to ask the doorman for help, she groaned when she saw the desk was empty.

Maybe she should take this as a sign that coming over here was a bad idea?

She sucked in a breath. No. Their situation was too personal to talk about at Mancini's. And she wanted to yell. She wanted to vent all her pent-up frustrations and maybe even throw a dish or two. She had to talk to him now. Alone.

She walked over to the desk and eyed the phone. Luckily, one of the marked buttons said Penthouse. She lifted the receiver and hit the button.

After only one ring, Rafe answered. "Hello?"

She sucked in a breath. "It's me. Daniella. I'm in your lobby and don't know how to get up to your penthouse."

"Pass the bank of elevators we used to get to the condo I showed you and turn right. I'll send my elevator down for you."

"Don't I need a key?"

"I'll set it to return. You just get in."

She did as he said, walking past the first set of elevators and turning to find the one for the penthouse. She stepped through the open doors and they swished closed behind her.

Riding up in the elevator with its modern gray geometric-print wallpaper and black slate floors, she was suddenly overwhelmed by something she hadn't considered, but should have guessed.

Rafe was a wealthy man.

Watching the doors open to an absolutely breathtaking home, she tried to wrap her brain around this new facet of Rafe Mancini. He wasn't just sexy, talented and mercurial. He was rich.

And she was about to yell at him? She, who'd always been poor? Always three paychecks away from homelessness? She'd never, ever considered that maybe the reason he didn't think anything permanent would happen between them might be because they were so different. They lived in two different countries. They had two different belief systems. And now she was seeing they came from two totally different worlds.

Rafe walked around a corner, holding two glasses of wine.

"Chianti." He handed one to her and motioned to the black leather sofa in front of a stacked stone fireplace in the sitting area.

Unable to help herself, she glanced around, trepidation filling her. Big windows in the back showcased the winking lights of the village. The black chairs around a long black dining room table had white upholstered backs and cushions. Plush geometric-patterned rugs sat on almost-black hardwood floors. The paintings on the pale gray walls looked ancient—valuable.

It was the home of a wealthy, wealthy man.

"Daniella?"

And maybe that's why he thought he could influence her with money? Because she came from nothing.

That made her even angrier.

She straightened her shoulders, caught his gaze. "Are you trying to buy me off?"

"Buy you off?"

"Get me to stop saying no to a relationship by bribing me with a big, fat salary?"

He laughed and fell to the black sofa. "Surely this is a first. An employee who complains about too much money." He shook his head with another laugh. "You said you wanted to be compensated for relocating. You said you wanted to be general manager. That is what a general manager makes."

"Oh." White-hot waves of heat suffused her. Up until this very second, everything that happened with reference to her job at Mancini's had been fun or challenging. He pushed. She pushed back. He wanted her for his restaurant. She made demands. But holding the check, hearing his explanation, everything took on a reality that had somehow eluded her. She was general manager of a restaurant. *This* was her salary.

He patted the sofa. "Come. Sit."

She took a few steps toward the sofa, but the lights of the village caught her attention and the feeling of being Alice in Wonderland swept through her.

"I never in my wildest dreams thought I'd make this much money."

"Well, teachers are notoriously underpaid in America, and though you'd studied a few things that might have steered you to a more lucrative profession, you chose to be a teacher."

Her head snapped up and she turned to face him. "How do you know?"

He batted a hand. "Do I look like an idiot? Not only did I do due diligence in investigating your work history, but also I took a look at your college transcripts. Do you really think I would have given you such an important job if you didn't have at least one university course in accounting?"

"No." Her gaze on him, she sat on the far edge of the sofa.

His voice became soft, indulgent. "Perhaps in the jumble of everything that's been happening I did not make myself clear. I've told you that I intend to be one of the most renowned chefs in Europe. I can't do that from one restaurant outside an obscure Tuscan village. My next restaurant will be in Rome. The next in Paris. The next in London. I will build slowly, but I will build."

"You'd leave Mancini's?" Oddly, the thought actually made her feel better.

"I will leave Mancini's in Tuscany when I move to Rome to build Mancini's Rome." He frowned. "I thought I told you this." His frown deepened. "I know for sure I told you that Mancini's was only a stepping stone."

"You might have mentioned it." But she'd forgotten. She forgot everything but her attraction to him when he was around. She'd accused him of using promotions to cover his feelings for her. But she'd used her feelings for him to block what was really going on with her job, and now, here she was, in a job so wonderful she thought she might faint from the joy of it.

"With you in place I can move to the next phase of my business plan. But there's a better reason for me to move on. You and I both worry that if we do something about our attraction, you will be hurt when it ends and Mancini's will lose you." He smiled. "So I fix."

"You fix?"

"I leave. Once I start my second restaurant, you will not have to deal with me on a day-to-day basis." His smile grew. "And we will understand each other because we'll both work in the same demanding profession. You will understand if I cancel plans at the last minute."

This time the heat that rained down on her had nothing to do with embarrassment. He'd really thought this through. Like a man willing to shift a few things because he liked her.

"Oh."

"There are catches."

Her gaze jumped to his. "Catches?"

"Yes. I will be using you for help creating the other restaurants. To scout sites. To hire staff. To teach them how to create our atmosphere. That is your real talent." He held her gaze. "That is also why your salary is so high. You are a big part of Mancini's success. You created that atmosphere. I want it not just in one restaurant, but all of them, and you will help me get it."

The foster child taught not to expect much out of life, the little girl who learned manners only by mimicking what she saw in school, the Italian tourist who borrowed Louisa's clothes and felt as though she was playing dress up every day she got ready for work, that girl quivered with happiness at the compliment.

The woman who'd been warned by him that he would hurt her struggled with fear.

"You didn't just create a great job for me. You cleared the way for us to have an affair."

Rafe sighed. "Why are you so surprised? You're beautiful. You're funny. You make me feel better about myself. My life. Yes, I want you. So I figured out a way I could have you."

She sucked in a breath. It was heady stuff to see the lengths he was willing to go to be with her. And she also saw the one thing he wasn't saying.

"You like me."

"What did you think? That I'd agonize this much over someone I just wanted to sleep with?"

She smiled. "You agonized?"

He batted a hand in dismissal. "You're a confusing woman, Daniella."

"And you've gone to some pretty great lengths to make sure we can...see each other."

His face turned down into his handsome pout. "And you should appreciate it."

She did. She just didn't know how to handle it.

"Is it so hard to believe I genuinely like you?"

"No." She just never expected he would say it. But he said it easily. And the day would probably come when those feelings would expand. He truly liked her and she was so in love with him that her head spun. This was not going to be an affair. He was talking about a relationship.

Happiness overwhelmed her and she couldn't resist. She set her wineglass on the coffee table and scooted beside him.

A warm, syrupy feeling slid through Rafe. But on its heels was the glorious ping of arousal. Before he realized what she was about to do, she kissed him. Quick and sweet, her lips met his. When she went to pull back, he slid his hand across her lower back and hauled her to him. He deepened their kiss, using his tongue to tempt her. Nibbling her lips. Opening his mouth over hers until she responded with the kind of passion he'd always known lived in her heart.

He pulled away. "You play with fire."

Her tongue darted out to moisten her lips. Temptation roared through him and all his good intentions to take it slowly with her melted like snow in April. He could have her now. In this minute. He could take what he greedily wanted.

She drew a breath. "How is it playing with fire if we really, really like each other?"

She was killing him. Sitting so warm and sweet beside him, tempting him with what he wanted before she was ready.

Still, though it pained him, he knew the right thing to do.

"So we will do this right. When you are ready, when you trust me, we will take the next step."

Her gaze held his. "When I trust you?"

"*Sì.* When I feel you trust me enough to understand why we can be lovers, you will come to my bed."

Her face scrunched as she seemed to think all that through. "Wait...this is just about becoming lovers?"

"Yes."

"But you just said you wouldn't worry that much about someone you wanted to sleep with." She caught his gaze. "You said you agonized."

"Because we will not be a one-night stand. We will be lovers. Besides, I told you. I don't do relationships."

"You also said that you'd never have a romance with an employee." She met his gaze. "But you changed that rule."

"I made accommodations. I made everything work."

"Not for me! I don't just want a fling! I want something that's going to last."

His eyebrows rose. "Something that will last?" He frowned. "Forever?"

"Forever!"

"I tried forever. It did not work for me."

"You tried?"

"*Sì.*"

"And?"

"And it ended badly." He couldn't bring himself to explain that he'd been shattered, that he'd almost given up his dream for a woman who had left him, that he'd been a ball of pain and confusion until he pulled himself together and realized his dreams depended on him not trusting another woman with his heart or so much of his life.

"*Cara*, marriage is for other people. It's full of all kinds of things incompatible with the man I have to be to be a success."

"You *never* want to get married?"

"No!" He tossed his hands. "What I have been saying all along? Do you not listen?"

She stood up. The pain on her face cut through him like a knife. Though he suddenly wondered why. He'd always known she wanted security. He'd always known he couldn't give it to her. He couldn't believe he'd actually tried to get her to accept less than what she needed.

He rose, too. "Okay, let's forget this conversation happened. It's been a long day. I'm tired. I also clearly misinterpreted things. Come to Mancini's tomorrow as general manager."

She took two steps back. "You're going to keep me, even though I won't sleep with you?"

"Yes." But the sadness that filled him confused him. He'd had other women tell him no and he'd walked away unconcerned. Her *no* felt like the last page of a favorite book, the end of something he didn't want to see end. And yet he knew she couldn't live with his terms and he couldn't live with hers.

CHAPTER TWELVE

AGREEING THAT HE was right about at least one thing—she was too tired, too spent, to continue this discussion—Dani walked to the elevator. He followed her, hit the button that would close the door and turned away.

She sucked in a breath and tried to still her hammering heart. But it was no use. They really couldn't find a middle ground. It was sweet that he'd tried, but it was just another painful reminder that she had fallen in love with the wrong man.

She squeezed her eyes shut. She'd be okay—

No, she wouldn't. She'd fallen in love with him. Unless he really stayed out of Mancini's, she'd always be in love with him. Then she'd spend her life wishing he could fall for her, too. Or maybe one day she'd succumb. She'd want him so much she'd forget everything else, and she'd start the affair he wanted. With the strength of her feelings, that would seal the deal for her. She'd love him forever. Then she'd never have a home. Never have a family. Always be alone.

She thought of the plane ticket tucked away somewhere in her bedroom in Louisa's house. Now that she knew he wanted nothing but an affair, which was unacceptable, she could go home.

But she didn't want to go home. She wanted to run Mancini's. He'd handed her the opportunity with her general managership—

And he was leaving. Maybe not permanently, but for the next several years he wouldn't be around every day. Most of the time, he'd be in other cities, opening new restaurants.

Wouldn't she be a fool to leave now? Especially since she had a few days before she had to use that ticket. Maybe the wise thing to do would be to use this time to figure out if she could handle working with him as the boss she only saw a few times a month?

The next day when she walked in the door and felt the usual surge of rightness, she knew the job was worth fighting for. In her wildest dreams she'd never envisioned herself successful. Competent, making a living, getting a decent apartment? Yes. But never as one of the people at the top. Hiring employees. Creating atmosphere. Would she really let some feelings, one *man*, steal this from her?

No! No! She'd been searching for something her entire life. She believed she'd found it at Mancini's. It would take more than unrequited love to scare her away from that.

When Emory sat down with her in between lunch and dinner and showed her the human resources software, more of the things she'd learned in her university classes tumbled back.

"So I'll be doing all the admin?"

Emory nodded. "With Rafe gone, setting up Mancini's Rome, I'll be doing all the cooking. I won't have time to help."

"That's fine." She studied the software on the screen, simple stuff, really. Basically, it would do the accounting for her. And the rest? It was all common sense. Ordering. Managing the dining room. Hiring staff.

He squeezed her hand. "You and me…we make a good team."

Her smile grew and her heart lightened. She loved Emory.

Even tempered with the staff and well acquainted with

Rafe's recipes, he was the perfect chef. As long as Rafe wasn't around, she would be living her dream.

She returned his hand squeeze. "Yeah. We do."

When she and Emory were nearly finished going over the software programs, Rafe walked into the office. As always when he was around, she tingled. But knowing this was one of the things she was going to have to deal with, because he wasn't going away permanently, she simply ignored it.

"Have you taught her payroll?"

Emory rose from his seat. "Yes. In fact, she explained a thing or two to me."

Rafe frowned. "How so?"

"She understands the software. I'm a chef. I do not."

Dani also rose from her chair. "I've worked with software before to record grades. Essentially, most spreadsheet programs run on the same type of system, the same theories. My boyfriend—" She stopped when the word *boyfriend* caught in her throat. Emory's gaze slid over to her. But Rafe's eyes narrowed.

She took a slow, calming breath. "My ex-boyfriend Paul is a computer genius. I picked up a few things from him."

Rafe turned away. "Well, let us be glad for him, then."

He said the words calmly, but Dani heard the tension in his voice. There were feelings there. Not just lust. So it wouldn't be only her own feelings she'd be fighting. She'd also have to be able to handle his. And that might be a little trickier.

"I've been in touch with a Realtor in Rome. I go to see buildings tomorrow."

A look passed between him and Emory.

Emory tucked the software manual into the bottom bin of an in basket. "Good. It's time to get your second restaurant up and running." He slid from behind the desk. "But right now I have to supervise dinner."

He scampered out of the room and Rafe's gaze roamed over to hers again. "I'd like for you to come to Rome with me."

Heat suffused her and her tongue stuck to the roof of her mouth. "Me?"

"I want you to help me scout locations."

"Really?"

"I told you. You are the one who created the atmosphere of this Mancini's. If I want to re-create it, I think you need to be in on choosing the site."

Because that made sense and because she did have to learn to deal with him as a boss, owner of the restaurant for which she worked, she tucked away any inappropriate longings and smiled. "Okay."

She could be all business because that's what really worked for them.

The next day, after walking through an old, run-down building with their Realtor, Rafe and Dani stepped out into the bright end-of-February day.

"I could do with a coffee right now."

He glanced at her. In her sapphire-blue coat and white mittens, she looked cuddly, huggable. And very, very, very off-limits. Her smiles had been cool. Her conversations stilted. But she'd warmed up a bit when they actually began looking at buildings.

"Haven't you already had two cups of coffee?"

She slid her hand into the crook of his elbow, like a friend or a cousin, someone allowed innocent, meaningless touches.

"Don't most Italians drink something like five cups a day?"

When he said, "Bah," she laughed.

All morning, their conversation at his apartment two nights ago had played over and over and over in his head. She wanted a commitment and he didn't. So he'd figured out a way they could be lovers and work together and she'd rejected it. He'd had to accept that.

But being with her this morning, without actually being allowed to touch her or even contemplate kissing her was making him think all kinds of insane things. Like how empty his life was. How much he would miss her when he stopped working at the original Mancini's and headquartered himself in Rome.

So though he knew her hand at his elbow meant nothing, he savored the simple gesture. It was a safe, nonthreatening way to touch her and have her touch him. Even if he did know it would lead to nothing.

"Besides, I love coffee. It makes me warm inside."

"True. And it is cold." He slid his arm around her shoulders. Her thick coat might keep her toasty, but it was another excuse to touch her.

They continued down the quiet street, but as they approached a shop specializing in infant clothing, the wheels of a baby stroller came flying out the door and straight for Daniella's leg. He caught her before she could as much as wobble and shifted her out of the way.

The apologetic mom said, *"Scusi!"*

Dani laughed. In flawless Italian she said, "No harm done." Then she bent and chucked the chin of the baby inside the stroller. "Isn't she adorable!"

The proud mom beamed. Rafe stole a quiet look at the kid and his lips involuntarily rose as a chuckle rumbled up from the deepest part of him. "She likes somebody's cooking."

The mom explained that the baby had her father's love of all things sweet, but Rafe's gaze stayed on the baby. She'd caught his eye and cooed at him, her voice a soft sound, almost a purr, and her eyes as shiny as a harvest moon.

A funny feeling invaded his chest.

Dani gave the baby a big, noisy kiss on the cheek, said

goodbye to the mom and took his arm so they could resume their walk down the street.

They ducked into a coffeehouse and she inhaled deeply. "Mmm…this reminds me of being back in the States."

He shook his head. "You Americans. You copy the idea of a coffeehouse from us, then come over here and act like we must meet your standards."

With a laugh, she ordered two cups of coffee, remembering his choice of brews from earlier that morning. She also ordered two scones.

"I hope you're hungry."

She shrugged out of her coat before sitting on the chair he pulled out for her at a table near a window. "I just need something to take the edge off my growling stomach. The second scone is for you."

"I don't eat pastries from a vendor who sells in bulk."

She pushed the second scone in front of him anyway. "Such a snob."

He laughed. "All right. Fine. I will taste." He bit into the thing and to his surprise it was very good. Even better with a sip or two of coffee. So tasty he ate the whole darned thing.

"Not quite the pastry snob anymore, are you?"

He sat back. He truly did not intend to pursue her. He respected her dreams, the way he respected his own. But that didn't stop his feelings for her. With his belly full of coffee and scone, and Daniella happy beside him, these quiet minutes suddenly felt like spun gold.

She glanced around. "I'll bet you've brought a woman or two here."

That broke the spell. "What?" He laughed as he shifted uncomfortably on his chair. "What makes you say that?"

"You're familiar with this coffeehouse. This street. You were even alert enough to pull me out of the way of the oncoming stroller at that baby shop." She shrugged. "You might not have come here precisely, but you've brought women to Rome."

"Every Italian man brings women to Rome." He toyed with his now-empty mug. He'd lived with Kamila just down the street. He'd dreamed of babies like the little girl in the stroller.

"I told you about Paul. I think you need to tell me about one of your women to even the score."

"You make me sound like I dated an army."

She tossed him an assessing look. "You might have."

Not about to lie, he drew a long breath and said, "There were many."

She grimaced. "Just pick one."

"Okay. How about Lisette?"

She put her elbow on the table, her eyes keen with interest. "Sounds French."

"She was."

"Ah."

"I met her when she was traveling through Italy…" But even as he spoke, he remembered that she was more driven than he was. *He* had taken second place to *her* career. At the time he hadn't minded, but remembering the situation correctly, he didn't feel bad about that breakup.

"So what happened?"

He waved a hand. "Nothing. She was just very married to her career."

"Like you?"

He laughed. "Two peas in a pod. But essentially we didn't have time for each other."

"You miss her?"

"No." He glanced up. "Honestly, I don't miss any of the women who came into and walked out of my life."

But he had missed Kamila and he would miss Dani if she left. He'd miss her insights at the restaurant and the way she made Mancini's come alive. But most of all he'd miss her smile. Miss the way she made *him* feel.

The unspoken truth sat between them. Their gazes caught, then clung. That was the problem with Dani. He felt for her the same things he had felt with Kamila. Except stronger. The emotions that raced through him had nothing to do with affairs, and everything to do with the kind of commitment he swore he'd never make again. That was why he'd worked so hard to figure out a way they could be together. It was why he also worked so hard to steer them away from a commitment. This woman, this Dani, was everything Kamila had been…and more.

And it only highlighted why he needed to be free.

He cleared his throat. "There was a woman."

Dani perked up.

"Kamila." He toyed with his mug again, realizing he was telling her about Kamila as much to remind himself as to explain to Dani. "She was sunshine when she was happy and a holy terror when she was not."

Dani laughed. "Sounds exciting."

He caught her gaze again. "It was perfect."

Her eyes softened with understanding. "Oh."

"You wonder how I know I'm not made for a relationship? Kamila taught me. First, she drew me away from my dream. To please her, I turned down apprenticeships. I took a permanent job as a sous-chef. I gave up the idea of being renowned and settled for being happy." Though it hurt, he held her gaze. "We talked about marriage. We talked about kids. And one day I came home from work and discovered her things were gone. *She* was gone. I'd given up everything for her and the life I thought I wanted, and she left without so much as an explanation of why."

"I'm sorry."

"Don't be." He sucked in a breath, pulled away from her, as his surety returned to him. "That loss taught me to be careful. But more than that it taught me never to do anything that jeopardizes who I am."

"So this Kamila really did a number on you."

"Were you not listening? There was no number. Yes, she broke my heart. But it taught me lessons. I'm fine."

"You're wounded." She caught his gaze. "Maybe even more wounded than I am."

He said, "That's absurd," but he felt the pangs of loss, the months of loneliness as if it were yesterday.

"At least I admit I need someone. You let one broken romance evolve into a belief that a few buildings and success are the answers to never being hurt. Do you think that when you're sixty you're going to look around and think 'I wish I'd started more Mancini's'? Or do you think you're going to envy your friends' relationships, wish for grandkids?"

"I told you I don't want those things." But even as he said the words, he knew they were a lie. Not a big pulsing lie, but a quiet whisper of doubt. Especially with the big eyes of the baby girl in the stroller pressed into his memory. With a world of work to do to get his chain of restaurants started, what she said should seem absurd. Instead, he saw himself old, his world done, his success unparalleled and his house empty.

He blinked away that foolish thought. He had family. He had friends. His life would never be empty. That was Dani's fear, not his.

"Let's go. Mario gave me the address of the next building where we're to meet him."

Quiet, they walked to his car, slid in and headed to the other side of the city. More residential than the site of the first property, this potential Mancini's had the look of a home, as did his old farmhouse outside Monte Calanetti.

He opened the door and she entered the aging building before him. Mario came over and shook his hand, but Dani walked to the far end of the huge, open first floor. She found the latch on the shutters that covered a big back window. When she flipped it, the shutters opened. Sunlight poured in.

Rafe actually *felt* the air change, the atmosphere shift. Though the building was empty and hollow, with her walking in, the sunlight pouring in through a back window, everything clicked.

This was his building. And she really was the person who brought life to his dining rooms. He'd had success of a sort without her, but she breathed the life into his vision, made it more, made it the vision he saw when he closed his eyes and dreamed.

Dani ambled to the center of the room. Pointing near the door, she said, "We'd put the bar over here."

He frowned. "Why not here?" He motioned to a far corner, out of the way.

"Not only can we give customers the chance to wait at the bar for their tables, but also we might get a little extra drink business." She smiled at him as she walked over. "Things will be just a tad different in a restaurant that's actually in a residential area of a city." Her smile grew. "But I think it could be fun to play around with it."

He crossed his arms on his chest to keep from touching her. He could almost feel the excitement radiating from her. While he envisioned a dining room, happy customers eating *his* food, he could tell she saw more. Much more. She saw things he couldn't bring into existence because all he cared about was the food.

"What would you play around with?"

Her gaze circled the room. "I'm not sure. We'd want to keep the atmosphere we've build up in Mancini's, but here we'd also have to become part of the community. You can get some really great customer relations by being involved with your neighbors." She tapped her finger on her lips. "I'll need to think about this."

Rafe's business instincts kicked in. He didn't know what she planned to do, but he did know whatever she decided, it would probably be good. Really good. Because she had the other half of the gift he'd been given.

He also knew she was happy. Happier than he'd ever seen her. Her blue eyes lit with joy. Her shoulders were back. Her steps purposeful. Confidence radiated from her.

"You want Mancini's to be successful as much as I want it to be successful."

She laughed. "I doubt that. But I do want it to be the best it can be." She glanced around, then faced him again. "In all the confusion between us, I don't think I've ever said thank-you."

"You wish to thank me?"

"For the job. For the fun of it." She shrugged. "I need this. I don't show it often but deep down inside me, there's a little girl who always wondered where she'd end up. *She* needed the chance to be successful. To prove her worth."

He smiled. "She'll certainly get that with Mancini's."

"And we're going to have a good time whipping this into shape."

He smiled. "That's the plan."

Her face glowed. "Good."

He said, "Good," but his voice quieted, his heart stilled, as he suddenly realized something he should have all along. Kamila had broken his heart. But Dani had wheedled her way into his soul. His dream.

If he and Dani got close and things didn't work out, he wouldn't just spend a month drinking himself silly. He'd lose everything.

CHAPTER THIRTEEN

THE NEXT DAY in the parking lot of Mancini's, Dani switched off the ignition of Louisa's little car, knowing that she was two days away from D-day. Decision day. The day she had to use her return ticket to New York City.

Being with Rafe in Rome had shown her he respected her opinion. Oh, hell, who was she kidding? Telling her about Kamila had been his way of putting the final nail in the coffin of her relationship dreams. It hurt, but she understood. In fact, in a way she was even glad. Now that she knew why he was so determined, she could filter her feelings for him away from her longing for a relationship with him and into his dream. He needed her opinion. He wanted to focus on food, on pleasing customer palates. She saw the ninety thousand other things that had to be taken care of. Granted, he'd chosen a great spot for the initial Mancini's. He'd fixed the building to perfection. But a restaurant in the city came with different challenges.

Having lived in New York and eaten at several different kinds of restaurants, she saw things from a customer's point of view. And she knew exactly how she'd set up Mancini's Rome restaurant.

She *knew.*

The confidence of it made her forget all about returning to New York, and stand tall. She entered the kitchen on her way to the office, carrying a satchel filled with pictures she'd printed off the internet the night before using Louisa's laptop.

This was her destiny.

Then she saw Rafe entering through the back door and her heart tumbled. He wore the black leather jacket. He hadn't pulled his hair into the tie yet and it curled around his collar. His eyes were cool, serious. When their gazes met, she swore she could feel the weight of his sadness.

She didn't understand what the hell he had to be sad about. He was getting everything he wanted. Except her heart. He didn't know that he already had her love, but their good trip the day before proved they could work together, even be friends, and he should appreciate that.

Everything would be perfect, as long as he didn't kiss her. Or tempt her. And yesterday he'd all but proven he needed her too much to risk losing her.

"I have pictures of things I'd like your opinion on."

Emory looked from one to the other. "Pictures?"

Rafe slowly ambled into the kitchen. "Dani has ideas for the restaurant in Rome."

Emory gaped at him. "Who cares? You have a hundred-person wedding tomorrow afternoon."

Dani's mouth fell open. Rafe's eyes widened. "We didn't cancel that?"

"We couldn't," Emory replied before Dani said anything, obviously taking the heat for it. "So I called the bride's mother yesterday and got the specifics. Tomorrow morning, we'll all come here early to get the food prepared. In the afternoon Dani and I will go to the wedding. I will watch your food, Chef Mancini. Your reputation will not suffer."

Rafe slowly walked over to Dani. "You know we cannot do this again!"

"Come on, Chef Rafe." She smiled slightly, hoping to dispel the tension, again confused over why he was so moody. "Put Mr. Mean Chef away. I got the message the day you fired me over this." With that she strode into the office, dumped her satchel on the desk and swung out again. She thought of the plane ticket in her pocket and reminded herself that in two days she wouldn't have that option. When he yelled, she'd have to handle it.

"I'll be in the dining room, checking with Allegra on how things went yesterday."

Rafe sagged with defeat as she stormed out. He shouldn't have yelled at her again about the catering, but everything in his life was spinning out of control. He saw babies in his sleep and woke up hugging his pillow, dreaming he was hugging Daniella. The logical part of him insisted they were a team, that a real relationship would enhance everything they did. They would own Mancini's together, build it together, build a life together.

The other part, the part that remembered Kamila, could only see disaster when the relationship ended. When Kamila left, he could return to his dream. If Dani left, she took half of his dream with her.

He faced Emory. "I appreciate how you have handled this. And I apologize for exploding." He sucked in a breath. "As penance, I will go to the wedding tomorrow."

Emory laughed. "If you're expecting me to argue, you're wrong. I don't want to be a caterer, either."

"As I said, this is penance."

"Then you really should be apologizing to Dani. It was her you screamed at."

He glanced at the door as he shrugged out of his jacket. She was too upset with him now. And she was busy. He would find a minute at the end of the night to apologize for his temper. If he was opting out of a romance because he needed her, he couldn't lose her over his temper.

But she didn't hang around after work that night. And the next morning, he couldn't apologize because they weren't alone. First, he'd cooked with a full staff. Then he'd had to bring Laz and Gino, two of the busboys, to the wedding to assist with setup and teardown. They drove to the vineyard in almost complete silence, every mile stretching Rafe's nerves.

Seeing the sign for 88 Vineyards, he turned down the winding lane. The top of a white tent shimmered in the winter sun. Thirty yards away, white folding chairs created two wide rows of seating for guests. He could see the bride and groom standing in front of the clergyman, holding hands, probably saying their vows.

He pulled the SUV beside the tent. "It looks like we'll need to move quickly to get everything set up for them to eat."

Dani opened her door of the SUV. "Not if there are pictures. I've known brides who've taken hours of pictures."

"Bah. Nonsense."

Ignoring him, she climbed out of the SUV.

Rafe opened his door and recessional music swelled around him. Still Dani said nothing. Her cold shoulder stung more than he wanted to admit.

A quick glance at the wedding ceremony netted him the sight of the bride and groom coming down the aisle. The sun cast them in a golden glow, but their smiles were even more radiant. He watched as the groom brought the bride's hand to his lips. Saw the worship in his eyes, the happiness, and immediately Rafe thought of Daniella. About the times he'd kissed her hand. Walked her to her car. Waited with bated breath for her arrival every morning.

He reached into his SUV to retrieve a tray of his signature ravioli. Handing it to Laz, he sneaked a peek at Daniella as she made her way to the parents of the bride, who'd walked out behind the happy couple. They smiled at her, the bride's mom talking a million words a second as she pointed inside the tent. Daniella set her hand on the mom's forearm and suddenly the nervous woman calmed.

He watched in heart-stealing silence. A lifetime of rejection had taught her to be kind. And one failed romance had made him mean. Bitter.

As he pulled out the second ravioli tray, Dani walked over.

"Apparently the ceremony was lovely."

"Peachy."

"Come on. I know you're mad at me for arranging this. But at the time, I didn't know any better and in a few hours all of this will be over."

He sucked in a breath. "I'm not mad at you. I'm angry with myself—" *Because I finally understand I'm not worried about you leaving me, or even losing my dreams. I'm disappointed in myself* "—for yelling at you yesterday."

"Oh." She smiled slowly. "Thanks."

The warm feeling he always got when she smiled invaded every inch of him. "You're welcome."

Not waiting for him to say anything else, she headed inside the white tent where the dinner and reception would be held. He followed her only to discover she was busy setting up the table for the food. He and Laz worked their magic on the warmers he'd brought to keep everything the perfect temperature. Daniella and Gino brought in the remaining food.

And nothing happened.

People milled around the tables in the tent, chatting, celebrating the marriage. Wine flowed from fancy bottles. The mother of the bride socialized. The parents of the groom walked from table to table. A breeze billowed around the tent as everyone talked and laughed.

He stepped outside, nervous now. He'd never considered himself wrong, except that he'd believed giving up apprenticeships for Kamila had made him weak. But setback after setback had made Dani strong. It was humbling to realize his master-chef act wasn't a sign of strength, but selfishness. Even more humbling to realize he didn't know what to do with the realization.

Wishing he still smoked, he ambled around the grounds, gazing at the blue sky, and then he turned to walk down a cobblestone path, only to find himself three feet away from the love-struck bride and groom.

He almost groaned, until he noticed the groom lift the bride's chin and tell her that everything was going to be okay.

His eyebrows rose. They hadn't even been married twenty minutes and there was trouble in paradise already?

She quietly said, "Everything is not going to be okay. My parents are getting a divorce."

Rafe thought of the woman in pink, standing with the guy in the tux as they'd chatted with Dani at the end of the ceremony, and he almost couldn't believe it.

The groom shook his head. "And they're both on their best behavior. Everything's fine."

"For now. What will I do when we get home from our honeymoon? I'll have to choose between the two of them for Christmas and Easter." She gasped. "I'll have to get all my stuff out of their house before they sell it." She sucked in a breath. "Oh, my God." Her eyes filled with tears. "I have no home."

Rafe's chest tightened. He heard every emotion Dani must feel in the bride's voice. No home. No place to call her own.

A thousand emotions buffeted him, but for the first time since he'd met Dani he suddenly felt what she felt. The emptiness of belonging to no one. The longing for a place to call her own. And he realized the insult he'd leveled when he'd told her he wanted to sleep with her, but not keep her.

"I'll be your home." The groom pulled his bride away from the tree. "It's us now. We'll make your home."

We'll make your home.

Rafe stepped back, away from the tree that hid him, the words vibrating through him. But the words themselves were nothing without the certainty behind them.

The strength of conviction in the groom's voice. The promise that wouldn't be broken.

We'll make your home.

"Let's go inside. We have a wedding to celebrate."

She smiled. "Yes. We do."

Rafe discreetly followed them into the tent. He watched them walk to the main table as if nothing was wrong, as the dining room staff scrambled to fill serving bowls with his food and get it onto tables.

The toast of the best man was short. Rafe's eyes strayed to Daniella. He desperately wanted to give her a home. A real one. A home like he'd grown up in with kids and a dog and noisy suppers.

This was what life had stolen from her and from him. When Kamila left, she hadn't taken his dream. She'd bruised him so badly, he'd lost his faith in real love. He'd lost his dream of a house and kids. And when it all suddenly popped up in the form of a woman so beautiful that she stole his breath, he hadn't seen it.

Dear God. He loved her. He loved her enough to give up everything he wanted, even Mancini's, to make her dreams come true. But he wouldn't have to give up anything. His dream was her dream. And her dream was now his dream.

Their meal eaten, the bride and groom rose from the table. The seating area was quickly dismantled by vineyard staff, who left a circle of chairs around the tent and a clear floor on which to dance.

The band introduced the bride and groom and he took her hand and kissed it before he led her in their dance.

Emotion choked Rafe. He'd spent the past years believing the best way to live his dream was to hold himself back, forget love, when the truth was he simply needed to meet the right woman to realize his dream would be hollow, empty without her.

"Hey." Daniella walked up beside him. "Dinner is

over. We can dismantle our warmers, take our trays and go home."

He faced her. Emotions churned inside him. Feelings for Dani that took root and held on. He'd found his one. He'd fired her, yelled at her, asked her to become his lover. And she'd held her ground. Stood up to him. Refused him. Forced him to work by her terms. And she had won him.

But he had absolutely no idea how to tell her that.

She picked up an empty tray and headed for his SUV. Grabbing up another empty tray, he scurried after her.

"I've been thinking about our choice."

She slid the tray into the SUV. "Our choice?"

"You know. Our choice not to—"

Before he could finish, the busboys came out of the tent with more trays. Frustration stiffened his back. With a quick glance at him, Dani walked back to the noisy reception for more pans. The busboys got the warmers.

Simmering with the need to talk, Rafe silently packed it all inside the back of his SUV.

Nerves filled him as he drove his empty pans, warmers and employees to Mancini's. When they arrived, the restaurant bustled with diners. Emory raced around the kitchen like a madman. Daniella pitched in to help Allegra. Rafe put on his smock, washed his hands and helped Emory.

Time flew, as it always did when he was busy, but Rafe kept watching Daniella. Something was on her mind. She smiled. She worked. She teased with staff. But he heard something in her voice. A catch? No it was more of an easing back. The click of connection he always heard when she spoke with staff was missing. It was as if she were distancing herself—

Oh, dear God.

In all the hustle and bustle that had taken place in the past four weeks, she'd never made the commitment to stay.

And she had a plane ticket for the following morning.

The night wound down. Emory headed for the office to

do some paperwork. Rafe casually ambled into the dining room. As the last of the waitstaff left, he pulled a bottle of Chianti from the rack and walked around the bar to a stool.

He watched Dani pause at the podium, as if torn between reaching for her coat and joining him. His heart chugged. Everything inside him froze.

Finally, she turned to him. Her lips lifted into a warm smile and she sashayed over.

Interpreting her coming to him as a good sign, he didn't give himself time to think twice. He caught her hands, lifted both to his lips and said, "Pick me."

Her brow furrowed. "What?"

"I know you're thinking about leaving. I see it on your face. Hear it in your voice. I know you think you have nothing here but a job, but that's not true. I need you for so much more. So pick me. Do not work for me. Pick me. Keep me. Take *me*."

Her breath hitched. "You're asking me to quit?"

"No." He licked his suddenly dry lips. He'd known this woman only twenty-four days. Yet what he felt was stronger than anything he'd ever felt before.

"Daniella, I think I want you to marry me."

Dani's heart bounced to a stop as she yanked her hands out of his.

"What?"

"I want you to marry me."

She couldn't stop the thrill that raced through her, but even through her shock she'd heard his words clearly. "You said *think*. You said you *think* you want to marry me."

He laughed a bit as he pulled his hand through his hair. "It's so fast for me. My God, I never even thought I'd want to get married. Now I can't imagine my life without you." He caught her hand again, caught her gaze. "Marry me."

His voice had become stronger. His conviction obvious.

"Oh." She wanted to say yes so bad it hurt to wrestle the

word back down her throat. But she had to. "For a month you've said you don't do relationships. Now suddenly you want to marry me?"

He laughed. "All these years, I thought I was weak because I gave Kamila what she wanted and she left me anyway. So I made myself strong. People saw me as selfish. I thought I was determined."

"I understand that."

"Now I see I *was* selfish. I did not want to lose my dream again."

"I understand that, too."

He shook his head fiercely. "You're missing what I'm telling you. I might have been broken by her loss, but Kamila was the wrong woman for me. I was never my real self with her. I was one compromise after another. With you, I am me. I see my temper and I rein it back. I see myself with kids. I see a house. I long to make you happy."

Oh, dear God, did the man have no heart? "Don't say things you don't mean."

"I never say things I don't mean. I love you, Daniella." He reached for her again. "Do not get on that plane tomorrow."

She stepped back, so far that he couldn't touch her, and pressed her fingers to her lips. Her heart so very desperately wanted to believe every word he said. Her brain had been around, though, for every time that same heart was broken. This man had called Paul's proposal a stopgap measure…yet, here he was doing the same thing.

"No."

His face fell. "No?"

"What did you tell me about Paul asking to marry me the day before I left New York?"

He frowned.

"You said it was a stopgap measure. A way to keep me." He walked toward her. "Daniella…"

She halted him with a wave of her hand. "Don't. I feel

foolish enough already. You're afraid I'm going to go home so you make a proposal that mocks everything I believe in."

She yearned to close her eyes at the horrible sense of how little he thought of her, but she held them open, held back her tears and made the hardest decision of her life.

"I'm going back to New York." Her heart splintered in two as she realized this really was the end. They'd never bump into each other at a coffee shop, never sit beside each other in the subway, never accidentally go to the same dry cleaner. He lived thousands of miles away from her and there'd be no chance for them to have the time they needed to really fall in love. He'd robbed them of that with his insulting proposal.

"Mancini's will be fine without me." She tried a smile. "*You* will be fine without me." She took another few steps back. "I've gotta go."

CHAPTER FOURTEEN

DANI RACED OUT of Mancini's, quickly started Louisa's little car and headed home. Her flight didn't leave until ten in the morning. But she had to pack. She had to say goodbye to Louisa. She had to give back the tons of clothes her new friend had let her borrow for her job at Mancini's.

She swiped at a tear as she turned down the lane to Palazzo di Comparino. Her brain told her she was smart to be going home. Her splintered heart reminded her she didn't have a home. No one to return to in the United States. No one to stay for in Italy.

The kitchen light was on and as was their practice, Louisa had waited up for Dani. As soon as she stepped in the kitchen door, Louisa handed her a cup of tea. Dani glanced up at her, knowing the sheen of tears sparkled on her eyelashes.

"What's wrong?"

"I'm going home."

Louisa blinked. "I thought this was settled."

"Nothing's ever settled with Rafe." She sucked in a breath. "The smart thing for me is to leave."

"What about the restaurant, your job, your destiny?"

She fell to a seat. "He asked me to marry him."

Louisa's eyes widened. "How is that bad? My God, Dani, even I can see you love the guy."

"I said no."

"Oh, sweetie! Sweetie! You love the guy. How the hell could you say no?"

"I've been here four weeks, Louisa. Rafe is a confirmed bachelor and he asked me to marry him. The day before I'm supposed to go home. You do the math."

"What math? You have a return ticket to the United States. He doesn't want you to go."

Dani slowly raised her eyes to meet Louisa's. "Exactly. The proposal was a stopgap measure. He told me all about it when we talked about Paul asking me to marry him. He said Paul didn't want to risk losing me, so the day before I left for Italy, he'd asked me to marry him."

"And you think that's what Rafe did?"

Her chin lifted. "You don't?"

Rafe was seated at the bar on his third shot of whiskey when Emory ambled out into the dining room.

"What are you doing here?"

He presented the shot glass. "What does it look like I'm doing?"

Emory frowned. "Getting drunk?"

Rafe saluted his correct answer.

"After a successful catering event that could have gone south, you're drinking?"

"I asked Daniella to marry me. And do you know what she told me?"

Looking totally confused, Emory slid onto the stool beside Rafe. "Obviously, she said no."

"She said no."

Emory laughed. Rafe scowled at him. "Why do you think this is funny?"

"The look on your face is funny."

"Thanks."

"Come on, Rafe, you've known the girl a month."

"So she doesn't trust me?"

Emory laughed. "Look at you. Look at how you've treated her. Would you trust you?"

"Yeah, well, she's leaving for New York tomorrow. I didn't want her to go."

Emory frowned. "Ah. So you asked her to marry you to keep her from going?"

"No. I asked her to marry me because I love her." He rubbed his hand along the back of his neck. "But I'd also told her that her boyfriend had asked her to marry him the day before she left for Italy as a stopgap measure. Wanting to tie her to him, without giving her a real commitment, he'd asked. But he hadn't really meant it. He just didn't want her to go."

Emory swatted him with a dish towel. "Why do you tell her these things?"

"At the time it made sense."

"Yeah, well, now she thinks you only asked her to marry you to keep her from going back to New York."

"No kidding."

Emory swatted him again. "Get the hell over to Palazzo di Comparino and fix this!"

"How?"

Emory's eyes narrowed. "You know what she wants… what she needs. Not just truth, proof. If you love her, and you'd better if you asked her to marry you, you have to give her proof."

He jumped off the stool, grabbed Emory's shoulders and noisily kissed the top of his head. "Yes. Yes! Proof! You are a hundred percent correct."

"You just make sure she doesn't get on that plane."

Dani's tears dried as she and Louisa packed her things. Neither one of them expected to sleep, so they spent the night talking. They talked of keeping in touch. Video chatting and texting made that much easier than it used to be. And

Louisa had promised to come to New York. They would be thousands of miles apart but they would be close.

Around five in the morning, Dani shoved off her kitchen chair and sadly made her way to the shower. She dressed in her own old raggedy jeans and a worn sweater, the glamour of her life in Tuscany, and Louisa's clothes behind her now.

When she came downstairs, Louisa had also dressed. She'd promised to take her to the airport and she'd gotten ready.

But there was an odd gleam in her eye when she said, "Shall we go?"

Dani sighed, knowing she'd miss this house but also realizing she'd found a friend who could be like a sister. The trip wasn't an entire waste after all.

She smiled at Louisa. "Yeah. Let's go."

They got into the ugly green car and rather than let Dani drive, Louisa got behind the wheel.

"I thought you refused to drive until you understood Italy's rules of the road better."

Stepping on the gas, Louisa shrugged. "I've gotta learn some time."

She drove them out of the vineyard and out of the village. Then the slow drive to Florence began. But even before they went a mile, Louisa turned down an old road.

"What are you doing?"

"I promised someone a favor."

Dani frowned. "Do we have time?"

"Plenty of time. You're fine."

"I know I'm fine. It's my flight I'm worried about."

"I promise you. I will pull into the driveway and be pulling out two minutes later."

Dani opened her mouth to answer but she snapped it closed when she realized they were at the old farmhouse Maria the real estate agent had shown her and Rafe. She faced Louisa. "Do you know the person who bought this?"

"Yes." She popped open her door. "Come in with me."

Dani pushed on her door. "I thought you said this would only take a minute."

"I said two minutes. What I actually said was I promise I will be pulling out of this driveway two minutes after I pull in."

Dani walked up the familiar path to the familiar door and sighed when it groaned as Louisa opened it. "Whoever bought this is in for about three years of renovations."

Louisa laughed before she called out, "Hello. We're here."

Rafe stepped out from behind a crumbling wall. Dani skittered back. "Louisa! *This* is your friend?"

"I didn't say he was my friend. I said I knew him." Louisa gave Dani's back a little shove. "He has some important things to say to you."

"I bought this house for you," Rafe said, not giving Dani a chance to reply to Louisa.

"I don't want a house."

He sighed. "Too bad. Because you now have a house." He motioned her forward. "I see a big kitchen here. Something that smells like heaven."

She stopped.

He motioned toward the huge room in the front. "And big, fat chairs that you can sink into in here."

"Very funny."

"I am not being funny. You," he said, pointing at her, "want a home. I want you. Therefore, I give you a home."

"What? Since a marriage proposal didn't keep me, you offer me a house?"

"I didn't say I was giving you a house. I said I was giving you a home." He walked toward the kitchen. "And you're going to marry me."

She scrambled after him. "Exactly how do you expect to make that happen?"

She rounded the turn and walked right into him. He caught her arms and hauled her to him, kissing her. She made a token protest, but, honestly, this was the man she couldn't resist.

He broke the kiss slowly, as if he didn't ever want to have to stop kissing her. "That's how I expect to make that happen."

"You're going to kiss me until I agree?"

"It's an idea with merit. But it won't be all kissing. We have a restaurant. You have a job. And there's a bedroom back here." He headed toward it.

Once again, she found herself running after him. Cold air leeched in from the window and she stopped dead in her tracks. "The window leaks."

"Then you're going to have to hire a general contractor."

"Me?"

He straightened to his full six-foot-three height. "I am a master. I cook."

"Oh, and I clean and make babies?"

He laughed. "We will hire someone to clean. Though I like the part about you making babies."

Her heart about pounded its way out of her chest. "You want kids?"

He walked toward her slowly. "*We* want kids. We want all that stuff you said about fat chairs and good-smelling kitchens and turning the thermostat down so that we can snuggle."

Her heart melted. "You don't look like a snuggler."

"I'll talk you into doing more than snuggling."

She laughed. Pieces of the ice around her heart began to melt. Her eyes clung to his. "You're serious?"

"I wouldn't have told Louisa to bring you here if I weren't. I don't do stupid things. I do impulsive things." He grinned. "You might have to get used to that."

She smiled. He motioned for her to come closer and when she did, he wrapped his arms around her.

"I could not bear to see you go."

"You said Paul only asked me to marry him as a stop-gap measure."

"Yes, but Paul is an idiot. I am not."

She laughed again and it felt so good that she paused to revel in it. To memorize the feeling of his arms around her. To glance around at their house.

"Oh, my God, this is a mess."

"We'll be fine."

She laid her head on his chest and breathed in his scent. She counted to ten, waited for him to say something that would drive her away, then realized what she was really waiting for.

She glanced up at him. "I'm so afraid you're going to hurt me."

"I know. And I'm going to spend our entire lives proving to you that you have no need to worry."

She laughed and sank against him again. "I love you."

"After only four weeks?"

She peeked up again. "Yes."

"So this time you'll believe me when I say it."

She swallowed. Years of fear faded away. "Yes."

"Good." He shifted back, just slightly, so he could pull a small jewelry box from the pocket of his jeans. He opened it and revealed a two-carat diamond. "I love you. So you will marry me?"

She gaped at the ring, then brought her gaze to his hopeful face. When he smiled, she hugged him fiercely. "Yes!"

He slipped the ring onto her finger. "Now, weren't we on our way back to the bedroom?"

"For what? There's no bed back there."

He said, "Oh, you of no imagination. I have a hundred ways around that."

"A hundred, isn't that a bit ambitious?"

"Get used to it. I am a master, remember?"

"Yeah, you are," she said, and then she laughed. She was

getting married, going to make babies…going to make a *home—in Italy.*

With the man of her dreams.

Because finally, finally she was allowed to have dreams.

* * * * *

RETURN OF THE
ITALIAN TYCOON

JENNIFER FAYE

To Michelle Styles, an amazing friend, who taught me so much, including that the important part of writing was what I decided to do after the dreaded "R".
Thank you!

CHAPTER ONE

"CAN I SMELL YOU?"

Kayla Hill's fingers struck the wrong keys on her computer. Surely she hadn't heard her boss correctly—her very serious, very handsome boss. "Excuse me. What did you say?"

Angelo Amatucci's tanned face creased with lines as though he were deep in thought. "Are you wearing perfume?"

"Uh…yes, I am."

"Good. That will be helpful. May I have a smell?"

Helpful? With what? She gave up on answering an email and turned her full attention to her boss, who moved to stand next to her. What in the world had prompted him to ask such a question? Was her perfume bothering him? She sure hoped not. She wore it all the time. If he didn't like it or was allergic to it, she thought he'd have mentioned it before now.

Kayla craned her neck, allowing her gaze to travel up over his fit body, all six-foot-plus of muscle, until she met his inquisitive eyes. "I'm sorry but I… I don't understand."

"I just finished speaking with Victoria Van Holsen, owner of Moonshadows Cosmetics. She has decided that her latest fragrance campaign, even though she painstakingly approved it each step of the way, just won't do."

"She doesn't want it?" Kayla failed to keep the astonishment out of her voice.

A muscle in his jaw twitched. "She insists we present her with a totally new proposal."

"But this is a Christmas campaign. Everything should be finalized, considering it's already March." Then, real-

izing that she was speaking to a man with far more experience, she pressed her lips together, silencing her rambling
thoughts.

"Now that information about her competitor's upcoming
holiday campaign has been leaked, she wants something
more noteworthy—something that will go viral."

"I thought the campaign was unique. I really like it."
Kayla truly meant it. She wasn't trying to butter up her
boss—that was just an unexpected bonus.

"The fact of the matter is, Victoria Van Holsen is a
household name and one of our most important clients.
Our duty is to keep her happy."

It was the company's motto—the client's needs come
first. No matter what. And if Kayla was ever going to rise
up the chain from her temporary detour as the personal assistant to the CEO of Amatucci & Associates Advertising
to her dream job as an ad executive on Madison Avenue,
she could never forget that the clients were always right.
It didn't matter how unreasonable or outrageous their re-
quests might be at times, keeping them happy was of the
utmost importance.

"How can I help?"

"Stand up."

His face was devoid of emotion, giving no hint of his
thoughts.

She did as he asked. Her heart fluttered as he circled her.
When he stopped behind her and leaned in close, an army
of goose bumps rose on her skin. Her eyes drifted closed as
a gentle sigh slipped across her lips. Angelo Amatucci truly
did want an up close and personal whiff of her perfume.

He didn't so much as touch a single hair on her, but she
could sense him near her neck. Her pulse raced. If this most
unusual request had come from anyone else, she'd swear
they were hitting on her. But as Mr. Amatucci stepped to
the front of her, his indifferent expression hadn't changed.
Her frantic heart rate dipped back to normal.

There had never been any attempt on his part to flirt with her. Though his actions at times could be quite unpredictable, they were always ingenuous. She deduced that his sudden curiosity about her perfume had something to do with the Van Holsen account. But what could he be thinking? Because there was no way she was wearing a Moonshadows fragrance. One ounce of the stuff would set her back an entire paycheck.

"It seems to have faded away." A frown tugged at his lips.

"Perhaps this will be better." She pulled up the sleeve of her blue suit jacket and the pink blouse beneath it before holding out her wrist to him. "Try this."

His hand was warm and his fingers gentle as he lifted her hand to his face. Her heart resumed its frantic tap dancing in her chest. *Tip-tap. Tip-tap.* She wished it wouldn't do that. He was, after all, her boss—the man who held her career aspirations in the palm of his very powerful hand. A man who was much too serious for her.

Still, she couldn't dismiss that his short dark wavy hair with a few silver strands at the temples framed a very handsome, chiseled face. His dark brown eyes closed as he inhaled the fragrance, and she noticed his dark lashes as they swept down, hiding his mesmerizing eyes. It was a wonder some woman hadn't snatched him up—not that Kayla had any thoughts in that direction.

She had narrowly escaped the bondage of marriage to a really nice guy, who even came with her Mom's and Dad's stamp of approval. Though the breakup had been hard, it had been the right decision for both of them. Steven had wanted a traditional wife who was content to cook, clean and raise a large family. Not that there was anything wrong with that vision. It just wasn't what she envisioned for her future. She wanted to get out of Nowhereville, USA, and find her future in New York City.

When Mr. Amatucci released her arm, she could still

feel warmth where his fingers had once been. Her pulse continued to race. She didn't know why she was having this reaction. She wasn't about to jeopardize her rising career for some ridiculous crush on her boss, especially when it was perfectly obvious that he didn't feel a thing for her.

His gaze met hers. "Is that the only perfume you wear?"

She nodded. "It's my favorite."

"Could I convince you to wear another fragrance?"

He was using her as a test market? Interesting. She could tell him what he wanted to hear, but how would that help him develop a new marketing strategy? She decided to take her chances and give him honest answers.

"Why would I change when I've been using this same perfume for years?"

He rubbed his neck as she'd seen him do numerous times in the past when he was contemplating new ideas for big accounts. And the Van Holsen account was a very big account. The fact that the client had the money to toss aside a fully formulated ad campaign and start over from scratch was proof of their deep pockets.

Mr. Amatucci's gaze was still on her, but she couldn't tell if he was lost in thought. "How long have you worn that fragrance?"

"Since I was a teenager." She remembered picking out the flower-shaped bottle from a department store counter. It was right before her first ever school dance. She'd worn it for every special occasion since, including her first date with Steven. And then there was her high school graduation followed by her college commencement. She'd worn it for all the big moments in her life. Even the day she'd packed her bags and moved to New York City in search of her dreams.

"Talk to me." Mr. Amatucci's voice cut through her memories. "What were you thinking about just now?"

She glanced hesitantly at him. In all of the weeks she'd worked as his PA, they'd never ventured into a conversation that was the slightest bit personal. Their talks had always centered around business. Now, he'd probably think she was silly or sentimental or both.

"I was thinking about all the times in my life when I wore this perfume."

"And?"

"And I wore it for every major event. My first date. My first kiss. My—" A sharp look from him silenced her.

"So your attachment to the fragrance goes beyond the scent itself. It is a sentimental attachment, right?"

She shrugged. "I guess so."

She'd never thought of it that way. In fact, she'd never given her perfume this much thought. If the bottle got low, she put it on her shopping list, but that's as far as her thoughts ever went.

"So if our client doesn't want to go with a sparkly, feel-fabulous-when-you-wear-this campaign, we can try a more glamorous sentimental approach. Thanks to you, we now have a new strategy."

She loved watching creativity in action. And she loved being a part of the creative process. "Glad I could help."

He started to walk away, then he paused and turned back. "You were just promoted to a copywriter position before you took this temporary assignment as my PA, right?"

She nodded. What better way to get noticed than to work directly for one of the biggest names in the advertising industry.

"Good. You aren't done with this project. I want you to dig into those memories and write out some ideas—"

"But don't you have a creative team for this account?" She wanted to kick herself for blurting out her thoughts.

Mr. Amatucci sent her a narrowed look. His cool, professional tone remained unchanged. "Are you saying you aren't interested in working on the project?"

Before she could find the words to express her enthusiasm, his phone rang and he turned away. She struggled to contain her excitement. This was her big opening and she fully intended to make the most of it.

This was going to work out perfectly.

A smile tugged at Kayla lips. She'd finally made it. Though people thought she'd made a big mistake by taking a step backward to assume a temporary position as Mr. Amatucci's PA, it was actually working out just as she'd envisioned.

She'd gone after what she wanted and she'd gotten it. Well, not exactly, but she was well on her way to making her dreams a reality. With a little more patience and a lot of hard work, she'd become an account executive on New York's famous Madison Avenue in the exclusive advertising agency of Amatucci & Associates.

Her fingers glided over the keyboard of her computer as she completed the email to the creative department about another of their Christmas campaigns. Sure it was only March, but in the marketing world, they were working months into the future. And with a late-season snowstorm swirling about outside, it seemed sort of fitting to be working on a holiday project.

She glanced off to the side of her computer monitor, noticing her boss holding the phone to his ear as he faced a wall of windows overlooking downtown Manhattan. Being on the twenty-third floor, they normally had a great view of the city, but not today. What she wouldn't give to be someplace sunny—far, far away from the snow. After months of frigid temperatures and icy sidewalks, she was most definitely ready for springtime.

"Have you started that list?" Mr. Amatucci's piercing brown gaze met hers.

Um—she'd been lost in her thoughts and hadn't even realized he'd wrapped up his phone call. Her gaze moved from his tanned face to her monitor. "Not yet. I need to finish one more email. It shouldn't take me long. I think your ideas for the account are spot-on. Just wait until the client lays her eyes on the mock-ups."

Then, realizing she was rambling, she pressed her lips firmly together. There was just something about being around him that filled her with nervous energy. And his long stretches of silence had her rushing to fill in the silent gaps.

Mr. Amatucci looked as though he was about to say something, but his phone rang again. All eyes moved to his desk. The ringtone was different. It must be his private line. In all the time she'd been working for him, it had never rung.

It rang again and yet all he did was stare at the phone.

"Do you want me to get it?" Kayla offered, not sure what the problem was or why Mr. Amatucci was hesitant. "I really don't mind."

"I've got it." He reached over and snatched up the receiver. "Nico, what's the matter?"

Well, that was certainly a strange greeting. Who picked up the phone expecting something to be wrong? Then, realizing that she was staring—not to mention eavesdropping—she turned her attention back to the notes she'd been rewording into an email. She glanced up to see Mr. Amatucci had turned his back to her. He once again faced the windows and spoke softly. Though the words were no longer distinguishable, the steely edge of his voice was still obvious.

She looked at the paper on her desk, her gaze darting over it to find where she'd left off. She didn't want to sit here with her hands idle. No, that definitely wouldn't look good for her.

She was sending along some of Mr. Amatucci's thoughts about the mock-up of an ad campaign for a new client—a very demanding client. The account was huge. It would go global—like most of the other accounts her boss personally handled. Each of his clients expected Mr. Amatucci's world to revolve around them and their accounts. He took their calls, no matter the time—day or night. Through it all, he maintained his cool. To say Angelo was a workaholic was being modest.

As a result, he ran the most sought-after advertising agency in the country—if not the world. Stepping off the elevator, clients and staff were immediately greeted by local artists' work and fresh flowers. The receptionist was bright and cheerful without being annoying. Appointments were kept timely. The quality of the work was exemplary. All of it culminated in Amatucci & Associates being so popular that they had to turn away business.

"*Cosa!* Nico, no!" Mr. Amatucci's hand waved about as he talked.

Her boss's agitated voice rose with each word uttered. Kayla's fingers paused as her attention zeroed in on the man who never raised his voice—until now. He was practically yelling. But she could only make out bits and pieces. His words were a mix of English and Italian with a thick accent.

"Nico, are you sure?"

Had someone died? And who was Nico? She hadn't heard Mr. Amatucci mention anyone with that name, but then again, this call was on his private line. It was highly doubtful that it had anything to do with business. And she knew exactly nothing about his personal life—sometimes she wondered if he even had one.

"Marianna can't be pregnant!" The shouts spiraled off into Italian.

Pregnant? Was he the father? The questions came hard and fast. There was a little voice in the back of her mind that told her she should excuse herself and give him some privacy, but she was riveted to her chair. No one would ever believe that this smooth, icy-cool man was capable of such heated volatility. She blinked, making sure she hadn't fallen asleep and was having some bizarre dream. But when her eyes opened, her boss was standing across the room with his hand slicing through the air as he spoke Italian.

The paramount question was: Who was Marianna?

Angelo Amatucci tightened his grip on the phone until his fingers hurt. This had to be some sort of nightmare and soon he'd wake up. Could it be he'd been working a bit too much lately? Perhaps he should listen to the hints from his business associates to take a break from the frantic pace. That would explain why just moments ago when he'd been examining Ms. Hill's perfume—a scent he found quite inviting—that he'd been tempted to smooth his thumb along the silky skin of her wrist—

"Angelo, are you listening to me?" Tones of blatant concern laced Nico's voice, demanding Angelo's full attention. "What are we going to do?"

Nico was his younger brother by four years, and though their opinions differed on almost everything, the one area where they presented a unified front was their little sister, Marianna—who wasn't so little anymore.

"There has to be another answer to this. You must have misunderstood. Marianna can't be pregnant. She's not even in a serious relationship."

"I know what I heard."

"Tell me again."

"I wanted her to taste the wine from the vineyard. I think it's the best we've ever produced. Just wait until you try some—"

"Nico, tell me about Marianna."

"Yes, well, she has looked awfully pale and out of sorts since she returned home after her year of traveling. I thought she'd done too much partying—"

"*Accidenti!* She wasn't supposed to waste the year partying." Unable to stand still a moment longer, Angelo started to pace again. When his gaze met the wide-eyed stare of Ms. Hill, she glanced down at her desk. He made a point of turning his back to her and lowering his voice. "She was sent to Australia to work on the vineyards there and get more experience in order to help you. If I'd have known she planned for it to be a year of partying, I'd have sent for her. I could have put her to work at the office."

Nico sighed. "Not everyone is like you, big brother. We aren't all driven to spend every last moment of our lives working."

"And you didn't do anything about her being sick?"

"What was I supposed to do? I asked if she needed anything. She said no, that it was some sort of flu bug. What else was I supposed to do?"

Angelo's hand waved around as he flew off in a string of Italian rants. Taking a calming breath, he stopped in front of the windows and stared blindly at the snow. "And it took her confessing she was pregnant for you to figure it out?"

"Like you would have figured it out sooner? What do either of us know about pregnant women…unless there's something you haven't told me?"

"Don't be ridiculous!" Angelo had no intention of getting married and having a family. Not now. Not ever.

"She didn't have any choice but to come clean when I offered her some wine. She knew she couldn't drink it. Hard to believe that you and I will be uncles this time next year."

"Don't tell me you're happy about this development?"

"I'm not. But what do you want me to do?"

"Find out the father's name for starters."

"I tried. She's being closemouthed. All she said was that she couldn't drink the wine because she's eight weeks pregnant. Then she started to cry and took off for her room."

"Didn't you follow? How could you have just let her get away without saying more?"

"How could I? I sure don't see you here trying to deal with an emotional pregnant woman."

How had things spun so totally out of control? Angelo's

entire body tensed. And more importantly, how did he fix them? How did he help his sister from so far away?

Angelo raked his fingers through his hair. "She has to tell you more. How are we supposed to help if we don't even know which man is the father. She isn't exactly the sort to stay in a relationship for long."

"Trust me. I've tried repeatedly to get his name from her. Maybe she'll tell you."

That wasn't a conversation Angelo wanted to have over the phone. It had to be in person. But he was in the middle of overseeing a number of important projects. Now was not the time for him to leave New York. But what choice did he have? This was his baby sister—the little girl he remembered so clearly running around with a smile on her face and her hair in braids.

But a lot of time had passed since he'd left Italy. Would she open up to him? The fact his leaving hadn't been his idea didn't seem to carry much weight with his siblings, who were left behind to deal with their dysfunctional parents. Though he dearly missed his siblings, he didn't miss the constant barrage of high-strung emotions of his parent's arguments and then their inevitable reunions—a constant circle of epic turmoil.

Maybe the trouble Marianna had got herself into was some sort of rebellion. With their parents now living in Milan, there was only Nico at home to cope with their sister. And to Nico's credit, he never complained about the enormous responsibility leveled solely on his shoulders.

Now that their parents had moved on, Angelo didn't have any legitimate excuse to stay away. But every time the subject of his visiting Monte Calanetti surfaced, he pleaded he had too much work to do. It was the truth—mostly. Perhaps he should have tried harder to make more time for his siblings.

Stricken with guilt, anger and a bunch of emotions that Angelo couldn't even name, he couldn't think straight. As the oldest brother, he was supposed to look out for his brother and sister. Instead, he'd focused all of his time and energy on creating a thriving, wildly successful company.

In the process, he'd failed their wayward and headstrong sister.

And now her future would forever be altered.

He owed it to Marianna to do what he could to fix things. But how could he do that when he was so far away?

CHAPTER TWO

THIS ISN'T GOOD. Not good at all.

Kayla pressed Save on the computer. She needed to give Mr. Amatucci some space. She reached for her wallet to go buy a—a—a cocoa. Yes, that would suit the weather outside perfectly.

She got to her feet when her boss slammed down the phone. He raked his fingers through his short hair and glanced at her. "Sorry about that. Where were we?"

The weariness in his voice tugged at her sympathies. "Um…well, I thought that I'd go get some um…cocoa—"

"The Van Holsen account. We were talking about how we need to put a rush on it."

"Um…sure." She sat back down.

Kayla wasn't sure how to act. She'd never before witnessed her boss seriously lose it. And who exactly was Marianna? Was it possible Mr. Amatucci really did have a life outside this office—one nobody knew about? The thought had her fighting back a frown. Why should it bother her to think that her boss might have fathered a baby with this woman? It wasn't as if they were anything more than employee and employer.

Mr. Amatucci stepped up to her desk. "I'll need to go over this with you tomorrow afternoon."

"Tomorrow?"

She knew that he asked for the impossible at times and this happened to be one of those times. He'd caught her totally off guard. It'd take time to think out innovative ideas for the new campaign platform. And she had an important meeting that night, but there was no way she was telling her boss about that.

Mr. Amatucci arched a brow at her. "Is that going to be a problem?"

"Uh...no. No problem." She would not let this opportunity pass her by. "I'll just finish up what I was working on, and I'll get started."

He paused as though considering her answer. "On second thought, it'd be best to go over your ideas first thing in the morning."

"The morning?"

His gaze narrowed in on her, and she wished that her thoughts would quit slipping across her tongue and out her mouth. It certainly wasn't helping this situation. She was here to impress him with her capabilities, not to annoy him when he was obviously already in a bad mood.

"Ms. Hill, you seem to be repeating what I say. Is there some sort of problem I should be aware of?"

She hated that he always called her Ms. Hill. Couldn't he be like everyone else in the office and call her Kayla? But then again, she was talking about Angelo Amatucci— he was unlike anyone she'd ever known.

He was the first man to set her stomach aquiver without so much as touching her. She'd been so aware of his mouth being just a breath away from her neck as he'd sniffed her perfume. The memory was still fresh in her mind. Was it so wrong that she hadn't wanted that moment to end?

Of course it was. She swallowed hard. He was her boss, not just some guy she'd met at a friend's place. There could never be anything serious between them—not that he'd ever even noticed her as a desirable woman.

"Ms. Hill?"

"No, there won't be a...uh...problem." Who was she kidding? This was going to be a big problem, but she'd work it out—somehow—some way.

Her gaze moved to the windows and the darkening sky. With it only nearing the lunch hour, it shouldn't be so dark, which could only mean that they were going to get pounded with more snow. The thought of getting stuck at the office turned her nervous stomach nauseous.

Snow. Snow. Go away.

He gazed at her. "I didn't mean to snap at you—"

"I understand. You've got a lot on your mind."

"Thank you."

His gaze continued to hold hers. The dark depths of his eyes held a mystery—the story of the real man behind the designer suits and the Rolex watches. She had to admit that she was quite curious about him—more than any employee had a right to about her very handsome, very single boss. And that odd phone call only made her all the more curious. Maybe he wasn't as single as she'd presumed. The jagged thought lodged in her throat.

Mr. Amatucci's steady gaze met hers. "You're sure you're up for this project?"

She pressed her lips together, no longer trusting her mouth, and nodded. She'd have to reschedule tonight's meeting for the fund-raiser.

"Good. If you need help, feel free to ask one of the other PAs to take over some of your other work. The Van Holsen account is now your priority."

He gathered his tablet computer and headed for the door. "I've got a meeting. I'll be back later."

"Don't worry. I've got this."

Without a backward glance, he strode out of the room, looking like the calm, cool, collected Angelo Amatucci that everyone respected and admired for his creative foresight. But how he was able to shut down his emotions so quickly was totally beyond her.

What was she going to do about her meeting tonight? It didn't help that she'd been the one to set it up. Somehow she'd been put in charge of the Inner City League after-school program fund-raiser. The program was in a serious financial bind. ICL was a great organization that kept at-risk kids off the streets after school while their parents were still at work.

Kayla had been volunteering for the past year. Helping others was how her parents had raised her. They had always been generous with their spare time and money—not that they had much of either. Kayla may have hightailed it out of Paradise, Pennsylvania, as soon as she could, but there was still a lot of Paradise in her. And she'd swear that she got more back from the kids and the other volunteers than she ever gave to any of them. For a girl who was used to living in a small town of friends, it was a comfort to have such a friendly group to keep her from feeling isolated in such a large city of strangers.

There was no way she could reschedule tonight's meeting. They were running out of time until the charity concert and there was still so much to plan. Somehow she had to make this all work out. She couldn't let down the kids nor could she let down her boss. The thought of Angelo Amatucci counting on her felt good.

Not only was he easy on the eyes, but she really enjoyed working with him, even if he was a bit stiff and withdrawn most of the time. But now that she'd witnessed him emotionally charged, she couldn't help but wonder what it'd be like to get up close and personal with him.

Angelo shook his head.

Marianna pregnant! Impossible.

Okay, so it wasn't impossible, but why had she been acting so irresponsible? It wasn't as if she was married or even considering it. She changed romantic interests faster than he changed ties—never getting too serious—until now. Nico didn't even know the father's name. What was up with that?

"What do you think, Mr. Amatucci?"

He glanced up at his youngest and most promising account executive. This was a meeting to discuss the campaign for a new sports car that was going to be revealed later that year. The car was quite nice and was sure to create a buzz of attention.

But for the life of him, Angelo couldn't keep his mind wrapped around business—no matter how important the account. His head was in Italy at the village of Monte Calanetti—where he should be dealing with his sister's life-changing event.

Angelo glanced down at the presentation on his digital tablet and then back at the account executive. "I think you still have work to do. This presentation is flat. It isn't innovative enough. There's nothing here to sway a twentysomething consumer to take out a sizable loan on top of their college debt in order to have this car. I want the 'must have' factor. The part that says if I have this car all of my friends will be envious. This isn't just a car—this is a status symbol. Do you understand?"

Mike glanced down and then back at Angelo. "But this is what the client asked for."

"And it's your job to push the envelope and give the client something more to consider—to want." Maybe he'd been too quick in his determination that Mike was going to be an asset to Amatucci & Associates—unlike Kayla, who was constantly proving she was an independent thinker. "Try again."

Mike's mouth started to open but out of the corner of Angelo's eye he could see the copywriter give a quick shake of his head. Mike glanced back at Angelo. He nodded his agreement.

"Good. I expect to see something new in forty-eight hours."

Again the man's mouth opened but nothing came out. His lips pressed together, and he nodded. Now if only Angelo could handle his little sister in the same no-nonsense manner. He liked when things were easy and uncomplicated.

But now, with time to cool down, he realized that his only course of action was to return home—to return to Italy. His gut knotted as he thought of the expectations that he'd failed to fulfill. Back in Monte Calanetti he wasn't viewed as someone successful—someone influential. Back home he was Giovanni's son—the son who'd fled his family and their way of life, unlike his younger brother who took great pride in their heritage.

With the meeting concluded, Angelo made his way back to his office. With the decision made to leave first thing in the morning, he had to figure out how to handle his current workload. His clients would never accept having their accounts turned over to anyone else. They paid top dollar for one-on-one attention, and they would accept nothing less.

In order for him to stay on top of everything while traveling abroad, he needed someone who was good in a crisis, levelheaded and an independent worker. Kayla's beautiful face immediately sprang to mind. Could she be the answer?

He hesitated. She did have a habit of being a bit too chatty at times. But this was an emergency. Allowances would have to be made.

More importantly, he was impressed with her work ethic and her attention to details. She was hungry and eager—two elements that would serve her well. And best of all, she had an easy way with people—something that might come in handy on this trip.

He stopped next to her desk. "Ms. Hill." She glanced up. Her green eyes widened. How had he missed their striking shade of jade until now? He cleared his throat, focusing back on the business at hand. "How's the Van Holsen account coming?"

Color pinked her cheeks. "Mr. Amatucci, I... I haven't gotten to it yet. The phone has been ringing and I've been sending out information for some other accounts."

She looked worried as though she'd done something wrong. For the first time, Angelo wondered if everyone who worked for him was intimidated by him. He didn't like the thought of Ms. Hill being uncomfortable around him. He knew he wasn't an easy man to get to know, but he didn't like the thought of striking fear in the hearts of his employees.

"Relax. That's fine. Besides you'll have plenty of time to brainstorm on the flight."

"Excuse me. The flight?"

Since when did he speak without thinking it through first? It had to be this mess with Marianna. It had him off-kilter. "Something urgent has come up. I need to travel to Italy. And I need a competent person to accompany me."

"Me?" Excitement lit up her whole face. Before today, he'd never noticed that behind those black-rimmed reading glasses were not only mesmerizing green eyes but also a beautiful face—not that he was interested in her, or anyone. Ms. Hill clasped her hands together. "I've never been to Italy. I'd love it."

"Good. That's what I was hoping you'd say." But suddenly he wasn't sure spending so much time alone with her was such a good idea, especially now that he'd noticed the unique color of her mesmerizing eyes and her intoxicating scent. He swallowed hard. But it was too late to back out now. "You need to understand this trip will be business only, not a holiday."

"Understood."

"If you go, you'll need to be committed to your work 24/7. We can't afford to miss any deadlines. Is that acceptable?"

She hesitated and, for a moment, he worried that she would back out.

But then Ms. Hill's head bobbed. "I can do it."

"Make sure you are ready to go first thing in the morning."

"As in tomorrow morning?"

He nodded. "And expect to be gone for at least a week—

maybe two." Her mouth gaped and her eyes widened. It was obvious that he'd caught her off guard. But she wasn't the only one to be surprised today—by so many things.

When he'd approved her transfer to be his temporary PA, he'd made it perfectly clear that he demanded 100 percent focus and commitment from his employees. It was that extra push and attention to detail that put Amatucci & Associates head and shoulders above the competition.

If you wanted to be the best, you had to give it your all. And that is what he expected from all of his employees, even if it meant dropping family, hobbies and extracurricular activities in order to focus on the job. What he was asking of Kayla was no different than he'd ask of anyone.

When she didn't jump to accept his offer, he had no patience to wait for an answer. "That won't be a problem, will it?"

From the little he knew about his assistant, she didn't have a family. At least not in the city. And he hadn't seen or heard any hints of a man in her life. Maybe she was more like him than he'd originally thought.

Or was there something else bothering her? Was it the incident with the perfume? Perhaps that hadn't been one of his better moves. He was used to following his instincts when it came to his creative process, but there was something about his assistant that had him leaning a little closer to her slender neck and, for the briefest second, he'd forgotten the reason. His mind had spiraled in a totally inappropriate direction. That wouldn't happen again. He'd see to it.

After all, she wasn't his type. Her nondescript business suits, the way she pulled back her hair and the way she hid her luminous green eyes behind a pair of black-rimmed glasses gave off a very prim, old-fashioned persona. So why was he letting one unexplainable moment bother him?

"I could make arrangements to go, but I have so much work to do on the Van Holsen account—"

"If that's your only objection, then don't worry. The account can wait one day. In fact, take the rest of the day off. I expect to see you at the airport at 6:00 a.m.. Unless you'd like me to pick you up on the way."

"Uh, no." She shook her head vehemently. "I'll find my own way there."

He felt a bit obligated. He was, after all, asking her to drop everything on a moment's notice to help him out. He needed to make a concerted effort to be a little friendlier. "Are you sure? It's really no problem to swing by your place."

"You don't even know where I live."

"True. But since you're going out of your way to help me, I wouldn't mind going out of my way for you."

"Thank you. I appreciate it." She smiled, easing the stress lines from around her mouth.

Angelo found his attention straying to her kissable lips coated with a shimmery light pink gloss. Okay, so not every aspect of her was prim and proper. A fantasy of her pulling off her glasses and letting down her hair played in his mind. Realizing the direction of his wayward thoughts, he halted them.

With effort, his gaze rose over the light splattering of freckles on her pert nose to her intense green eyes. How had he failed to notice her beauty up until today? Had he been that absorbed in his work that he'd failed to see what was standing right in front of him?

He cleared his throat. "I'll pick you up at say five-thirty?"

"Mr. Amatucci—"

"If we're going to travel together, we should at least be on a first name basis. Please, call me Angelo." Now where in the world had that come from? He made a point of keeping his distance from his employees. But then again, he was taking her home with him, where she would meet his family, and that broke all of his professional rules. He reconciled himself with the fact that Kayla's time working for him was limited—soon his regular PA would be back. So maybe he could afford to bend the rules a bit.

"And please call me Kayla." She smiled again, and this time it reached her eyes, making them sparkle like fine jewels.

"We're going to my home in Italy. It's a small village in the Tuscany countryside—Monte Calanetti."

"I'm afraid I've never heard of it, but then again, I've never had the opportunity to travel abroad. Is it big? The village that is?"

He shook his head. "The last time I saw it— granted it has been quite a while—but it was as if time had passed it by. It is rather small and quaint. It is entirely a different world from New York City. Now, are you still interested in going?"

She hesitated and he worried that he'd have to come up with an alternate plan. As of right now, he didn't have one. He needed someone who was familiar with his accounts and wouldn't need a bunch of hand-holding. Kayla was his only viable option. He wasn't one to beg, but at this particular moment he was giving it serious consideration.

Her dimpled chin tilted up. "Yes, I am. It sounds like it'll be a great adventure."

"I don't know about that. The reason I'm going there isn't exactly pleasant, but then again, that isn't for you to worry about. You need to go home and pack."

"Okay. But what should I plan on wearing for the trip? Business attire?"

"Definitely something more casual. There won't be any business meetings, so use your best judgment." He had no doubt her casual attire was as dull and drab as her suits. Not that it mattered to him what she wore so long as she was ready to work.

Kayla gathered her things, and then paused. "Before I leave, should I make plane reservations?"

He shook his head. "No need. We'll take my private jet."

Her pink lips formed an O but nothing came out. And for a moment, he let himself wonder what it'd be like to kiss those full, tempting lips. Not that he would, but he could imagine that one kiss just wouldn't be enough. Something told him that lurking beneath that proper and congenial surface was a passionate woman—

Again, he drew his thoughts up short. The last thing he needed was to notice her feminine qualities. He wasn't about to mix business with pleasure. No way.

CHAPTER THREE

FLUFFY CLOUDS FLOATED past the jet's windows.

They'd soon be touching down in Italy.

A giddy excitement bubbled up in Kayla's chest as she glanced across the aisle at Mr. Amatucci—er—Angelo. She still had a problem remembering to call him by his given name after referring to him as Mr. Amatucci for so long. Being on a first-name basis left her feeling unsettled—not exactly sure how to act around him. If anything, Angelo was even more quiet and reserved than before. Had he sensed her attraction to him?

Impossible. She hadn't said or done anything to betray herself. She smoothed a hand over her gray skirt. She was worrying for nothing.

Just act normal.

She glanced at her boss. "Do you know how long until we arrive?"

Angelo turned in his leather seat to look at her. "What did you say?"

"I was wondering how long we have until we land in Italy."

"Not much longer." His dark gaze dipped to the pen and paper in her lap. "Are you working?"

"I am." Her body tensed as she read over her scribbled notes for the Van Holsen account. She didn't have anything innovative enough to measure up to the Amatucci standard. "I thought this would be a good time to flesh out some ideas."

"And you like doing it longhand?"

"I think better that way." She'd never really taken the time to consider her creative process, but yes, now that she thought about it, she did always start with pen and paper. She didn't move to the computer until she had a fully functioning idea.

"Is that for the Van Holsen account?"

"Yes, I've been doing what you suggested and going with a nostalgic appeal."

"Good. Can I see what you've come up with so far?"

She glanced down at all of her scribbles and half thoughts. And then her eyes caught sight of his name scrolled out in cursive. Her heart clenched. *What in the world?*

She must have done it while she'd been deep in thought. Immediately, her pen started crossing it out. The last thing she needed was for her boss to think she had a crush on him. That would be the end of her career.

"I… I don't exactly have anything solid yet." She was going to have to be careful in the future of what she wrote down just in case Mr. Curious decided to peer over her shoulder.

"I could help you. Let me see what you have." He held out his hand.

She really didn't want to hand over her notepad, but what choice did she have if she wanted to stay in his good graces? She glanced down at the scratched-out spot and squinted. She could still see his name—all fourteen letters. But that was because she knew it was there. She ran the pen over it a few more times.

With great hesitation, she handed over the legal pad. Angelo's acute gaze skimmed over the page. Her palms grew moist. He took his time reading, but he paused as he reached the bottom. That was where she'd vigorously scratched out his name, almost wearing a hole in the page.

"I'm guessing that you've ruled out this idea?" He gestured to the blob of ink.

"Most definitely. It wouldn't have worked."

"Are you sure? Maybe you should tell me what it was,

and then we can see if there's any value in pursuing it?"
He sent her an expectant look.

"Honestly, it's not worth the effort. I was totally off the
mark with it." A man like Angelo, who could have a gorgeous model or movie star on each arm, would never be
interested in someone as plain and boring as herself.

He let the subject go and turned back to her notes while
she sat there realizing just how "off the mark" her imagination had wandered. No way was she going down that
romantic path again, even if it was paved with rose pet-
als. All it'd do was lead her into making a commitment—
having a family—everything she'd left behind in Paradise.
She wanted to be different—she wanted to be professionally successful. She needed to show everyone back in her
hometown that she'd made her dreams come true.

And then Angelo's gaze lifted to meet hers. She should
glance away but the intensity of his gaze held her captive.
Her heart raced. He didn't say anything, which was just as
well, because she doubted she could have strung two words
together. Had he figured out what she'd scribbled on the
page? *Please, not that.* But then again, he didn't look upset.
Instead, he looked like—like what? The breath hitched in
her throat. Was he interested in her?

He glanced away and shook his head. "Sorry about that.
Something you wrote down gave me an idea for the campaign, but then it slipped away."

Silly girl. What made her think he'd ever look at her that
way? And why would she want him to? It'd be the beginning of the end of her rising career—her dream.

Get a grip, Kayla.

"No problem." She held out her hand, willing it not to
shake. "If you let me have the pad back, I'll work on getting my thoughts more organized. Maybe we can discuss
them as soon as we get situated in Italy." She wasn't quite
sure where their accommodations would be since Angelo

had personally handled the travel arrangements, but she was certain they would be nice.

"Sounds good. Just because we're out of town doesn't mean we should fall behind on our work. I don't plan to be here long—just long enough to take care of some personal business. If we're lucky, perhaps I can wrap it up in a day or two."

What had happened to a week—maybe two? Disappointment assailed her. But it would be for the best. After all, it'd get her home sooner to make sure the ICL fund-raiser was moving along without too many snags. But she still couldn't shake the disappointment.

He'd missed this.

Angelo maneuvered the low-slung sports car over the windy roads of the Tuscany hillside toward his home in Monte Calanetti. He was grateful to be behind the wheel. It helped to center his thoughts. On the plane, he'd noticed his assistant in the most unexpected way. With her peaches-and-cream complexion, he'd been tempted to reach out and caress her smooth skin. But it was her green, almost-jade eyes that sparkled and hinted at so much more depth to the woman than he already knew—or would expect to know. The last thing he needed to do was get distracted by his assistant.

Actually, now that he'd noticed her—really noticed her—it was getting harder and harder to keep his mind on business around her. Perhaps bringing her on this trip wasn't his best decision, after all, but it was a necessity. He needed her help. He assured himself that, in the end, it would all work out as long as he stayed focused on the business at hand.

Thankfully, Kayla was just temporary help until his assistant returned from maternity leave. Then life would get back to normal. As far as he was concerned, that wouldn't be soon enough.

"This is wonderful."

The sound of Kayla's excited voice drew him out of his thoughts. He took his eyes off the roadway for just a moment to investigate what she found so fascinating, but he only saw vegetation. "Sorry. I missed it."

"No, you didn't. It's this. The long grass and the trees lining the roadway. It's beautiful."

What? The woman had never been outside of the city? He supposed that was possible. He honestly didn't know much about her other than her excellent work ethic. That, in and of itself, would normally be enough for him, but since they were traveling together, what would it hurt to know a little more?

"Is this your first time outside New York City?"

"I'm not a native New Yorker."

They had something else in common. Still, after all of those years living in New York, it was home to him now. He thrived on the constant energy that flowed through the city. He couldn't imagine living anywhere else. "Where does your family live?"

He could feel her curious gaze on him, but he didn't turn to her. "They live in a small town in Pennsylvania."

"So you really didn't move all that far from home."

"That's not what my parents think."

He glanced at her and saw she'd pressed her lips together in a firm line. Something told him that she hadn't meant to share that bit of information. But why? What else was she holding back?

"Your parents aren't crazy about the big-city life?"

There was a moment of hesitation as though she were trying to figure out how to answer him. "It's not New York so much as the fact that I'm not in Paradise anymore. They had my whole life planned out for me, but I rejected it."

"You must have had one of those chopper mothers I've heard about."

Kayla laughed. The sound was melodious and endearing. In that moment, he realized that he'd never heard her laugh before. He really liked it and hoped she'd do it more often, but for the life of him, he had no idea what he'd said to cause such a reaction.

"Do you mean a helicopter mom?"

He shrugged. "I guess. I knew it was something like that."

"My mom wasn't too bad. I know friends that had mothers who were much more controlling. But my mom is pretty good."

Wait. Something wasn't adding up. He pulled to a stop at an intersection. If he went straight ahead, it'd lead them up the hill to the village. But if he veered to the right, it'd take them to Nico's boutique vineyard—their childhood home.

Checking the rearview mirror and finding no traffic behind them, he paused and turned to her. "So if your mother is so great, why did you flee to the big city?"

Kayla shifted in her seat as though she were uncomfortable—or was it that he was digging too deep into personal territory? He knew what that was like—wanting to keep a firm lid on the past. But he couldn't help himself. There was just something about Kayla that intrigued him—and it went much deeper than her beauty. He was genuinely interested in her as a person.

Her voice was soft when she spoke, and he strained to hear. "I didn't live up to my parents' expectations."

That was so hard to believe. He was a very particular employer, and Kayla lived up to and in some areas exceeded his expectations. "Do they know what a wonderful job you've done at Amatucci & Associates?"

Her gaze widened. "You really think so?"

Angelo didn't realize he'd kept his approval of her work under wraps. Then again, he wasn't the sort of man to go on about someone's performance. Yet, in this moment, something told him that Kayla really needed to hear his evaluation of her performance.

"I think you've done an excellent job—"

"You do?" She smiled brightly and practically bounced in her seat before clasping her hands together.

"I do—"

A horn beeped behind them.

The interruption was a welcome one. This conversation was getting a little too emotional for his comfort. He thought for a moment that in her glee she might throw her arms around him. He didn't do hugs—no way—and certainly not with an employee. He couldn't—wouldn't—let the lines between them blur.

Angelo eased the car forward, focusing once again on the road and his destination. He urged himself to ignore the funny feeling Kayla's obvious excitement had given him. He trained his thoughts on the scene he'd be walking into at the vineyard. His fingers tightened on the black leather steering wheel.

On second thought, maybe he should have dropped Kayla off at the hotel before venturing out here. But he hadn't exactly been thinking straight—not since Nico had dropped the bombshell that their little sister was about to have a baby. Angelo was about to become an uncle. He wasn't sure how he felt about that. He'd worked so hard to distance himself from his family—from his emotionally charged parents and their chaotic marriage. But now that they'd moved, what excuse did he have to stay away from his birthplace—the home of his brother and sister?

"Is this the way to the village?" Kayla sat up a little straighter.

"No, this is the way to my brother's vineyard."

"Oh, how exciting. I've never visited a vineyard. I can't wait to see it. I bet it's beautiful like those magazine photos. Will we be staying there?"

"No." Angelo's tone was brusquer than he'd intended, but her endless chatter combined with his pending reunion had him on edge.

He chanced a glance her way and found her eyes had widened in surprise. He couldn't blame her, but how did he explain his family dynamics to her? Then again, why did he feel a need to explain his family at all?

"It'll be best if we stay at a hotel in the village. I'm not sure if the internet at the vineyard has been updated." There, that sounded like a valid reason for them to have some space between him and his siblings.

"Oh, I hadn't thought about that. I know the Van Holsen account needs to be updated as soon as possible. I already contacted the art department and let them know that a whole new strategy will be coming their way."

"Good. I want everything to move ahead without delay."

Whether he liked it or not, he'd been right to bring Kayla along on this trip. She was efficient and quite good at her job. Now, if only he could be just as professional and keep his mind from meandering into dangerous territory. However, the more time he spent around her, the more he found himself being anything but professional.

CHAPTER FOUR

THE CAR TURNED to the right and lurched forward. Kayla grabbed for the door handle. She had no idea that the vineyard would be so far out in the country, but then again, this was her first trip to Italy. In fact, other than one business trip to Canada, this was her first expedition out of the country.

"Welcome to Calanetti Vineyard."

Kayla glanced around, taking in the neat lines of grapevines. "Does all of this belong to your brother?"

"No. His vineyard is just a small portion of this land, but he produces some of the highest quality wine in the country."

"And you grew up here?"

"I did." Angelo pulled the car to a stop in front of a two-story villa. The home featured earth tones that blended in well with the land. "My brother will be expecting us. I phoned him from the airport."

As if on cue, the front door of the villa swung open and a man stepped out. Kayla did a double take—it was like looking at a slightly younger version of Angelo. The man approached the car wearing an easy smile. His eyes were dark brown like his brother's, but there was an easiness in them. They were quite unlike Angelo's dark and mysterious eyes.

When Nico opened the car door for her and held out his hand, she accepted his offer. Then she noticed the biggest difference of all. Instead of her stomach quivering with nervous energy in response to Nico's touch, she had no reaction at all. What did that mean? How could two men who looked so much alike have her reacting in such opposite ways?

It had to be that Angelo was her boss. That must be it. There was simply no other reasonable explanation for the electric charge that Angelo gave her every time she felt his gaze on her or when their fingers brushed as they passed papers back and forth.

"Benvenuta." Nico's voice carried a thick, warm Italian accent. When she sent him a puzzled look, he smiled. *"Scusi.* Welcome."

She smiled back, immediately liking Angelo's brother. "I'm so glad to be here."

"My brother doesn't bring many visitors home. In fact, you are the first. You must be special—"

"Nico, this is my assistant." Angelo frowned at his sibling.

Nico's dark brows rose and then a knowing smile pulled at his lips. "I hope my brother doesn't work you too hard while you're in Italy. There's so much to see. I'd love to give you a tour of the vineyard—"

"She doesn't have time for that stuff. She's here to work." Any hint of the easiness Angelo had displayed in the car was gone—hidden behind an impenetrable wall. "Now where is Marianna?"

"I don't know."

"What? Didn't you tell her that I was on my way?"

"I did." Nico folded his arms over his broad chest and lifted his chin. "I think that's the reason she left so early this morning without even bothering to grab a bite to eat. I haven't seen her since, but then again, I haven't looked for her, either."

"You let her walk away—?"

"What did you want me to do? Lock her in her room?"

"Maybe if you'd have done that a while ago, we wouldn't be in this mess."

Nico's arms lowered and his shoulders straightened. "You're blaming me for this?"

Angelo's body visibly tensed. "Yes…no. If only I'd have known something was wrong, I could have…"

"Could have what?"

Kayla's gaze darted between the two men who glared at each other. It was time to do something and fast. "This certainly is a beautiful place you have here." She acted as though she were totally oblivious to the torrent of undercurrents. "Angelo told me you produce some of the finest wine in Italy."

At last, the brothers quit glaring at each other. Nico turned to her. "My brother got that much right. I'd be happy if you'd sample some while you're here."

"I'd be honored."

This palpable tension certainly wasn't what she'd been expecting for a family reunion, but then again, after overhearing the heated conversation when Nico had phoned the office, she shouldn't be too surprised. She turned her attention to her always-in-control boss, who looked as though he was about to lose his cool edge and have a meltdown. *Intriguing.* There was definitely a lot more to him than what she'd witnessed so far.

"I should have come back before now." There was a weary, pained toned to Angelo's voice. "I let the past keep me away."

Nico turned back to his sibling. "What happened to you was a long time ago. It wasn't right, but a lot has changed since then. You no longer have an excuse to stay away."

"But I still have a company to run. I don't have time to drop everything and travel halfway around the globe to check up on things. As far as I knew, everything was all right."

"Maybe if you didn't work all the time and bothered to call occasionally, you'd know how things were going around here."

Questions crowded into Kayla's mind—questions that were absolutely none of her business. But that didn't stop her from wondering what had happened to drive Angelo away from his family. He obviously loved them or he wouldn't have let his cool composure slide. And what caused him to keep his emotions under lock and key in the first place?

Angelo raked his fingers through his hair. "Maybe I should have called more."

"Yes, you should have."

The thud of a door slamming shut punctuated Nico's words. Kayla hesitantly glanced off in the distance as a young woman marched toward them. Her brown hair was wild and curly as it fluttered in the breeze. Her lips pressed into a firm line and her eyes narrowed in on the two men. This must be Marianna.

"Enough!" The woman came to a stop between Angelo and Nico. "You two are being ridiculous. Anytime you both want to quit with the overprotective-brother routine, we can talk."

Though she was at least a foot shorter than her brothers, Marianna certainly didn't hesitate to step between them. Something told Kayla that little sister wasn't a shrinking violet with these two as her brothers. She'd definitely have to be strong-willed. Silently Kayla cheered her on.

Angelo's broad chest puffed up before he sighed. When he spoke, his voice was much gentler. "Marianna, if only I'd known—"

"Stop." The young woman pressed her hands to her hips and pulled back her slender shoulders. "Neither of you are to blame for my choices."

Angelo's brows drew together in a formidable line. "But—"

"I'm not done." Her shoulders remained ramrod straight. "I'm a grown woman, if you hadn't noticed. But then again, you've been off in the States and missed the fact that I've grown up. Maybe if you'd spent more time here, you'd have realized this."

Kayla's heart went out to Angelo. He'd obviously made mistakes where his family was concerned, and they weren't shy about calling him out on it. In his eyes, she could see pain and regret. Beneath his hard, protective shell lurked a vulnerable man.

Angelo's stance eased and his head lowered. "I know I should have been here for you—"

"No. This isn't what I want." Marianna shook her head, sending her hair flying. "I don't need you feeling guilty. I need you to understand that I can make my own decisions."

"See, I told you," Nico piped in. "Trying to deal with her isn't as easy as it sounds."

Angelo turned to his brother. "Maybe if you'd have told me sooner—"

Nico's dark brows drew together in a formidable line. "Told you—I tried calling you but I always got your voice mail. And you didn't call back."

"I... I was getting around to it."

Nico shook his head in disbelief. "I'm glad to know where I fit on your list of priorities."

"You don't understand." Angelo rubbed the back of his neck. "You don't know what it's like to have a lot of people relying on you to produce cutting-edge promotions and other people looking to you for a paycheck. It's not as easy as it sounds to run a successful company."

Nico expelled a disgusted sigh. "And you think turning this place into a renowned boutique vineyard has been easy? Yet I still found time to call you."

"Your message never said it was important."

"Stop!" Marianna pushed Angelo back. "You aren't helping anything by coming here and fighting with Nico."

Angelo took a deep breath and blew it out. "I know I wasn't here when you needed me, but I'm here now. Let me help."

Kayla watched all of this in utter amazement. She never would have guessed her boss was capable of such a wide range of emotions. So then why did he strive at the office for such an unflappable persona? What was she missing?

Kayla was about to introduce herself to Marianna, when the young woman stared up at Angelo and said, "And I wish you weren't here now. Not like this. Not with all of the fighting." When Angelo's brows rose and his mouth opened but nothing came out, Marianna added, "I don't want to play referee." Her hand moved protectively to her still-flat stomach. "It isn't good for the baby."

Angelo and Nico looked at each other as though neither had considered how their fighting would stress their sister—their pregnant sister.

Marianna moved to look at both of her brothers. "I'm fully capable of taking care of myself."

Nico rolled his eyes. Angelo crossed his arms but refrained from saying anything.

"I hope you'll both give me some space."

Angelo's brows rose. "But first, we want to know the name of the father."

"That's none of your business."

Nico stepped forward. "It is our business if he thinks he's going to get our sister pregnant and then just walk away."

Marianna's face filled with color.

Angelo pressed his hands to his sides. "We deserve the right to speak to this guy. He needs to know that we expect him to step up and do his part—"

"And I expect you both to mind your own business." Marianna started for the house.

Enough was enough. The time had come to make a hasty exit. It was obvious that Marianna was in over her head and that her brothers were only making the situation worse.

When Angelo turned to follow his sister, Kayla moved swiftly in front of him. "I'm not feeling so good." It wasn't totally a lie—her stomach was in knots watching the Amatucci siblings squabble. "Could you take me to the hotel?"

Angelo's worried gaze moved from her to his sister to her. "Sure." He turned to Nico. "We need to talk more."

"I figured as much."

"I'll be back after we get settled."

Nico shrugged. "I'll be here. I can't speak for Marianna."

"I don't think she needs anyone to speak for her. She certainly does have a mind of her own. Even if it gets her in trouble."

"She always was strong-willed. I think she's a lot like Mama."

"Agreed."

At last the two had something they agreed on—their little sister's character. And now that things were on a good note, it was definitely time to say goodbye.

Kayla cleared her throat, hoping to gain Angelo's attention. When he didn't turn her way, she proceeded to say, "Angelo, are you ready to go?"

She'd have rather had a tour of the vineyard and stretched her legs, but not under these strained circumstances. She couldn't help but wonder if it was the situation with their sister that had them at odds or if they had a history of not getting along.

Angelo glanced her way. "It was a long trip. I suppose you would like to lie down for a bit."

"That would be nice." She turned to Nico, who was still eyeing his brother with obvious agitation. "It was so nice to meet you. I hope that we'll see each other again."

"I suppose that'll depend on my brother and whether he trusts you with me—"

"Nico. Enough." Angelo's voice held an obvious note of warning. "We'll be staying at the Hotel Villa Bellezza. If Marianna cools down, phone me."

Angelo quietly followed her to the car and opened the door for her. "I'm sorry you had to witness that."

"Don't be." She searched for words of comfort. "Families are messy. It's what happens when people love each other. And I saw a lot of love back there."

"You did?"

"Most definitely." She stepped past him and got in the car.

She'd never met anyone who could get under her boss's skin like Nico. The man appeared to have needling his big brother down to a fine art. There was so much more to the polished, successful businessman standing next to her than she'd ever imagined. And she was anxious to know more.

CHAPTER FIVE

KAYLA GRIPPED THE armrest tightly.

The line of cypress trees was no more than a blur as Angelo accelerated away from the vineyard. He didn't say a word as they zigzagged through the valley before starting their ascent up a hillside. The vegetation was so green and lush that she couldn't imagine there was a village, much less a five-star hotel, within miles of here.

"I need to apologize." Angelo's voice broke the awkward silence. "I didn't mean to have you witness our family drama."

"It's okay. I know how families can be." She couldn't help but want to know more about him and his family. "Your parents, do they live around here?"

He shook his head, keeping his eyes on the road. "They left the vineyard to us kids and moved to Milan. It was best for everyone."

Kayla wasn't sure what to say to that. Obviously there wasn't a close relationship between him and his parents. Did she even want to know why? It'd just move them further from boss and employee and into a new relationship—one that she didn't want to examine too closely.

Angelo downshifted for a curve. "I know that you come from a close-knit family, so it'd be hard for you to understand a family that functions better apart than together."

Kayla was surprised that he kept talking about his private life when she hadn't even asked him anything. It was as if these thoughts were pent up inside him, and he needed to get them out if he was to have any peace.

She searched frantically for words of comfort. "Every family is different. Not better. Not worse. Just different."

"But this is my fault." His palm smacked the steering wheel. "I shouldn't have left for New York to go to college. I should have found a way to stay here. Marianna was so young when I left, and my parents—well, they were so consumed with each other that they didn't have time to worry about anyone else."

"I'm sure they did their best."

He shook his head. "You don't know my parents. They are the most passionate people I know. And not in a good way. One minute they love each other and the next they are getting divorced. That's the end. They never want to see each other again. To say our childhoods were unstable is putting it mildly."

Kayla struggled to keep her mouth from gaping open. Her parents were the most mild-mannered couple. Their voices were rarely raised to each other, and they still gazed lovingly at each other like a couple of starstruck teenagers. Kayla knew they wanted her to experience the same sort of love and happiness. That's why she didn't hold it against them for trying to guide her life. It's just that she was different. There was so much more to life than love, marriage and babies. And she wanted to experience all of it.

Angelo cleared his throat, but his voice still rumbled with emotion. "I just couldn't take any more of their fighting and making up. It was so unnerving to never know if my parents were passionately in love or on the verge of calling their divorce attorneys. And there was no way I could take Nico with me—not that he'd have gone. He has this unbreakable tie to the vineyard—to the village. He never would have done what I did. And maybe he's right. Maybe if I'd stayed then Marianna wouldn't be alone and having a baby."

"It's not your fault." Kayla resisted the urge to reach out to him. "Your sister is a grown woman. She has to be allowed to make her own choices. Right or wrong. You couldn't have prevented this."

"But maybe if I'd been here, she'd have felt like she still had a family that loves her. Then she wouldn't have taken off on this trip of hers only to let some smooth-talking guy take advantage of her." Angelo's body noticeably stiffened.

"I'm fairly certain that no one could take advantage of your sister. She seems quite strong, like her brothers. She just needs some time to sort things out."

He sighed. "I'm sure she's plenty confused. And I suppose Nico and I did nothing to help by arguing. It's just that every time my brother and I get together, we disagree. We are very different. That's why I reserved us a suite at the hotel. I knew staying at the vineyard would just lead to more drama, and that's the last thing any of us need."

"But you two didn't argue at the end."

"That's because we both agree that Marianna needs both of us—whether she likes it or not."

"Good. Maybe you can build on that."

"Perhaps."

She decided that enough had been said for now on that subject. Angelo needed time to calm down. "Is the hotel far from here?"

"No. It's just at the rise of the hill." His voice had returned to its normal reserved, unemotional tone.

"Really. I never would have guessed. I can't wait to see the village." But if Angelo was serious about this being a productive trip, she wasn't sure that she'd get to see much of Italy. The thought dampened her mood. "Do you think I'll have some time to look around the village?"

He glanced at her before turning back to the road. "There really isn't much to see."

She'd beg to differ with him. Everything about Italy was special for this American girl. This was the biggest adventure of her life. How could he think this place was anything but special?

"I... I've never been here before. I was just hoping to sneak in some sightseeing."

"As long as you get your work done, I don't care what you do with your free time."

Oh, good!

As the car climbed the hill, Angelo pulled to the side for an older truck that was barreling toward them. Once back on the road, the car's tire dropped into a rut and bounced Kayla. The seat belt restrained her, but her bare thigh brushed against his hand as it gripped the gearshift. Heat raced up her leg, under her skirt and set her whole body tingling.

"Sorry about that." He quickly moved his hand back to the steering wheel.

Had he noticed their touch? Had it affected him, too? Was that why he'd moved his hand? Or was she just being ridiculous? Definitely being ridiculous. She knew when men were interested in her, and Angelo certainly wasn't. A frown pulled at her lips.

So why then did it bother her? Sure, he was the most handsome man she'd ever laid eyes on. But, he was her boss—the key to her career. She wouldn't—she couldn't—let some ridiculous crush get in her way after everything she'd sacrificed to get here.

Time to think about something else.

"I didn't have time to do any research before we left New York. What should I see while I'm here?"

He shrugged. "Honestly, there's nothing special about Monte Calanetti. It's just small and old."

"I'm used to small towns. I grew up in one. And there's always something special about them."

He glanced her way and his dark brow rose. "What was special about your town?"

"A number of things." She wasn't sure that she wanted to delve into this subject with him. She'd finally got past her homesickness. The way she'd done that was by not thinking of her hometown and what made it special.

"Such as?"

She shook her head. "Never mind."

Before he could question her more, she spotted what she thought was the edge of Monte Calanetti. "Are we here?"

"We are."

She stared out the windshield, not exactly sure what to expect. There was a tall wall. As they eased past it she found rustic buildings of earth tones similar in color to Nico's villa. People stopped and glanced their way as though trying to figure out if they should know them.

As more and more people turned to stare, Kayla couldn't hold back her curiosity any longer. "Why are they staring?"

He shrugged. "It must be the car."

"The car?"

"Yeah, you know because it's a sports car. They probably don't see many around here."

"Oh." She glanced over at him. Was he sitting up a little straighter? And was his chin tilted just a little higher? *Interesting*. "The village looks quite intriguing. And small enough to explore on foot."

Angelo didn't say anything. He just kept driving. And sadly he didn't offer her a guided tour. She forced herself not to frown. Then again, why should he bend over backward for her? She was, after all, merely an employee. They weren't even friends. Though little by little, she was getting to know Angelo better and better. In fact, she'd learned more about him in the past forty-eight hours than she had in the past two months while working as his assistant.

The car slowed as they eased through a wrought iron gate and up the short paved drive to a two-story building. The outside was plain but there was an elegance in its simplicity. Beneath a black awning, a bronze plaque off to the side of the front door read: Hotel Villa Bellezza. The place looked old but well kept. It reminded her of maybe a duke's grand house. She couldn't wait to check out the inside.

A young man in a black uniform rushed outside and opened her door for her. He smiled at her before his gaze moved to Angelo. The smile dimmed. She had the feeling that the young man had jumped to the wrong conclusion—that she and Angelo were a couple, here for a romantic tryst. Nothing could be further from the truth. But for the first time, she imagined what it might be like if Angelo were to look at her as a woman—a woman he desired. The thought rolled around in her mind at a dizzying pace.

Angelo moved to her side and spoke softly in her ear. "Are you okay?"

His voice drew her from her thoughts. She swallowed and hoped she succeeded in composing herself. "Yes."

"Are you sure? You're a little pale."

She patted his arm, not a good move as her fingertips tingled where they made contact. "I'm fine. Honest."

Or she would be, once she quit fantasizing about her boss. He obviously wasn't attracted to her. He saw her as nothing more than his temporary assistant, and that's the way it'd have to remain if she hoped to convince him of her talents.

While Angelo took care of registering them, she took in her surroundings. The modest exterior had not prepared her for the beauty of the interior. The floor was gleaming marble while the walls and ceiling were masterpieces of art with ornate parquet. Kayla had to force her mouth to remain closed instead of gaping open. She'd never stayed anywhere so fancy.

She couldn't even imagine how much this visit would cost Angelo. And the fact that he could afford to stay in a place such as this without even batting an eye impressed her. They sure didn't have anything like this back in Paradise. Wait until she told her mother and father about this.

CHAPTER SIX

THERE WAS NO time for fun and games.

Angelo didn't get to the top of his profession by taking time off. Now that they were settled into their suite and Kayla had rested for a bit, they needed to get back to work. As he waited for her to join him, he couldn't help but wonder what she made of his clash with his brother. He shouldn't have taken her to the vineyard. What had he been thinking?

Yet on the car ride here, she hadn't seemed to judge him. Instead, she'd acted as though she cared. It was as if she understood him. Her reaction surprised him. He wasn't used to letting people into his personal life. But from the moment he'd asked her to join him on this trip, the lines between personal and professional had become irrevocably blurred.

Kayla entered the common room between their bedrooms. Her auburn hair was loose and cascaded down past her shoulders. Her glasses were off and she was no longer wearing the drab gray business suit. Instead, she was wearing pink capris and a white cotton sleeveless top, which showed off her creamy shoulders and slender arms.

The breath hitched in his throat. Who was this gorgeous woman? And what had happened to his nondescript assistant?

"I hope you don't mind that I changed?"

Wow! All he could do was stare. It was as if she were some sort of butterfly who'd just emerged from a cocoon.

Kayla settled on the couch with her laptop. She gave him a strange look as though wondering why he had yet to say a word. The problem was he didn't know what to say. Ever since they'd left New York, the ground had been shifting under his feet. Now it was as though a fissure had opened up and he was teetering on the edge, scrambling not to get swallowed up.

She didn't appear to be too disturbed by his standoffishness, which was good. Before he took a seat anywhere near her, he had to get a hold on his rambling thoughts. Kayla wasn't just any woman. He couldn't indulge in a romantic romp with her, and then go about his life.

He was her boss and, more important, he couldn't afford to lose her because she was good—really good at her job. He'd already had ideas of promoting her, but he wasn't sure that she was ready to be advanced quite yet. He wanted to see how she handled the Van Holsen account, since he'd given her a lot of room to show him her stuff.

The tight muscles in his chest eased and he was able to breathe easier. Concentrating on work always relaxed him and put him back in his groove. Work was logical for the most part and it lacked emotions, again for the most part, depending on the client. But since he was the boss, he was able to hand off the more excitable clients to other account executives.

That was it. Focus on business and not on how appealing he found her. "How's the Van Holsen account coming?"

She glanced over the top of her laptop. "Thanks to your help, I think I've come up with some innovative ideas. Would you care to take a look?"

His gaze moved to the cushion next to her on the couch and his body tensed. He was being ridiculous. She wasn't the first beautiful woman that he'd been around. What in the world had got into him today? It had to be his return home. It had him feeling out of sorts.

Time to start acting like Angelo Amatucci, the man in charge. "Sure. I'll have a look."

He strode over to the couch and took a seat. Kayla handed over the laptop and their fingers brushed. Hers were soft, smooth and warm. A jolt of awareness zinged up his arm and the air hitched in his lungs. *Stay focused.* He didn't dare turn to look at her. Instead, he focused his gaze on the computer monitor.

He read over her ideas for the new fragrance campaign and was truly impressed. Not only had she taken his ideas and expanded upon them, but she'd also inserted some of her own. He loved her initiative. Kayla was exactly the kind of innovative person that he wanted at Amatucci & Associates. Talented people like Kayla were the assets that would keep his company one of the most sought-after advertising agencies in the world.

"This is really good." He turned to her. When her green gaze met his, the rest of his thoughts scattered.

"You really like it?"

He nodded. His line of vision momentarily dipped to her pink frosted lips before meeting her gaze again. He struggled for a nonchalant expression. "I think you've captured a touching nostalgic note with a forward-thinking view. This should capture both the new and old consumer."

Her tempting lips lifted into a broad smile that lit up her eyes. "Now we just have to hope the client will approve."

"I wouldn't worry about that. Send this along to the art department and have them start working on some mockups."

Her smile dimmed a bit. "You're sure about this?"

"Of course I am. Don't look so surprised. You don't think you got the position as my assistant just because you're beautiful, do you?"

Now why in the world had he gone and said that? But it was the truth. She was stunning. In fact, he was considering changing the dress code at the office. He really enjoyed this different look on her. Then again, if she looked this way in the office, he'd never get any work done.

Color bloomed on her creamy cheeks. "You think I'm beautiful?"

He stared back into her eyes longer than was necessary.

In that moment, his ability to speak intelligently was debatable. He merely nodded.

"No man has ever called me that."

At last finding his voice, Angelo said, "I'm having a hard time believing that."

"Steven was more matter-of-fact and sparing on compliments. It wasn't that he was a bad man. In fact, it's quite the opposite. He was really good to me. He just wasn't good with flowery words."

"This Steven, he's from Paradise, too?"

She nodded. "High-school sweethearts."

"The man must need glasses badly to have missed your beauty. Both inside and out. Is he still your boyfriend?" Part of Angelo wanted her to say yes to put a swift end to this surreal moment, but a much stronger part wanted her to be free.

"We…we broke up before I moved to New York."

The field was wide-open. Exhilaration flooded through Angelo. His hand reached out, stroking the smooth, silky skin of her cheek. The backs of his fingers skimmed down over her jaw, and then his thumb ran over the plumpness of her bottom lip. Her sudden inhale drew air over his fingers.

In her eyes, he noted the flames of desire had been ignited. She wanted him as much as he wanted her. And in that moment, he didn't want to think—he just wanted to act. He wanted to forget everything and enjoy this moment with the girl with wavy red hair.

His heart pounded as he leaned forward. He needed her and her understanding ways more than he imagined possible. Their lips met. He was a man who knew what he wanted and he wanted Kayla. Yet he fought back the urge to let loose with his mounting need. Instead, his touch was tentative and gentle. He didn't want to do anything to scare her away—not now that he had her exactly where he wanted her.

Kayla's lips were rose-petal soft. And when she opened them up to him, a moan grew deep in his throat. She tasted sweet like chocolate. He'd never been a fan of candy until this moment. Now he couldn't get enough of her sugary sweetness.

His arms wrapped round her curvy form, pulling her close. The gentle scent of perfume wrapped around them— the teasing scent that he hadn't been able to forget since that day in the office. It was as though she'd cast some sort of magical spell over him.

In the next instant, his phone vibrated in his pocket, zapping him back to his senses. He pulled back and Kayla's confused gaze met his. He couldn't blame her. He was just as confused by what had happened.

He held up a finger to silence her inevitable questions— questions for which he had no answers. Because there was no way he was falling for her. Getting involved with her— with anyone—meant dealing with a bunch of messy emotions. The last thing in the world he wanted to do was end up like his parents. Just the memory of their turbulent life had Angelo immediately working to rebuild the wall between him and Kayla. He just couldn't—wouldn't—subject anyone to such miserable instability.

Angelo glanced down at the screen to see his brother's name pop up. Hopefully his sister had confessed all. Angelo couldn't wait to confront the man who'd walked away from his responsibilities.

Angelo lifted the phone to his ear. "Nico, do you have a name yet?"

There was a distinct sigh. "Is this how you answer your phone these days? Too important for a friendly greeting before diving into the heart of the matter?"

Angelo's back teeth ground together. He quickly counted to ten, okay maybe only to five, before addressing his sibling. "Hello, Nico. What did Marianna say?"

"Nothing."

He was losing his patience. "But why did you call?"

"You and Kayla need to return to the villa. Now. I'll explain everything when you both get here." The line went dead.

Angelo slipped the phone back into his pocket. He turned to Kayla, whose face was still filled with color. "We have to go."

"What happened?"

"I don't know. That was Nico and he summoned us back to the villa. It must be Marianna. I just pray there aren't complications with the baby." Before they left he needed to clear the air about their kiss that never should have happened. "Listen, about the kiss, I crossed a line. I... I don't know what I was thinking."

A myriad of expressions crossed over her face. "It's forgotten."

He didn't believe her. "Can we talk about it later?"

"I'd rather not. There's nothing to say. Besides, you have more important things to deal with." She jumped to her feet and moved away from him. "You should get going. I'll be fine here."

"Nico requested you, too." Angelo held back the startling fact that he'd feel better facing this crisis with her next to him.

Kayla pressed a hand to her chest. "But why me?"

"I don't know. But we have to go."

"Okay. Just let me grab my shoes and purse." She rushed back to her room.

Angelo got to his feet and paced back and forth. Of course he was worried about his sister, but there was something else fueling his inability to sit still—Kayla's off-the-cuff dismissal of his kiss.

The women he was used to spending time with never brushed off his advances, though each of them knew his rules in advance—nothing serious. So why did that rule not apply here? Probably because Kayla was off-limits. She was his assistant. He couldn't forget that going forward—no matter how much his personal life spun out of control while in Italy.

From this point forward, Kayla was off-limits.

CHAPTER SEVEN

HER THOUGHTS RACED so fast that it unsettled her stomach.

Kayla stared out of the passenger window as she clasped her hands tightly together. Angelo expertly guided the rented sports car along the narrow, tree-lined road. How in the world had she lost control of the situation?

She inwardly groaned. As fantastic as that kiss had been, it couldn't have come at a worse time. Angelo at last had noticed her work and complimented her professionally. And what did she turn around and do, stare at him like some lovesick teenager—encouraging him to kiss her.

Sure, she was wildly attracted to him. What woman with a pulse wasn't? He was gorgeous with that short, dark hair, olive skin and dark, sensual eyes. But he was her boss— the man in charge of her professional future—her dreams.

She couldn't afford any more blunders. She had to remain aloof but professional. Surely it wasn't too late to correct things between them. At least he hadn't mentioned anything about sending her back to New York on the next plane, but then again they'd rushed out of the hotel so quickly that he didn't have time to think of it. His thoughts were on his sister.

Kayla sure hoped there wasn't anything wrong with Marianna. This was the first time Kayla had ever witnessed Angelo visibly worried. He obviously cared a great deal for his family though he never let on at the office—when he was working he was 100 percent professional—

So then what happened back there at the hotel?

Angelo pulled the car to a skidding halt in front of the villa. Before she could summon an answer to that nagging question, Angelo had her car door opened. She would figure it out later. Right now, she would offer her support in whatever capacity to Angelo's family.

Nico rushed into the drive. "About time you got here."

"We came right away." Angelo frowned at his brother. "What's the matter with Marianna?"

"Marianna?" Nico's brows drew together in a questioning look. "This has nothing to do with our sister."

"Then why in the world did you have us rush over here?" Angelo's voice took on a sharp edge.

Kayla breathed a sigh of relief. She had no idea what Nico wanted, but she was fully relieved that mother and baby were okay. However, she did have to wonder why Nico wanted her here? Was he hoping that she'd play referee?

Nico's eyes opened wide and his face became animated. "You are never going to believe this—"

"I might if you'd get to the point."

Nico smiled in spite of his brother's obvious agitation. "What would you say if I told you that I was just approached by representatives of Halencia? Monte Calanetti has just made the short list of locations for the royal wedding of Prince Antonio and Christina Rose."

Angelo rolled his eyes. "Nico, this is no time for joking around—"

"I'm not. I'm perfectly serious."

Kayla's mouth gaped open. A royal wedding. Wow! She really was in Europe because nothing like this ever happened back in the States. Wait until she told her family. They would never believe it.

Her gaze moved to Angelo. He still wasn't smiling. In fact, he didn't look the least bit excited about this news. She had absolutely no ties to this village and she was over-the-moon happy for them. So why was he so reserved?

Angelo pressed his hands to his trim waist. "You called us back here to tell us this?"

"Brother, you're not understanding. The royal family of Halencia wants us to make a pitch as to why Monte Calanetti should be the location for the soon-to-be king and his intended bride's wedding."

"And?"

Nico shook his head. "What aren't you understanding? This is where you come in. You and Kayla. This is what you two do for a living—pitch ideas, convince people to go with the products you represent. That's what we need."

Nico wanted Angelo and her to help? Really? For a royal wedding?

The breath caught in her throat as she held back a squeal of excitement. If she'd ever wanted a chance to stand out and gain a promotion, this was a prime opportunity. Plus, it'd mean continuing to work with Angelo. But once they got back to New York, away from this romantic countryside, things would go back to normal. Wouldn't they?

Surely they would. This project was huge. It was amazing. An honest-to-goodness royal wedding. She didn't even know where they'd begin, but she couldn't contain her excitement. She'd show Angelo how good an ad executive she could be. Just wait and see.

Pitch a wedding to royalty?

Angelo had never done such a thing. Weddings weren't his thing. He knew nothing about love and romance. He was highly unqualified for this project. But he wasn't about to admit any of this to Nico. No way. So how was he supposed to get out of this?

Nico smiled as he led them straight through the modestly decorated villa that still looked much the same as it did when he'd been a child. Once everyone was situated on the veranda with cold drinks, Nico turned to him. "So what do you think?"

"About what?"

"You know, coming up with a pitch for the village?"

Angelo wanted to tell his brother that he was too busy and that he couldn't possibly fit it into his schedule. He highly doubted his brother would hear him. Nico had selective hearing when he wanted something bad enough—like Angelo being a silent investor in the vineyard.

Angelo turned to Kayla to see what she thought about the idea, hoping she'd make some excuse to get them out of this situation. But her green eyes sparkled with excitement. How wrong could he have been to look to her for support? Was there a woman alive who didn't get excited about weddings? Or was it the part about pitching it to a real-life prince that had caught her full attention?

Angelo's gut tightened when he thought of Kayla being starstruck over the royal prince. He shrugged off the uneasy sensation. It was none of his concern. Besides, it wasn't as if she was attracted to him. She couldn't dismiss their kiss fast enough.

His jaw tensed as he recalled how easily she'd brushed off their moment. He could have sworn she'd been as into him as he was into her. It just showed how little he understood women.

He drew up his thoughts, refusing to dwell on the subject. In the meantime, Kayla had engaged his brother in light conversation about the vineyard and how it'd been their childhood home. Angelo looked around the place and was truly impressed by what his brother had done to bring this place back to life. It looked so different than when they were kids, when the place was dying off.

Angelo had actually thought that his brother was crazy for wanting to devote his time and money into reviving the vineyard, but with Nico's determination, he'd made a go of the place. In fact, this boutique vineyard might not produce a large quantity of wine, but what it did produce was of the finest quality. Angelo kept his private wine collection stocked with it. Calanetti wines impressed a great number of influential guests that he'd entertained.

The chime of Kayla's laughter drew his thoughts back to the moment. Nico was entertaining her with a tale from when they were kids. As the oldest, Angelo had always been put in charge of his siblings while his parents went out. But this one time, Angelo hadn't been paying attention and they'd sneaked off. What Nico failed to add, and what he probably didn't know, was that had been one of Angelo's scariest moments—not knowing what had happened to his brother and sister.

"Are you telling them about the royal wedding?" Marianna joined them. Her face was a bit on the pale side and there were shadows beneath her eyes.

Nico leaned back in his chair. "I just told Angelo about it. He's thinking it over."

Marianna turned to Angelo. "You have to think it over? But why? This will be the biggest thing you've ever done."

"You really want me to do the pitch?"

She nodded. "Please. It would be so wonderful for everyone. Couldn't you just this once help your family?"

Guilt landed squarely on his shoulders with the force of a full wine barrel. He owed his brother and sister this. It'd put Monte Calanetti on the map. And the benefits the village would reap from the royal wedding taking place here were countless.

But he was already fully obligated. And he couldn't do it all on his own. He'd need help. A good copywriter. His gaze strayed to Kayla. He'd already witnessed just how talented she was with words and images. He could easily imagine her taking on some more of his workload, allowing him time to work on the wedding proposal.

They'd have to work closely together—closer than ever. There was no way he'd let her loose with the company's most important clients. But would they be able to manage it after the kiss?

"So what do you say, Angelo?" Nico looked at him. "The village is all abuzz with the news, and you know that pitching a wedding isn't my area of specialty."

"Please Angelo, will you do it?" Marianna looked at him, openly pleading with him with her eyes.

He'd never been good at telling her no. And now that she was standing there carrying some stranger's baby—some man that his sister wouldn't even introduce to their family—his resistance to her plea was nonexistent. If playing host to a royal wedding made her happy, how could he deny it to her? The decision for once was quite simple.

"Okay. I'll do it."

"You will?" The words echoed around the patio.

"Why does everyone sound so shocked? It'll be good publicity for the firm." But that wasn't his reason for agreeing—it was to see the smiles on the two women in his life... and his brother.

Marianna launched herself into his arms. Warmth swelled in his chest. He may not have been here to protect her and watch over her as he should have been, but at least he could give her something to look forward to while she sorted out the rest of her life.

Marianna pulled back and sent him a watery smile. "Thanks."

He turned to Kayla. She looked like an excited kid on Christmas Eve. "How about you? Are you up for taking on some more responsibility?"

Kayla didn't waste a moment before uttering, "Definitely. Just tell me what needs done."

"Good." He turned to his brother. "It looks like you've hired yourself a team. I'll get started on the pitch as soon as we get back to New York."

"New York?" Nico's brows gathered together.

"Yes, that's where we work. I'll send through what I come up with, but it's going to take me a little time. I have a rush project that I—we—have to wrap up—"

"This can't wait. You have to get started on it right away."

Angelo didn't like the worried tone of his brother's voice. "Why? What haven't you told us?"

Nico got to his feet. "Does anyone need anything else to drink?"

Angelo knew a stalling tactic when he saw one. "Nico, spit it out. What is the catch?"

After Nico finished refilling Kayla's iced tea, he turned to his brother. "The catch is the pitch has to be completed in no more than three weeks' time."

"Three weeks." Angelo leaned back in his chair. "You sure don't give a person much time."

"And—"

"There's more?"

Nico nodded. "The presentation has to be given to the royal family at the palace in Halencia."

Nico sank down into his chair while Angelo charged to his feet. "This changes everything. I wasn't planning to stay in Italy for three weeks. Nico, don't you understand? I have a business to run."

"You're the boss. Can't you put someone else in charge while you're here?"

Angelo never sloughed off his work on other people. He stayed on top of things. Some people called him a control freak. He considered it the only way to keep the company on track. "That's not the point. There are certain things only I can do."

"The point is that when we need you, you're never here." Nico got to his feet and faced him. "Why should I have thought this would be any different?"

His brother's words were pointed and needled at his guilt. "That's not fair. I've lent you money for the vineyard—"

"This isn't about you writing out a check. I'm talking about you personally investing yourself—your time—in something that's important to your family."

Angelo turned to Marianna, looking for support, but she moved to Nico's side. When he sought out Kayla, she was busy studying her iced tea glass with such intensity that it was as if she'd never seen glassware before. He was alone in this. He knew what he should do, but it was so hard to just hand over the reins of the company he'd built from the ground up.

Three weeks was a long time to be away. And yet it wasn't much time to create a compelling campaign for a wedding—a royal wedding. It had just started to sink in what a big deal this really was for his brother and sister, and the village, plus it would be amazing for his company— that is if they won the pitch.

Angelo raked his fingers through his hair. Letting go of the reins at Amatucci & Associates went against every business instinct. Yet, he couldn't turn his back on his siblings again. "Okay. I'll stay."

Marianna turned to Kayla. "Will you stay, too?"

"Yes, Kayla," Nico chimed in. "Will you help my brother? I get the feeling that he won't be able to do it without you."

Kayla's eyes flashed with surprise. "I don't know that I need to stay in Italy to do it."

"It'd be most convenient," Marianna pointed out. "I'm sure Angelo will need your input. After all, we're talking about a wedding. And my brothers, well, they aren't exactly romantic."

"Hey!" Nico and Angelo protested in unison.

Both women burst out in laughter. Angelo supposed the dig was worth it as his sister's face broke into a smile. And when he turned to Kayla, the happiness reflected in her eyes warmed a spot in his chest. She was a very beautiful woman. Why, oh, why did it have to be now when they were practically attached at the hip that he truly realized his attraction to her?

When she caught him staring, the breath hitched in his throat. He should glance away, but he couldn't. He was in awe of her. Was it being away from the office that had him more relaxed about the proper conduct between employer and employee? Nonsense. He knew what he was doing. He could keep this together.

He gazed directly at the woman who took up more and more of his thoughts. "Well, don't keep us in suspense. Will you remain in Italy and lend a hand?"

CHAPTER EIGHT

THIS WAS A very bad idea.

But it was so tempting. How could she let such a rare opportunity pass her by?

Kayla worried her bottom lip. Though she wouldn't be working directly on the royal wedding, she'd be close at hand. Perhaps she could add an idea here and there. Oh, what she wouldn't give to actually work on the project itself. Yet, she understood with the magnitude of a royal wedding that only the best of the best would work on the project, and that meant Angelo.

But she was needed back in New York. The ICL fund-raiser was quickly approaching, and seeing as it was her idea—it was her responsibility to make sure it went off without a hitch. However, she had put Pam, an associate at the after-school program, in charge while she was gone. And how much could possibly go wrong in three weeks?

"Please say you'll stay." Marianna looked so hopeful. "I could use someone on my side against my brothers, who think they know everything."

That sold her. Marianna could definitely use some help keeping her brothers in line while she figured out her next move. "Okay, I'll stay."

Everyone smiled except Angelo.

Aside from the fund-raiser, there was nothing waiting for her back in New York, not even a goldfish. When she wasn't at the office, she was at the after-school program helping kids with their homework followed by a game of dodgeball or basketball or volleyball. She wasn't very good at any of the games, but she gave it her best effort.

For the moment, she was giving herself permission to

enjoy Italy before she set to work. And this was the perfect place to start. She'd love to see more of the vineyard, and it'd give Angelo some private time with his siblings.

"Would you mind if I had a look around the vineyard?" Kayla's gaze met Nico's.

"My apologies. I should have offered to give you a tour earlier. I've had other thoughts on my mind—" his gaze strayed to his sister and then back to her "—with uh…the royal wedding."

"That's okay. I totally understand." Kayla got to her feet. "I've never been to a vineyard before. I'll just show myself around."

"Nonsense. Angelo can give you the grand tour while I make some phone calls and spread the good news. And make sure he shows you the chapel." Nico turned a smile to Angelo. "You can handle that, can't you, brother?"

Angelo's jaw tightened, but he didn't argue. Kayla took that as progress between the brothers. Not wanting to give Angelo time to change his mind, she set off for the vines, hoping Angelo would follow.

He did, and he proved to be quite an insightful guide. He explained to her the difference between a larger vineyard and this boutique vineyard. While Nico produced fewer barrels of wine—less than five thousand cases a year— it was carefully processed to the highest quality with the least amount of oxidation.

As much as the history and current production of wine interested her, it was the bell tower in the distance that drew her attention. She headed for the weathered building that sat on the other side of the wall that lined the edge of the vineyard. "Is this the chapel your brother mentioned?"

"Yes. Nico and I explored it as kids. We considered it our castle. I was the king and Nico was the daring knight fighting off dragons." Angelo smiled at the long-forgotten memory.

"You and your brother must have had a lot of fun."

"Now that I think about it, we did have some good times."

She smiled. "This looks like a great place for an adventure. Can we go inside the chapel?"

"It's nothing you'd be interested in."

"Sure I would." Her steps grew quicker as she headed for the opening in the wall that led to the little chapel. Maybe this was her chance to let Angelo know that she'd be more than willing to help with the wedding pitch—in fact, this was the opportunity of a lifetime. Now, how did she broach the subject with Angelo?

She stopped next to the four steps that led to two tall, narrow wooden doors. It looked as though time had passed it by. Okay so it needed a little TLC, but it had a charm about it that transcended time. "Your brother is so lucky to have this piece of history on his land. Imagine all of the weddings and christenings that must have taken place here."

"Technically it's not on Nico's land." Angelo pointed over his shoulder to the wall. That divides the vineyard. The other side is Nico's."

"So who owns this land, then?"

"This is Palazzo di Comparino. Its owner, Signor Carlos Bartolini, recently passed away. From what I understand, there's a young woman staying there now."

"You know this chapel gives me an idea—it'd be perfect for the royal wedding."

"I don't know." Angelo rubbed his chin. "It needs work."

She pulled open one of the doors and peered inside at the rows of pews. The place was filled with dust and cobwebs. "It's nothing that can't be done rather easily." This was her chance to put herself out there. "You know I could help you with the pitch."

Angelo didn't immediately respond. The breath hitched in her throat as she waited—hoping that he'd latch on to her offer. The experience from working on such a prestigious project had immeasurable potential, from a promotion at Amatucci & Associates to making her résumé stand out— head and shoulders above the rest.

"I don't think so. You'll have enough to do with the other accounts that need looking after." The disappointment must have filtered across her face because his stance eased and his voice softened. "I appreciate the offer, but I don't want you getting overwhelmed."

It teetered on the tip of her tongue to ask him if this had anything to do with the kiss, but she hesitated. She couldn't bring herself to tarnish that moment. The memory of how his eyes had devoured her before his lips had claimed hers still made her heart race.

If it wasn't the kiss, why was he turning away her offer of help? Was it just as he said, not wanting to give her too much work? Or did he feel she wasn't up to the task of working on something so important?

With the wind temporarily knocked out of her sails, she turned back to the villa. She wasn't giving up. She would show Angelo that she was invaluable.

What was the problem?

Two days later, Angelo paced around the hotel suite. He needed a fresh approach to the wedding. It had to be something amazing—something unique to Monte Calanetti that would appeal to a prince and his intended bride. But what?

He was stuck. This had never happened to him before. He inwardly groaned as his mind drew a total blank. This was ridiculous. He clenched his hands into tight balls. He had absolutely nothing. And that was so not like him.

He liked to think outside the box. He liked to push boundaries and experiment, but all he could think of was why would anyone would want to get married in Monte Calanetti? What special qualities did they see in the village for it to make the royals' short list?

He poured himself a cup of the now-lukewarm coffee.

The silence of the suite was getting to him. Kayla had cleared out early that morning, claiming she wanted some fresh air while she worked on the mock-ups for the Van Holsen account and answered emails. She'd been great about taking on additional responsibilities, allowing him time to brainstorm. Not that it was helping him much.

In fact, she'd done such an exceptional job that maybe he should see what she could do with this wedding stuff. After all, she was a girl, and didn't they all dream about their weddings?

Suddenly the image of Kayla in a white dress formed in his mind. His body tensed. As quickly as the image came to him, he vanquished it. She'd be a beautiful bride, but for someone else. He wasn't getting married—ever.

Determined to stay on point and to get her input on the wedding, he headed downstairs to the pool area. He opened the door and stepped outside, momentarily blinded by the bright sunlight. Once his vision adjusted, he glanced around, quickly locating his assistant. She was at a shaded poolside table. She lifted her head and smiled, but it wasn't aimed at him.

She wasn't alone. A young man stood next to her table. Angelo's gut knotted. He told himself that it was because she was supposed to be working, not flirting. His only interest was in her getting her work done in a timely fashion. But as the chime of her laughter carried through the gentle breeze, Angelo's mouth pulled into a frown.

He strode toward the table. Kayla didn't even notice him approach as she was captivated by the young man.

Angelo cleared his throat. "Hello, Kayla."

Both heads turned his way. Kayla's eyes opened wide with surprise. The young man drew himself up to his full height as though he was about to defend his right to be flirting with Kayla. The guy had no idea that Angelo had no intention of challenging his right to gain Kayla's attention. After all, it would be for the best if she was interested in someone—as long as it wasn't him. But that would all have to wait, because right now she was on the clock. And he needed her help.

Angelo used his practiced professional voice, the one that let people know that he meant business. "How's the Van Holsen account coming?"

"Uh, good. Dino was just asking about the royal wedding."

"He was?" Angelo stepped between Kayla and the young man. "What do you want to know?"

The young man glanced down, not meeting Angelo's direct gaze. "I... I was just curious if the rumor was true that they might pick Monte Calanetti for the wedding."

"It is. Is there anything else?"

Dino shrugged his shoulders. "I guess not."

"Good. Kayla has work to do now. If you'll excuse us."

"Uh, sure." Dino leaned to the side to look at Kayla. "I'll see you around."

"Bye."

Angelo took a seat next to Kayla. "It seems you've found yourself an admirer."

"Who? Dino?" She shook her head. "He was just interested in what I knew about the royal wedding, which wasn't anything more than he's heard through the grapevine. How's the pitch for the wedding coming?"

"Good." *Liar.*

He wasn't about to admit that he, Angelo Amatucci, couldn't come up with a dynamic pitch that would turn the prince's and his bride's heads. No way. What would Kayla think of him? No. Scratch that. He didn't want to know what she'd think. She'd probably laugh at him.

"I'm glad to hear it's going well. I know that I'm not the only one who's anxious for the pitch. Imagine a royal wedding. The whole world will be watching it and you'll have played a big part in it."

"Not a big part."

"You're too modest. You're like the village hero now."

Just what he needed was more pressure. He swallowed down his uneasiness. "You're assuming that the prince will choose this village, and that's a big leap."

"But why wouldn't they pick Monte Calanetti? From the little I've seen, I think it's a lovely village."

"That's just because you didn't grow up here."

Her green eyes widened. "You really didn't like living here?"

He shook his head, but he wasn't going to get into the details of his childhood or his strained relationship with his parents. Kayla had already been privy to more about his private life than anyone else ever. But something told him that his family secrets were safe with her.

Not in the mood to talk anymore about this village or dwell on the fact that he'd wasted two days without coming up with anything striking or fascinating, he decided to turn the conversation around. "How is the work going?"

CHAPTER NINE

COULD SHE PRETEND she hadn't heard Angelo?

Kayla had spent a large chunk of time at this poolside table. With most of the guests either off sightseeing or attending other engagements, it was a peaceful place for her to jot out more ideas for the Van Holsen account. But after going back and forth between the art department and the very demanding client, they were still missing the mark.

It didn't help that her ideas for the Van Holsen account had stalled. For the past half hour or so, she'd been jotting out ideas for the fund-raiser back in New York. The event was their last hope to keep the after-school program going for so many at-risk kids and it was weighing heavy on her mind. There were still so many details to iron out.

And as exciting as it was to be working with Angelo Amatucci on what could be the project to catapult her career, she couldn't forget the children. They were relying on her to make their lives a little better by raising money to keep their facility open.

"Kayla, did you hear me?"

The sound of Angelo's voice startled her back to the here and now. "Sorry. I just had a thought."

"About the account?"

She nodded. "It's coming along."

"Why don't you tell me what you have so far and we can work on it together?"

She glanced down at her closed notebook. "That's okay. I know you have more important things to concentrate on. I've got this."

Angelo's dark brows drew together. "Listen, I know that

things haven't exactly been right between us since, well, you know…the kiss. If that's still bothering you—?"

"It's not." Yes, it was. But not the way he was thinking. The kiss had been better than she'd ever imagined. And she knew that it could never happen again. She had too much on the line to risk it all by fooling around with her boss.

The truth of the matter was the pad of paper also contained her thoughts for the benefit concert. Angelo had a strict policy about not taking on charity accounts—he believed there were too many good causes and not enough time to help them all. Kayla couldn't understand his stance, but then again she'd never been in charge of a large company. Maybe there was more to it than what she knew.

The one thing she did know was that she couldn't let Angelo find out that she was organizing a fund-raiser while on this trip. She didn't want him to have a reason not to consider her for a promotion or worse yet to have her replaced as his assistant. She wasn't sure how he would handle the situation. In all of her time at Amatucci & Associates, she'd never witnessed anyone going against company policy. Angelo was a man no one wanted to cross.

"I'm just jotting out some ideas. Nothing specific yet." She caught herself worrying her bottom lip, hoping he wouldn't take exception to her not coming up with something more concrete. After all, they were on a timetable and the clock was ticking. "I spent the morning on the phone with the art department and Mrs. Van Holsen—"

His brows drew together into a formidable line. "Why didn't you get me?"

"I… I didn't want to disturb you. I'm supposed to be here to lighten your load."

He shook his head. "I can't spend all of my time on one campaign. That isn't fair to the other clients. I have to stay on top of everything. Next time you speak with a client, I expect to be in on the call. Understood?"

"Yes."

He let the subject go as he continued on with some other business items. "By the way, while I was on the phone with the office I mentioned that we'd been unavoidably detained in Italy, but I didn't go into specifics. I don't want any rumors starting up that we put off longtime clients in favor of this royal wedding pitch. I won't risk my company's reputation for something that is never going to happen."

Kayla's mouth gaped before she caught it and forced her lips together. "Is that really what you think?"

He nodded. "Pretty much."

"But why?"

"Well, I can't see what a royal couple would find so endearing about Monte Calanetti. I think everyone, including my brother and sister, are getting worked up over something that will never happen."

"I don't understand. If that's truly what you think then why go to all of the bother to delay your return to New York and work on a campaign that you're certain will fail?"

He shrugged. "It's an obligation that I owe them." He raked his fingers through his hair. "I owe it to Nico and Marianna—you know, for skipping out on them. For letting them fend for themselves with parents who were more wrapped up in their marital drama than worrying about their children."

"I'm sorry—"

"Don't be. I didn't tell you any of that so you'd feel sorry for me. In fact, I don't know why I mentioned it at all."

"I'm glad you did. I'd like to think that we've become more than coworkers." When she met his drawn brows, she realized that she'd said more than she should have. "I... I don't mean about the kiss. I just thought we might be friends, too."

A wave of relief washed over his face easing the stress lines. "I would like that."

"You would?"

Slowly he nodded, and then a smile tugged at his lips. "Yes, I would."

She couldn't help but smile back. She noticed how the worry lines bracketing his eyes and mouth smoothed. She'd never seen him look so worried before. Why would that be? He was amazing at creating winning pitches. He was amazing in a lot of ways.

Realizing that she was staring, she turned away, but by then, her heart was beating faster than normal. Images of the kiss they'd shared clouded her mind. She'd tried to put it out of her head, but the memory kept her awake late into the night. What had it meant? Had it meant anything? Because there was no way that a wealthy, successful businessman who could have his choice of women would fall for his assistant.

Kayla reached for a tall, cool glass of iced tea. "Would you like something to drink? I could go and get you something."

"Thanks. But I'm all right." He looked at her as though studying her. "Can I ask what direction you think the wedding pitch should take?"

"Really?" She sat up straighter. "You want my input?"

He nodded. "I thought you might have some ideas that I hadn't thought of."

"I do…have ideas, that is." She struggled to gather her thoughts.

"I'm listening."

She'd done a lot of thinking about this—probably too much, considering she hadn't even been invited to help with the royal pitch until now. "I'm thinking that regardless of whether they go big or small, they're going to want elements that play into an elegant yet traditional event."

"That's true. If they wanted a contemporary feel, they certainly wouldn't come to Monte Calanetti." He rubbed the back of his neck.

"What's bothering you?"

"I'm just trying to figure out why this village made the short list for the royal wedding. I mean, there's nothing special here. I've gone round and round with this, but I still have no answer. It's not like it has amazing history like Rome or the heartbeat of the nation like Milan or the stunning architecture of Venice. This is a little, old village."

"And it's tripping you up when you're trying to come up with a unique pitch."

Angelo hesitated as though he wasn't sure whether or not to confide in her. Then he sighed. "Yes, it's giving me a bit of a problem. No matter which way I go at it, I just can't find that special quality that will put Monte Calanetti head and shoulders above the other locations."

Kayla smiled and shook her head. "You just don't see it because you take this place for granted. It's your home, but to outsiders, it's something special."

His gaze met hers. "You think it's special?"

She decided a neutral stance was best. "I haven't made up my mind yet."

"Then how can you tell me that I'm blind to what's in front of me when you haven't even made up your mind?" His voice held a disgruntled tone.

She smiled, liking the fact that she could get past his polished persona and make him feel real genuine emotions. "I mean that I need to see the village." When he opened his mouth to protest, she held up her hand, stopping him. "And driving straight through it to get to the hotel does not count. It was more of a blur than anything."

"What are you saying?"

"I'm saying that tomorrow you and I will start exploring Monte Calanetti. You can tell me all about it. You know, the little things that a tourist wouldn't know—the parts that make the village special."

"Don't be too disappointed when it doesn't live up to your expectations."

"I think you'll actually end up surprising yourself."

His gaze narrowed in on her. "You really want to walk all through the village?"

She nodded. "If you want to come up with a winning pitch to make all of the citizens, not to mention your brother and sister very happy, you're going to have to see it differently."

"I'm not sure that's possible. But if you insist on it, I will give you the grand tour."

"I would like that."

"Now, if you'll excuse me, I promised to swing by my brother's villa. He wants to show me the latest improvements at the winery." He got to his feet. "Of course, if you'd like to accompany me, you're welcome."

Kayla glanced down at her rather sparse list of notes. "I think my time would be better spent here doing some research."

"You're sure?"

She nodded. "I am. But thank you for the invite."

The truth was, she and Angelo were getting along a lot better than they had in the office. She'd been working for him for weeks now and they'd only ever addressed each other with mister and miss, but now they were on a first-name basis. And then there was that kiss…er…no she wasn't going to think about it. No matter how good it was or how much she wished that he'd kiss her again—

Her thoughts screeched to a halt. Did she want him to kiss her again? She turned to watch his retreating form. His broad shoulders were evident in the linen suit jacket. His long, powerful legs moved at a swift pace, covering the patio area quickly.

Yes, she did want to be kissed again. Only this time she wanted him to kiss her because he wanted her and not because he was exhausted and stressed after a run-in with his siblings. But that couldn't happen. She needed this job.

A quick fling with her boss in the warm sunshine of

Tuscany wasn't worth throwing away her dreams—the rest of her life. No matter how tempting Angelo might be, she just couldn't ruin this opportunity.

And she couldn't return to Paradise as a failure.

CHAPTER TEN

WHY EXACTLY HAD he agreed to this?

The last thing Angelo wanted to do was take a stroll through Monte Calanetti. It was like taking a walk back through history—a history that he preferred not to dwell on. Still, he had to admit that having Kayla along would make the journey back in time a little more tolerable, but he still didn't see how it was going to help him create a winning pitch.

He paced back and forth in the hotel lobby, waiting for Kayla to finish getting ready for their outing. He'd also wanted to check with the front desk to make sure that extending their stay wouldn't be an issue.

"Mr. Amatucci, you're in luck." The concierge strode up to him. "We've just had a cancellation. And with a bit of juggling we've been able to keep you and your assistant in your suite of rooms." The young man, who was polished from the top of his short cut hair down to his spiffed-up dress shoes, looked quite pleased with himself. "Is there anything else I can do for you?"

"Actually there is." Angelo wasn't sure it was a good idea, but he decided that Kayla deserved a night out for being such a good sport. "I've heard that Mancini's is quite a popular restaurant."

"Yes, it is. We're so lucky to have had Raffaele Mancini return to the village. Mancini's is so popular that they only take reservations."

That's what Angelo suspected. "Would you mind making a reservation for myself and my assistant for tomorrow evening?"

The concierge's face creased with worry lines.

"Is there a problem?"

"Well, sir. They're usually booked well in advance."

Angelo wasn't used to being put off. Even in New York he didn't have a problem getting into the most popular restaurants. How in the world was it that he was being turned down in little old Monte Calanetti? Impossible.

"Do you know who I am?"

The young man's eyes opened wide, and then he nodded.

Angelo got the distinct impression that the young man didn't have a clue who he was or what power he wielded outside of the Tuscany countryside. He felt as though he'd stepped back in time, becoming a nobody who faded into the crowd. With his pride pricked, he gave the young man a pointed look. But he knew that he was letting his past get the best of him. He swallowed down the unwarranted agitation. Of course the young man didn't know him. The concierge wasn't much more than a kid.

Angelo decided upon a new approach. "Forgive me. My tone was uncalled-for just now. When you call for the reservations, tell them that the owner of Amatucci & Associates is requesting a table as we are considering including them in the pitch for the royal wedding."

Maybe he had put it on a little thick just now, but he wanted—no, he needed to prove to everyone including himself that he had far surpassed everyone's expectations of him—especially his father's. Angelo's gut churned at the memory of his father turning to him in anger and saying, *You'll never amount to anything.*

"Yes, sir." The concierge attempted a nervous smile. "I'll do that right away. I had no idea, sir—"

"It's okay." Angelo tipped the young man handsomely to make up for his brusqueness. "I just need you to know that this dinner is very important." But suddenly Angelo was no longer talking about business or proving himself to the villagers or even the royal wedding. His mind was on Kayla. He liked making her happy, and he was hoping this dinner would earn him another smile or two.

"I'll get right on it, sir."

"Thank you. I appreciate it."

Angelo moved over to the small sitting area in the lobby to wait for Kayla. Just about to reach for the newspaper to find out what was going on around the world, Angelo caught a movement out of the corner of his eye. Curious to see if it was Kayla, he turned.

His gaze settled on her slender form. He stood transfixed as he took in her beauty. Kayla's auburn wavy hair hung loose and flowed down over her shoulders. A pair of sunglasses sat atop her head like a hair band. Her face was lightly made up and her reading glasses were nowhere in sight. A sheer tan cardigan covered her arms while beneath was a lacy white tank top. She looked so stunning that all of the villagers would be too busy trying to figure out if she was a movie star to take any notice of him.

"Is everything all right with the suite?" She stopped next to him.

He swallowed hard and glanced away, telling himself to relax. This was still the same Kayla that he'd been working closely with for weeks. He gazed at her again, trying to see her as the levelheaded assistant that he'd come to rely on. Spending the day with her, leisurely strolling about was going to be a struggle. He just had to keep in mind that they had a mission to accomplish—a royal wedding to brainstorm.

"Angelo?" She sent him a concerned look.

"Um…sorry. Yes, the suite is ours for the duration."

She pressed a hand to her chest. "That's good. You had me worried for a moment there."

"Nothing at all to worry about. Are you ready for your grand tour?"

She smiled and nodded. "Yes, I am. I'm really looking forward to it."

Without thinking, he extended his arm to her. Surprise lit up her eyes but in a blink it was gone. She slipped her arm in his. He didn't know why he'd made the gesture. It just felt right. So much for the promise he'd made himself to remain professional around her. They hadn't even left the hotel and he was already treating her like…like… Oh, whatever.

Angelo led her out of the hotel into the sunshiny afternoon. He had to admit that it was nice to get away from the stress of the wedding pitch. The whole project had ground to a complete halt. He sure hoped this outing would refill his creative well. If nothing else, maybe it would help him relax so he could start brainstorming again.

He glanced over to find Kayla taking in their surroundings. "I thought we would walk since the village isn't far from here."

"Sounds fine by me. I've been cooped up in the hotel long enough. Back in New York, I'm used to doing a lot of walking."

"Really. Where do you walk?" He didn't know why but he was truly interested.

"I walk to the subway and then to the office. Sometimes, if the weather is right, I will duck out at lunch and stretch my legs."

"So you truly like to walk."

She nodded. "It sure beats eating like a bird. If you hadn't noticed, I do enjoy food." She rubbed her flat abs. "Especially pasta."

"Would you like to try some of the best Italian food in the region?"

"Definitely."

"Good. From what I've heard, you should be impressed with the restaurant I've chosen."

"Is it far from here?"

"Not at all. In fact, it's right here in Monte Calanetti. We have reservations for tomorrow night."

"I can't wait."

"Good. Consider it a date."

When her fine brows rose and her eyes glittered with unspoken questions, he realized he'd blundered. But he didn't take back the words. He liked the thought of having a friendly date with her.

They walked a bit before Kayla spoke. "What's it called?"

"Mancini's. It's an exclusive IGF-starred restaurant on the outskirts of the village. The chef is a friend of my brother's."

"This friend of your brother's, is he from around here?"

"Yes, he grew up here. After Raffaele achieved international success with his cooking, he returned to open his own restaurant. I suspect he was anxious to try running his own place, but I'm surprised he didn't start his business in one of the cities like Rome or Milan."

"Perhaps he just wanted to be home again. Have you really never considered moving back here?"

Angelo gave a firm shake of head. "Not even once."

"Don't you like it here?"

"It…it has a lot of memories. Not all of them good ones."

Angelo remembered how he'd been turned away from his home and told not to return. The buried memories came flooding back to him. The loud arguments between his parents. His brother and sister upset. And then there was the last time he came to his mother's defense. He'd experienced many a row with his father before that life-altering one—the one where his father threw him out of the house, telling him that he was old enough to make it on his own.

When Angelo had turned a pleading stare to his mother, she'd told him that he was a smart, strong young man and that it was time to make his way in life. That was when he'd had no choice but to follow his dreams. With the aid of his inheritance from his grandfather combined with his meager savings, he'd set out for New York.

Though he hated to leave his brother and sister, he didn't have a choice. His father was a stubborn man who wouldn't back down from an argument. And Angelo wasn't about to live any longer with his parents and their dysfunctional relationship. In fact, he hadn't even come back to Monte Calanetti to visit until his mother and father had moved to Milan. He had no intention of seeing his father again.

"I'm sorry. I didn't mean to upset you."

Kayla's voice drew him out of his thoughts. "What? Um…oh, you didn't."

She sent him an I-don't-believe-you look but said nothing more. They continued toward the village in silence. It felt so strange to be back here—when he'd left all of those years ago, he'd sworn that he'd never return. And he hadn't for a long time.

The truth was he missed his brother and sister. But he rarely made the journey home. It was too hard. There were too many unsettling memories lurking about, and he just didn't have the same draw to this place that his brother and sister did. He didn't understand Nico's need to cling to their heritage, not when there were so many adventures outside of Monte Calanetti to experience.

"This is beautiful." Kayla stood at the crumbling rock wall that surrounded the village, which was perched high upon a hill. "What an amazing view. What's with the wall?"

"The village is centuries old and used to be a stronghold against attacks."

"I couldn't imagine there being unrest here. I mean, did you ever see anything so peaceful?" There was a distinct note of awe in Kayla's voice. "There's something almost magical about it."

"I used to think that, too."

"You did?"

He nodded, recalling days of long ago. "I used to come to this spot when I was a kid." What he failed to mention is that he came here to get away from his parents' arguing.

"I'd pretend that I was the defender of the kingdom. Many sword battles took place where you're standing."

"Really? So you were Sir Lancelot?" She eyed him up as though imagining him in a coat of armor.

He was no knight—not even close to it. He'd just been a kid trying to escape the battlefield between his parents, but he didn't want to get into any of that. A gentle breeze rushed past them and he willed it to sweep away the unsettling memories. He didn't want the past to ruin this day.

"Look." She pointed to a flock of little birds as they took flight. They soared up into the sky, circled and swooped low before rising again. "Aren't they beautiful?"

He was never a bird-watcher, but he had to admire the symmetry of their movements. He couldn't help but wonder what else he'd been missing. His gaze strayed back to Kayla. How had he missed noticing how amazing she was both inside and out?

"And listen."

He did as she asked. "I don't hear anything."

"Exactly! There's nothing but the rustle of the leaves. It's so freeing."

Now that he could agree on. He'd been searching for quietness like this ever since he'd moved to New York, but he'd never been able to find it—until now. "It clears the mind."

"Good. We want clear heads when we tour Monte Calanetti." She turned and pointed off in the distance. "I just love the rows of grapevines. I wonder how they get the lines so straight."

"I'm betting if you were to ask Nico that he'd tell you anything you want to know about running a vineyard. He's very proud of his work."

"You mean all of that is Nico's land?"

Angelo nodded. "It has been passed down through the family. When my father couldn't make a go of it, they passed the land down to us kids. I was already working in New York and Marianna was too young, so Nico stepped up. He's worked really hard to rebuild the vineyard and make a name for the wine."

"Hardworking must be a trait of the Amatucci men."

"Some of them anyhow." His father wasn't big on work, which was evident by the poor condition of the vineyard when he'd handed it over to his children. "Come on. I thought you wanted to see Monte Calanetti."

"I do."

With Kayla's hand still tucked in the crook of his arm, Angelo took comfort in having her next to him. This was his first stroll through the village since that dreadful day when his father cast him out of their family home. These days when he returned to Italy, he either stayed in the city or at the villa. He just wasn't up for the curious stares or worse the questions about why he left.

As they strolled through the village, Angelo warned himself not to get too comfortable with Kayla. Soon this vacation illusion would end, and they'd be back in New York, where he'd transform back into Mr. Amatucci and she'd once again be Ms. Hill. Everything would once again be as it should.

CHAPTER ELEVEN

NEVER ONE TO lurk in the shadows, Angelo led Kayla into the center of Monte Calanetti. Their first stop was at the *caffè* shop. He'd never met a woman who loved coffee as much as Kayla. She savored each sip before swallowing. He loved to watch her facial features when she'd take her first sip—it was somewhere between total delight and ecstasy. He longed to be able to put that look on her face...and not with coffee...but with a long, slow, deep, soul-stirring kiss.

He'd given up the futile effort of fighting his lustful thoughts for Kayla. He couldn't lie to himself. He found her utterly enchanting. And as long as he stuck with his daydreams of holding her—of kissing her passionately—they'd be fine. It wasn't as if she could read his mind.

They stepped out of the shop and onto the busy sidewalk. As they started to walk again, he reminded himself not to get too caught up in having Kayla by his side. She was the absolute wrong person for him to have a dalliance with beneath the Tuscany sun. He was her escort—her friend—nothing more. He forced his thoughts to the quaint shops that offered such things as locally grown flowers and to-die-for baked goods. There was a little bit of everything. And he could tell by the rapt stare on Kayla's face that she was enthralled by all of it.

"Angelo, is that you?"

They both stopped at the sound of a woman's excited voice. Angelo glanced over his shoulder to see an older woman rushing toward them. She looked vaguely familiar.

"It is you." The woman couldn't be much more than five feet tall, if that. She beamed up at him. "I knew you'd come back."

It took him a moment, but then the woman's gentle smile and warm eyes clicked a spot in his memory—Mrs. Caruso. He hadn't seen her since he was a teenager. Back then, she'd had long dark hair that she kept braided over one shoulder. Now, her dark hair had given way to shades of gray, and instead of the braid, her hair was pinned up.

Kayla elbowed him, and at last, he found his voice. "Mrs. Caruso, it's good to see you."

"What kind of greeting is that?" She grabbed him by the arms and pulled him toward her. When he'd stooped over far enough, she placed a hand on either side of his head, and then kissed each cheek. "You've been gone much too long. You've been missed."

She pulled him back down to her and gave him a tight hug. He hugged her back. Heat warmed his face. He wasn't used to public displays of affection...no matter how innocent they might be. This would never happen back in the States. But then again, Monte Calanetti was a lifetime away from New York City, and the same rules didn't seem to apply here.

They chatted for a bit as she asked one question after the other about what he'd been doing with himself. The years rolled away as she put him at ease with her friendly chatter. The best part was that she really listened to him—as she'd done all of those years ago when he was a kid. Mrs. Caruso and her husband ran the local bakery. They'd never had any children of their own. Angelo always suspected that it wasn't from the lack of wanting or trying. Without little ones of her own, she'd doted on the kids in the village.

"You are going to do the royal wedding pitch, aren't you?" She smiled and clapped her hands together as though she'd just solved the world's problems.

"Nico asked me to work on it. My assistant and I just extended our stay here in order to work up a presentation for the royal family."

"Wonderful!" Mrs. Caruso beamed. "Now I'm more

certain than ever that the village will host the wedding. Everyone will be so grateful to both of you."

"I don't know about that—"

"You're just being modest. You always were." Mrs. Caruso's gaze moved to Kayla. "Now where are my manners? Angelo, introduce me to your girlfriend."

His girlfriend? Hadn't she heard him say Kayla was his assistant? His gaze moved from her to Kayla, who was smiling. Why wasn't she correcting the woman? Was she just being polite? Or should he be concerned that she was taking this friendly outing far too seriously?

"Hi, I'm Kayla." She held out a hand while Angelo struggled to settle his thoughts. "I'm actually Mr. Amatucci's assistant."

Mrs. Caruso's brows rose as her gaze moved back and forth between them. "I could have sworn that you two were— Oh, never mind me. I'm just so glad that you're both here to help with the wedding."

They promised to stop by the bakery soon and moved on down the walkway. He still didn't know why Mrs. Caruso would think they were a couple. Then he glanced down to where Kayla's hand was resting on his arm. Okay, so maybe from the outside the lines in their relationship appeared a bit blurred, but they knew where they stood. Didn't they?

He swallowed hard. "I'm sorry about back there with Mrs. Caruso jumping to conclusions about us."

"It's okay. It was a natural mistake."

A natural mistake? Wait. What exactly did that mean?

He glanced over at Kayla. "But you know that you and I…that we're, um…that nothing has changed. Right?"

She smiled up at him. "Relax. We're just two business associates enjoying a stroll through the village. It's a mission. We have to learn as much about this place as possible so that you can do some brainstorming about the pitch when we return to our suite."

She said all of the right things, but why did they sound

so wrong to his ears? Maybe he was just being hypersensitive. He took a deep breath and blew it out. "Exactly." Now he needed to change the subject to something a little less stressful. "Mrs. Caruso certainly seemed hopeful about the royal wedding."

"She did. It seems as if the whole village is buzzing with excitement about it."

"I just hope they don't end up disappointed."

She lightly elbowed him. "They won't be. You'll see to that."

At this particular moment, she had a lot more faith in his abilities than he did. "I don't know if I'm that good. This is just a small village and we're talking about a royal wedding—the sort of thing they write about in history books."

"And who better to sell the royal couple on the merits of Monte Calanetti?" She gazed up at him with hope in her eyes. "You just need to loosen up a bit and enjoy yourself."

"I am relaxed." As relaxed as he got these days.

She sighed and shook her head. "No, you aren't. Let down your guard and enjoy the sun on your face."

"Why is this so important to you?"

"Because I want you to really see Monte Calanetti and get excited about it." Her gaze met his and then dipped to his mouth. "I think if you're passionate about something it will show."

The temperature started to rise. He knew what she was thinking because he was thinking the same thing. He zeroed in on her inviting lips. He was definitely feeling passionate. Would it be wrong to kiss her again?

Someone bumped his shoulder as they passed by, reminding him that they were in the middle of the village. Not exactly the place for a passionate moment or even a quick peck. Besides, he couldn't give her the wrong impression. He didn't do relationships.

Before he could decide if he should say something,

Kayla slipped her arm in his and they started to walk again. They made their way around the piazza, taking in the various shops from a shoe boutique to a candy shop. Monte Calanetti offered so much more than he recalled.

Maybe it wasn't quite the small backward village he'd conjured up in his memory—the same village where he'd once got into a bit of mischief with harmless pranks. Those were the carefree days that he hadn't known to appreciate as they flew by.

"What are you smiling about?" Kayla sent him a curious look.

He was smiling? He hadn't realized his thoughts had crossed his face. "I was just recalling some antics I'd gotten into as a kid."

"Oh, tell me. I'd love to hear."

"You would?" He wouldn't think something like that would interest her. When she nodded, he continued. "There was this one time when I glued a coin to the sidewalk outside the market. You wouldn't believe how many people tried to pry it free."

Her eyes twinkled. "So you didn't always play by the rules."

He shrugged. "What kind of trouble did you get into?"

"Me? Nothing."

"Oh, come on, confess. There has to be something."

She paused as though giving it some serious consideration. "Well, there was this one time the neighborhood boys attached some fishing line to a dollar. It was similar to what you did. They'd lay it out in front of my parents' market, and when someone went to pick up it up, they'd tug on the line."

"See, I knew you weren't as innocent as you appeared."

"Hey, it wasn't me. It was them. I... I was just watching."

"Uh-huh." He enjoyed the way her cheeks filled with color. "It's good to know you have some spunk in you. That will come in handy in this business."

* * *

Kayla was in love—with the village, of course.

Brilliant sunshine lit up the heart of Monte Calanetti. The piazza was surrounded by a wide range of small shops to satisfy even the most discerning tastes. But it was the large fountain in the center of the village square that drew Kayla's attention. She tugged on Angelo's arm, leading them toward it.

The focal point of the fountain was a nymph draped in a cloak. She held a huge clamshell overhead. The sunshine sparkled and danced over the fine billowing mist from the continuous jets of water. Kayla stopped at the fountain's edge. She smiled, loving the details of the sculpture that included a ring of fish leaping out of the water.

"I take it you like the fountain." Angelo's deep voice came from just behind her. "You know there's a tradition that if you toss a coin and it lands in the shell, you get your wish."

Her gaze rose to the clamshell—suddenly it didn't look quite so big. "You'd have to be awfully lucky to get it all the way up there."

"Why don't you give it a try?"

"I… I don't think so. I was never good at those types of things."

Angelo held a coin out to her. "Here you go." His fingers pressed the money into her palm. "I made a wish once and it came true."

"Really?" She turned to him. "What was it?"

He shook his head. "You aren't supposed to tell your wish."

"But that doesn't apply if your wish has already come true. So, out with it."

The corner of his very inviting lips lifted. "Okay. I wished that someday I'd get to travel the world."

"Wow. It really did come true." She thought really hard, but was torn by what she should wish for. She could wish for the fund-raiser to be a huge success. Or she could wish for her promotion to ad executive. But fountains should be for fanciful dreams.

"Don't look so worried. Turn around."

She did as he said. The next thing she knew, his body pressed to her back—his hard planes to her soft curves. His breath tickled her neck. Her heart thumped and her knees grew weak. Thankfully he was there holding her up.

His voice was soft as he spoke. "You make the wish and I'll help you get the coin in the shell. Ready?"

She nodded. Together with their hands touching, they swung. The coin flipped end over end through the air.

Let Angelo kiss me.

Plunk! The coin landed in the clamshell.

"We did it!"

At that moment, Angelo backed away. "Did you ever doubt it?"

"I couldn't have done it without you." She turned around, hoping her wish would come true.

"Did you make your wish?"

Disappointment washed over her. Of course he wasn't going to kiss her. She'd let herself get caught up in the moment. That wouldn't happen again.

"We should keep moving." She turned to start walking. "We don't want to miss anything."

"Wait." He reached out for her hand. "Aren't you going to tell me what you wished for?"

"Um…no. I can't." When he sent her a puzzled look, she added, "If I tell you, it won't come true."

"Well, we wouldn't want that to happen."

Her hand remained in his warm grasp as they continued their stroll. Was it her imagination or was Angelo's icy professional persona melting beneath the Tuscany sun? She smiled. He was definitely warming up.

CHAPTER TWELVE

SIMPLY *CHARMING*.

At this particular moment, Kayla had no better word for it. And she wasn't just talking about the village. She gave Angelo a sideways gaze. Handsome, thoughtful and entertaining. "Quite a combo."

"What?"

Oops! She hadn't meant to vocalize her thoughts. "I... I was just thinking Monte Calanetti has quite an amazing combination of old-world charm and modern day functionality."

They meandered away from the fountain. On the edge of the piazza, they passed by a well that she was certain had seen its days of women gathering to fill their buckets. While waiting for their turn, she imagined they'd shared the happenings of the village—the historic form of gossiping around the water cooler. It was so easy to envision how things used to be. Something told Kayla that this village hadn't changed a whole lot over the years.

The sunshine warmed the back of her neck, but it was Angelo's arm beneath her fingertips that warmed her insides. She resisted the urge to smooth her fingers over his tanned skin. She was in serious danger of forgetting that he was her boss—the key to her future promotion.

As the bell towers rang out, Kayla stared at the cobblestone path that wound its way between the brick buildings. A number of the homes had flower boxes with red, yellow and purple blooms. There were also flowerpots by the various shaped doors painted in every imaginable color. In other places, ivy snaked its way along the bricks. This area was quite picturesque and made Kayla forget that she was in the center of the village.

A rustling sound had her glancing upward. She craned her neck, finding fresh laundry fluttering in the breeze. She couldn't help but smile. It was a lovely, inviting sight. But as much as she liked it, it was the man at her side that she found utterly captivating.

Angelo Amatucci might be icy cool in the office, but she'd found that once he thawed out, he was a warm, thoughtful man. Not that she was falling for his amazing good looks or his dark, mysterious eyes. Her priority was her career—the reason she'd left her home in Paradise. And she wasn't about to ruin her future by throwing herself at her boss.

She chanced a quick glance his way. But then again—

No. She pulled her thoughts up short. This wasn't getting her anywhere.

She was supposed to be touring Monte Calanetti to get ideas for the wedding pitch. If they were going to sell the royal couple on this location for the wedding, she needed to know as much about it as possible. And of what she'd seen so far, she loved it. This village and its occupants would give the wedding an old-world feel with lots of heart.

The villagers sent puzzled glances their way as though they should know who Angelo was but couldn't quite place his face. And then there were a few people that ventured to ask if he was indeed Angelo. When he confirmed their suspicions, he wasn't greeted with a simple hello or a mere handshake; instead, he was yanked into warm hugs. She could see the frown lines etched on his face, but to his credit he didn't complain. There were even a few tears of happiness from the older women who remembered him when he was just a young boy.

Angelo took her hand in his as though it were natural for them. Kayla liked feeling connected to him—feeling his long fingers wrapped around hers.

"I'm sorry about that." Angelo started walking again. "I didn't expect anyone to remember me."

"You must have spent a lot of time in the village as a kid."

"I did. It was my escape from the monotony of work-ing around the vineyard." His jaw tensed and a muscle twitched.

"I take it that's why you let your brother have the run of Calanetti Vineyards?"

He nodded. "Nico is as passionate about the winery as I am with advertising. How about you? Do you have any brothers or sisters?"

Kayla shook her head. "My parents wanted more chil-dren, but that didn't work out. So with me being an only child, they heaped all of their hopes and dreams onto me."

"Hmm…sounds a bit daunting for one person."

"It is. That's why I had to leave Paradise."

"Somehow I just can't imagine life in Paradise could be such a hardship."

She shrugged. "It's great. The people are wonderful. It's the perfect place to raise kids."

"But you weren't ready for kids?"

The thought of taking on that sort of responsibility still overwhelmed her. "I have to figure out me first and ac-complish some things on my own before I can be there 24/7 for others. And my parents, as much as I love them, didn't understand this."

"They wanted you to graduate high school and settle down."

She nodded. "They had it all planned out. I'd get mar-ried, have lots of kids and when the time came my husband and I would take over the family store."

"Doesn't sound so bad."

"No. It isn't. But I always had a dream of going to col-lege and making a name for myself. I wanted to move to the city. I wanted to climb the corporate ladder. I wanted to—"

She bit off her last words. Heat rushed up her neck and warmed her face. She couldn't believe that she'd gotten so comfortable around Angelo that she'd just rambled on about her dreams. For a moment, she'd forgotten that she was talking to her boss.

Not good, Kayla. Not good at all.

She freed her hand from his. It was time she started acting like his employee, not his girlfriend. The time had come to get back to reality.

Angelo stopped walking and turned to her. "What aren't you saying? What do you want to do?"

"Um…nothing. It's no big deal. Let's keep going. I want to see the whole village." She turned to start walking again.

Angelo reached out, catching her arm in his firm grip. "Not so fast." She turned back, glancing up at his serious gaze. "Kayla, talk to me." His hand fell away from her arm. "I've told you all sorts of things that I don't normally share with people. I'd like to know what you were about to say and why you stopped. Surely by now you know that you can trust me."

Could she trust him? She supposed it depended on the subject. With her safety—most definitely. With her dreams—perhaps. With her heart— Wait, where had that come from?

"Kayla, what is it?"

She wasn't good at lying so that left her with the truth, but she didn't know how Angelo would take it. "I came to New York because I wanted…er… I want to be an ad executive."

His brows scrunched together. "And?"

She shrugged. "And that's it."

"That's what you didn't want to tell me?"

Her gaze moved to the cobblestone walkway. "It's just that I got comfortable around you and forgot to watch what I was saying."

"Oh, I see. Since I'm the boss, you feel like you have to screen what you say to me?"

She nodded.

"How about this? For the duration of this trip, I'm not

your boss. We're just business associates or how about friends? Would you like that?"

Her gaze met his and she found that he was being perfectly serious. "But what about when we return to New York?"

"Obviously things will have to change then, but for right now, I'd like to just be Angelo, not Mr. Amatucci. I'd forgotten what it's like just to be me again."

"And I like you calling me Kayla." Her gaze met his. Within his eyes she found a comforting warmth. "Consider yourself a friend."

He held out his hand to her. She accepted it. A shiver of excitement raced up her arm. They continued to stare deep into each other's eyes, even though it was totally unnecessary. She knew she should turn away. She knew that it was the proper thing to do with her boss. But as he'd just pointed out they were friends—for now.

His voice grew deeper. "I couldn't think of a better friend to have."

Her heart fluttered in her chest. What had just happened?

Angelo turned and tucked her hand back in the crook of his arm. Why did it suddenly feel as though their relationship had just taken a detour? How would they ever find their way back to just being boss and employee now?

Monte Calanetti is a diamond in the rough.

Had that thought really just crossed his mind?

Before he'd left the hotel a few hours ago, he'd envisioned Monte Calanetti as he had when he was a child—suffocating with its traditional ways and its resistance to growth and to modernization. But somehow, with Kayla by his side, he'd seen the village from a different perspective —he'd seen it through her very beautiful, very observant eyes. With her passion and romantic tendencies, she might just be the key he needed to pull this wedding pitch together. But did he dare ask for her help?

Sure, she had talent. He'd witnessed it firsthand with the Van Holsen account. But did he trust her with a project that was so important to his family? After all, his brother and sister, not to mention the entire village, were counting on him to represent them properly to the royal couple. But how was he supposed to do that when he kept hitting one brick wall after the other?

They walked some more before Kayla turned to him. "Thank you for showing me your hometown. I love it."

"Really?" He failed to keep the surprise from his voice.

"Of course I do. How could you not? Not only that but it has the most delicious aromas and it's so peaceful." Just then two scooters whizzed by them. "Okay, so it isn't totally peaceful."

"You'll get used to them. Scooters are very popular around here."

A couple more scooters zoomed down the road causing Kayla to step into the grass. She took a moment, taking in her surroundings. "Is this where you went to school?"

Angelo glanced at the back of the building off in the distance. The years started to slip away. "Yes, it is."

"I bet you were a handful back then."

As a young kid, he'd been the complete opposite of the way he is now. "I believe the word they used was *incorrigible*."

Now why had he gone and admitted that? Letting down his defenses and opening up about his past would only lead to confusion and misunderstandings, because sharing was what people did when they were getting serious. And that wasn't going to happen. He refused to let it happen. No matter how ripe her lips were for a kiss. Or how her smile sent his pulse racing.

"You probably picked on all of the girls and pulled on their ponytails."

He shook his head. "Not me. I didn't have time for girls, not until I was a bit older."

"And then I bet you broke a lot of hearts."

He wasn't sure about that, but there was one girl, Vera Carducci, and he'd had the biggest crush on her. He hadn't thought of her in years.

"See. I was right." Kayla smiled triumphantly.

"Actually, I was the one who got dumped."

"That's so hard to believe—"

"It's the truth." Why did he feel the need to make Kayla believe that his life was far from idyllic? What was it about her that had him letting down his guard? He had to do better. He couldn't let her get too close. It'd only cause them pain in the end.

Kayla walked over to a tree in the school yard. Her fingers traced over the numerous carvings from initials to hearts. "Was this the kissing tree?"

He nodded, suddenly wishing they were anywhere but here.

"I bet your initials are here…somewhere." Kayla's voice drew him back to the present. "Want to point me in the right direction?"

"Actually, they aren't here."

Her eyes opened wide. "Really? I thought for sure that you would have been popular with the girls."

He shrugged, recalling his fair share of girlfriends over the years. But he'd never kissed them here. Not a chance.

"Surely you stole a kiss or two." Her gaze needled him for answers.

"Not here."

"Why not?"

Oh, what did it matter if he told her? It wasn't as if there was any truth to the legend. It was all a bunch of wishful thinking.

"There's some silly legend attached to the tree that says whoever you kiss here will be your soul mate for life."

Kayla's green eyes widened with interest. "Really? And you don't believe it?"

He shook his head. "It's just an old wives' tale. There's nothing to it."

"And yet you've made a point not to kiss anyone here." She stepped closer to him. "If you don't believe in such superstitions, prove it."

His pulse kicked up a notch. Why was there a gleam in her eyes? Was she challenging him? Did she really expect him to kiss her here?

Instead of the idea scaring him off, it actually appealed to him. His gaze dipped to her lips. Kayla was the only woman he had ever contemplated kissing here—wait, when did that happen? He gave himself a mental jerk, but it didn't chase away the tempting thought.

What was it about Miss Kayla Hill that had him wishing there were such things as happily-ever-afters instead of roller-coaster relationships? He'd had so much turbulence in his life that he couldn't stand anymore. But Kayla was different. She had a calming presence.

This wasn't right. He should make it perfectly clear that he was no Romeo, but the way she kept staring at him, challenging him with her eyes, filled him with a warm sensation. He didn't want it to end. What would it hurt to let her remain caught up in her romantic imaginings?

Without thinking about the pros and cons of what he was about to do, he dipped his head and caught her lips with his own. Her lips were soft and pliant. He wrapped his arms around her slender waist and pulled her to him. She willingly followed his lead. Her soft curves pressed to him and a moan swelled deep in his throat. How in the world was he ever going to let her go? He'd never felt anything this intense for anyone—ever.

He wanted to convince himself that it was because she was forbidden fruit—his assistant. But he couldn't buy that. There was something so special about her that he couldn't diminish the connection with such a flimsy excuse. He knew as sure as he was standing there in a liplock with her that if their situation were different and he wasn't her boss that he'd still desire her with every fiber of his body.

His mouth moved over hers, slow at first. Yet when she met him move for move, the desire burning in him flared. Her mouth opened to him and she tasted sweet like the sun-ripened berries she'd sampled back in the village. He'd never tasted anything so delectable in his life. He doubted he'd ever experience a moment like this again.

There was something so special about Kayla. It was as though no matter what he did, she could see the real him. But could she see his scars, the ones that kept him from letting people get too close?

Her hands slid up over his shoulders and wrapped around the back of his neck. Her touch sent waves of excitement down his spine. He wanted her. He needed her. But his heart and mind were still guarded.

If he let her get any closer, she'd learn of his shame—of his ultimate pain—and then she'd pity him. Pity was not something that he could tolerate. He was Angelo Amatucci. A self-made man. He needed no one's sympathy. He needed no one.

Anxious to rebuild that wall between them, he braced his hands on her hips and pushed her back. Her eyes fluttered open and confusion showed in them.

"We should head back to the hotel. I... I have work to do."

Disappointment flashed in her eyes. "Oh. Okay."

He retraced their steps. "I have a conference call this afternoon."

Kayla fell in step beside him. He should say something. Explain somehow. But he didn't know what to say because that kiss left him utterly confused by the rush of emotions she'd evoked in him. Somehow, some way, she'd sneaked past his well-placed barriers and with each smile, each touch, she was getting to him. That wasn't part of his plan.

Unable to decide what to do about his undeniable attraction to his assistant, he turned his attention to something much less stressful—the village. For the first time, he saw its charms. Kayla had opened his eyes to everything he'd blocked out, from the amazing artisans, to the detailed architecture, to the warm and friendly people. He had so much to work with now. The pitch would be amazing if he could pull it all together, even though he was still unsure about the wedding aspect.

Still, Monte Calanetti had some of the best food in the world. It was sure to impress even the royal couple. And to be truthful, he was quite anxious to try Raffaele's restaurant—if the rumors were anything to go by, it was out of this world.

Although his desire to go to dinner had more to do with Kayla than the food. He hungered for more of her melodious laugh and her contagious smiles. Though he shouldn't, he'd come to really enjoy her company.

As productive as they were, working as a team, he was enjoying getting to know her on a personal level. After all, it wasn't as if this thing, whatever you wanted to call it, would carry over to New York. He'd make sure of it. But what would it hurt to enjoy the moment?

CHAPTER THIRTEEN

ANGELO SWIPED HIS key card and opened the suite door for Kayla. When she brushed past him, he noticed the softest scent of wildflowers. He inhaled deeply, enjoying the light fragrance as he followed her into the room, wishing he could hold on to her delicate scent just a little longer.

When she stopped short, he bumped into her. He grabbed her shoulders to steady her. She turned in his arms and gazed up at him with those big luminous green eyes. His heart pounded in his chest.

"Wasn't the afternoon wonderful?"

Was it his imagination or was her voice soft and sultry? And was she looking at him differently? Or was it that he wanted her so much that he was projecting his lusty thoughts upon her?

He swallowed down the lump in his throat. "Yes, it was a really nice day."

"Thank you so much for spending the day with me. I promise to pay you back." She stood up on her tiptoes and leaned forward.

She was going to repeat their kiss. His heart pounded. His brain told him that it shouldn't happen, but his body had other thoughts. He started to lean forward—

Buzz. Buzz. His phone vibrated in his pocket, breaking the spell.

He pulled back. After retrieving the phone from his pocket, he checked the screen. "It's the conference call. I have to take it. Can we talk later?"

He moved to his room to take the call in private. He actually welcomed the interruption. It gave him time to figure out how to handle this change of dynamics with Kayla.

The phone call dragged on much longer than he'd anticipated. When he finally disconnected the call, he found Kayla was still in the suite working on her laptop.

He cleared his throat and she glanced up, but her gaze didn't quite reach his. "Sorry about the interruption."

"No problem." Her voice didn't hold its normal lilt. She lifted her reading glasses and rested them on her head.

As much as he'd like to pretend that the kiss hadn't happened, he couldn't. It was already affecting their working relationship and that was not acceptable. "I need to apologize. That kiss…back at the tree, it shouldn't have happened. You must understand that it can't happen again."

"Is that what you really want?"

"Yes. No. I don't know." He raked his fingers through his hair. "Maybe I was wrong about this. Maybe it'd be better if you flew back to New York."

"What?" She jumped to her feet. Her heated gaze was most definitely meeting his now.

"This isn't going to work between us." He glanced away, knowing he'd created this problem. "We can't keep our hands off each other. How are we supposed to concentrate on all of the work we have to get done?"

She stepped up to him and poked him in the chest. "You're not firing me. I won't let you—"

"Wait. Who said anything about firing you?" He wrapped his hand around her finger, fighting off the urge to wrap his lips around it. "Certainly not me. You are very talented. Do you honestly think that I'd sack you over a kiss or two—kisses that I initiated?"

"Then what?" She pulled her finger from his hold as though she'd read his errant thought. "You don't think you can keep your hands to yourself around me?"

"Yes… I mean, no." He absolutely hated this feeling of being out of control—of his emotions or whatever you called it ruling over his common sense. "You confuse me."

"How so?" Her gaze narrowed in on him. When he didn't answer her, she persisted. "Tell me. I want to know."

He sighed. "It's nothing. Just forget I said anything."

"What is this really about? It has to be about more than just a kiss."

His gaze lifted and met hers head-on. How could she understand him so well? No other woman had ever seen the real him—they'd always been more interested in having a good time. But then again, he'd gone out of his way to hook up with women who didn't have serious, long-term plans where he was concerned.

His strong reaction to Kayla was due to a lot more than just the kiss. She made him feel things—want things—that he had no business feeling or wanting. And the way she'd moved him with that passionate kiss hadn't done anything to settle him. It had only made him want her all the more. What was up with that? He'd never desired a woman with every single fiber of his being. Until now.

Kayla stepped closer and lowered her voice. "Angelo, I think we've grown close enough on this trip that you can talk to me and know that it won't go any further. Tell me what's eating you up inside."

He knew what she was after—the secrets of his past. But was he ready for that? Did he have the courage to peel back those old wounds? Was he ready to deal with her reaction? Could he stand having her think less of him?

The answer was a resounding no.

Angelo inhaled a deep breath and blew it out. He wasn't prepared to open that door. It wasn't as if they were involved romantically. They didn't have a future, just the here and the now.

But there was something else…

He needed her—well…er…her help. He couldn't do this wedding pitch alone. The admission twisted his gut in a knot. He was not a man accustomed to reaching out to others.

He made a point of being the man handing out assignments, making suggestions and overseeing operations. He was never at a loss for how to accomplish things—especially an advertising pitch. This was supposed to be his area of expertise—his specialty.

What was wrong with him? Why couldn't he come up with a solid pitch? And what was Kayla going to think of him when he made this request? Would she think less of him?

Wanting to get it over with, he uttered, "I need your assistance."

"What?" Her brow creased. "Of course I'll help you. That's what I'm here for." She took a seat on the couch. "What do you need?"

His gaze met hers briefly, and then he glanced away. "I… I'm having issues with this pitch. Weddings and romance aren't my thing." That much was the truth. He avoided weddings like the plague—he always had a prior business engagement. "I thought maybe you'd have some experience with them."

"Well, um… I have a bit of experience." Her cheeks took on a pasty shade of white.

"You don't look so good. I'll get you something to drink."

"You don't have to wait on me. I can get it."

She started to get up when he pressed a hand to her shoulder. "I've got this."

He retrieved a bottle of water from the fridge and poured it in a glass for her. This was his fault. He'd had her gallivanting all around Monte Calanetti in the sun. She must have worn herself out.

He moved to her side and handed over the water. "Can I get you anything else?"

She shook her head. "Thanks. This is fine."

He sat down beside her as she sipped at the water. "I'm sorry if I pushed you too hard in the village. I should have brought you back here sooner—"

"No, that's not it. The visit was perfect. I wouldn't have changed anything about it." She sent him a smile, but it didn't quite reach her eyes.

"I don't believe you. There's something bothering you." He stopped and thought about it. "And it started when I mentioned the wedding pitch. Do you feel that I'm expecting too much of you?"

"That's not it." She placed a hand on his knee. The warmth of her touch could be felt through his jeans. "I'm just a bit tired."

"Are you sure that's all it is? It doesn't have anything to do with your broken engagement?"

Her eyes widened. "That's been over for a long time. I've moved on."

Moved on? Surely she wasn't thinking those kisses—that they'd somehow lead to something. He swallowed hard and decided it was best to change topics. "Have you made many friends since you moved to New York?"

"I haven't had much time. But I made a few at the after-school program." She pressed her lips together and turned away.

He was missing something, but he had no idea what that might be. "What do you do at this after-school program?"

She shrugged. "It's no big deal. So what can I do to help you with the wedding pitch?"

"Wait. I'd like to hear more about this program. What do you do? And how do you have time?" It seemed as if she was always in the office working long hours without a complaint.

"I do what is necessary. It all depends on the day and how many volunteers show up. Sometimes I help with homework and do a bit of tutoring. Other times I play kickball or a board game."

"You do all of that on top of the overtime you put in at the office?"

"It's not that big of a deal." She toyed with the hem of her top. "I don't have anything waiting for me at home, so why not put my spare time to good use?"

"You shouldn't dismiss what you do. There are very few people in this world who are willing to go out of their way for others. It's impressive."

Her eyes widened. "You really think so?"

"I do. Why do you seem so surprised?"

"It's just that at the office you've banned employees from taking on charitable accounts."

"It has to be that way." He raked his fingers through his hair. "There are only so many hours in the workday. I write out enough checks each year to various organizations to make up for it."

Kayla nodded, but she certainly didn't seem impressed. Uneasiness churned in his gut. Maybe she would be more understanding if she knew the amount of those checks.

"I'm sure those organizations appreciate the donations."

Guilt settled over him. What was up with that? It wasn't as if he didn't do anything. He just couldn't afford the time to take on more accounts—especially for free. He was still working on growing Amatucci & Associates into the biggest and the best advertising firm. Speaking of which, he needed to get moving on this pitch. Time was running out before his trip to Halencia.

"I need to ask you something."

She reached for the glass of water. "Ask away. Then I need to go check my email. I'm waiting on some responses about the Van Holsen account."

He shook his head, thinking this was a bad idea. "Never mind. You have enough to deal with."

She arched a thin brow at him. "You can't back out now. You have me curious."

He just couldn't admit to her that he had absolutely no direction for the pitch. Three wasted days of jotting down ideas and then realizing that they were clichéd or just plain stupid—certainly nothing that he would present to the royal family.

"If it doesn't bother you—you know, because of your broken engagement—I wanted to ask you some wedding questions."

She reached out and squeezed his hand. "I appreciate you watching out for my feelings but talking about weddings won't reduce me to tears. I promise. Let's get started."

His gaze met hers and his breath caught in his throat. He was going to have to be really careful around her or he just might be tempted to start something that neither of them was ready for. And once he got something started with her, he wasn't sure he'd ever be able to end it when reality crashed in around them.

CHAPTER FOURTEEN

THIS IS IT!

At last, it was her big break.

Kayla grinned as she sat by the pool the next day. She could hardly believe that at last her plans were all coming together. If only she could keep her attraction to Angelo under wraps. Was that even possible at this point?

Who'd have thought that the wish she'd made at the fountain would actually come true?

Angelo had kissed her—again.

Her eyelids drifted closed as her thoughts spiraled back to their amazing day beneath the Tuscany sun. The day couldn't have gone any better. She'd always treasure it. And then there had been that mind-blowing, toe-curling kiss—

"And what has you staring off into space with a smile on your face?"

Kayla glanced up to find Angelo gazing at her. "Um… nothing. I… I mean I was thinking about the wedding."

"How about the Van Holsen account? We don't want to forget about it."

"Of course not. I've sent out the new concepts to the art department."

"Good." He took a seat next to her. "You know if you're having problems you can talk to me?"

Was he referring to personal problems? Or business ones? Since they'd arrived in Italy the lines had blurred so much that she wasn't sure. But she decided that it was best for her career to take his comment as a purely professional one.

"I understand." She smoothed her hands down over her white capris. "And so far the accounts are all moving along.

I should have some drafts back from the art department this afternoon to run by you."

"Sounds good. Can I see what you've come up with so far for the royal wedding?"

She pushed her notebook over to him. "Go ahead."

The seconds slowly passed as his gaze moved down over the first page. "But this is all about Monte Calanetti." He shoved aside the pages. "There's nothing here about the wedding itself. Nothing sentimental or romantic."

Oh, boy.

This was not the start she'd imagined. She swallowed a lump in her throat. To be honest, she wasn't ready to present her ideas to him. They were only partial thoughts—snippets of this and that.

She'd have to think fast on her feet if she wanted him to keep her on this account, because she wasn't about to let this opportunity slip through her fingers. She leveled her shoulders and tilted her chin up, meeting his frown. "I think the main focus should be all about the location."

"You do?"

She nodded. "The royal couple have already been taken by the village's charm." Kayla lowered her voice and added, "I was taken by it, too. It'd be the perfect backdrop for a wedding. And that's the part I think we should exploit."

Angelo's eyes widened and he was quiet for a moment as though considering her words. "What issues do you have with basing the pitch on the wedding itself? You know with all of the pomp and circumstance. We could even throw in a horse-drawn carriage for good measure."

Kayla smiled, loving the idea of six white horses leading a shiny white carriage with gold trim. And then her imagination took a wild turn and there was Angelo next to her in the carriage. Her insides quivered at the thought. Then, realizing that she was getting off point, she gave herself a mental jerk.

"We don't know anything about what the bride wants for the actual ceremony. But we need to show them that no matter whether it is a big, splashy affair, which seems most reasonable considering it's a royal wedding, or whether they want something smaller and more intimate, that Monte Calanetti can be quite accommodating."

Angelo leaned back and crossed his arms as he quietly stared at her. He was taking her suggestions seriously. She inwardly cheered. Not about to lose her momentum, she continued. "No matter what the size of the ceremony, we need to show them that we are willing to work with the bride. We need to show them that the whole community will come together to make it a day that neither of them will ever forget."

"So you think our approach should be two-pronged, showing the village both as intimate and accommodating."

Kayla nodded. "The tour you gave me was a great start. But if we are going to sell the royals on the virtues of this village, I think we need to dig deeper."

Angelo nodded. "Sounds reasonable. What do you have in mind?"

Before she could continue, her phone vibrated on the table. She'd turned off the ringer, not wanting to bother anyone else who was around the pool.

"Do you need to get that?" Angelo's gaze moved from her to the phone.

"Um...no."

Angelo cocked a brow. "It could be the office."

"I already checked my voice mail and sorted everything that needs attention." She wanted to get back to their conversation, but he kept glancing at her phone. Knowing he wasn't going to let up on this subject until he found out why she was so hesitant to answer, she grabbed her phone and checked the ID. Just as she'd suspected, the call was from the States but it wasn't the office—it was Pam, the woman handling the fund-raiser while Kayla was in Italy.

"It's nothing urgent." Kayla would deal with it later.

"Are you sure?"

"I am." This wasn't Pam's first call of the day nor would it likely be her last.

Why was Angelo looking at her that way? It was as though he could see that she was holding something back. And the last thing Kayla needed was for him not to trust her. Because this royal wedding was the opportunity of a lifetime. She planned to grasp it with both hands and hold on tight. Having Angelo make her an official part of this pitch would be the validation she needed to show her parents that she'd made the right decision with her life. At last, they'd be proud of her and her choices.

"Okay." He waved away the phone and grabbed for her notebook again. "You need to add more detail to these notes."

"I will, but I was thinking we need to visit each of the establishments in the village again. I could write up very specific notes about their specialties—things that will be hard to find elsewhere—items that the village is especially proud of."

His eyes lit up. "And I know exactly where we'll start."

"You do?" She smiled, knowing he liked her ideas. "Where?"

"Mancini's. You did bring something pretty, formal—Oh, you know what I mean."

"A little black dress?"

"Yes, that will do nicely. We have reservations at seven. Consider it a research expedition during which I want to hear more of your thoughts."

Her mounting excitement skidded to a halt upon his assurance that this evening would be all about business. She didn't know why she should let it bother her. This is what she wanted—for things to return to a business relationship. Wasn't it?

* * *

Time flew by far too fast.

A week had passed since their dinner at Mancini's. Angelo had been quite impressed with the service and most especially the food. What Raffaele was doing spending his time here in the countryside was beyond Angelo. The man was a magician in the kitchen. He could head up any restaurant that he set his sights on from Rome to New York. Although, it was lucky for Angelo, because Mancini's award-winning menu was going to be the centerpiece of the pitch.

Angelo stood in the middle of the hotel suite. He really liked what he saw. His gaze zeroed in on Kayla. They'd had a couple of tables brought in. The room had been rearranged so that the area loosely resembled an office more than a relaxing, posh hotel room. And it seemed to be helping them to stay on track.

Feeling the pressure to get this right, Angelo had relented and had Kayla pass along some of their other accounts to his top ad executive. Their attention needed to be centered on the wedding, especially since he'd already lost time spinning his wheels. One of the accounts they had retained was Victoria Van Holsen's account. The woman simply wouldn't deal with anyone but himself or Kayla. Victoria, who was quite particular about who she dealt with, had surprisingly taken to Kayla's sunny disposition. It seemed no one was immune to Kayla's charms—him included.

There was so much more to Kayla than he'd given her credit for when he'd hired her as his temporary assistant. Sure, her résumé had been excellent and her supervisors had nothing but glowing reports about her. Still, he was so busy rushing from meeting to meeting, cutting a new deal and approving the latest cutting-edge promotion that he never had time to notice the girl behind the black-rimmed glasses and the nondescript business suits.

While in Italy, he'd witnessed firsthand her passion for her work. She invigorated him to work harder and dig deeper for fresh ideas to top her own, which was nearly impossible as she came up with ideas for the wedding that never would have crossed his mind. To say she was a hard worker was an understatement. She was amazing and it wasn't just her work ethic that fascinated him.

Her smile lit up his world like the golden rays of the morning sun. And when he would lean over her shoulder, he'd get a whiff of her sweet, intoxicating scent. It conjured up the image of a field of wildflowers in his mind and always tempted him to lean in closer for a deeper whiff.

Then there were times like now, when she was concentrating so hard that her green eyes grew darker. She lifted her hand and twirled a long red curl around her finger. He noticed that she did this when she was unsure of something. He wondered what was troubling her now.

He moved closer. "Need some help?"

She glanced up with a wide-eyed stare as though she'd been totally lost in her thoughts. "Um...what?"

This wasn't the first time she'd been so lost in her thoughts that she hadn't heard him. "I said, would you like some help?"

"Sure. I was contemplating the piazza. I'm thinking it should play a prominent part in the wedding processional."

Her words sparked his own imagination. They made a great couple...um, team. He couldn't remember the last time he'd felt this invigorated. "How about having a horse-drawn carriage circle the fountain, giving the villagers a chance to cheer on the future queen?"

"I don't know. The bride will be a bundle of nerves. I don't know if she'll want to spend the time waving at people—"

"Sure she will."

Kayla sent him a doubtful look. "What would you know about weddings?"

"Nothing." His jaw tightened. And he planned to keep it that way. "You're forgetting one important thing."

"And what's that?"

"The villagers are the part that makes the village special."

A smile eased the worry lines on her face. "I'm glad you were paying attention while on our tour. And if the bride is willing, I think the villagers should play a prominent role in the festivities."

"And along the route there could be large royal flags waving in the breeze—"

"No. That's too impersonal." Her eyes sparkled. "What if we hand out small complimentary flags to the onlookers to welcome the newest member of the royal family?"

Angelo paused as he considered the idea. "I like it. It'll be a sea of color."

"I also think the chapel should be included in the pitch." Before he could utter a word, she rushed on. "The place is so beautiful. Sure it needs some work, but it has such a romantic feel to it. Just imagine it filled with roses— No, make that lilies. And the glow of the candles would add to the magic. Can't you just imagine it all?"

"No." He didn't believe in magic or romance. They were just fanciful thoughts. "I can't imagine anyone wanting to get married in such a dump—"

"It's not a dump!"

He ignored her outburst. "Besides, you're forgetting that I talked to the new owner and she wants nothing to do with the wedding."

"And that's it…you're just giving up? She could change her mind."

What was Kayla getting so worked up for? He wasn't making up these problems. "The chapel is crumbling. We are not putting it in the pitch. The royal couple would laugh us out of the room if we presented it—"

"They would not." Her words were rushed and loud. "They'd love its charm."

His muscles tensed. He hated conflict. "We're not using it!"

Her fine brows drew together as she crossed her arms. "You're making a mistake!"

He wasn't used to people challenging his decisions and they certainly didn't raise their voice to him. This argument was ending now. "This is my company—my decision! We're not including the chapel." When she went to speak, he added, "End of story."

She huffed but said nothing more.

For a while, they worked in an uncomfortable silence. He kept waiting for Kayla to rehash their disagreement, but she surprised him and let it go. He didn't know how much time had passed when they started to communicate like normal again.

Angelo rubbed his jaw. "Perhaps our best option is to take all of these photos and do a workup of each setting. We can have sketches made up of how each wedding scenario would work. Nothing sells better than letting the client see it with their own eyes. I'll have the art department start on it right away. They'll be on solid overtime until our meeting with the happy couple."

"You never said— Where is the meeting? At Nico's villa?"

"No. The meeting is in Halencia. It's an island not far from here."

"Oh, how exciting. You must be nervous to be meeting a real prince and his bride."

"Me? What about you?"

"What about me?"

"You're part of this team. You'll be going, too. I hope you have something in your suitcase suitable for a royal meeting. If not, perhaps you can find an outfit or two in the village."

Kayla's mouth gaped open and he couldn't help but chuckle. She looked absolutely stunned. Surely she didn't think that he'd put her to all of this work and then leave her behind. He was never one to take credit for another person's work, and he wasn't about to start now. Kayla deserved this honor.

But he sensed something else was on her mind. He could see the subtle worry lines marring her beautiful complexion when she didn't think he was looking. He had no doubt she was still smarting over his unilateral decision to scrap the chapel proposal. She had to accept that he knew what he was doing.

Just then a cell phone vibrated, rattling against the tabletop. Not sure whose phone it was, Angelo headed for the table in time to witness Kayla grabbing her phone and turning it off without bothering to take the call. She'd been doing it a lot lately.

He cleared his throat. "You know, just because I'm here doesn't mean you can't take a phone call from home now and then."

She shook her head. "It…it was nothing."

"Are you sure about that? I get the distinct feeling that the call was definitely something."

"I told you it's nothing important." Her voice rose with each syllable. "Why are you making such a big deal of it?"

"I just thought it might be important."

Her gaze didn't meet his. Her voice was heated and her words were rushed. "It's nothing for you to worry about. Besides, we have work to do."

He'd never witnessed Kayla losing her composure—ever. What was wrong with her? And why wouldn't she open up to him?

"Kayla, if you need a break—"

"I don't." She ran her fingers through her long red curls before twisting the strands around her fingertip. "Can we get back to work?"

His jaw tightened. These heated exchanges reminded him of his parents, and not in a good way. Kayla had just reinforced his determination to remain single. He wanted absolutely nothing to do with a turbulent relationship.

"Work sounds like a good idea." He turned to his laptop. Before he could even type in his password, Kayla softly called out his name. In fact, her voice was so soft that he was sure he'd imagined it. He glanced over his shoulder to find her standing next to him.

Her gaze was downcast and her fingers were laced together. "I'm sorry for snapping. I didn't mean to grouch at you. I... I—"

Before she could go any further, he uttered, "It's okay. We're both under a lot of pressure, working night and day to get this pitch perfected."

Her eyes widened in surprise. "Thanks for understanding. It won't happen again."

He didn't doubt that she meant it, but he was a realist and knew that blowups happened even in the best of relationships. So where did they go from here?

When he didn't immediately say anything, she added, "The phone call was a friend. I'll deal with it later."

Not about to repeat their earlier argument, he let her comment slide. "Then let's get back to work. We have the menu to work into the layout."

He didn't miss the way she played with her hair—the telltale sign she was nervous. Oh, that call was definitely something important. All of his suspicions were now confirmed. So what could be so important that it had her jumping for the phone, and yet she refused to take the call in front of him? A boyfriend? But she'd already stated categorically that she didn't have one, and he believed her.

So what had her nervous and fidgeting with her hair? What didn't she want him to know? And why was he more concerned about her blasted phone calls and mysterious ways than he was about this presentation that was quickly approaching?

He really needed to get his head in this game or Monte Calanetti would lose the pitch before they even gave their presentation in Halencia. But with Kayla so close by it was difficult at times to remember that she was here to work and not to fulfill his growing fantasies.

Moonbeams danced upon the window sheers as Kayla leaned back in her chair. They'd been working on this pitch night and day, trying to make it beyond amazing. A yawn passed her lips. Not even coffee was helping her at this point.

"You should call it a night." Angelo stared at her over the top of his laptop. "I've got this."

Not about to let him think she wasn't as dedicated to this project as he was, she said, "If you're staying up, so am I."

He sent her an I-don't-believe-you're-so-stubborn look. "If you insist—"

"I do." She crossed her arms. Even that movement took a lot of effort.

He arched a brow, but he didn't argue. "How about we take a break? I'm starved."

"Sounds good to me, but I don't think there's any room service at this hour."

"Who needs room service? There's still half of a pizza in the fridge."

"Oh. I forgot."

In no time, Angelo warmed them each a couple of slices in the microwave in their kitchenette. After handing her a plate, he moved to the couch. "Sorry, I can't provide you anything else."

"This is plenty. It reminds me of my college days. Leftover pizza for breakfast was a common staple in the dorms."

Angelo leaned back, kicked off his loafers and propped his feet up on the coffee table. There was no longer any boss/employee awkwardness between them. Being closed up in a hotel suite, no matter how fancy, left no room for cool distances. In fact, they'd shared some passionate disagreements over the pitch, which only led them to better, outside-the-box ideas. But it was far too late for any passionate conversations—at least the professional ones.

"I'm surprised your parents let you go to college." Angelo's voice roused her from her exhaustion-induced fantasy.

"Why?"

"Because they had your life planned out to be a wife, to be a mom and to take over the family business. Why spend the money and time on an advanced degree if you weren't going to use it?"

The fact that Angelo Amatucci, star of Madison Avenue, was truly interested in her life sent her heart fluttering. "It was hard for them to object when I won an academic scholarship. Plus, they knew I had my heart set on earning a degree. My guess is they thought I'd go, have fun with my friends for a few years and eventually realize my place was with them in Paradise." Her gaze met his. "Didn't your parents expect you to return to Italy after you graduated college?"

He glanced away as he tossed his plate of half-eaten pizza onto the table. "My family is quite different from yours. Their expectations weren't the same."

"I have a hard time believing that, after seeing how much your brother and sister miss you. Maybe you can slow down and fly here more often."

"I don't know." He rubbed the back of his neck. "I'd have to find someone to help with the special accounts—someone the clients would trust."

"Do you have anyone in mind?"

His steady gaze met hers, making her stomach quiver.

"I have an idea or two. And how about you? Is Amatucci & Associates just a stepping-stone for you? Do you have other plans for your future?"

"I'm exactly where I want to be."

His gaze dipped to her lips and then back to her eyes. "That's good to know. I want you here, too." He glanced away. "I mean at the company. You've become really important to me." He cleared his throat. "To the company. You know, it's really late. Let's call it a night and pick up where we left off tomorrow. You know, with the pitch."

Kayla sat there quietly as her normally calm, composed boss tripped and fell over his words. She wanted to tell him to relax because she liked him, too—a lot. The words teetered on the tip of her tongue when he jumped to his feet and moved across the room to shut down his computer.

Disappointment settled in her chest. Shouting her feelings across the room just didn't seem right, nor did she have the guts to do it. And by the rigid line of his shoulders, he wasn't ready to hear the words. She had to accept that the fleeting moment had passed—if it had truly been there at all.

She tried to tell herself that it was for the best. Taking a risk on revealing her feelings to Angelo was putting all of her hopes and dreams on the line, but she wasn't much of a gambler. She liked sure bets. At the moment, the odds were really good that she'd gain a promotion if they pulled off this royal pitch. And that's what she needed to focus on—not on the way Angelo's intense gaze could make her stomach do a series of somersaults.

CHAPTER FIFTEEN

THIS COULDN'T BE HAPPENING.

Two days before Angelo's private jet was scheduled to sweep them off to the Mediterranean island of Halencia, Kayla received yet another phone call from Pam. However with Angelo hovering so close by and forever checking over her shoulder to see the progress she was making with their pitch, she couldn't answer the call. No way. No how.

Kayla sent the call to voice mail before returning to the email she was composing. But a thought had been nagging at her that perhaps after their talk Angelo might have changed his stance on the company doing some charity work. There were so many worthy causes out there that really could use the power of Amatucci & Associates to make a difference. And she wasn't just thinking of her beloved after-school program.

There were countless other organizations that were worthy of a helping hand. Perhaps it was worth a shot. What was the worst that could happen? He would tell her to drop the subject and get back to work? Because surely at this point he wouldn't fire her, would he?

"You've done a really good job with this pitch." And she meant it. Angelo was very talented and creative. If he weren't, he wouldn't be at the top of his game. "It might be a nice idea if you'd considered implementing a charity program at the office. I know a lot of people would be willing to help—"

"No."

Just a one-word answer? Really? Kayla tried to accept it as his final word, but she was having problems swallowing such a quick dismissal. Why did he have to be so close-minded? Was he that worried about his bottom line?

She stared at him. How was it possible that the same man who had escorted her around the village and had shared some of his childhood memories with her could be opposed to helping charities? There had to be something more to his decision.

Maybe if she understood, she could change his mind—make him see that charities needed his special kind of help. Not everyone was gifted in getting the word out in so many different capacities from tweeting to commercials and radio spots. Not to mention that Angelo had an army of contacts in Hollywood willing to help him when needed.

"Why are you so opposed to the idea of helping out charity organizations?"

"You just aren't going to let this go, are you?"

She shook her head. How could she be honest with him about what had her distracted when she knew that it would put her job in jeopardy? Maybe if she understood his reasons, it would bridge the divide. "Explain it to me."

He raked his fingers through his hair and pulled out a chair next to her. "When I came to the States, I was alone. I didn't know anyone. And I'll admit that it wasn't easy and there were a few scary moments."

This certainly wasn't the explanation that she was expecting, but she liked that he was opening up to her, little by little. "I can't even imagine what that must have been like for you. I mean, I moved to New York City and I didn't know a soul here, but I was only a car ride away from my family. You practically moved halfway around the world."

"I didn't have a choice." His lips pressed together into a firm line as though stopping what was about to come out of his mouth.

"What do you mean?"

"Nothing. It's just that when I was in school, I got caught up in the football team and my dream of graduating college started to fade into the rearview mirror. Now granted, that isn't the same as working for a charitable organization, but

I learned a valuable lesson—if I wanted to be the best at whatever I decided to do, I had to commit myself 100 percent. I couldn't let myself get distracted."

Was that happening to her with the fund-raiser? Was she spreading herself too thin? Was she trying to cover too many bases?

She didn't want to accept that she was setting herself up to fail. He had to be wrong. "Couldn't you have done both in moderation?"

"You're not understanding me—I had to succeed—I had to be the best to get anywhere in New York City. Competition is fierce and if I failed, I couldn't go home."

"Sure you could have—"

"You don't know what you're talking about." His intense stare met hers, warning her not to delve further into that subject. "The point is that I know what happens when people become distracted for any reason—no matter how good the cause. They lose their focus. Their ambition dwindles. And that can't happen to Amatucci & Associates. I hate to say it, but it's a cutthroat business. If we lose our edge, the competitors will swoop in and steal away our clients."

Between the lines she read, if she lost her edge—if she didn't give 100 percent—she'd lose her dream. She'd fail and return to Paradise with her tail between her legs. Her stomach twisted into a queasy knot.

She clasped her hands together. Knowing all of this, there was no way she was about to confess to Angelo that she was spending every free moment handling a fund-raiser that seemed to hit one snag after the next. He'd think she wasn't dedicated to her career—that couldn't be further from the truth.

She cleared the lump from the back of her throat. "And that's why you compromise and write generous checks each year to the various organizations?"

He nodded. "I didn't say I wasn't sympathetic. But the office policy stands. End of discussion."

She was more than happy to change subjects, and he'd touched upon one that she was most curious about. "And your parents—"

"Are not part of this discussion."

They might not be, but that didn't mean that she didn't understand a whole lot more about them now. At last, the pieces of his family life started to fall into place. She had wondered why they weren't at the villa to greet Angelo. Nor were they around to help their daughter cope with her unplanned pregnancy. There was definitely discord, and it must run quite deep if Angelo still wasn't ready to broach the subject.

Something told her that he'd closed himself off from that part of his life and focused on his business not so much because he was worried about losing focus, but rather because he found his business safe. It lacked the ability to wound him the way family could do with just a word or a look. That was why he was so cold and professional most of the time. It was his shield.

That was no way to live. There was so much more in life to experience. And she desperately wanted to show him that…and so much more.

But how was she to help him if he wasn't willing to open up?

"Help! I don't know what to do. Everything is ruined."

Kayla's heart lurched at the sound of Pam's panicked voice. She gripped the phone tightly and reminded herself that Pam tended to overreact. Things with the ICL fundraiser had been going pretty well. Ticket sales were still lagging but the radio spots were helping. What could be wrong now?

"Pam, slow down."

"But we don't have time."

"Take a deep breath. It can't be as bad as you're thinking."

"No, it could be worse." Pam sniffled.

Okay. What had happened this time? Did Pam lose another file on her computer? Or misplace the phone number for the manager of the headline band? Pam did blow things out of proportion.

"Pam, pull yourself together and tell me what happened." While Kayla hoped for the best, she steeled herself for a catastrophe.

"They canceled."

Kayla sat up straight, knocking her empty water glass over. Surely she hadn't heard correctly. "Who canceled?"

"The band." Pam started to cry again.

Impossible. "The band quit?"

"Yes! What are you going to do?" She hiccupped.

"But they can't just quit. We have an agreement—a contract."

"That...that's what I said. They said there was a clause or some sort of thing in there that let them back out."

Kayla rubbed her forehead. This couldn't be happening. What was she supposed to do about it all the way in Italy?

"I... I just can't do this anymore. Everyone is yelling at me." The sniffles echoed across the Atlantic. "I can't."

Oh, no. She couldn't have Pam backing out on her, too. "Calm down." Kayla's hands grew clammy as she tightened her hold on the phone. "You can't quit. The kids are counting on us. We can't let them down."

"But what are you going to do? You have to fix this. I can't."

Kayla wanted to yell that she didn't know but that the whining wasn't helping anyone. "I don't know yet. What did the band say was the problem?"

"They got a contract with some big band to be the opening act on a cross-country tour. They leave before the concert."

It'd certainly be hard to compete with a national tour.

Most likely this was the band's big break and Kayla's heart sank, knowing that wild horses couldn't hold them back. And to be honest, she couldn't blame them. This was what they'd been working toward for so long now. But none of that helped her or the fund-raiser.

Kayla struggled to speak calmly. "Just sit tight. I'll think of something."

"You know of another band that can fill in at the last minute?"

She didn't have a clue where to find a replacement. In fact, she'd totally lucked into that first band. A friend of a friend knew the band manager, who liked the idea of free publicity. Where in the world would she locate another band?

"I need time to think." Kayla said, feeling as though the world was crumbling around her.

"But what do I tell people?"

"Tell them that we'll have an announcement soon."

Kayla ended the call. Her mind was spinning. She didn't know how she was going to save the event. The enormity of the situation was only beginning to settle in. With no headline act, there was no point. The tickets would have to be refunded. The Inner City League after-school program would cease to exist.

All of those at-risk kids would be turned away.

No! She refused to fail them. Visions of Gina's smiling face, Patrick's pout when she didn't have time to throw the ball with him and Lilly's anxious look as she'd handed Kayla a new drawing filled her mind. And there were so many more faces—all counting on her to come through for them.

Something splashed her hand. Kayla glanced down to see a tear streak down the back of her hand. She lifted her fingers and touched her cheek, finding it damp. At that moment, she heard the door to the suite open. She took a deep calming breath and dashed the back of her hands across her cheeks.

"I'm back." Angelo's deep voice echoed through the large room. "Did I miss anything?"

Talk about a loaded question. "Um...no." She struggled to sound normal as she kept her back to him. She blinked repeatedly and resisted the urge to fan her overheated face. "Nothing much happened around here."

"You were right about approaching my brother." He paused. "Kayla?"

"Yes."

"Is there a reason I'm talking to the back of your head?" She shook her head. "I'm just finishing up an email."

"Do you want to hear this?"

"Um...yes. Of course. I can do two things at once."

There was an extended pause as though he was deciding if she were truly interested or not. "Well, I asked Nico for permission to offer up his vineyard as one of the sites for the wedding. The photographer from the village is stopping by tomorrow to take some professional photos."

"I'm glad the meeting went smoothly between you and your brother. What about the new owner of the neighboring vineyard? What did you say her name was?"

"Louisa something or other." He rubbed the back of his neck. "I talked to her about using her vineyard, since it's larger than Nico's place, but she was adamant that she wants absolutely nothing to do with the wedding."

"Really? How odd."

"Not as odd as this."

"What do you mean?" Kayla hated putting on this pretense, but she knew that he would never abide her splitting her work hours between the royal wedding and a charity event. He'd already made that abundantly clear.

"You won't face me and there's something off with your voice." His approaching footsteps had her body tensing. He knelt down next to her. He placed a finger beneath her chin and turned her face to his. "Now tell me, what's got you upset?"

His voice was so soft and comforting. All she wanted to do in that moment was lean into his arms and rest her face in the crook of his neck. She wanted to feel the comfort and security of his strong arms holding her close. She wanted him to tell her that everything would be all right—that they would work together to find a solution.

But none of that could or would happen. Angelo would never understand how she'd knowingly gone behind his back to work on this fund-raiser instead of focusing solely on the royal wedding. She'd never be able to justify her actions to his satisfaction.

"I'm fine." Her gaze didn't meet his.

"You're not fine. Not by a long shot." As though he'd been privy to her thoughts, he reached out and pulled her to him.

She shouldn't do this. It wasn't right. But her body had other thoughts and willingly followed his lead. Her cheek pressed against the firmness of his shoulder and she inhaled the spicy scent of his cologne mingled with his male scent. It was quite intoxicating.

Her eyes drifted closed and for a moment she let go of everything. The silent tears streamed down her cheeks. She took comfort in the way Angelo's hands rubbed her back. It wove a spell over her and relaxed muscles that she hadn't realized were stiff.

"I'm sorry for working you too hard."

She dashed her fingers over her cheeks and pulled back. "You aren't making me work this hard—I want to do it. I want to do everything to make our pitch stand out."

He ran his hands up her arms, sending goose bumps racing down her skin. "But not to the point where you've worn yourself to a frazzle. Look at you. You've gotten yourself all worked up."

She shook her head. No matter how much she wanted

to open up to him, she couldn't. They only had two days until they had to catch a plane to Halencia, and they still didn't have a completed pitch. And what they had didn't sparkle. And it didn't scream "pick me." There was something missing, but she just couldn't put her finger on it. And now, add to it the problem with the fund-raiser and she was at a total loss.

"Kayla, if you won't talk to me, how can I help?"

Her gaze met his, and she saw the worry reflected in his eyes. "You can't."

"Why don't you give me a chance?"

He just wasn't going to let this go. His eyes begged her to open up to him—to trust him. But she couldn't give up her dream of being the sort of person that Angelo Amatucci would want as an ad executive—she'd given up everything to follow this dream. She couldn't return to Paradise and face her parents as a failure.

"The truth is I... I have a headache." And that wasn't a lie. The stress of everything had her temples pounding.

He studied her for a moment as though weighing her words. "Did you take anything for it?"

"I was about to, but I hadn't made it there yet."

Angelo nodded as though he knew what needed to be done. "Go lie down on the couch and rest—"

"But I have stuff that needs done—"

"Later. Right now, you're going to rest. I'll get some medication for you."

His thoughtfulness only made her feel worse—about everything—most especially that she couldn't open up to him. She was certain that he would have some amazing suggestion that would save the fund-raiser, but she just couldn't risk everything she'd worked for. Instead, she'd have to pray for a miracle.

CHAPTER SIXTEEN

He was as ready as he would ever be.

Angelo kept telling himself that, hoping it would sink in.

As the royal limo ushered them through the streets of Halencia toward the palace, Angelo stared out the window. Mounting tension over this meeting had his body stiff. This sort of reaction was unfamiliar to him. Usually he was calm, cool and collected. He was the expert when it came to marketing. But ever since he'd let his guard down around Kayla, he'd lost that cool aloofness that he counted on when doing business.

She'd gotten past his defenses and had him connecting with his emotions. He just hoped he hadn't lost his edge—the confidence needed to execute a pitch and sell the buyer on his—er—their ideas.

The flight had been a short one as Halencia was just a small island nation not far off the coast of Italy. Angelo had noticed how Kayla kept to herself, working on her computer. He had no idea what she'd been working on because at that point the pitch had been locked in. They had the talking points nailed down and the graphics were in order. He'd made sure to include what he considered the key element—a sample menu from Raffaelle's restaurant. All combined, he hoped this pitch would clinch the royal couple's interest.

Kayla had even insisted on bringing along some of the baked goods for the royal couple to sample. They were fresh baked that morning and delivered to their hotel suite. He'd tried to taste them, but Kayla had smacked his hand away with a warning glance. Everyone in Monte Calanetti was excited and more than willing to do their part to help.

But Kayla had him worried. She'd been so quiet on the flight here. And now as she leaned against the door of the limo with her face to the window, the bubbly woman who toured Monte Calanetti was gone. He didn't recognize this new person.

He cleared his throat. "Are you feeling all right?"

Kayla turned to him, the dark circles under her eyes were pronounced. His gut tightened.

She smiled, but her lips barely lifted at the corners. "Sure. I'm fine."

He wasn't going to argue the point when it was obvious that she was anything but fine. "You did an excellent job preparing the pitch."

She shrugged. "I don't know. I guess it all depends on what the royal couple says."

He shook his head. "It doesn't matter whether they chose Monte Calanetti or not for the wedding, I know for a fact that you went above and beyond for this project." He hated how his praise seemed to barely faze her. She'd worn herself out and he'd been so busy trying to tie up all of the loose ends for this pitch that he'd failed to notice.

On the flight to Halencia, he'd been mulling over how to recognize Kayla's tremendous effort. He decided to share part of it with her now. "And when we get back to New York, you'll be rewarded for your accomplishments not only with the royal pitch but also with the success of the Van Holsen account."

Her eyes widened. "Really? I… I mean thank you."

Before she could say more, her phone buzzed. She swiped her finger over the screen and frowned. Her fingers moved rapidly over the touch screen as her frown deepened.

Even Angelo had his limits. Work could wait. They were almost at the palace and having her upset was not going to be a good way to start their meeting with the royal couple. He reached out and snagged her phone from her.

She glanced up and her mouth gaped open. Then her lips pressed together into a firm line and her gaze narrowed.

She held out her hand. "It's important."

"It can wait."

"No, it can't."

The car slowed as they eased through the gates leading up the drive to the palace. "We're here. Forget the rest of the world and enjoy this adventure. It isn't every day you get a royal invitation to a palace."

Kayla turned to the window as they wound their way up the paved drive lined with statues and greenery. It was very prestigious and yet it wasn't overly pretentious. In fact, he found it quite a fitting reflection of their nobility. He just hoped that they'd find the prince and his bride to have the same unassuming demeanor.

When the palace came into view, Angelo was taken by surprise at the enormity of it. The palace stood three stories high and appeared to be a large square with towers at each corner. The outside was painted a sunny yellow while the numerous windows were outlined in white. Grand, sweeping stairs led the way to a large patio area with two enormous doors in the background that granted access to the palace.

There weren't that many things in life that still took Angelo's breath away, but he had to admit that this palace was an amazing piece of architecture. And with the abundance of greenery and bright flowers, it was definitely like stepping into paradise. He couldn't even imagine what it must be like calling this place home.

The car swung up the drive and stopped right in front of the palace. To one side was a garden with a fountain in the center. It was quite inviting. He could easily imagine taking Kayla for a stroll through it after dinner as the setting sun cast a watermelon hue over the sky. They'd stop to admire a flower and she'd turn to him. The breeze would rush through her hair as her gaze would meet his. Then his attention would move to her lips. No words would be necessary as they'd lean into each other's arms.

"Angelo, this is amazing."

Kayla's voice jerked him from his daydream, which was in fact amazing. "Um…yes. This is quite beautiful."

"Is this your first visit?"

"It is. I've never done business in this part of the world before." Though he had done business in a great many other countries.

As beautiful as the grounds were, Angelo's attention was drawn back to Kayla. He had plans for her. A surprise after their big presentation. At first, he'd been hesitant, but now, seeing how weary she was, he was certain that he'd made the right decision. He just hoped she would relax long enough to enjoy it.

He still had the feeling that she was keeping something from him—something that was eating at her. But what was it? Was she worried that he'd make another move on her?

The thought left him feeling unsettled. Granted, he wasn't that good at reading women. They were forever a mystery to him, but he'd swear that she was into him and his kisses. She'd come alive in his arms. He was certain that he hadn't imagined that. So then, what had her putting an unusually big gap between them in the limo?

He was impressive.

Kayla sat in one of the plush chairs in the palace's state room. Instead of taking a closer view of the ornate ceiling with large crystal chandeliers, the red walls with white trim, the huge paintings of historical figures or the priceless statues on pedestals, her entire attention was focused on Angelo as he stood in the front of the room in his freshly pressed navy suit and maroon tie. Every inch of him looked as if he'd just stepped off the cover of a men's magazine. He was definitely the most handsome man she'd ever laid her eyes on.

And his presentation was truly impressive. If this didn't sell the royal couple on the benefits of holding the royal wedding in Monte Calanetti, then nothing would. Angelo's talk was informative while containing bits of entertainment. Sure, he'd gone over it with her back in Italy, but somehow here in front of the royal prince and his bride, it seemed so much more special—more dynamic.

"Monte Calanetti offers a variety of services from a world-renowned chef to the most delicious bakery." Angelo moved off to the side while Kayla started the slideshow presentation on a large high-definition screen. "You can see here an overview of the village—"

With the slideshow up and running, Kayla's thoughts spiraled away from the presentation she knew verbatim. Instead, she was amazed by the man making the presentation. Though he didn't have the best one-on-one people skills, he was truly amazing when he was selling an idea. His voice was strong, sure and unwavering. His tone was cajoling. And his posture was confident but not cocky. No wonder he was the best in the business.

So then how in the world was he so inept when it came to dealing with people—people like his family? People like her? Why did he have to make it so tough to get close to him?

Why couldn't he let his guard down and take a chance on love like the crown prince and his Cinderella bride? Kayla's gaze moved to the soon-to-be couple, envious that they seemed to have it all—success, stability and most of all love.

But as they sat there surrounded by their staff, Kayla didn't see any telltale signs of love. There were no clasped hands. No loving gazes when they thought no one was looking. No nothing.

Kayla gave herself a mental jerk. She was overthinking things. Of course they were being all businesslike. This was their wedding—a wedding that would have all of the world watching. That had to be their focus right now.

Still, there was something that nagged at her about the couple, but she brushed it off. Whatever it was—bridal nerves or such—it was absolutely none of her business. She had enough of her own problems.

He'd nailed it.

Angelo wore an easy smile. The presentation had gone without a hitch. Everything had fallen into place just as he'd practiced it over and over again with Kayla in their hotel suite. He had a good feeling that Monte Calanetti would be in serious contention for the site of the royal wedding.

After the slideshow presentation was over, Angelo asked, "Are there any questions?"

"Yes." The bride, Christina Rose, sat up straight. "I didn't see anything in your presentation about the chapel. I'm particularly interested in it."

Angelo's gut knotted. He'd been wrong. His gaze sought out Kayla. He was certain that she'd be wearing an I-told-you-so look. But her chair was empty? Where had she gone? The next thing he knew Kayla was standing next to him. What in the world?

"Hi. I'm Kayla." She sent him an I've-got-this smile. "The chapel is my part of the presentation."

He moved away and went to take a seat. What in the world did Kayla have up her sleeve? He thought they'd settled this back in Monte Calanetti—no chapel presentation. His back teeth ground together as he remembered that call had been his.

Angelo leaned back in his chair while Kayla put photos of the chapel up on the screen with a pitch that he'd never heard before, but it sounded like music to his ears. So the little minx had gone behind his back and done exactly what he'd told her not to do.

And he couldn't be happier.

After Kayla finished her short presentation, the bride

spoke up again. "The chapel—you mentioned that it had just switched ownership—the new owner—have they approved the use of it for the wedding?"

Seriously? That had to be the first question. Kayla's gaze momentarily strayed to him. He had no help to offer her, but he was anxious to see how she handled the question.

Kayla laced her fingers together. "At this moment, we have not obtained a release for the use of the chapel." The bride's face creased with frown lines. That was definitely not a good sign. "Knowing the chapel is of particular interest to you, we will make it a priority to secure its use for the wedding."

The young woman's eyes lit up, but she didn't say anything as she glanced over at the crown prince. He didn't speak to Kayla, either, but rather conversed softly with his advisors, who had a list of questions.

Kayla handled the inquiries with calm and grace. Angelo couldn't have done any better. She certainly was full of surprises, and he couldn't be happier having her by his side.

It wasn't until much later that Angelo walked with her toward their rooms. This was their first chance to talk privately since the presentation. As they strolled along the elegant hallways, Kayla waited anxiously to hear Angelo's thoughts on how she'd handled her part of the meeting. She hoped he wasn't too upset about her ignoring his dictate about the chapel.

Angelo stopped and turned to face her. "Stop looking so worried. You did an excellent job today."

"I did?"

He nodded. "I owe you an apology for not listening to you and a thank-you for being so prepared."

"Really? Even though I didn't do what you said?"

He gazed deep into her eyes. "I think you have excellent instincts and the courage to follow them. You've got what it takes to have a very bright future."

In her excitement, she threw her arms around him. He had no idea how much she needed this one perfect moment.

Coming back to earth, she grudgingly let go of him and stepped back. "Thank you for the opportunity."

"You earned it. And you did well by knowing all of the answers to their questions. And you took notes of things that particularly interested them. I couldn't have done any better."

"You really mean that? You're not just saying these things to make me feel better."

He chuckled. "Did anyone ever tell you that you don't take compliments well?"

She shrugged. "I guess I'm still wound up."

"We make a great team."

It was the first time he'd ever referred to them in that manner and she liked it. She really liked it. More than that, she liked him a lot—more than was wise. But that didn't stop her heart from pounding in her chest when he gazed deeply into her eyes.

He was going to kiss her—again. She should turn away. She should pretend she didn't know that he was interested in her. But her body had a will of its own, holding her in place. She knew that nothing good would come of it, but she wanted him to kiss her more than she wanted anything in that moment.

Angelo turned and continued down the hallway. The air that had been caught in her lungs rushed out. What had happened? It took her a second to gather her wits about her, and then she rushed to catch up to him.

They continued on in silence until they stopped outside her bedroom door. He turned to her again. "Thank you for everything. If I had done this alone, I wouldn't have stood a chance of winning their favor. You were my ace in the hole."

His gaze caught and held hers.

"I… I was?"

He nodded and stepped closer. "How could anyone turn you down?"

Her heart pitter-pattered harder and faster. She didn't want this moment to end—not yet. It was her very own fairy tale. "Do you want to come inside?"

He tucked a loose curl behind her ear. Then the back of his fingers grazed down her cheek. "I don't think that would be a good idea. We're expected at dinner with the royal couple. It wouldn't look right if we were late."

The hammering of her heart drowned out her common sense. Because when he was looking at her that way and touching her so sweetly, all she could think about was kissing him—

She lifted up on her tiptoes and pressed her lips to his. He didn't move at first and she wondered if there was some way that she had misread the situation. But then his arms wrapped around her and pulled her hard against him. She'd been here before, but it never failed to excite her. He was thoughtful, sweet and kind. Nothing like her boss at the office. This was a different side of him, and she found him utterly irresistible.

Angelo braced his hands on her hips, moving an arm's length away. "We need to stop now or we are never going to make it to that dinner."

"Who needs dinner?" There was only one thing she was hungry for at that moment and she was staring at him.

"Don't tempt me." He smiled at her. "I don't think that would help our pitch." He pressed a kiss to her forehead and proceeded down the hallway to his room.

In that moment, Kayla felt lighter than she had in days. Suddenly anything seemed possible. Maybe she'd given up on the fund-raiser too soon. She pressed a hand to her lips. Perhaps everything would work out in the end, after all.

She sure hoped so.

CHAPTER SEVENTEEN

"I DON'T UNDERSTAND."

Kayla's gaze narrowed in on Angelo as they stood beneath the crystal chandelier in the marble foyer. He'd been acting mysterious ever since they'd given their pitch to the royal couple the day before. Was it the kiss? It couldn't be. He hadn't been distant at the royal dinner. In fact, he'd been quite attentive—even if the evening hadn't ended with any more kisses.

"Trust me." His dark eyes twinkled with mischief. "You will understand soon enough."

"It'd be easier if you'd just tell me where we're going. If this has something to do with the pitch, you should tell me. I would have brought my laptop. Or at least I could have grabbed my tablet."

"You don't need it." He took her hand and guided her out the door, down the palace steps and into an awaiting limo. "Trust me."

"But how do I know if I'm dressed appropriately. The only formal clothes I have with me I wore yesterday for the pitch and then the dinner with the royal couple. I thought that we'd be leaving today."

"I've delayed our departure."

He had? She didn't recall him mentioning anything to her. Then again, she'd been so caught up in her thoughts lately that she might have missed it.

"Don't worry. I ran it past your boss." He winked at her. "He's fine with it."

"He is, huh?" She wondered what Angelo was up to and why he was in such a good mood. "But why aren't we flying back to Italy? I thought you'd be anxious to wrap things up there before we return to New York."

"It can wait."

She had absolutely no idea where they were headed.
The curiosity was eating at her. But the driver knew. She
turned to the front to ask him.

"Don't even think of it," Angelo warned as though he
knew exactly what she intended. "He's been sworn to se-
crecy."

Her mouth gaped open. Angelo really did know what
she was thinking. Thankfully he didn't know everything
that crossed her mind or else he'd know that she'd gone
against his express wishes and worked on the fund-raiser
during work hours.

And worst of all, her efforts were for naught. She'd
reached out to everyone she could think of, but she had
yet to come up with another big-name band on such short
notice. But ever the optimist, she wasn't canceling the event
until the very last minute. There just had to be a way to
help the kids.

"Hey, no frowning is allowed."

She hadn't realized that her thoughts had transferred to
her face. "Sorry. I was just thinking of all the work I should
be doing instead of riding around with you."

"You'll have plenty of time for work later. In fact, when
we return to New York I imagine that you'll have more
work than you'll ever want."

She sent him a quizzical look. Was he trying to tell her
something?

"Quit trying to guess. You aren't going to figure out
our destination."

The car zipped along the scenic roadway. Angelo was
totally relaxed, enjoying the terrific view of the tranquil
sea. But she couldn't relax. Not yet. Not like this. Not with
the fate of the fund-raiser hanging over her head.

Kayla desperately wanted to ask Angelo for help, but she
just couldn't bring herself to trust him, knowing his adamant stance on such matters. But if she didn't ask Angelo

for help, what did that say about their relationship? Did it mean what they'd shared meant nothing?

The thought left a sour taste in her mouth. The Angelo she'd got to know so well here in Italy put his family above his own needs even at the risk of one of his most important accounts. But that was his family? And she was what?

She had absolutely no answer.

Realizing that he was still holding her hand, her heart thumped. She was certainly more than his assistant—but how much more?

He turned to her. Their gazes caught and held. Her heart started to go *tap-tap-tap*. Oh, yes, she was definitely falling for her boss.

But what would happen when this trip was over? What would their relationship be like when they returned to the reality of their Madison Avenue office? Or worse yet, what if he found out that she'd been working on the fund-raiser instead of devoting all of her attention to her work?

"Relax. Everything will be okay." Angelo raised her hand to his lips and pressed a gentle kiss to the back of her hand.

Her stomach shivered with excitement. Throwing caution to the wind, she uttered, "When you do that, relaxing is the last thing on my mind."

"In that case…" He pulled her close and with her hand held securely in his, he rested his arm on his leg. His voice lowered. "You can get as worked up as you like now."

His heated gaze said a hundred things at once. And all of them made her pulse race and her insides melt. He wanted her. Angelo Amatucci, the king of Madison Avenue, was staring at her with desire evident in his eyes.

If she were wise, she would pull away and pretend that none of this had happened. But her heart was pounding and her willpower was fading away. She'd been resisting this for so long that she was tired of fighting it—tired of denying the mounting attraction between them.

Maybe this thing between them wouldn't survive the harsh glare of the office, but that was days away. They were to remain in Italy until the royal couple had all of the inquiries answered and their decision made. In the meantime, what was so wrong with indulging in a most delightful fantasy?

Once again, Angelo seemingly read her mind—realizing that she'd come to a decision. He turned to her and leaned forward. His lips were warm as they pressed to hers. Her eyes drifted closed as her fingers moved to his face, running over his freshly shaved jaw. His spicy aftershave tormented and teased. It should be illegal for anyone to smell so good. A moan bubbled up in the back of her throat.

The car stopped, jostling them back to the here and now. Angelo was the first to pull away. Disappointment coursed through her. Her eyes fluttered open and met his heated gaze.

"Don't look so disappointed. There will be time for more of this later." He smiled and her discontentment faded away. "Remember, I have a surprise for you."

"Did I forget to tell you that I love surprises?"

He laughed. "I was hoping you would."

She glanced out her window, finding nothing but lush greenery, flowers and trees. She struggled to see around Angelo, but with his arm draped loosely around her, she couldn't see much.

"I can't see." She wiggled but his strong arm kept her next to him—not a bad place to be, but she was curious about their location. "Where are we?"

"My, aren't you impatient? You'll soon see."

She couldn't wait. Though she still had problems to resolve, for just this moment she let them shift to the back of her mind. She might never have this kind of experience again, and she didn't want to miss a moment of it. And it had nothing to do with the surprise that Angelo had planned for her.

It had everything to do with the man who could make her heart swoon with those dark, mysterious eyes.

Mud. Seriously.

Angelo frowned as he sat submerged in a mud bath. He felt utterly ridiculous. This was his first trip to a spa, and though he'd set up the appointment for Kayla, he'd thought he might find out what he was missing. After all, Halencia was known for its world-renowned spa. It ought to be renowned for the exorbitant prices and, worse yet, the cajoling he had to do to get an appointment at the last moment. He'd finally relented and name-dropped—the prince's name certainly opened up their schedule quickly. But it had been worth it when Kayla's face lit up.

He glanced sideways at her as she leaned back against the tub's ledge with her eyes closed. Her long red wavy hair was twisted up in a white towel, safe from this muck. She definitely wasn't the prim-and-proper girl that he'd originally thought her to be when he'd hired her as his temporary assistant. No, Kayla definitely had a bit of a naughty, devil-may-care attitude. And that just intrigued him all the more.

"I'm sorry." Angelo didn't know what else to say. "I guess I should have done more research before making the reservations, but we were so pushed for time with the royal pitch that it just slipped my mind."

Kayla lifted her head. "It's really no problem. I'm enjoying myself."

"But how was I to know that they would set us up for a couple's spa day?"

Her eyes lit up. Her smile stretched into a grin and her eyes sparkled with utter amusement.

"Hey, you aren't inwardly laughing at me, are you?"

"Who? Me? No way." She clutched her bottom lip between her teeth as her shoulders shook.

He wasn't used to being the source of entertainment, but she certainly seemed to be enjoying herself. He supposed that made it worth it. Although, when he'd found out what was involved in the deluxe package, he did think that she was going to balk and walk away. But he'd been worried for no reason.

Kayla wasn't shy. In fact, she could be quite bold. The memory of her in hot pink lacy underwear before she'd stepped into the mud had totally fogged up his mind. Although, when he'd had to strip down to his navy boxers, he'd been none too happy. How could he have overlooked the need to bring swimsuits? Talk about taking down each other's defenses and getting down to the basics.

"What are you thinking about?"

He turned to Kayla, finding her studying him. "Nothing important. So, are you enjoying your trip?"

"Definitely. But…"

"But what?"

"I get the feeling that you aren't enjoying it. Why is that? Is it because of your sister's situation?"

He shrugged. "I suppose that has something to do with it."

"What else is bothering you? I'd think after being gone for so long that you'd be happy to be back in Italy."

"And you would be wrong. Returning to Monte Calanetti and interacting with my siblings and villagers is one of the hardest things I've ever had to do."

She arched an eyebrow and looked at him expectantly.

Why had he opened his mouth? He didn't want to get into this subject. It would lead to nothing but painful memories. And he couldn't even fathom what Kayla would think of him after he told her the truth about his past—about how he ended up in New York.

She reached out her hand and gripped his arm. "You know that you can talk to me. Openness and honesty are important to a relationship—even a friendship or whatever this is between us. Besides, I'm a really good listener."

Even though they were submerged in this mineral mud

stuff, her touch still sent a jolt up his arm and awakened his whole body. After telling himself repeatedly that she was off-limits, he wanted her more with each passing day. He turned and his gaze met hers.

She was the most beautiful woman he'd ever laid his eyes on and it wasn't just skin-deep. Her beauty came from the inside out. She was kind, thoughtful and caring. She was everything he would ever want in a woman—if he were interested in getting involved in a serious relationship.

But he wasn't. He jerked his gaze back to the large window that gave an amazing view of the Mediterranean Sea, but it wasn't the landscape that filled his mind—it was Kayla. She consumed far too many of his thoughts.

"Angelo, talk to me." Her voice was soft and encouraging.

For the first time in his life, he actually wanted to open up. And though his instinct was to keep it all bottled up inside, he wondered if that was the right thing to do. Maybe if Kayla, with her near-perfect home life, were to see him clearly she wouldn't look at him with desire in her eyes.

But could he do it? Could he reveal the most horrific episode in his life? More than that, could he relive the pain and shame?

He gazed into Kayla's eyes, finding compassion and understanding there. He swallowed hard and realized that perhaps he had more strength than he gave himself credit for. Though taking down his ingrained defenses to expose the most vulnerable part of himself would be extremely hard, he firmly believed it would be for the best. If it would put an end to this thing between him and Kayla, how could he hold back?

He cleared his throat. "Remember when I told you that I left Italy to go to school in the States?"

She nodded. "It's the bravest thing I've ever heard. I couldn't have done it—"

"But the thing is… I didn't do it because I wanted to."

Her brows drew together. "What are you saying?"

"My father and I didn't get along and that's putting it mildly." Angelo's body tensed as his mind rolled back in time. "My parents have always had a rocky relationship. On and off. Divorcing and remarrying." He shook his head, chasing away the unwelcome memories. "It was awful to listen to them."

He stopped and glanced at Kayla, whose expression was one of compassion. And then she did something he didn't expect. She reached over, grabbed his arm again and slid her hand down into the mud until she reached his hand. She laced her fingers tightly around his and gave him a big squeeze.

He exhaled a deep breath and continued. "My father is not a small man and he can be quite intimidating. When I'd had enough and my mother needed help with his temper, I... I'd step between them. My father did not like that at all."

"You don't have to tell me this."

"Yes, I do." He'd started this and he was going to see it through to the end. "It didn't matter what I did, it was never up to my father's expectations. I don't think there was anything I could have done to please him. And by the time I graduated school, I was done trying. And he was done trying."

"One day he blew up at me for not doing something in the vineyard. His bad mood spilled over to my mother— this was one of their good periods, so she didn't want to ruin things with him. When I tried to intervene between him and her by trying to soothe him, my father...he...he threw me out."

Kayla's fine brows rose. "But surely he calmed down and let you back in."

Angelo shook his head as he stared blindly out the window. Suddenly he was back there on that sunny day. His father had pressed a meaty hand to Angelo's chest, sending him stumbling out the front door. His mother's expression was one of horror, but she didn't say a word—not one thing—to contradict her husband. Instead, she'd agreed with him. Angelo's hurt had come out as anger. He'd balled up his hands and lifted them, taunting his father into a fight. But his father had told him that he wasn't worth the effort. How did a father do that to his son? How did he turn his back on him?

Angelo blinked repeatedly. "He told me that I was worthless and that I would never amount to anything. And then he told me to never darken his doorway again. He closed the door in my face."

"But your mother—"

"Wanted to make her husband happy. Don't you get it? Neither of them…they…didn't want me." His gut tightened into a knot and the air caught in his lungs as he fought back the pain of rejection.

This is where Kayla would turn away—just like his parents. She would know he was damaged goods. Not even his own parents could love him. He couldn't face Kayla. He couldn't see the rejection in her eyes.

"So you just left?" Her voice was soft.

He nodded. "I wasn't about to go back."

"But you were just a kid."

"I was man enough to make it on my own. I didn't have a choice. I couldn't live with him after that. And he didn't want me there. Nico brought my clothes to me, and with the money I'd saved from odd jobs over the years and my inheritance from my grandfather, I left. If it wasn't for Nico and Marianna, I'd have never looked back."

"And this is why you avoid serious relationships?"

He shrugged. "There isn't any point in them. The relationship will fail and somebody will get hurt. It's best this way."

"Best for who? You? You know that not everyone will treat you like your parents."

Suddenly he turned to her. His gaze searched her eyes. What was she saying?

Her warm gaze caressed him. "You can't keep yourself locked away from love because you're afraid. Some things are worth the risk."

She is worth the risk.

He leaned over and dipped his head, seeking out her lips. Every time he thought he'd learned everything there was to know about Kayla, she surprised him again. What did he ever do to deserve her?

He deepened the kiss. She responded to his every move. Her heated touch was melting the wall of ice inside him that he used to keep everyone out. Every second with their lips pressed together and their fingers intertwined was like a soothing balm on his scarred heart.

He needed her. He wanted her. He…he cared oh, so much about her.

A person cleared their throat in the background. "Do you need anything?"

Yeah, for you to leave.

Fighting back a frustrated groan, Angelo pulled back. If it wasn't for their attendant, he might have continued that kiss to its natural conclusion. Yes, he'd have definitely followed her into the shower and finished it.

In what seemed like no time, they were ushered from the mud bath into a shower and then into a private Jacuzzi. Angelo didn't know what to do with his hands. Well, he knew what he wanted to do with them, but with their attendant floating in and out, those plans would have to wait for later. For now, he stretched his arms along the rim of the tub and pulled her close to him. He just needed to feel that physical connection.

"Are you enjoying yourself?" He just had to be sure.

"This is perfect. Thank you."

"Well, not quite perfect. I did overlook the need for swimsuits." The heat of embarrassment crept up his neck.

"And miss seeing you in your boxers?" She waggled her brows at him. "I think it worked out perfectly."

"But you had to ruin your...um, clothes. They're all stained now."

"Oh, well. It was worth the sacrifice."

"Don't worry. I'll make sure to replace your...things." Why did he get so tripped up around her? It wasn't like him. But then again, everything was different when he was around Kayla.

"Will you be picking them out yourself?" Her eyes taunted him.

"Sure. Why not?"

"Do you have much experience with women's lingerie? And exactly how will you know what sizes to get?"

Boy, this water was starting to get hot—really hot. "Fine." His voice came out rough, and he had to stop to clear his dry throat. "I'll give you the money and you can get what you need."

She grinned at him. "I never thought of you as the kind to take the easy way out."

He had the distinct feeling there was no winning this conversation. No matter which way he went, he was doomed. "I'll make you a deal."

"Oh, I like the sound of this. Tell me more."

"We'll go together. I'll pick them out, but you have to promise not to wear them for anyone else."

Her eyes widened and then narrowed in on him. "Why, Mr. Amatucci, are you hitting on me?"

"I must be losing my touch if it took you this long to figure it out." He didn't even wait for her response before his head dipped and he caught her lips with his own.

Their relationship was unlike anything he had known previously—he never tired of Kayla. In fact, he missed her when she wasn't next to him. And her kisses, they were sweet and addicting.

What was wrong with him? He never acted like this.

And he never took part in flirting. He never had to. Normally women gravitated to him and things were casual at best. But with Kayla it was different—he was different. He barely recognized himself. It was as if he'd let down his shield of Mr. Angelo Amatucci, Madison Avenue CEO, and could at last be himself.

However, Kayla had taught him that a relationship didn't have to be turbulent like his parent's relationship. She'd opened his eyes to other possibilities. She'd shown him through her patience and understanding that, with openness and honesty, things didn't have to be kept bottled up inside until they exploded.

She hadn't been afraid to voice her disagreement over ideas for the wedding pitch. Nor had she been shy about vocalizing her objection to his no-charity-projects rule at the office. And though he hadn't agreed with her on some of the things, he'd been able to communicate it without losing his temper. Was it possible that he wasn't like his parents? Or was Kayla the key to this calm, trusting relationship?

He wasn't sure what it was, but the one thing he was certain about was that he wanted to explore this more—this thing that was growing between them.

When their attendant entered the room, they pulled apart. Disappointment settled in his chest. But the thought of picking up where they'd left off filled him with renewed vigor. This wasn't the end—it was just the beginning.

"I just have one question." Kayla gave him a puzzled look. "What exactly are we supposed to wear when we leave here? Please don't tell me that we're going commando."

He burst out laughing at the horrified look on her face.

"Hey, this isn't funny."

"Relax. I have another surprise waiting for you."

The worry lines on her face eased. "You do? Aren't you a man of mystery today?"

"I try."

"So tell me what it is."

He shook his head. "Just relax and let the water do its magic. You'll learn about your next surprise soon enough."

CHAPTER EIGHTEEN

CINDERELLA.

Yep, that's exactly how Kayla felt as she stepped out of the limo. Her nails were freshly manicured, her face was done up by a makeup artist and her hair was swept up with crystal-studded bobby pins. And that was just the beginning.

Angelo had surprised her with a gorgeous navy blue chiffon dress. Wide satin straps looped over her shoulders while a pleated bodice hugged her midsection. The tea-length skirt was drawn up slightly in the front while the back of the skirt flirted with her ankles. The thought that Angelo had picked it out for her and that it fit perfectly amazed her.

And there was lingerie—she wasn't even going to ask how he got all of her sizes right. Heat tinged her cheeks. Some things were best left unknown. Her silver sandals, though a bit tight, looked spectacular. And he'd even thought to present her with a sparkly necklace and earrings. The man was truly Prince Charming in disguise.

She looped her hand through the crook of his arm as he escorted her into a very posh restaurant. Tall columns, a marble floor and white table linens greeted them. Palms grew in large urns. The soft lighting and instrumental music made the ambience quite romantic. When the maître d' led them to the back of the restaurant and out a door, she wondered where they were going.

She soon found them standing on the terrace overlooking the Mediterranean Sea. A sweet floral scent filled the air. Kayla glanced up to find a wisteria vine woven through an overhead trellis. The beautiful bunches of delicate purple flowers were in full bloom. Lanterns hung from chains and gave off a soft glow. The whole setup was just perfect for a first date—this was a date, wasn't it?

Her gaze strayed to Angelo. What exactly had been his intention in giving her this magical day? Suddenly she decided she didn't want to analyze it—she just wanted to enjoy it.

The maître d' stopped next to a table by the railing. The view was spectacular, but even that word didn't cover the magnificence of the sight before her. The sea gently rolled inland, lapping against the rocks below the balcony. The glow of the sinking sun danced and played with the water, sweeping away her breath. She didn't know such a beautiful place existed on earth.

"If this is a dream, I don't want to wake up."

Angelo smiled at her. "Trust me. I'm having the same dream and I have no intention of waking up anytime soon."

"You have made this a day I'll never forget."

"Nor will I."

She continued to stare across the candlelit table at Angelo, who was decked out in a black tux that spanned his broad shoulders—the place where'd she'd been resting her head not so long ago. Even his dark hair was styled to perfection. Her fingers itched to mess up the thick strands while losing herself in another of his kisses. But that would have to wait until later. It would be the sweetest dessert ever.

The maître d' presented the menus and explained the wine list to Angelo before walking away. Everything sounded delightful.

Angelo peered over the menu at her. "I hope you brought your appetite."

She nodded, eating him up with her eyes. This was going to be a very long dinner.

However much Kayla wanted to throw caution to the wind, there was still a small hesitant voice in the back of

her mind. And try as she might, it was impossible to ignore. She'd worked so hard to get to where she was at Amatucci & Associates—did she really want to jeopardize her
dreams? And worse yet, if she did continue to thrive there,
would she always wonder if her flourishing was due to the
fact that she'd had a fling with her boss?

"Did I tell you how beautiful you look?" The flickering
candlelight reflected in his dark eyes as he stared across
the table at her.

"You don't look so bad yourself."

"You mean this old thing?" He tugged on his lapel. "I
just grabbed it out of the back of my closet."

His teasing made her laugh. Maybe she'd worry about all
of the ramifications tomorrow. "Is it possible that we never
have to go back to New York? Couldn't we just live here in
this little piece of heaven and never let the moment end?"

"Mmm... I wish. I've never enjoyed myself this much.
But we can make the most of our time here." His eyes
hinted at unspoken pleasures that were yet to come. "You
know if we weren't in public and there wasn't a table separating us, I'd finish that kiss we started back at the spa."

Her stomach shivered with the anticipation. "Then I
guess I have something more to look forward to."

"We both do."

Like Cinderella swept away in her carriage...

The limo moved swiftly over the darkened roadway back
to the palace. All Kayla could remember of the dinner was
staring across the table at her date. Angelo had presented
one surprise after the other, and somewhere along the way,
she'd lost her heart to him.

She didn't know when her love for him had started. It
was a while back. Maybe it was when she first witnessed
how much Angelo cared about his family. Or maybe it was
when he'd given her a tour of his village and told her about
pieces of his past—finally letting down that wall he kept

between them. Then somewhere, somehow, Angelo Amatucci had sneaked into her heart.

Kayla loved him wholly and completely.

The revelation shook her to her core. Part of her wanted to run from him—from these feelings. They had the power to destroy everything she'd built for herself back in New York. But how did she turn off the powerful emotions that Angelo evoked in her? And did she want to?

Just a look and he had her heart racing. Her body willingly became submissive to his touch. And she reveled in the way he'd looked at her back at the spa. He had no idea that her insides had been nothing more than quivering jelly when she stripped down to her undies. But when his eyes had lit up with definite approval and then desire, her nervousness was quickly forgotten.

In his eyes, she saw her present and her future. She saw a baby with Angelo's dark eyes and her smile. Startlingly enough, the thought didn't scare her off. In fact, she liked it. Maybe it was never the idea of a family that frightened her, but rather she'd had her sights set on the wrong man.

"Hey, what has you so quiet?" Angelo reached out and pulled her to his side.

"Nothing." *Everything.*

"I hope you had a good day."

"It was the best." She turned her head and reached up, placing a kiss on the heated skin of his neck. There was a distinct uneven breath on his part.

His fingers lifted from her shoulder and fanned across her cheek. "No, you're the best."

They both turned at once and their lips met. There was no timidity. No hesitation. Instead, there was a raw hunger—a fiery passion. And it stemmed from both of them. Their movements were rushed and needy. Their breath mingled as their arms wrapped around each other. Reality reeled away as though it was lost out there in the sea.

Right now, the only thing Kayla needed or wanted was

Angelo. If they were to have only this one moment together, she wanted it to be everything. She wanted memories that would keep her warm on those long lonely winter nights back in New York.

Angelo moved his mouth from hers. His hands held her face as his forehead rested against hers. His breathing was ragged. "I don't want to leave you tonight."

She knew her response without any debate. "I don't want you to go."

For once, she was going to risk it all to have this moment with the man she loved—even if he didn't love her back.

The limo pulled to a stop at the foot of the palace's sweeping white stairs that were lit with lanterns trailing up each side. Angelo didn't follow protocol. He opened the door before the driver could make it around the car. Angelo turned back and held out his hand to help her to her feet.

With both of them smiling like starstruck lovers, they rushed up the steps and inside the palace. Brushing off offers of assistance from the staff, hand in hand they swiftly moved to the second floor. They stopped outside her bedroom door and Angelo pulled her close. His mouth pressed to hers. He didn't have to say a word; all of his pent-up desire was expressed in that kiss.

When he pulled back, he gazed into her eyes. "Are you sure about this?"

She nodded and opened the door. She'd never been so sure about anything in her life. She led the way into the room. This would be a night neither of them would ever forget.

CHAPTER NINETEEN

WHAT IN THE world had he let happen?

Angelo raked his fingers through his hair, not caring if he messed it up or not. He'd already messed things up big-time with Kayla. In the bright light of the morning sun, he stood on the balcony of his suite in the royal palace. He'd woken up in the middle of the night after a nightmare— a nightmare he'd thought he'd done away with long ago.

After leaving Italy, he'd had nightmares about his father turning him out—of his father throwing his clothes out in the drive and telling him that he was not welcome there ever again. In his dream, and in real life, his mother had cried, but she didn't dare go against her husband's wishes even if it meant sacrificing one of her own children.

But last night his nightmare had been different. It was Kayla who'd turned him away. She'd told him that she never wanted to see him again. He'd begged and pleaded, but she'd hear none of it. Her face had been devoid of emotion as she slammed the door in his face. With nowhere to go, he'd walked the dark streets of New York. When a mugger attacked him, Angelo had sat up straight in bed. His heart had been racing and he'd broken out in a cold sweat.

Angelo gave his head a firm shake, trying to erase the haunting images. Of course, he knew that he wasn't going to end up homeless, but he also knew that the dream was a warning of looming trouble. If his own parents could turn him out, why couldn't Kayla? How could he risk getting close to her, knowing how unreliable relationships could be? After all, his own parents were quite familiar with the divorce courts as they broke up and got back together on a regular basis. Angelo's chest tightened.

The only thing he could do was end things with Kayla—quickly and swiftly. There was no way to put the genie back in the bottle, but that didn't mean that they had to continue down this road—no matter how tempted he was to do just that. He couldn't put his tattered heart on the line only to have it shunned again. The price was just too high.

A knock at his door alerted him to the fact that their car was waiting to take them to the airstrip. It was time to return to Italy. More than that, it was time to face Kayla. He didn't know what to say to her—how to explain that everything they'd shared was a big mistake.

By the time he made it downstairs, Kayla was already in the car. Not even the clear blue sky and the sight of the beautiful gardens could lighten his mood. He was in the wrong here. Things had spiraled totally out of control yesterday, and it had been all his doing.

"Good morning." He settled in the seat next to her, making sure to leave plenty of room between them.

Her face was turned away. "Morning."

That was it. The only conversation they had as his luggage was loaded in the rear. Time seemed suspended as he waited for the car to roll down the driveway. This was going to be a very long trip back to Italy. And a very quiet one.

It wasn't until they were on his private jet and airborne that he realized ignoring the situation wasn't going to make it go away. They still had to work together.

"We need to talk."

Kayla turned to him. "Funny you should pick now to talk."

"What's that supposed to mean?"

"It means that you didn't have time to talk last night. You had one thing on your mind and now that you've gotten it, you want to give me the big kiss-off."

"Hey, that's not fair. I didn't set out to hurt you. You were as willing for last night as I was."

"You didn't even have the decency to face me this morning. You slunk away in the middle of the night."

"That's not true." Not exactly. "I couldn't sleep and I didn't want to wake you up." The truth was that he'd never gone back to sleep after that nightmare. He just couldn't shake the feeling of inevitable doom.

She eyed him up. "So then I jumped to the wrong conclusion? You weren't trying to get away from me?"

The hurt look in her eyes tore at him. This was all about him, not her. She was wonderful—amazing—perfect. He just wasn't the guy for her. But how did he make that clear to her?

He got up from his seat and moved across the aisle and sat beside her, still not sure what to say. Somehow, someway he had to say the right words to make her realize that she was amazing, but they just weren't going to have more than they'd shared yesterday.

He resisted the urge to pull her into his arms and kiss away the unhappiness written all over her face. Instead, he took her hand in his. "Kayla, you are the most wonderful woman I have ever known. And yesterday was very special. I will never ever forget it—"

"But you don't want to see me again." She jerked her hand away.

"No—I mean yes." He blew out a breath. "I'm not the man to settle down into a serious relationship."

"Is that what you tell all of your women?"

"No. It's not." She eyed him with obvious disbelief reflected in her eyes. "I'm telling you the truth. I never let anyone get this close to me."

She crossed her arms. "Then why me? Why did I have to be the one that you let get close only to reject me after one night?"

Frustration balled up in his gut—not at her, at himself for being unable to explain this properly. He'd been a scared young man with no one to turn to for help. Thank goodness for his inheritance or else he never would have been able to make it in the States. But did either of his parents care? No. Did they ever write or phone? No. Not until he'd made it on his own did he hear from his mother—she was marrying his father again and she wanted him to be there. Angelo didn't bother to respond. The only family he acknowledged these days was his brother and sister.

He didn't need a romantic relationship. Love was overrated. His business gave him happiness and a sense of accomplishment—that was all he'd ever need.

And somewhere along the way, he'd stumbled upon his explanation to Kayla. "You have to understand that for years now the only thing I've had to count on in my life was my career, and then it was my business. I've put everything I am into it—"

"But what does that have to do with me—with us?"

He reached out as though to squeeze her arm, but when her eyes widened, he realized that he was making yet another mistake and pulled back. "One of the reasons that Amatucci & Associates was able to grow so rapidly into a top advertising firm is that I gave it 110 percent of my attention—to the point of spending many nights on the couch in my office."

Her eyes grew shiny and she blinked repeatedly. "So what you're saying is that your company is now and will always be more important to you than me."

Is that what he was saying? It sure sounded much harsher when she said it. His gut twisted in a painful knot, knowing that he couldn't be the man worthy of her heart.

"You have to understand. I'm losing my edge. I fumbled this wedding pitch. If it wasn't for you, it would have been a disaster. The thing is I don't fumble accounts. I always maintain my cool. I keep my distance so that I am able to view projects objectively. But since we've been in Italy—since that first kiss—I haven't been able to maintain a professional distance. I've been all over the place, and that can't happen—I can't lose focus. It's what keeps me ahead of my competitors."

He did his best work when he relied on his head and not his heart. It was all of the talk about romance and weddings that had him thinking there was something between him and Kayla. That was all. Exhaustion and too much talk of love.

"I really need to work now." Kayla's voice was icy cold and dismissive.

"Do me a favor." He wanted to say something to lighten her mood.

"Depends."

"Remind me to stay far, far away from any other accounts where there's a wedding involved."

She didn't smile. She didn't react at all. Her head turned back to her computer.

He felt compelled to try again to smooth things over. Was that even possible at this point? "Is there anything I can help you with?"

Her narrowed gaze met his straight on. "You've helped me quite enough. I can handle this on my own. I'm sure you have something requiring your objective view and professional distance."

He moved back to his seat on the other side of the aisle. The fact that she was throwing his own words back in his face hurt. But he deserved it and so much more. He'd lost his head while in Halencia and now Kayla was paying the price.

For the rest of the flight, Kayla didn't say a word, and though he longed for her understanding—he had to accept that it was too much for her to take in. There was a part of him that wasn't buying it, either. It was the same part of him that couldn't imagine what his life was going to be like without her in it.

He leaned back in his seat, hearing the wheels of the plane screech as they made contact with the tarmac. Instead of returning to Italy, he longed to be in New York—a return to a structured, disciplined work atmosphere.

Back at the office there'd be no cucumber waters with sprigs of mint and the most adorable woman dressed in nothing more than a white fluffy robe that hid a lacy hot pink set of lingerie. His mouth grew dry as he recalled how Kayla had stared at him over the rim of her glass with those alluring green eyes.

He drew his thoughts to a sharp halt. He reminded himself that his regular PA should be returning from her maternity leave soon—real soon. If he could just keep it together a little longer, his life would return to normal. But why didn't that sound so appealing any longer?

It doesn't matter.

Kayla kept repeating that mantra to herself, wishing her heart would believe it. Three days had passed since she'd woken up alone after a night of lovemaking. How could Angelo just slip away into the night without a word? Did he know how much it would hurt her? Did he even give her feelings any consideration?

It doesn't matter.

Today was the day they learned whether their royal wedding pitch had been accepted or not. Kayla replayed the presentation in her head. She couldn't help wondering—if she hadn't been so distracted by the problems with the fundraiser and with her growing feelings for Angelo could she have done more? She worried her bottom lip. For months and months, she'd done everything to be the best employee, and now that it counted, she'd lost her focus. She'd let herself fall for her boss's mesmerizing eyes, devilish good looks and charms.

It doesn't matter.

Dismissing their time together was his choice. Why should she let it bother her? She didn't need him. She squeezed her eyes shut, blocking out the memories of being held in his arms—of the tender touch of his lips. How could such a special night go so terribly wrong? Had she totally misread what Angelo had been telling her?

None of it matters!

She had important work to do. Angelo had just departed for his brother's villa to speak to him about their sister. Kayla had declined his stilted offer to take her with him. She may have made a mess of things with Angelo, but there was still time to pull together the after-school program fund-raiser.

Kayla focused on the email she was composing to the manager of another New York City band. She could only hope they had a cancellation because the most popular bands were booked well into the future. With her name typed at the bottom, she reread it, making sure it contained plenty of appeals to the man's generous side. After all, who could possibly turn down a group of needy kids? She sure couldn't. Once she was certain there weren't any typos, she pressed Send, hoping and praying that this appeal to the Spiraling Kaleidoscopes would turn things around.

Her thoughts immediately turned to her faltering career at Amatucci & Associates. She grabbed frantically for some glimmer of hope that there was a way to get back to their prior boss-employee relationship. But every time Angelo looked at her, her heart ached and her mind went back in time to those precious moments they'd spent together, wondering if any of it was real.

Ending things now was for the best. It was all of this talk about a wedding that had filled her head with these ridiculous romantic notions. And after working so closely with Angelo these past few weeks, it was only natural that she would project them onto him. The truth was that she wasn't ready to fall in love with him—or anyone. She didn't want to settle down yet. She still had her dreams to accomplish and her career to achieve.

A message flashed on the computer screen. She had a

new email. Her body tensed and she said a silent prayer that it would be good news.

She positioned the cursor on the email and clicked, opening the message on to the screen:

To: Kayla Hill
From: Howard Simpson
RE: Spiraling Kaleidoscope Booking
Thanks so much for thinking of us for your fund-raiser. I am sorry but we are already booked solid for that weekend, in fact, we're booked for the month. Next time consider booking well in advance.

The backs of Kayla's eyes stung. She continued to stare at the email, wishing the letters would rearrange themselves into an acceptance letter, but they refused to budge. This was it. She was out of ideas and out of time. No other band at this late date was going to be available.

Another email popped into her inbox.

To: Ms. Kayla Hill
From: Ms. Stephanie Dyer, Public Relations, Paper Magic Inc.
RE: ICL after-school program fund-raiser
It has recently come to our attention that the fund-raiser no longer has a headline performer. And it is therefore with great regret that we will have to pull our sponsorship...

Her vision blurred. She'd made a mess of everything. And she had no idea how she was ever going to face the children of the after-school program and tell them that she'd let them down—that the doors of the center were going to close.

Just then the door of the suite swung open. It must be the maid. Kayla swiped a hand across her cheeks and sniffled.

She was a mess. Hopefully the cleaning lady wouldn't notice. And if she did, hopefully she wouldn't say anything.

"I'll just move out of your way." Kayla closed her laptop, preparing to move down to the pool area to work.

"Why would you have to get out of my way?"

That wasn't the maid's voice. It was Angelo's. He was back. But why?

When she didn't say a word, he moved to her side. "Kayla, what's the matter?"

She didn't face him. "I… I thought you were the maid."

"Obviously, I'm not. I forgot my phone so I came back. I didn't want to miss a call from the royal family about the pitch."

"Oh, okay." She kept her head down and fidgeted with the pens on the table.

"Kayla, look at me."

She shook her head.

"Kayla." He knelt down next to her.

Oh, what did it matter? She lifted her face to him. "What do you need?"

"I need you to explain to me what's wrong." The concern was evident in the gentleness of his voice. "I thought we had everything worked out between us."

"Is that what you call it?" He really wanted to know? Then fine. She'd tell him. "I call it ignoring the big pink elephant in the middle of the room."

But that wasn't the only reason she'd been crying. It seemed in the past few days that everything she cared about was disintegrating.

"Kayla, talk to me."

His phone chimed. Saved by the bell so to speak. He checked the caller ID and then held up a finger for her to wait. He straightened and moved to the window, where he took the call.

This was her chance to escape his inevitable interrogation. She didn't know where she would go. Suddenly gelato sounded divine. So what if she was wallowing in her own misery? She deserved some sugary comfort—until she figured out what to do next.

She moved to her room to splash some water on her face, repair her makeup and grab her purse. When she was ready to go, there was a knock at her door. She knew it was Angelo. She sighed. Why couldn't he just leave well enough alone?

"Kayla, we need to talk."

CHAPTER TWENTY

"No, WE DON'T." Kayla moved to the door and swung it open. "Not unless it's about work. Other than that we have nothing to say."

Frown lines bracketed Angelo's face. "Did I hurt you that much?"

She glared at him. He really didn't expect an answer, did he? "Please move. I'm on my way out."

He moved aside and she passed by. She'd reached the exterior doorknob when he said, "Kayla, that was the prince's representative on the phone."

That stopped her in her tracks. Her heart pounded in her chest. *Please don't let the wedding fall through, too.* She turned and scanned Angelo's face. There were no hints of what had transpired on the phone.

"And…"

"The royal couple is steadfast in their decision that the chapel must be a part of the wedding. The bride was totally taken with the place. From what I understand that's the reason Monte Calanetti was placed on the short list."

"Did you try again to talk Louisa into letting them use it?"

His face creased with worry lines. "I did. And no matter what I said, she wanted no part of the wedding."

Kayla worried her bottom lip. This wasn't good. Not good at all. "This is all my fault. I shouldn't have let the royal couple believe we could deliver something that we obviously can't."

"It's not your fault. I thought that Louisa would change her mind. What I don't understand is why she's so adamant to avoid the royal wedding. Aren't all women romantics at heart?"

"Obviously not. And it's my fault. Everything is falling apart because of me."

Kayla's chin lowered. How could this be happening? Instead of helping everyone, she was about to let them all down. Most of all, she was about to let down the man she loved—correction, the man she worked for.

Angelo stepped up to her and grabbed her by the shoulders. "I've had enough of the riddles. There's more going on here than the royal wedding. I want to know what it is. Let me help you."

Her heart wanted to trust him. It wanted to spill out the problems so that they could work together to solve them. Perhaps it was time she let go of her dream of being an ad executive at Amatucci & Associates.

The price for her career advancement was far too steep. In her haste to escape her home and make a name for herself, she feared that she'd lost a part of herself. Now she realized that deep down where it counted, she still had the same principles that she'd been raised with. Her caring hometown and loving family had shown her what was truly important in life.

And the fact was she could never be happy as an ad executive, knowing she'd stepped over other people's hopes and dreams to get there. It was time to put her faith in Angelo's kindness and generosity.

She needed his help.

Why wouldn't she let him in?

Why did she insist on refusing his help?

Then Angelo remembered how their night of lovemaking had ended. His jaw tightened as he recalled how badly he'd handled that whole situation. No wonder she didn't trust him. If the roles were reversed, he'd feel the same way. But he couldn't give up. He couldn't just walk away and leave her upset.

"I know you don't have any reason to trust me, but if

you'll give me a chance, I'd like to help." His tone was gentle and coaxing. "I did my best for Nico and Marianna when they asked me—"

"But they are family. And…and I'm, well, just an employee."

His thumb moved below her chin and tilted her face upward until their gazes met. "I think you know that you're much more than that."

It was in that moment the air became trapped in his lungs. In her worried gaze he saw something else—something he hadn't expected to find. And it shook him to his core.

He saw his future.

It was in that moment that he realized just how much she meant to him.

He, the man who was intent on remaining a bachelor, had fallen head over heels, madly, passionately in love with his assistant. She was everything he'd been trying to avoid. Excitable, emotional and compassionate. The exact opposite of the cool, collected businessman image he'd created for himself.

The how and the when of these emotions totally eluded him. The startling revelation left him totally off-kilter and not sure what to say or do next. All that kept rolling through his mind was…

He, Angelo Amatucci, loved Kayla Hill.

"Angelo, what is it?"

"Um…nothing. And don't try changing the subject. We were talking about you and what has you so upset."

She breathed out an unsteady breath. "It's the emails."

"What emails? From the office?"

She shook her head. "Emails from the band's manager and the sponsors. Everyone's pulling out and…and it's in shambles—"

"Whoa. Slow down. I think we better take a seat and you need to start at the beginning."

Once seated on the couch, everything came bubbling to the surface. She told him about how she was involved with the after-school program. It came out about how the program was about to lose their lease unless they could come up with money to cover a hefty increase in the lease. And then she told him that she was heading up a fund-raiser—a big fund-raiser.

In fact, he'd heard about the fund-raiser. It was all over the radio and the papers. At the time, he'd been surprised his company hadn't been approached for a donation, but now he knew why.

"And this fund-raiser, you've been organizing it while you were here in Italy?"

She nodded. "I didn't have a choice."

So this is what she'd been hiding from him. "And you didn't think to mention it?"

"I thought about it." His mouth opened to respond but she cut him off. "And don't you dare blame this on me. I tried." Her voice rose and her face filled with color. "Every time I mentioned helping a charitable organization, you didn't want any part of it. Me not telling you before now is as much your fault as mine. I couldn't risk my job."

His voice rose. "You thought I'd fire you?"

She shouted back. "Wouldn't you have? Correction, aren't you going to now that you know?"

What he wanted to do was leave. Kayla was loud, emotional and making him extremely uncomfortable. She had him raising his voice—something he avoided at all costs. In that moment, he had flashbacks of his parents' endless arguments. He refused to end up like them.

He started for the door. The walls started to close in on him.

"Where are you going?"

"Out." His head pounded.

"And my job?"

"I don't know." He honestly didn't. He was torn between

his newfound feelings for her and the fear that they'd end up miserable like his parents. The pain in his temples intensified.

He stormed out the door, covering as much ground as he could cover with no destination in mind. He just had to get away from the arguing.

Over the years he'd worked so hard to control as much of his life as possible—keeping it the exact opposite of his emotional, turbulent parents. And then in one afternoon, he found himself back exactly where he'd started—in the middle of a heated relationship. That was unacceptable. His home and his office were kept orderly and on an even keel. Everything was how he wanted it—so then why couldn't he control his own traitorous heart?

CHAPTER TWENTY-ONE

HAD SHE BEEN FIRED?

Impossible.

But she was resigning from Amatucci & Associates effective as soon as she completed this one final task. Kayla sat across from Louisa Harrison on her patio. The Tuscany sun beamed bright overhead, but Louisa had the white table shaded by a large yellow umbrella. The woman was quiet, reserved and poised. Not exactly the easiest person to get to know.

"Thank you so much for taking the time to see me." Kayla fidgeted with the cup of coffee that Louisa had served just moments ago.

"I'm new here so I don't get much company."

Kayla gazed up at the huge palazzo. "Do you live here alone?"

Louisa nodded.

"You must get lonely in this big place all by yourself." Kayla pressed her lips together, realizing she'd once again said too much. "Sorry. I shouldn't have said that. Sometimes I don't think before I speak."

"It's okay. Most people probably would get lonely." Louisa played with the spoon resting on the saucer. "I moved here to get away from the crowd in Boston."

So Louisa wanted to be alone—perhaps that was the reason for her refusing to host a royal wedding that would bring a huge crowd of onlookers, not to mention the press. So was Louisa an introvert? Or was there another reason she preferred a quiet atmosphere?

First, Kayla had to build some friendly bridges. Hopefully she'd do a better job of that going forward. She genuinely liked Louisa. And she felt sorry for the woman, being so secluded from life.

And then a thought struck Kayla—if she wasn't careful and didn't stop pushing people away, she might end up alone just like Louisa. First, she'd shoved away her ex because she just didn't share his vision of the future. And now, there was Angelo, who had given her one amazing opportunity after the next. And how did she repay him but by having an utter meltdown.

She hadn't spoken to him since he'd stormed out of their suite that morning. He'd never returned. And she'd been so busy losing her cool that she never did get to ask him for help with the fund-raiser.

At the moment, though, she had to focus on Louisa. "You know, we have something in common. I'm new here, too. Except I'm not staying. I'm only here on a business trip with my boss, Angelo Amatucci."

Louisa's cup rattled as she placed it on the saucer. "I met Mr. Amatucci. I suppose he sent you here to convince me to change my mind about the royal wedding?"

Kayla could hear the obvious resistance in Louisa's voice. She'd have to tread lightly if she were to learn anything. "Actually, he didn't send me. He doesn't even know I'm here."

Louisa's eyes widened. "Then why have you come?"

"I need to be honest with you. I am here about the use of the chapel."

Louisa's mouth pressed together in a firm line and she shook her head. "I haven't changed my mind. I told Mr. Amatucci numerous times that I wouldn't agree to it."

"But I was wondering if there was something we could do to make the idea acceptable to you. The fact of the matter is this event could really help the village's economy. And the royal couple is adamant about using the chapel. If it's not available, they'll move on to the next village on their list."

Surprise reflected in the woman's eyes. "It's really that important?"

Kayla nodded. "I haven't lied to you so far. I need you to believe me now."

Louisa's light blue gaze met hers. "I do believe you. As much as I'd like to help, I just can't do it."

Kayla leaned forward. "If you tell me the problem, maybe I can find a way around it."

"I… I just can't have all of those people and reporters poking around here."

Something told Kayla that Louisa had spent more time in front of the paparazzi's cameras than she preferred. Her sympathy went out to the woman, but there had to be a compromise. "What if I make it my personal mission to ensure that you aren't photographed or even mentioned in the press coverage?"

Louisa's eyes opened wide. "You can do that?"

"Remember, we are dealing with royalty here. They have far-reaching hands. I'll let them know about your stipulation, and I'm sure they'll be able to handle the press."

There was a moment of silence. "If you're sure. I suppose it'd be all right."

Kayla resisted the urge to reach out and hug the woman, not wanting to scare her off. Instead, she leaned forward and squeezed Louisa's arm.

"Thank you." Kayla sent her a smile. "Now, if you don't mind, I'd love to hear more about your plans for this place. It's absolutely beautiful here."

Kayla sat back and sipped her coffee. She was happy that she could provide Angelo with this parting gift. With her resignation already typed up on her laptop, it was time for her to print it out.

That evening, Angelo had plans to dine with his brother and sister. While he was off having some family time, she would catch a plane home. Her moment beneath the Tuscany sun was over, and it was time to face the harsh reality of being jobless and heartbroken.

CHAPTER TWENTY-TWO

THIS HAS TO WORK.

Angelo sat in the back of a limousine outside Kayla's apartment. He'd been trying to call her ever since he'd found her resignation letter and the hotel suite empty, but she wasn't taking his calls. He'd just arrived in New York earlier that day after wrapping things up in Italy. Thanks to Kayla, Monte Calanetti was hosting the royal wedding.

He'd have left earlier but he couldn't. Nico and Marianna had been counting on him to stay until the royal decree was announced. Now that he and his siblings had achieved a peaceful relationship, it was as if they were truly a family again—something Angelo hadn't known how much he'd missed. And though Marianna still refused to divulge the name of the father of her baby, she knew without a doubt that both he and Nico were there for her—to support her no matter what decision she made about her future.

He'd returned to New York with orders from his brother and sister to track down Kayla and sweep her off her feet.

Since she'd been gone, he'd had time to realize how black-and-white his life was without her in it. He'd overreacted when he realized that he loved her. But now that he'd come to terms with the depth of his emotions, he hoped what he had planned was enough for her to give him—give them—a second chance.

Thanks to Kayla's very helpful assistant, who was a romantic at heart, he and Pam had secretly been able to piece the fund-raiser back together. And Kayla had been notified that a very special sponsor would be sending a car to escort her to the event.

He hated waiting. It seemed like forever since he'd last

laid his eyes on her. He wanted to march up to her apartment and beg her forgiveness, but he couldn't take the chance that she'd slam the door in his face. Worst of all, she'd end up missing her big night at the fund-raiser. He couldn't let that happen.

Instead, he'd stayed behind in the limo and sent up his driver with instructions not to mention that he was waiting. He needed a chance to talk to Kayla face-to-face. There was so much that he wanted to say—to apologize for—but he still hadn't found the right words.

The car door swung open and Kayla slid in the car next to him. She wore the navy dress he'd given her for their date in the Mediterranean. It hugged all of her curves and dipped in just the right places. It left him speechless that any woman could look so good.

When her gaze landed on him, her eyes opened wide. "What are you doing here?"

"What does it look like?"

Her gaze scanned his dark suit. "It looks like…like you're set for a night on the town."

"And so I am."

"Well, it can't be with me. I'm quite certain that it goes against your rules to date an employee."

"Ah, but what you're forgetting is that you're no longer an employee of Amatucci & Associates." He sighed. "We need to talk."

"Now's not the time. I have a fund-raiser to attend. Alone." She reached for the door handle, but before she could open it, the car started moving.

"And it looks like I'm your ride."

Her gaze narrowed in on him. "Angelo, there's nothing left to say. You said it all back in Tuscany."

"Not everything. Why did you quit without even talking to me?"

"First, I have a question for you. I thought it was strange when an internationally acclaimed rock band wanted to play for our fund-raiser on short notice. No one would tell me how Slammin' Apples heard about our need for help. Now I know. It was you, wasn't it?"

He wasn't so sure by the tone of her voice if this was going to go his way or not. "I was the one who called in a favor or two to have the band show up tonight."

"That isn't just any band. They are amazing. They've won national awards."

Angelo was going to take this all as a good sign. "I'm glad that you are pleased."

Her brows gathered together. "I didn't ask for your help."

"Kind of like how I didn't ask for your help with gaining permission from Louisa to use the chapel."

She shrugged. "I don't quit in the middle of projects."

He hoped this news would thaw her demeanor. "And thanks to you, Monte Calanetti is the official host of the royal wedding."

"Really?" A big smile bowed her lips and eased her frown lines. "I mean, I'm really happy for them."

"I knew you would be. Nico and Marianna send along their sincerest thank-yous." This was his chance to fix things. "I'm sorry about what was said in Tuscany. I never ever meant for you to quit. I need to make things right. You're far too talented to let go."

The light in her eyes dimmed. He'd obviously not said the right thing. For a man who made his fortune coming up with just the right words to turn people's heads and convince them to buy certain products or ideas, why was he messing this up so badly? Why couldn't he find the words to tell Kayla what she truly meant to him?

And then he knew what it was—what was holding him back. He was afraid that she wouldn't feel the same. He didn't want her to close the door on him as his parents had done so many years ago.

But still, he had to do it. He had to put himself out there if he ever wanted to win Kayla back. And that was something he most definitely wanted. After their month in Tuscany —he couldn't imagine another day without Kayla's sunny smile or her beautiful laugh.

Yet before he could sort his thoughts into words, the car pulled to a stop. Without waiting for the driver, Kayla swung the door open.

"Kayla, wait."

Without a backward glance, she faded into the sea of people waiting to get into the convention center. Though he rushed to get out of the car, by the time he did so she'd vanished—lost in the excited crowd.

He'd lost his chance to speak his piece. Maybe showing her how he felt would be better. He just hoped that his other surprise worked, because he just couldn't lose her now, not after she'd shown him that there was a different way to live—one with love in it.

CHAPTER TWENTY-THREE

KAYLA'S HEART ACHED.

She bit down on the inside of her lower lip, holding in the pain. Her legs were on automatic pilot as they kept moving one after the other, weaving her way through the throng of people. She didn't have a particular destination in mind. She just needed to put distance between her and Angelo before she crumbled in front of him.

After all they'd shared, how could Angelo look at her and see nothing more than an Amatucci & Associates asset? Was that truly all she was to him? The thought slugged her in the chest, knocking the breath from her.

And the sad thing was, for the longest time that's what she thought she'd wanted—Angelo to look at her and see her for all of her creative talent. But now things had changed—they'd changed considerably. Now she wanted him to see oh so much more—to see the woman that loved him with all of her heart.

After passing through security, she made her way to the front of the hall where the stage was set up. The kids of the ICL after-school program rushed up to her.

"Ms. Hill." Her name was repeated in chorus.

"Hi." With so many happy, smiling faces looking at her, it was like a temporary bandage on her broken heart. She forced a smile to her lips. "Is everyone here?"

"Yeah!"

The parents made their way up to her, shaking her hand and thanking her. She wanted to tell them that she hadn't done this, that it had been Angelo, but every time she opened her mouth to explain someone else thanked her.

And then her parents stepped in front of her. Her mother's eyes were misty as she smiled at her and her father looked at her. "You've done us proud."

They drew together into a group hug—something she'd grown up doing. No matter how old she got, some things didn't change.

Kayla pulled back. "But what are you two doing here?"

"Honey—" her mother dabbed at her eyes "—you don't think that we'd miss this after the invitation you sent."

Invitation? That she had sent? Something told her that Angelo had orchestrated this, too. Suddenly she wasn't so upset with him. For him to listen to her and give her this chance to show her parents what she'd accomplished while in New York touched her deeply. She wished he was around so that she could apologize for overreacting in the limo. More than that, she wanted to thank him.

The lights dimmed and one of the security guards approached her. They guided her through the barrier, around the stage and up a set of steps. When she stepped on the stage, she was awed by the number of people in the audience. She wondered if Angelo was out there somewhere or if he'd given up and gone home. The thought of him giving up on her left her deeply saddened.

Oh, boy. This wasn't good. She couldn't think about Angelo. Not here. Not now. She had to keep it together for all of the excited faces in the audience who were counting on her to pull this off. She'd made it this far—just a little longer.

And then as if perfectly timed, pink-and-silver balloons fell from the ceiling, scattering across the stage. *What in the world?*

The head of the outreach program stood at the microphone. Mr. Wilson was an older gentleman who'd already raised his family. Now he and his wife spent their time helping the children enrolled in the program.

"Kayla, join me." He turned to the audience. "Everyone,

please give the mastermind behind this amazing event a round of applause."

The clapping and cheers were unbelievable. And it would have been so much better if Angelo was standing next to her—after all, he'd been the one to save the fund-raiser. Not her.

As she peered at the countless smiling faces, her gaze connected with Angelo's. Her heart picked up its pace. What was he still doing here?

When quiet settled over the crowd, Mr. Wilson continued. "Kayla, would you like to say something?"

Though her insides quivered with nerves, she moved up to the microphone. Back at her apartment, she'd planned out what to say, but now standing here in front of thousands of people, including Angelo, the words totally escaped her.

She swallowed hard and relied on her gut. "I want to say a huge thank-you to everyone who helped with this event. Those people who helped with the planning and the organizing, please stand." Afraid to start naming names and forgetting someone, she stuck with generalities. "This was most definitely a group effort, and what a fabulous group. So please give them a round of applause."

She handed the microphone back to Mr. Wilson before she herself started clapping. Her gaze moved back to the last place she'd seen Angelo, but he was no longer there. She searched the immediate area but saw no sign of him. Her heart sank.

And then a familiar voice came across the speaker system. "Kayla, I know I say everything wrong when it comes to you. But I want you to know that I think you are the most amazing woman I've ever met."

Just then Angelo stepped on the stage and approached her. Her heart pounded in her chest. He stopped in front of her.

"What are you doing?" Heat flamed in her cheeks.

"Kayla, you've opened my eyes and my heart to the way

life can be if I let down my guard." He took her hand in his and gave it a squeeze. "I couldn't imagine doing that with anyone but you."

Kayla's eyes grew misty. It was a good thing that Angelo was holding her hand or she might have fallen over, because everything from her neck down felt like gelatin.

He handed the microphone back to Mr. Wilson as the band started to play. "Can I have this dance?"

He wanted to dance right here? Right now? In front of everyone?

Surely this all had to be a dream. If so, what did it matter if she accepted? She nodded and he pulled her into his arms as the band played a romantic ballad.

Angelo stared deeply into her eyes. "I never thought it was possible for me to feel this way, but I love you."

A tear of joy splashed on her cheek, a trait she inherited from her mother. "I love you, too."

"Does that mean I can rip up your resignation?"

"You still want me?"

"Always and forever."

EPILOGUE

Three months later...

"Do you have time for a new account?"

Kayla turned from her computer monitor to face Angelo. Was he serious? It was hard to tell as he was smiling at her. Ever since the charity concert, Angelo had been a different man in the office. He'd let his guard down and put on a friendly face, but one thing that hadn't changed was that he still expected perfection—or as close to it as anyone could get with their work.

"I don't know. Since we succeeded with the royal pitch, we've been flooded with new accounts. It really put Amatucci & Associates heads and shoulders above the competition."

"Yes, it did. And I couldn't have done it without you."

She knew that praise from Angelo didn't come willy-nilly. He truly had to mean it or he wouldn't say anything. "Thank you. But you were the driving force behind it."

"How about we just settle for 'you and I make a great team'?" He approached her and held out his hand to her.

She placed her hand in his, all the while wondering what he was up to. He pulled her gently to her feet, and then his hands wrapped around her waist. What in the world was up with him? He never acted this way at the office —ever.

"About this account—" he stared deep into her eyes, making her heart flutter "—if you decide to take it, it'll be all yours."

The breath hitched in her throat. Was he saying what she thought he was saying? "It'll be my first solo account?"

He smiled and nodded. "I thought that might get your attention."

As much as she wanted to spread her wings, she also didn't want to mess up. "Are you really sure that you want to give me so much responsibility?"

"I'm quite confident that you'll handle it perfectly. You are amazingly talented in so many ways." His eyes lit up, letting her know that his thoughts had momentarily strayed to more intimate territory.

She lightly swiped at his arm. "We aren't supposed to talk about those things at the office. What if someone overheard?"

"Then they'd know that I'm crazy about you."

She couldn't hold back a smile as she shook her head in disbelief at this side of Angelo, which had been lurking just beneath the surface for so long. "Now tell me more about this account. I'm dying to hear all about it before I make up my mind."

"It's a wedding."

"Are you serious?" He nodded and she rushed on. "I don't know. Don't you remember all of the headaches we had with the royal wedding? I couldn't imagine having a nervous bride lurking over my shoulder. I don't think I'd be good at mollifying a bridezilla."

"I don't think you give yourself enough credit. Look at how you handled me and opened my eyes to a thing or two."

"I know. Talk about a lot of hard work to get past your stiff, cold shell—"

"Hey!" His mouth formed a frown, but his eyes twinkled, letting her know that he was playing with her. "There's no need to throw insults."

"I wasn't. I was just stating the obvious." She grinned at him, letting him know that she was playing, too. "We could take an office poll and see which boss they like best—preItaly Mr. Amatucci or post-Italy?"

"I think we'll pass on that idea. Besides, you're going

to be too busy for such things now that you have this very special account."

"Special, huh? How special are we talking?"

Angelo reached into his pocket and pulled out a box. He dropped down to one knee. "Kayla, I love you. Will you be my bride?"

With tears of joy in her eyes, she nodded vigorously. "Yes. Yes, I will. I love you, too."

* * * * *

REUNITED BY A
BABY SECRET

MICHELLE DOUGLAS

With thanks to my fellow Romance authors
for creating such a strong and supportive community.
I can't begin to tell you how much I appreciate it.

CHAPTER ONE

MARIANNA AMATUCCI STARED at the door of the Grande Plaza Hotel's Executive Suite and swallowed. With her heart pounding in her throat, she backed up to lean against the wall opposite. A glance up and down the corridor confirmed she was alone. Up here at the very top of the hotel all was free from bustle, the very air hushed.

She patted her roiling stomach. *You will behave.* Usually by mid-morning her nausea had eased.

It wasn't morning sickness that had her stomach rebelling, though. It was nerves. She stared at the door opposite and her skin broke out in a cool sheen of perspiration. She twisted her hands together. She had nothing to fear. This was Ryan—blond-haired, blue-eyed, tanned surfer boy Ryan.

An image of his long-limbed beauty and sexy smile rose in her mind and her heart started to flutter in an altogether different fashion. She pressed one hand to her abdomen. *Mia topolino, your papà is utterly lovely.*

She moistened her lips. No, she had nothing to fear. Her news would startle him of course. Heavens, the shock of it still reverberated through her own being. But he'd smile that slow, easy smile, pull her into his arms and tell her it'd all be okay…and she'd believe him. He'd come to see that a child would be a blessing.

Wouldn't he?

The corridor swam. She blinked hard and chafed her arms, the chill of the air-conditioning seeping into her bones. She stared at the door and pressed steepled hands to her mouth? It was just…what on earth was Ryan doing in the *Executive Suite*? She couldn't square that with the

man she'd met on a Thai beach two months ago. A man
more at home in board shorts and flip-flops and his own
naked skin than a swish hotel that catered to Rome's elite.

Stupid girl! What do you really know of this man?

That was Angelo's voice sounding in her head. Not
that he'd uttered the words out loud, of course. But she'd
read them in his eyes in the same way she'd read the disappointment in Nico's. As usual, her brothers had a point.

What *did* she know of Ryan? She moistened her lips.
She knew he made love as if he had all the time in the
world. He'd made love to her with such a mixture of passion and tenderness he'd elicited a response from her that
had delighted and frightened her simultaneously. She'd
never forget their lovemaking. The week of their holiday
fling had been one of the best weeks of her life, and while
they'd made no plans to see each other again—too complicated with her in Italy and him in Australia—but...her
head lifted. Maybe this was fate?

Or maybe being pregnant has addled your brain?

And standing here wondering why on earth Ryan was
currently ensconced in the Executive Suite wouldn't provide her with an answer. Fortune smiled on men like
Ryan—men that oozed easy-going good humour and
warmth. The check-in clerk could simply have taken a
shine to him and upgraded him, or a friend of a friend
might've owed him a favour or...something. There'd be
a logical explanation. Standing out here tying herself in
knots was crazy, a delaying tactic.

She was no coward!

Marianna pushed away from the wall, wiped her palms
down her skirt and straightened her shirt before lifting her
hand and finally knocking. A thrill coursed through her.
She and Ryan might not have made plans to see each other
again, but he'd never been far from her thoughts during
the last two months and maybe—

The door opened and Marianna's breath caught and held, suspended between hard pounds of her heart. The haze in front of her eyes slowly dissolved, and in sluggish bewilderment her brain registered that the stranger standing in front of her dressed in a bespoke suit and a crisp cotton business shirt and tie was—

She blinked and peered up at him. 'Ryan?'

He leaned towards her and then frowned. 'Marianna?'

The stranger *was* Ryan! Her pulse jumped as she took in the dark blond hair, the blue-green eyes, and the sensual curve of his lips. Lips that had started to lift, but were suddenly pressed together into a grim straight line.

She stared at that mouth, at the cool light in his eyes. How different he seemed. Her stomach started to churn with a seriousness that forced her to concentrate on her breathing for a moment.

'What are you doing here?'

That was uttered in a voice she barely recognised. She dug her fingernails into her palms. *Smile. Please. Please just smile.*

Her inner pleading did no good. If anything, his frown deepened. She stared at him, unable to push a word out of a throat that had started to cramp. *Keep breathing. Do not throw up on his feet!*

He glanced away and then back at her, and finally down at his watch. 'I have a meeting shortly.'

A chill chased itself down her spine as her nausea receded. Why would he not smile?

'I wish you'd called.'

She reached out to steady herself against the doorjamb. He was giving her the brush-off?

He lifted his wrist to glance at his watch again. 'I'm sorry, but—'

'I'm pregnant!'

The words blurted out of her with no forethought, without any real volition, and with the force of one of Thailand's summer storms. Her common sense put its head in its hands and wept.

He stilled, every muscle growing hard and rigid, and then his eyes froze to chips of blue ice. 'I see.' He opened the door wider, but the expression on his face told her he'd have rather slammed it in her face. 'You'd better come in.'

She strode into the room with her back ramrod straight. Inside, though, everything trembled. This wasn't how it was supposed to go. She'd meant to broach the subject of her pregnancy gently, not slap him over the head with it.

She stopped in the middle of the enormous living room with its plush sofas and ornate tables and furnishings and pulled in a deep breath. Right. Take two. She touched a hand to her stomach. *Mia topolino, I will fix this.*

Setting her shoulders, she turned to face him, but her words dried on her lips when she met the closed expression on his face. It became suddenly evident that he wasn't going to smile and hug her. She did her best not to wobble. Couldn't he at least take her hand and ask her if she was okay?

Except…why would he smile at her when she stood here glaring at him as if he were the enemy? She closed her eyes and did what she could to collect herself, to find a smile and a quip that would help her unearth the man she'd met two months ago. 'I know this must come as a shock—'

'I take it then that you're claiming the child is mine?'

She took a step back, her poor excuse for a smile dying on her lips, unable to reconcile this cold, hard stranger with the laid-back man she'd met in Thailand. Fear had lived inside her ever since she'd discovered she was pregnant—and she was tired of it. Seizing hold of that fear now, she turned it into anger. 'Of course it's yours! Are you attempting to make some slur on my character?'

She didn't believe in slut-shaming. If *that* was what he was trying to do she'd tear his eyes out.

'Don't be ridiculous!'

Oh, so now she was ridiculous, was she? She could feel her eyes narrowing and her fingers curving into claws. 'I'm just over two months pregnant. Two months ago I was—'

'On a beach in Thailand!' He whirled away from her, paced across the room and back again. His pallor made her swallow. He thrust a finger at her, his eyes blazing. 'Pregnancy wasn't part of the plan.'

'There was a plan?' She lifted her hands towards the ceiling and let loose a disbelieving laugh. 'Nobody told me about any plan.'

'Don't be so obtuse!'

Ridiculous? Obtuse? Her hands balled to fists.

'We were supposed to…to just have fun! No strings! Enjoy the moment, live in the moment, before sailing off into the sunset.' He set his legs and stabbed another finger at her. 'That's what we agreed.'

'You think…' Her breath caught. She choked it back. 'You think I planned this?'

If anything the chill in his eyes only intensified.

Her brothers might think her an immature, irresponsible piece of fluff, but it knocked the stuffing out of her to find Ryan did too.

Maybe they're all right.

And maybe they were not! She slammed her hands to her hips. 'Look, I know this has come as a shock and I know it wasn't planned, but the salient fact is that I'm pregnant and you're the biological father of the child I'm carrying.'

Her words seemed to bow him although as far as she could tell not a single one of his muscles moved. She pressed a fist to her mouth before pulling it down and pressing both hands together. She had to think of the baby.

What Ryan thought of her didn't matter. 'It…it took me a little while to get my head around it too, but now…'

She trailed off. How could she tell him that she now saw the baby as a blessing—that it had become a source of excitement and delight to her—when he stared at her like that? The tentative excitement rose up through her anew. 'Oh, Ryan!' She took a step towards him. 'Is this news really so dreadful to you?'

'Yes.'

The single word left him without hesitation and she found herself flinching away from him, her hands raised as if to ward him off, grateful her baby was too young to understand its father's words.

Ryan's chest rose and fell too hard and too fast. His face had become an immobile mask, but the pounding at the base of his jaw told her he wasn't as controlled as he might like her to think.

It was all the encouragement she needed. She raced over to him and seized him by the lapels of his expensive suit and shook him. She wanted some reaction that would help her recognise him, some real emotion. 'We're going to have a baby, Ryan! It's not the end of the world. We can work something out.' He stood there like a stone and panic rose up through her. She couldn't do this on her own. 'For heaven's sake.' She battled a sob. 'Say something useful!'

He merely detached her hands and stepped back, releasing her. 'I don't know what you expect from me.'

That was when some stupid fantasy she hadn't even realised she'd harboured came crashing down around her.

You are such an idiot, Marianna.

A breath juddered out of her. 'You really don't want this baby, do you?'

'No.'

'The bathroom?' she whispered.

He pointed and she fled, locking the door behind her

before throwing up the crackers she'd managed for breakfast. Flushing the toilet, she lowered the lid and sat down, blotting her face with toilet paper until the heat and flush had subsided. When she was certain her legs would support her again, she stood and rinsed her mouth at the sink.

She stared at her reflection in the mirror. *Screw-up!* The accusation screamed around and around in her mind.

She didn't know that man out there. A week on a beach hadn't given her any insight into his character at all. She'd let her hormones and her romantic notions rule her…as she always did. And now she'd humiliated herself by throwing up in the Executive Suite of the Grande Plaza Hotel. It was all she could do not to scream.

With a superhuman effort, she pushed her shoulders back. She might be impulsive and occasionally headstrong, she might be having trouble reining in her emotions at the moment, but the one thing she could do was save face. Her baby deserved far more than that man out there had to give.

She rinsed her mouth one more time, and dried her hands before pinching colour back into her cheeks. With a nod at her reflection, she turned and flung the bathroom door open…and almost careened straight into Ryan standing on the other side, with his hand raised as if to knock.

She might not recognise him, but the familiarity of those lean, strong hands on her shoulders as he steadied her made her ache.

'Are you okay?' His words shot out short and clipped.

She gave a curt nod. He let her go then as if she had some infectious disease he might catch. It took a concerted effort not to snap out, *Pregnancy isn't contagious, you know?*

He stalked back out into the main room and she followed him. 'Can I order something for you? Food, tea… iced water?'

'No, thank you.' All she wanted to do now was get out of here. The sooner she left, the better. 'I—'

'The fact that you're here tells me you've decided to go ahead with the pregnancy.'

'That's correct.'

He shoved his hands into his pockets, his lips pursed. 'Did you consider alternatives like abortion or adoption?'

She had, so it made no sense why anger should rattle through her with so much force she started to shake. 'That's the male answer to everything, isn't it? Get rid of it…make the problem go away.'

He spun to her. 'We were *so* careful!'

They had been. They'd not had unprotected sex once. Her pill prescription had run out a month before she was due to return to Italy, though, and she'd decided to wait until she'd got home before renewing it. They'd used condoms, but condoms, obviously, weren't infallible.

Her heart burned, but she ignored it and straightened. Not that her five feet two inches made any impact when compared to Ryan's lean, broad six feet. 'I made a mistake coming here. I thought…'

What had she thought?

Anger suddenly bubbled back up through her. 'What's this all about?' She gestured to his suit and tie, his Italian leather shoes, angry with him for his stupid clothes and herself for her overall general stupidity. 'I thought you were…'

His lips twisted into the mockery of a smile. 'You thought me a beach bum.'

She'd thought him a wanderer who went wherever whim and the wind blew him. She'd envied him that. 'You had many opportunities to correct my assumption.'

He dragged a hand down his face. 'That week in Thailand…' He shook his head, pulling his hand away. 'It was an aberration.'

'Aberration?' She started to shake with even more force. 'As I said, I made a mistake in coming here.'

'Why didn't you ring?'

She tossed her head and glared. 'I did. A couple of days ago. I hung up before I could be put through…*to the Executive Suite*. It didn't seem the kind of news one should give over the phone.' It obviously wasn't the kind of news she should've shared with him at all. This trip had been an entirely wasted effort. *I'm sorry,* topolino. She lifted her chin. 'I thought you would like to know that I was pregnant. I thought telling you was the right thing to do. I can see, though, that a child is the last thing you want.'

'And you do?'

His incredulity didn't sting. The answer still surprised her as much as it did him. She moved to cover her stomach with her hand. His gaze tracked the movement. 'Ryan, let's forget we ever had this conversation. Forget I ever came here. In fact, forget that you ever spent a week on a beach with me.' *Aberration that it was!*

She turned to leave. She'd go home to Monte Calanetti and she'd build a wonderful life for herself and her child and it'd be fine. Just…fine.

'I don't know what you want from me!'

His words sounded like a cry from the heart. She paused with her hand outstretched for the door, but when she turned his coldness and impassivity hit her like a slap in the face. The room swam. She blinked hard. 'Now? Nothing.'

He planted his feet. 'What were you *hoping* for?'

She'd swung away from him and her hand rested on the cold metal of the door handle. 'I wanted you to hug me and tell me we'd sort something out.' What a wild fantasy that now seemed. She turned and fixed him with a glare. 'But I'd have settled for you taking my hand and asking me if I was all right. That all seems a bit stupid now, doesn't it?'

Anger suddenly screamed up through her, scalding her throat and her tongue. 'Now I don't even think you're any kind of proper person! What I want from you *now* is to forget you ever knew me. Forget all of it!' *Aberration?* Of all the—

'You think I can do that? You think it's just that easy?'

'Oh, I think *you'll* find it incredibly easy!'

She seized the vase on the table by the door and hurled it at him with all of her might. The last thing she saw before she slammed out of the room was the shock on his face as he ducked.

Ryan stared at the broken vase and the scattered flowers, and then at the now-closed door. *Whoa!* Had that crazy spitfire been the sweet and carefree Marianna? The girl who'd featured in his dreams for the last two months? The girl who'd shown up on the beach in Thailand and had blown him away with her laughter and sensuality?

No way!

He bent to retrieve the flowers and broken pieces of the vase. *Pregnant?* He tossed the debris into the wastepaper basket and stumbled across to the sofa. *Pregnant?* He dropped his head to his hands as wave after wave of shock rolled over him.

In the next moment he leapt up and paced the room in an attempt to control the fury coursing through him. She couldn't be! A child did not figure in his future.

Ever.

Him a father? The very idea was laughable. Not to mention an utter disaster. No, no, this couldn't be happening to him. He rested his hands on his knees and breathed in deeply until the panic unclamped his chest.

You can walk away.

He lurched back to the sofa. What kind of man would that make him?

A wise one?

He slumped, head in hands. What on earth could he offer a child? Given his background…

Money?

He straightened, recalling Marianna's shock at finding him ensconced in the Executive Suite wearing a suit and tie. A groan rose up through him, but he ground it back. He'd played out a fantasy that week on the beach. He'd played at being the kind of man he could never be in the real world.

One thing was sure. Marianna hadn't deliberately got pregnant in an attempt to go after his money. She hadn't known he had any!

Did she, though? Have money? Enough to support a baby?

Why hadn't he thought to check?

He passed a hand across his eyes. When he'd opened the door to find her standing on the other side, his heart had leapt with such force it had scared him witless. He'd retreated behind a veneer of professional remoteness, unsure how to handle the emotions pummelling him. He had no room for those kinds of emotions in his life. It was why he'd made sure they'd said their final farewells in Thailand. But…

Pregnant?

Think! He pressed his fingers to his forehead. She'd mentioned that her family owned a vineyard in Tuscany. It didn't mean she herself would have a lot of spare cash to splash out on a baby, though, did it?

He strode to the window that overlooked the gardens and rooftops of Rome with the dome of Saint Peter's Basilica in the distance, but he didn't notice the grandeur of the view. His hand balled to a fist. Had he really asked her if the baby was his? No wonder she'd lost her temper. It had been an inexcusable thing to say.

I'm pregnant.

She'd blurted it out with such brutal austerity. It had taken everything inside him to stay where he was rather than to turn and run. He'd wanted to do anything to make her words not be true. Who'd have thought such cowardice ran through his veins? It shouldn't be a surprise, though, considering whose genes he carried.

He dragged a hand down his face. When she'd stood there staring at him with big, wounded eyes, he'd had to fight the urge to drag her into his arms and promise her the world. That wasn't the answer. It wouldn't work. And he'd hurt her enough as it was.

He let loose a sudden litany of curses. He should've taken her hand and asked her how she was, though. He should've hugged her and offered her a measure of comfort. Shame hit him.

Now I don't even think you're any kind of proper person.

He didn't blame her. She might even have a point. He seized the room phone and punched in the number for Reception. 'Do you have a guest by the name of Marianna Amatucci staying here at the moment?'

'I'm sorry, Signor White, but no.'

Damn! With a curt thank-you, Ryan hung up. He flung open the door and started down the hallway, but his feet slowed before he reached the elevator. What did he think he was going to do? Walk the streets of Rome looking for Marianna? She'd be long gone. And if by some miracle he did catch up with her, what would he say?

He slammed back into his room to pace. With a start, he glanced at his watch. Damn it all to hell! Seizing his mobile, he ordered his PA to cancel his meetings for the rest of the morning.

He shook off his suit jacket, loosened his tie, feeling suffocated by the layers of clothing. His mind whirled, but one thought detached itself and slammed into him, making him flinch. *You're going to become a father.* He didn't want to become a father!

Too bad. Too late. The deed has been done.

He stilled. Marianna no longer expected his involvement. In fact, she'd told him she wanted him to forget they'd ever met. And she'd meant it. He ran a finger beneath his collar, perspiration prickling his scalp, his nape, his top lip. He could walk away.

Better still he could give her money, lots of money, and just…bow out.

His grandmother's face suddenly rose in his mind. It made his shoulders sag. She'd saved him—from his parents and from himself—but it hadn't stopped him from letting her down.

He fell onto the sofa. Why think of her now? He'd tried to make it up to her—had pulled himself back from the brink of delinquency. He'd buckled down and made something of himself. He glanced around at the opulence of the hotel room and knew he'd almost succeeded on that head. If he walked away now from Marianna and his child, though, instinct told him he'd be letting his grandmother down in a way he could never make up.

He'd vowed never to do that again.

You vowed to never have children…a family.

What kind of life would this child of his and Marianna's have? He moistened his lips. Would it be loved? Would it feel secure? Or…

Or would it always feel like an outsider? When parenthood became too much for Marianna would this child be shunted to one side and—?

No! He shot to his feet, shaking from the force of emotions he didn't understand. He would not let that happen. He didn't want to be a father, but he had a duty to this child. He would not abandon it to a life of careless neglect. He would not allow it to be overlooked, pushed to one side and ignored.

He swallowed, his heart pounding. He didn't have a clue about how to be a father—he didn't know the first thing about parenting, but… He knew what it was like to be a child and unwanted. He remembered his parents separating. He remembered them remarrying new partners, embracing their new families. He remembered there being no place for him in that new order. He hadn't fitted in and they'd resented this flaw in their otherwise perfect new lives. His lips twisted. His distrust and suspicion, his wariness and hostility, had been a constant reminder of the mistake their first marriage had been. They'd moved on, and it had been easier to leave him behind. *That* was his experience of family.

He would not let it be his child's.

He might not know what made a good father, but he knew what made a miserable childhood. No child of his was going to suffer that fate.

He slammed his hands to his hips. Right. He glanced at his watch and then rang his PA. 'I'd like you to organise a car for me. I'm going to Monte Calanetti tomorrow. I'll continue working remotely while I'm there so offer my clients new appointments via telephone conferencing or reschedule.'

'Yes, sir, would you like me to organise that for this afternoon's appointment as well?'

'No. I'll be meeting with Signor Conti as planned.' This afternoon he worked. He wasn't letting Marianna's bombshell prevent him from sealing the biggest deal of his career. He'd worked too hard to let the Conti contract slip from his fingers now. Clinching this deal would launch him into the stratosphere.

Conti Industries, one of Italy's leading car-parts manufacturers, were transitioning their company's IT presence to cloud computing. It meant they'd be able to access all points in their production chain from a single system. Every car-part manufacturing company in the world was watching, assessing, waiting to see if Conti Industries could make the transition smoothly. Which meant every car-part manufacturing company in the world had their eyes on him. If he pulled this off, then he could hand-pick all future assignments, and name whatever price he wanted. His name would be synonymous with success.

Finally he'd prove that his grandmother's faith in him hadn't been misplaced.

In the meantime… He fired up his laptop and searched for the village of Monte Calanetti.

CHAPTER TWO

RYAN GLANCED DOWN at the address he'd scrawled on the back of a Grande Plaza envelope and then at the driveway in front of him, stretching through an avenue of grapevines to a series of buildings in the distance. A signpost proudly proclaimed Vigneto Calanetti—the Amatucci vineyard. This was the place.

With a tightening of his lips, he eased the car forward, glancing from left to right as he made his way down the avenue. Grapevines stretched in every direction, up and down hillsides in neat ordered rows. They glowed green and golden in the spring sunshine and Ryan lowered the windows of the car to breathe in the fragrant air. The warm scents and even warmer breeze tormented him with a holiday indolence he had no hope of assuming.

Pulling the car to a halt at the end of the driveway, he stared. This was Marianna's home? Her heritage? All about him vines grew with ordered vigour. The outbuildings were all in good repair and the spick and span grounds gave off an air of quiet affluence. He turned his gaze to the villa with its welcoming charm and some of the tension drained from him.

Good. He pushed out of the car. He'd never doubted Marianna's assertion that she could stand on her own two feet, but to have all of this behind her would make things that much easier for her.

And he wanted things to be as easy for her as they could be.

A nearby worker saluted him and asked if he was wishing to sample the wines. Ryan cast a longing look at the cellar building, but shook his head. 'Can you tell me where

I might find Signorina Amatucci? Marianna Amatucci,'
he added. She'd mentioned brothers, but for all he knew
she might have sisters too.

The worker pointed towards the long, low-slung villa.

He nodded. *'Grazie.'* Every muscle tensed as he strode
towards it. He had to make Marianna see sense. He had
to convince her not to banish him from their child's life.

Once he reached the shade of the veranda, Ryan saw
that the large wooden front door stood open as if to welcome all comers. He stared down the cool shade of the
hallway and crossed his fingers, and then reached up and
pulled the bell.

A few moments later a tall lean figure appeared. He
walked down the hallway with the easy saunter of someone who belonged there. 'Can I help you?'

Ryan pulled himself up to his full height. 'I'm here to
see Marianna Amatucci.'

The suntanned face darkened, the relaxed easiness dis-
appearing in an instant. 'You're the swine who got her
pregnant!'

He'd already deduced from the hair—dark, and wavy
like Marianna's—that this must be one of her brothers.
A protective brother too. More tension eased out of Ryan's shoulders. Marianna should be surrounded by people
who'd love and support her.

A moment later he swallowed. Protective was all well
and good, but this guy was also angry and aggressive.

The two men sized each other up. The other man was
a couple of inches taller than Ryan and he looked strong,
but Ryan didn't doubt his ability to hold his own against
him if push came to shove.

Fighting would be far from sensible.

He knew that but, recalling the way Marianna had
thrown the vase at him yesterday, her brother might have
the same hot temper. It wouldn't hurt to remain on his

guard. He planted his hands on his hips and stood his ground.

'So…you have nothing to say?' the other man mocked.

'I have plenty to say…to Marianna.'

The brother bared his teeth. 'You don't deny it, then?'

'I deny nothing. All you need to know is that I'm here to see Marianna.'

'Do you have an appointment?'

He debated the merits of lying, but decided against it. 'No.'

'What if she doesn't want to see you?'

'What if she does?'

'I—'

'And if she doesn't want to see me, then I want to hear it from her.' He shoved his shoulders back and glared. 'I mean to see her, one way or another. Don't you think it would be best for that to happen here under your roof?'

The other man stared at him hard. Ryan stared right back, refusing to let his gaze drop. The brother swore in Italian. Ryan was glad his own Italian wasn't fluent enough for him to translate it. With a grim expression, he gestured for Ryan to follow him, leading him to a room at the back of the house that was full of rugs and sofas—a warm, charming, lived-in room. Light spilled in from three sets of French doors that stood open to a paved terrace sporting an assortment of cast-iron outdoor furniture and a riot of colour from potted plants.

Home. The word hit Ryan in the centre of his chest. This place was a home. He hadn't had that sense from any place since the day his grandmother had died. His lungs started to cramp. He didn't belong here.

Another man strode through one of the French doors. 'Nico, I—' He pulled up short when he saw Ryan.

Brilliant. Brother number two.

Brother number one—evidently called Nico—jerked a thumb at Ryan. 'This is Paulo.'

He glanced from one to the other. Marianna had told them his name was Paulo?

The second brother started towards him, anger rolling off him in great waves. Brilliant. This one was even taller than the first. Ryan set himself. He could hold his own against one, but not the two of them. He readied himself for a blow—he refused to throw the first punch—but at the last moment Nico moved between them, his hand on his brother's chest halting him.

Ryan let out a breath and then nodded. 'No. This is good.'

'Good?' brother number two spat out, his face turning almost purple.

'That Marianna has brothers who look out for her.'

The anger in the dark eyes that surveyed him turned from outright hostility to a simmering tension. 'You made her cry, you...' A rash of what Ryan guessed must be Italian insults followed. Brother number two flung out his arm, strode away, and then swung back to stab a finger at him. 'She returned here yesterday, locked herself in her room and cried. That is your fault!'

Ryan's shoulders slumped. He rubbed a hand across his chest. 'Yesterday...it was...it didn't go so well and she—' He pushed his shoulders back. 'I'm here to make it right.'

'What do you mean to do?' Nico asked. His voice had become measured but not for a second did Ryan mistake it for a softening.

'I mean to do whatever Marianna wants me to do.' Within reason, but he didn't add that caveat out loud.

Brother number two thrust out his jaw. 'But are you going to do what she *needs* you to do?'

He thrust his jaw out too. 'I will not *force* her to do

anything. I refuse to believe I know better than she does about what she needs. She's a grown woman who knows her own mind.'

The brothers laughed—harsh, scornful laughter as if he had no idea what he was talking about.

Ryan's every muscle tensed and he could feel his eyes narrow to slits as a dangerous and alien recklessness seized him. 'Have the two of you been bullying her or pressuring her in any way?'

Had they been pressuring her to keep the baby due to some outdated form of conservatism? Or... Had they been pressuring her to give the baby up because of scandal and—?

'And what if we have, Paulo?' brother number two mocked. 'What then?'

'Then I will beat the crap out of you!'

It was stupid, reckless, juvenile, but he couldn't help it. Marianna was pregnant! She needed calm and peace. She needed to take care of her health. She didn't need to be worried into an early grave by two overprotective brothers.

The brothers stared at him. Neither smiled but their chins lowered. Nico pursed his lips. The other rolled his shoulders. Ryan stabbed a finger first at brother number one and then at brother number two. 'Let me make one thing crystal clear. *I am not abandoning my child.* Marianna and I have a lot we need to sort out and we're going to do it without interference from either one of you.'

Raised voices drifted out across the terrace as Marianna marched towards the villa. She rolled her eyes. What on earth were Angelo and Nico bickering about now? She stepped into the room...

And froze.

Ryan!

A shock of sweet delight pierced through the numbness she'd been carrying around with her all day, making her tingle all over.

No! She shook it off. She would *not* be delighted to see him. Of all the low-down—

His gaze speared to her and the insults lining up in her mind dissolved.

'Hello, Marianna.' His voice washed over her like warm, spiced mead and she couldn't utter a single sound. She dragged her gaze away to glance at her brothers. Angelo raised a derisive eyebrow. 'Look what the cat dragged in, Marianna.' He folded his arms. 'Paulo.'

Ryan ignored his mockery to stride across to her. He took her hand in his and lifted it to his lips. Her heart fluttered like a wild crazy thing. 'Are you okay?' He uttered the words gently, his eyes as warm as the morning sun on a Thai beach.

While it wasn't a hug and an 'it'll all be okay' there was no mistaking the sincerity of his effort. She hadn't expected to see him again. Ever. She'd thought he'd have run for the hills.

'Marianna?'

She loved the way he said her name. It made things inside her tight and warm and loose and aching all at once. His grip on her hand tightened and she shook herself. 'Yes, thank you.' But the sudden sexual need that gripped had her reefing her hand from his. They were no longer Ryan and Mari, free and easy holidaymakers. They were Ryan and Marianna, prospective parents. That put a very different spin on matters and the sooner she got her head around that, the better.

This wasn't about him and her. It was about him and the baby. Did he want to be involved with the baby? If he did, and if he was sincere, then they would have to sort something out…come to some kind of arrangement.

Shadows gathered in Ryan's eyes. She swallowed, recalling the way she'd thrown the vase at him. 'And you? Are you okay?'

She watched him as he let out a slow breath. 'As you haven't thrown anything at me yet, then yes—so far, so good.'

Behind him, Nico groaned. 'You threw something at him?' he said in Italian.

'He made me angry,' she returned in her native tongue, trying not to wince at how rash and impetuous it must make her sound.

With a sigh she glanced back at Ryan. 'Have you been formally introduced to my brothers?'

'I've not had that pleasure, no.'

His tone told her they'd been giving him a hard time, but he didn't seem too fazed by it. A man who could hold his own against her two overprotective brothers? Maybe there were hidden depths to Ryan she had yet to plumb. *Let's hope so,* mia topolino. She wanted her baby to have a father who would love it.

She couldn't get her hopes up on that head, though. She recalled all the things he'd said yesterday and her stomach started to churn. He might just be here to offer her some kind of financial arrangement—to buy her off.

Keep your cool until you know for sure.

She tossed her head. She meant to keep her cool regardless.

She pulled herself back to the here and now and gestured. 'This is my oldest brother, Angelo, and this is Nico. He manages our vineyard.' She couldn't keep a thread of pride from her voice. She adored both of her brothers. 'And this—' she went to touch Ryan's arm and then thought the better of it '—is Ryan White.'

The men didn't shake hands.

Angelo gave a mock salute. 'Paulo.'

Ryan glanced down at her with a frown in his eyes. She waved a dismissive hand through the air. 'It is a stupid joke of theirs. Don't pay them any mind.'

'Marianna's boyfriends don't last too long,' Nico said. A deliberate jab, no doubt, at what he saw as her flightiness. 'Angelo and I decided long ago it was pointless remembering names.'

Angelo folded his arms. 'How long do you think this one will last, Nico?'

'Six weeks.'

'I'll give him four. He doesn't look as if he has what it takes to keep Mari's interest.'

'True. I can't see that he has anything more to offer her than any of the others.'

A clash of gazes ensued between the men and in some dark, dishonourable place in her heart the silent interchange fascinated her.

She tried to shake herself from under its spell. *What is wrong with you?*

With a snort, Ryan turned back to her. 'May I take you out to lunch?'

She glanced at Nico, who told her in Italian to take the afternoon off. 'Give him a chance.'

'You owe it to him, *bella*,' Angelo added.

What on earth…? She pulled in a breath, grateful her brothers spoke in their native tongue. She recalled the raised voices she'd heard when she'd approached the villa. 'How good is your Italian?' she asked Ryan.

'Very poor.' He glanced at Angelo and Nico. 'Which is probably a blessing.'

She folded her arms and glared at her brothers, reverting back to Italian. 'Did you put him up to this?'

Nico shook his head. 'But if this man is the father of your baby, you need to speak with him.'

'I did that yesterday!'

His gaze skewered her. 'Did you? Or did you merely drop your bombshell, throw a temper tantrum and run?'

Her face started to burn. It took an effort of will not to press her hands to her cheeks to cool them. Nico had a point.

Another thought slid into her then and she stared at each man in turn. If Angelo and Nico saw her dealing with the father of her prospective child maturely and responsibly, then that would help them see her as a responsible adult who could be trusted to make sensible decisions about her life, right? Not to mention the life of her unborn child. Maybe this was one way she could prove to them that she wasn't a failure or a flake.

She glanced down at her hands. Ryan *was* the father of her child. If he wanted to be a part of their baby's life...

Lifting her chin, she turned back to Ryan and reverted to English. 'I need to talk to Nico about the vines for a few minutes and then we can go for lunch.'

He nodded and glanced around. 'What if I wait over there?' He pointed to a sofa on the other side of the room.

She pressed her hands together. 'Perfect.' She wasn't so sure how perfect it was when Angelo followed him and took the seat opposite.

'Is there anything wrong with the vines?' Nico said, his face suddenly alive and intent.

'The soil is perfect! You have done an admirable job, Nico.'

'You set the groundwork before you left.'

Did he really believe that? Did he really think her an asset to the vineyard? She shook the thought off. She would prove herself to him. And Angelo. She was good at her job. 'The grapes are maturing as they should, but if the long-range weather forecast is to be believed, then we need to consider irrigating the northern slopes sooner than usual.'

'You mentioned last week something about new irrigation methods you'd picked up in Australia?'

She and Nico moved to the dining table to go over her report, but all the time her mind was occupied with Ryan. She heard him try to make small talk about the vineyard, but Nico asked her a question and she didn't hear Angelo's reply.

The next time she had a chance to glance up it was to see Ryan flicking a business card across to Angelo with the kind of mocking arrogance that would've done both of her brothers proud.

She dragged her attention back to Nico. 'From what I've seen so far, Nico, the vines are in great shape. I'll continue with my soil samples over the next week and checking the vines for any signs of pests or moulds, but...' she shrugged '...so far, so good. Seems to me we're on track for the fattest, juiciest grapes in the history of winemaking.'

It might've been an exaggeration, but it made her brother smile as it was supposed to. 'I'm glad you're home, Mari.'

Guilt slid in between her ribs at that. She'd been Irresponsible Marianna too long. She'd left Nico to run the vineyard on his own and now... She rubbed a hand across her chest. And now both of her brothers thought her an incompetent—a screw-up—that they needed to look after. They hadn't said as much, of course, but she knew.

'I'm not sure I like him.'

She glanced up to find Nico staring at Ryan.

She'd liked the man she'd met in Thailand. She'd liked him a lot. She hadn't liked the man she'd met at the Grande Plaza Hotel yesterday, though. Not one little bit. The man sitting on the sofa...she wasn't sure she knew *him* at all.

She touched Nico's arm. 'What matters is if I like him or not, I think, Nico.'

The faintest of smiles touched his lips. 'You always like them, Marianna...for a week or two.'

'This one is different.'

'Is he?'

Yes. He was the father of her unborn child.

He turned grey. 'Please don't prevent me from being a part of my child's life. I know I behaved badly yesterday and I know I'm not what you thought I was, but then you're not what I thought you were either.'

That arrow found its mark.

He leaned towards her, his eyes ablaze. 'I know what it's like to feel unwanted by one's parents.'

Something inside her stilled, and then started to ache at the pain he tried to mask in the depths of his eyes.

'I have no intention of letting a child of mine feel rejected like that.'

Yesterday, before their unfortunate meeting, she'd expected him to be a part of their child's life...regardless of anything else that might or might not happen between them. She passed a hand across her eyes and tried to still the sudden pounding of her heart. 'How do you think this can work?'

He captured her hand and forced her to look at him. The sincerity in his face caught at her. 'Marianna, I will do anything you ask of me. Anything except...' He swallowed.

'Except?'

'Walk away from our child. Or...'

'Or?'

'Marry you.'

She reclaimed her hand and glared. 'Who mentioned anything about marriage?'

'I didn't say I thought that's what you wanted. I—'

'Good! Because I don't! We don't even know each other!' A fact that was becoming increasingly clear. 'What kind of antiquated notions do you think I harbour?'

'Don't fly off the handle.' He glared right back at her. 'I thought it wise to make myself and my intentions clear. Your brothers seem very traditional and—'

'They're protective, not stupid! They wouldn't want me marrying some man just because I'm pregnant. For heaven's sake, women get pregnant all the time—single women. No one expects them to get married any more. No one thinks it's shameful or a scandal.'

He leaned towards her, his eyes intent. 'So your brothers haven't been pressuring you about the baby?'

'What are you talking about?'

He eyed her warily. 'Don't fly off the handle again.'

Her hands clenched. 'Do *not* tell me what to do.'

His eyes narrowed, turning cold and hard, and Marianna had to suppress a shiver, but she held her ground. He folded his arms and eased back. 'I was concerned your brothers might've been pressuring you to keep the baby when you didn't want to. Or, alternatively, pressuring you to give it away when you wanted to keep it.'

'They've been nothing but supportive.' She'd screwed up, again, but she had their support. They might think her a total write-off, but she would always have their support.

But if they were pressuring her, had Ryan meant to intervene on her behalf? The idea intrigued her.

She moistened her lips. 'What do *you* mean to pressure me to do?'

'It seems to me I have very little say in the matter.' He picked up his fork again, put it down. 'It's your body and your life that will be most immediately impacted. I'll support you in whatever decisions you make. If there's anything practical I can do, I hope you'll let me know.'

He made her feel like a spoilt child.

'Correct me if I'm wrong, but yesterday I was under the impression that you meant to keep the baby.' He frowned, looking not altogether pleased. 'Have you changed your mind?'

She shook her head. An unplanned pregnancy hadn't been part of her life plan, but... She'd always intended to become a mother one day. She'd just thought she'd be married to the man of her dreams first. Still, the moment the pregnancy test had confirmed that she was, indeed, pregnant, she'd been gripped by such a fierce sense of protectiveness for the new life growing inside her that, while she'd considered all of the options available to her, the only one that had made any sense to her *emotionally* was to keep her baby. To love it. To give it a wonderful life. 'I'm going to have this baby and I'm going to raise it and love it.'

He nodded. 'I know I've made it clear that I'm a lone wolf—I never intend to marry—but I do mean to be a father to this child.'

She rubbed her temples, unable to look at him. She finally picked up her cutlery and ate a bite of food.

He honed in on her unease immediately. 'What's wrong with that? Why do you have a problem with that?'

'Lone wolves don't hang around to help raise the young, Ryan. They hotfoot it to pastures greener.' Nothing he said made sense. 'If you intend to never marry, that's your business. But I don't see how you can be both a lone wolf and any kind of decent father.'

She raised her hands, complete with cutlery, heavenwards. 'To be a good father you need to be connected to your child, involved with it. When it needs you to, you have to drop everything at a moment's notice. You have to...' She met his gaze across the table. 'You have to put its needs above your own...even when you're craving solitude and no strings.'

He swallowed.

'A baby is just about the *biggest strings* that you can ever have.' She leaned towards him. 'Ryan, you will be bound to this child for life. Are you prepared for that?'

He'd gone pale. He stared back at her with eyes the colour of a stormy sea.

'For a start, how do you mean to make it work? How...?' She rubbed a hand across her brow. 'I can tell you how I

mean to make it work. I mean to stay here in Monte Calanetti where I have a good job, a family I love and a network
of friends. My entire network of support is here. What do
you mean to do—drop in for a few days here and there
every few months when you're between assignments?'

'I…'

She massaged her temples. 'I don't know what your
definition of a good father might be, but that's not mine.'

'Mine neither.' Hooded eyes surveyed her. 'You have
to realise I've only had a day so far to try and think things
through.'

He wanted her to cut him some slack, but…this was her
child's life they were talking about.

'I did have a thought during the drive up here,' he said.
The slight hesitancy in his voice coupled with the deep,
whisky tones made the flutters start up in her stomach.

She swallowed. 'Okay, run it by me, then.'

'What if I buy a house for you and the baby, and whenever I can get back here I can stay and spend time with
our child? I do mean to get back here as often as I can.'

He wanted what? She seized her fork and shoved luke-
warm *arancini* into her mouth to stop from yelling at him.
Yelling wouldn't be mature or adult. It wouldn't help their
child. Her grip on her cutlery tightened. Oh, but it would
be entirely understandable! Any innocent bystander would
surely agree?

'You don't like the idea?'

She shook her head and chewed doggedly.

'But the house would be yours and—'

He broke off when she pushed a whole half of an *arancini* ball into her mouth.

He rubbed a hand across his jaw. 'Okay, what's wrong
with that plan?'

It took her a moment of chewing and swallowing and

sipping of water before she could trust herself to answer with any equanimity. 'You don't ever mean to marry, no?'

His frown deepened. 'Right.'

'But it doesn't necessarily follow that I won't.'

He gazed at her blankly.

'The mother, her baby, her ex-lover and her husband,' she quipped. 'All under one roof? How cosy. *Not!*' She stabbed her fork at him. '*Not* going to happen.'

He dragged a hand down his face, before glancing back at her with eyes that throbbed.

'Ryan, I will organise my own life—my own house and furniture, not to mention my work. If you want contact with the baby, then that's fine. I have no intention of stopping you—but nor do I have any intention of being your glorified housekeeper while you do it. Buy a house in Monte Calanetti by all means. Feel free to hire a housekeeper and a nanny to help you with housework and the baby, but don't think you're going to cramp my life like that.'

'You mean to marry one day?'

Of all the things she'd just said, *that* was what he wanted to focus on? 'Of course I do.' And while they were on the topic… 'I mean to have more babies too.'

He paled. 'And do you think this future husband of yours will love our child?'

What kind of question was that? How on earth could he think it possible for her to fall in love with someone who wouldn't love her child too?

He sat back, his spine ramrod-rigid. 'My offer of a house wasn't meant to curtail your freedom. I can see now it was ill considered. You're right—it would never work. I'm sorry.'

Did he really want what was best for their baby? She recalled the way his eyes had flashed when he'd said he wouldn't let his child feel unloved or rejected. They were on the same side, but it didn't feel that way.

He pressed his lips together. 'We're going to have to learn to work together on this.'

'Yes.' At least they agreed about that.

He thrust a finger at her. 'And I can tell you now that I won't be foisting my child off onto some nanny.'

That scored him a few brownie points, but... 'What do you know about caring for a baby? Have you ever fed one and then burped it? Have you ever changed a diaper?'

He glanced away.

Marianna choked. 'Please tell me you've at least held one.'

He didn't answer, but his expression told its own story. Why on earth was he here? If he avoided children with the same ferocity he did marriage, why hadn't he run for the hills?

I know what it's like to feel unwanted.

Her heart suddenly burned for the small boy that was still buried deep in the man opposite her. He'd been hurt badly by his childhood, that much was evident, and he wanted to do better by his child. She couldn't help but applaud that.

'Hell, Marianna!' He swung back. 'I know nothing about babies or children. They're a complete mystery to me. But I can learn and I will love our child.'

For their baby's sake, she hoped he was right.

He'd gone so pale it frightened her. 'Can you teach me what I need to know?'

'Me?' The word squeaked out of her.

'There isn't anyone else I can ask.'

The implication of his lone-wolf ways hit her then and she gulped. It occurred to her that he might need this baby more than he realised. She gripped her hands together in her lap. Admittedly, she and he did have to learn to work together—that'd be in the best interests of their child. And seeing the two of them working things out together in a rational, *adult* way would put both Angelo's and Nico's minds at rest.

If Ryan really was willing to make an effort then…then their baby deserved to know him, to have him in its life. Her baby deserved to be loved by as many people as possible. And… She swallowed. And if Ryan did suddenly decide that he couldn't handle fatherhood, it'd be better to discover that now, before the baby was born.

You mean to test him to see if he's worthy?

Was that what she was doing?

Who's going to test you?

She closed her eyes.

'Is everything okay with your meals?'

Marianna's eyes sprang open to find Daniella frowning at their barely touched plates. 'The food is divine,' Marianna assured her.

The maître d' planted her hands on her hips. 'Would you like me to get Raffaele to prepare something else for you?'

'No, no, Daniella. Honestly, the food is wonderful. It's just…' Marianna pulled in a deep breath. 'Well, the fact of the matter is I'm pregnant, and food at the moment—any food—is a bit…iffy.'

Daniella stared, and then an enormous smile spread across her face. 'Marianna! What exciting news! Congratulations!'

She bent and hugged her and Marianna's throat thickened. 'I…thank you.'

The maître d' tapped a finger against her lips and then suddenly winked and wheeled away. Her smile speared straight into Marianna's heart. She swallowed and blinked hard. She stared down into her lap and fiddled with her napkin.

Ryan ducked his head and tried to catch her eye. 'Are you okay?'

'Uh-huh.' She nodded.

He brought a fist up to his mouth. 'Are you crying?'

Marianna lifted her napkin and buried her face in it for a moment, before drawing back and dabbing at her eyes.

Ryan stared at her as if he didn't have a clue what to do. He shuffled on his seat, but he didn't run. 'What's wrong?'

'Nothing's wrong. It's just…Daniella is the first person who's actually congratulated me and…and it was nice. The news of a baby should be celebrated.'

Ryan's face darkened. 'I thought you said your brothers had been supportive.'

'They have been, but…well, the pregnancy was obviously unplanned and…' They hadn't meant to make her feel as if she'd messed up. 'They've been worried about me.'

On the table, his hand clenched. 'And I acted like a damn jerk.'

She blew out a breath. She hadn't really given him much of a chance to act any other way.

Daniella returned with an enormous slice of chocolate cherry cake—Marianna's favourite. 'Compliments of the chef,' she said, setting it down with a flourish.

Darn it! Her throat went all thick again. Her emotions were see-sawing so much at the moment they were making her dizzy. 'Thank him for me,' she managed.

She promptly curved her spoon through it and brought it to her mouth, closing her eyes in ecstasy as the taste hit her. She opened them again to find Ryan staring at her as if mesmerised. A strange electricity started to hum through her blood.

They both glanced away at the same time.

Her heart pounded. Okay. In her mind she drew the word out. She and Ryan might be virtual strangers—in their real world incarnations—but they still generated heat. A lot of heat. She ate more cake. Ryan set to work on his fettuccine. They studiously avoided meeting each other's eyes.

If they were going to successfully co-parent, they were going to have to ignore that heat.

What a pity.

She choked when the unbidden voice sounded in her head. She was shameless!

'Everything okay?'

She pulled in a breath. 'If we want this to work, Ryan—'

'I for one *really* want it to.'

His vehemence made her feel less alone. She couldn't afford to trust it too deeply, to enjoy it too much, but...it was still kind of nice. 'Then we need to be really, *really* honest with each other, yes?'

He set his knife and fork down. 'Yes. Even when it proves difficult.'

'Probably especially when it proves difficult.' She pursed her lips. 'So, by definition, some of our conversations and discussions are going to be...difficult.'

The colour in his eyes deepened to a green that reminded her of a lagoon in Thailand where they'd spent a lazy afternoon. She swallowed and tried not to linger on what had happened after that swim when Ryan had taken her back to his beach hut.

'You want to hit me with whatever's on your mind?'

She dragged herself back.

The colour in his eyes intensified. 'I swear to you, Marianna, that I mean to do right by our baby. And by you too. I want to make things as easy for you as I can. I don't want you thinking you're in this alone.'

It was a nice sentiment but... She motioned to his plate. 'You can keep eating while I talk.'

The faintest of smiles touched his lips. 'If we're going

to have one of those difficult conversations it might be better if I don't. I wouldn't want to choke, now, would I?'

Her lips kicked up into a smile before she managed to pull herself back into line. 'I think there's an enormous difference between being a good father and being a man who holds the title of father.'

'I agree.'

'To be good at anything means working hard at it, don't you think?'

Again, he nodded. 'I'm not afraid of hard work, I promise you.' He met her gaze, his face pale but his eyes steady. 'What I'm afraid of is failure.'

His admission had her breaking out in gooseflesh as her own fears crowded about her. She chafed her arms. 'That's something I can definitely relate to.'

He shook his head. 'You're going to be a brilliant mother. You shouldn't doubt that for a moment. Already you're fighting for your baby's happiness—protecting it.'

But did it need protecting from Ryan?

'You will be a wonderful mother,' he repeated.

Her stomach screwed up tight. She hoped so.

His eyes suddenly narrowed. 'Are you afraid you won't be?'

'No,' she lied. 'Of course not.' She'd be just fine. She would! Besides, one of them feeling wobbly on the parent front was more than enough, thank you very much.

Ryan folded his arms. 'It hasn't been a terribly difficult discussion so far.'

Ah. Well. She could fix that. She pushed her cake to one side and pressed her hands together. 'Ryan, in Thailand I…' She faltered for a moment before finding her footing again. 'I was coming home to Italy after a year spent travelling and working through Australia. Thailand was my… last hurrah, so to speak. That holiday was about having no responsibilities, being young and free, and living in the moment before settling back into my real life.'

A furrow appeared on his brow. 'I understand that.'

'You are an incredibly attractive man.'

He blinked.

'But what we had in Thailand—all of that glorious sex…' He grinned as if in remembrance and it made her pulse skitter. 'It…it just doesn't belong here in my real world.'

He sobered as he caught her drift.

'If we're to successfully co-parent, then sex has no place in that. Friendship would be great if we can manage it. Sex would wreck that.'

'Too complicated,' he agreed.

She shook her head. 'It's actually incredibly simple. You never want to marry while I'd love to find the man of my dreams and settle down with him. If we make love here—in my real world—I would be in grave danger of falling in love with you.'

He shot back in his seat, his eyes filling with horror. The pulse in his throat pounded. 'I…' He gulped. 'That would be seriously unwise.'

She snorted. 'It'd be a disaster.' And if they were being honest… 'I doubt I'd make a particularly gracious jilted lover.'

He raised both hands. 'Point taken. We keep our hands to ourselves, keep things strictly platonic and…friendship.' He nodded vigorously. 'We focus on friendship.'

Ryan stared at Marianna, his heart doing its best to pound a way out of his chest. There couldn't be any sex between them. *Ever again.* She'd just presented him with his nightmare scenario and… Just, *no.* It would wreck everything.

He swallowed and tried to slow his pulse. If only he could forget the satin slide of her skin or the dancing delight of her fingertips as they travelled across his naked flesh, not to mention the sweet warm scent of her and the way he'd relished burying his face in her hair and breathing her in.

He stamped a lid on those memories and shoved them into a vault in his mind marked: *Never to be opened.*

Marianna lifted another spoonful of cake to her lips. He glanced at his fettuccine, but pushed the plate away, his stomach now too acid. Marianna had told him the food here was superb, world class, but it could've been sawdust for all he knew.

He glanced across the table and his gaze snagged hers. 'You really don't mean to make it difficult for me to see our child?'

Very slowly she shook her head. 'Not if you want to be involved.'

He wanted to be involved all right. He just didn't know what *involved* actually entailed. 'So…where do we go from here?'

She halted with a spoon of cake only centimetres from her mouth.

He tried not to focus on her mouth. 'I mean, what do we do next?'

She lowered her spoon. 'I don't really know. I…' She frowned and he went on immediate alert. It had to be better for her health and the baby's if she smiled rather than frowned.

Also, it had to be seriously bad for her health—her blood pressure—to go about hurling vases at people. He made a mental note to try and defuse all such high emotion in the future.

Her spoon clattered back to her plate and she gestured heavenwards with a dramatic flourish. 'It feels as if there must be a million things to do before the baby arrives!'

Were there? Asking what they were would only reveal the extent of his ignorance. He hadn't been able to shake off her horrified expression when she'd realised he'd never so much as held a baby. So, he didn't ask what needed doing. Instead he asked, 'What can I do?'

She folded her arms and surveyed him. She might only be a petite five feet two inches, but it took all of his strength to not fidget under that gaze.

'You really want to help?'

'Yes.' That was unequivocal. He *needed* to help.

'I plan to move out of the family home and into a cottage on the estate.'

He wondered if her brothers knew about this yet.

'It's solid and hardy, but I'd like to spruce up the inside with a new coat of paint and make everything lovely and fresh for the baby.'

It took a moment before he realised what she was asking of him. His heart started to thud. She'd told him that if he was serious about becoming a good father, his time would no longer be his own. His mouth dried. Could he do this?

He had to do this!

He reviewed his upcoming work schedule. He set his shoulders and rested both arms on the table. 'How would it be if I spent the next month—' *four whole weeks!* '—in Monte Calanetti? I can work remotely with maybe just the odd day trip back to Rome, and in my spare time I can help you get established in your cottage, help you set up a nursery...and in return you can tell me what you see as the duties and responsibilities of a good father?'

Her eyes widened, and he was suddenly fiercely glad he'd made the offer. 'You'd stay for a whole month?'

It wouldn't interfere with the Conti contract, and he didn't kid himself—he'd only have one chance to prove himself to the mother of his yet-to-be-born child, and he wasn't going to waste it. 'Consider it done,' he said.

CHAPTER FOUR

MARIANNA STARED AT him and Ryan found himself holding his breath, waiting for her answer...her verdict.

She folded her arms. 'That would help me out a lot.'

'And me,' he added, wanting her to remember that she'd just promised to tutor him in the arts of fatherhood.

She stared down at her cake and bit her lip. Her hair fell around her shoulders in a riot of dark waves, and it suddenly struck him how young she looked. He pushed his plate further away and glanced at her again. 'How old are you, Marianna?'

'Twenty-four.'

She was so young!

'And you?'

'Twenty-nine.' It was one of the many pieces of information they hadn't exchanged during their week in Thailand.

'If you researched me on the Internet, then you know what I do for a living.' As a specialist freelance consultant brought in, usually at the last moment, to turn the fortunes of ailing companies around, he enjoyed the adrenaline surge, the high-stakes pressure, and the tight deadlines. He shifted on his seat. 'What about you? What's your role at the vineyard? Are you a winemaker?'

She shook her head and those glorious curls performed a gentle dance around her face and shoulders. 'Nico is the vintner. I'm a viticulturist. I grow the grapes, look after the health of the vines.' She pushed a lock of hair behind her ear. 'The art of grape growing is a science.'

He knew she had a brain. It shouldn't surprise him that she used it. 'Sounds...technical.'

'I grew up on the vineyard. It's in my blood.'

The smile she sent him tightened his skin. He tried to ignore the pulse of sexual awareness coursing through him. That was *not* going to happen. No matter how much he might want her, he wasn't messing with her emotions.

'What?' she said.

He shook himself. 'So your job is stable? Financially you're...secure?'

He could've groaned when her face turned stormy.

He raised both hands. 'No offence meant. Difficult conversations, remember?'

She blew out a breath and slumped back, offered him a tiny smile that speared straight into the centre of him. 'I feel as if you're quizzing me to make sure I'm suitable mother material.'

'*Not* what I'm doing.' He'd be the least qualified person on earth to do that.

She kinked an eyebrow. 'No?'

He shook his head. 'When I said I wanted to make things easier for you, I meant in every way.'

He saw the moment his meaning reached her. The hand she rested on the table—small like the rest of her—clenched. He waited with an internal grimace and a kind of fatalistic inevitability for her to throw something at him.

In amazement he watched as her hand unclenched again. 'I keep forgetting that you don't really know me.'

He knew the shape of her legs, the dip of her waist and the curves of her breasts. He knew the feel of her skin and how she tasted. Hunger rushed through him. He closed his eyes. He had to stop this.

'One thing you ought to know is that I do have my pride.' She pulled in a breath and let it out slowly. 'I have both the means and the wherewithal to take care of myself and—' her hand moved to cover her still-flat stomach '—whoever else comes along. I have a share in Vigneto Calanetti, I'm a qualified viticulturist, I work hard and I draw a good salary. It may not be in the same league as what you earn, Ryan, but it's more than sufficient for both my and the baby's needs. I think you ought to know that if you were to offer me money it would seriously offend me.'

Right. That *was* good to know, but… 'What if I weren't offering it to you, but to the baby?'

She frowned and gestured to his plate. 'Are you finished?' At his nod she glanced across the room and caught the maître d's eye, wordlessly asking for the bill.

He let her distract herself with these things, but this money issue wasn't something he'd let her ignore indefinitely. He had a financial responsibility to this child—a responsibility he was determined to meet. He left a generous tip and followed Marianna to the cobbled street outside. He glanced at her and then glanced around. 'Your village is charming.'

It did what it was supposed to do—it cleared the frown from her face and perked her up. 'This was a stronghold back in medieval times. Many of the stones from the wall have since been used to build the houses that came after, but sections of the wall still stand. Would you like to walk for a bit?'

'I'd like that a lot. If you're not feeling too tired.'

She scoffed at that and set about leading him through cool cobbled streets that wound through the town with a grace that seemed to belong to a bygone age. He found himself entranced with houses made from stone that had mellowed to every shade of rose and gold, with archways leading down quaint alleys that curved intriguingly out of view. There were walled gardens, quirky turrets and fountains in the oddest places. And all the while Marianna pointed out architectural curiosities and regaled him with stories from local folklore. Her skill on the subject surprised him.

It shouldn't. Her quick wit and keen intelligence had been evident from their very first meeting.

Her enthusiasm for her subject made her eyes shine. She gestured with her hands as if they were an extension of her mind. His gut tightened as he watched her. Hunger roared through him...

He wrenched his gaze heavenwards. *For heaven's sake, can't you get your mind off sex for just ten minutes?*

'I'm boring you.'

He swung back to her. 'On the contrary, I'm finding all of this fascinating.' He refused to notice the shape of her lips. 'You obviously love your town.'

'It's my home,' she said simply. 'I love it. I missed it when I was in Australia.' She frowned up at him. 'Don't you love your home?'

Something inside him froze.

Her frown deepened. 'Where *is* your home, Ryan?'

'Have you heard the saying "Wherever I lay my hat, that's my home"? That pretty much sums me up.'

She halted, hands on her hips. 'But you have to live somewhere when you're between assignments. I mean, where do you keep your belongings?'

'I have office facilities in Sydney and London, and staff who work for me in both locations, but...' He shrugged.

Her eyes grew round. 'What? Are you telling me that you just live out of hotel rooms?'

'Suites,' he corrected.

'But—' She frowned. 'What about your car? Where do you keep that?'

'Whenever I need a car, I hire one.'

'Then what about the gifts people give you, your books and CDs, photographs, art you've gathered and... Oh, I don't know. The myriad things we collect?'

'I travel light. All I need is a suitcase and my laptop.'

She eased away from him, those dark eyes surveying

him. 'I wasn't so wrong about you after all,' she finally said. 'You are a kind of gypsy.'

She didn't look too pleased with her discovery. He shrugged. 'While we're on the subject of accommodation, perhaps you could recommend somewhere for me to stay while I'm in Monte Calanetti?'

She folded her arms and frowned at him for a long moment and then tossed her head, eyes flashing. 'Oh, that's easy.' She swung away and led him down an avenue that opened out into a town square. 'If you're going to help me get the cottage shipshape then you can stay there.'

His heart stuttered. 'With you?'

Some of his horror must've seeped into his voice because she swung back with narrowed eyes. 'Do you have a problem with that?'

'Not at all,' he assured her hastily. *Hell, yes!* How on earth was he going to avoid temptation when he was living with her? He rolled his shoulders. Not that he could ask the question out loud. Not when she stood glaring at him like that.

She turned and moved off, sending him a knowing glance over her shoulder. 'Considering the circumstances of our *acquaintance*, local traditions of hospitality demand I offer you a place to stay.'

What on earth was she talking about?

'If you don't stay at the vineyard, Ryan, tongues will wag.'

Ah. He didn't want to make things here in the village uncomfortable for her.

Her lips suddenly twitched. 'Of course, you could always stay in the main house with Angelo and Nico if you prefer.'

'No, no, the cottage will be great.'

She waved to a group of men on the other side of the square before leading Ryan to a bench bathed in warm spring sunshine. The square rose up around them in stone that glowed gold and pink. In the middle of the square stood a stone fountain—a nymph holding aloft a clamshell. It sent a glittering sparkle of water cascading, the fine mist making rainbows in the air. The nearby scent of sautéing onion, garlic and bacon tantalised his nose, reminding him of lunch and the abandoned conversation that he hadn't forgotten.

'In my country, Marianna, it's the law for a man to pay child maintenance to help look after his children. I expect it's the law here too. I *will* be giving you money. It's only right and fair that I contribute financially.'

Her mouth opened but he rushed on before she could speak. 'This is non-negotiable. I insist on contributing to my child's upkeep. I have my pride too.' She tried to butt in but he held up a hand. 'The money is not for you, it's for the baby.'

She folded her arms and slumped back against the bench, dark eyes staring towards the centre of the square. He couldn't help feeling he'd wounded her in some way. It didn't mean he wanted to unsay it. He had every intention of being financially accountable in this situation, but...

'None of that is to say that I believe for a single moment that you're not capable of looking after the baby on your own. Of course you are.'

Those dark eyes met his and he didn't understand the turmoil in their depths. 'Imagine for a moment I was one of your brothers. Wouldn't they want to contribute to the care of their child?'

Very slowly her chin and her shoulders unhitched. 'I suppose you're right.'

He let out a breath he hadn't known he'd been holding. Being around this woman was like negotiating a minefield. He didn't know from one moment to the next what would set her off. He dragged a hand back through his hair. What on earth had happened to the sweet sunny girl he'd met in Thailand?

She still had the same sweet curves, and when she smiled—

Stop it!

'So…' She pursed those luscious lips of hers and Ryan had to drag his gaze away. 'We've discussed the fact that you want to be involved in the baby's life, that you want to be a good father. We've talked about money, and settled that you're going to stay here in Monte Calanetti for the next month. We've organised where you're going to stay during that time. Is there anything else we need to tackle today?'

The dark circles beneath her eyes beat at him. He'd put them there. She'd returned here yesterday after their dreadful interview and cried. She'd probably barely slept a wink for worry. *His fault.*

'Maybe we should return to the vineyard. You can put your feet up and relax for a bit and—'

'Oh, for heaven's sake, Ryan, I'm pregnant not an invalid!'

Whoa. Okay. 'I, um…well, maybe I can put my feet up. I'm kind of beat after the drive from Rome.'

She swung to him, her eyes filling with tears. 'Oh, I'm sorry. Of course you're tired. What a dreadful hostess I'm proving to be.'

He prayed her tears wouldn't fall. He didn't want to deal with a sobbing woman. 'You, uh…you don't have to assume any role on my account.' If they were going to make this work then they had to drop pretences.

And he *had* to make it work. He had to learn how to be a good father to this child so that when Marianna found her true love and had more babies, he'd be there when she no longer had time for the cuckoo in the nest.

There was no doubt in his mind that when she did marry

and start a new family, this child could be cast aside. She wasn't as young as his mother had been when she'd become pregnant with Ryan, but she was still young. Marianna mightn't see it at the moment, but raising another man's baby would throw a pall over any life she tried to build with a new man. And Ryan vowed to be there for his child when that happened.

Marianna directed Ryan to park his car beneath the carport standing to one side of the villa—the villa that was her family home. He switched off the ignition and turned to her. 'Have you told your brothers about your plan to move?'

His tone told her he thought she'd have a fight on her hands. She bit back a sigh. Tell her something she didn't know. 'Not yet.'

'Would you like me there when you do?'

'No, thank you.' His earlier non-negotiable 'I'm paying for my child' still stung. Did he think her completely helpless? Did he think her utterly incapable of looking after her baby?

'When are you planning to move in?'

She lifted her chin. 'Tomorrow.' And nobody was going to stop her. But...

Pushing out of the car, she bit back a curse. What on earth had possessed her to offer him a room at the cottage? How relaxing was that going to be? *Not.*

She passed a hand across her forehead. It was just... She'd been utterly horrified when she'd learned how he lived his life. How could someone have no home? What kind of upbringing had this man had to have him still shunning the idea of a home?

If he wanted to co-parent he would need to create a home for their child, and she wanted him to experience at least a little of the welcoming atmosphere of a real home.

If he helped her to create that warm environment perhaps he could emulate it.

Unless he had his heart set on sticking to hotel rooms. *Suites*. Would a baby mind...or even notice? Heavens, a toddler would have a field day!

When she turned back to face him, however, it wasn't their child's welfare that occupied her thoughts. It was his. Her heart burned for him and she couldn't explain why, but for as long as he stayed here in Monte Calanetti she wanted to wipe away the memories of all of those impersonal anonymous hotel rooms and replace them with warmth and belonging.

Which, of course, made no sense at all.

Think with your head, not your heart.

You're too impulsive.

Those were the voices of her brothers.

She reached up to scratch between her shoulder blades. Maybe it was simply pregnancy hormones making her feel maternal early or something.

Speaking of hormones... She thought back to some of her reactions during lunch and grimaced. She wasn't exactly doing a great job at holding her emotions in check at the moment, was she?

Do you really think you can blame that on pregnancy hormones?

She flinched. Maybe she was as immature and irresponsible as her brothers seemed to think. Maybe she had no right becoming a mother. Maybe she'd be a terrible mother—

'What's wrong?'

She blinked to find Ryan right beside her. How had he known anything was wrong? She hadn't even been facing him. How could he be so attuned to her when he didn't really know her?

But he does know you. He knows every inch of your body intimately.

She gulped. *Don't think about that now.*

'Marianna.' He smoothed her hair back from her face before clasping her shoulders. 'If you're afraid of your brothers, then let me inform them of your intentions. I'll do anything you need me to.'

Except marry me.

That had her jerking out of his grip. She *didn't* want to marry him. 'I'm not afraid of Angelo and Nico, Ryan. It's just…I…' She spun away, swore and spun back. 'I feel as if I have constant PMS—as if some alien has taken over my mind and is making me behave irrationally. And it's taken over my body too. My breasts hurt. If I cross my arms, it hurts. If I reach up to get something from a shelf, it hurts. Putting a seat belt on is an exercise in agony, and I'm not even going to talk about the torture of putting on a bra. I…it's making me tetchy. And then I feel like I'm some kind of immature loser who can't deal with a bit of breast tenderness and some whacky hormones, and who's creating a whole lot of trouble for everyone else.'

She paused, running out of breath and Ryan's jaw dropped. 'Why didn't you say something earlier?'

'Because—' she ground her teeth together '—I should be bigger than it.'

'Garbage!' He reached out and cupped her face. 'I would hug you only I don't want to hurt you.' The sweet sincerity in his eyes melted something inside her. 'But let me tell you now that you're not a loser. You're warm and beautiful and brave.'

He thought her beautiful?

So that's the bit—out of all that he just said—that you latch onto, is it? Very mature.

She tried to ignore that critical inner voice.

'I don't feel brave,' she murmured. She didn't feel beautiful either, but she left that unsaid.

'I think you're wonderfully brave. I also think it understandable for you to be worried about the future. You shouldn't beat yourself up about that.'

'Okay,' she whispered.

With that, he drew away. She missed his touch, the brief connection they'd seemed to share. She shook it off and made herself smile. 'C'mon, I'll show you the cottage.'

'You want to do what?' Angelo shouted from where he set the table.

She bit back a sigh. The moment she'd informed her brothers that Ryan was coming to dinner, Angelo had cancelled his date with Kayla, and Nico had returned earlier than normal from the vineyard with a martial light in his eye. She'd figured, *In for a penny...*

'That's ridiculous!' Angelo slammed down the last knife and fork. 'Nico, talk sense into the girl.'

Marianna doggedly tossed the salad from her post at the kitchen bench.

'Mari—' Nico swung from where he turned steaks on the grill. '*This* is your home. *This* is where you belong.'

She turned at that. 'No, Nico, this is *your* home.' One day he'd fill it with a wife and children of his own, but his head rocked back at her words and he turned white. Her head bled a little for him. 'Turn the steaks,' she ordered and he did as she bid. 'I don't mean that as some kind of denial or as an indication that I don't feel welcome here. This is my childhood home. It will always be a haven for me. If I need it. Currently, though, I don't need a haven.'

'But—'

'No!' She spun back to Angelo. 'Do *you* feel as if this is your home? When you marry your beautiful Kayla, do *you* mean to settle in this house?'

He rolled his shoulders. 'That's different.'

'Why?' she fired back at him. 'Because you're a man?'

'Because I haven't lived here in years! I've built a different life for myself.'

'And what's wrong with me building a different life for myself?'

'Marianna,' Nico spluttered. 'You *do* belong here! You play a key role at Vigneto Calanetti—'

'But it doesn't mean I have to live under this roof. I'll still be living on the estate.'

Both brothers started remonstrating again. Marianna tossed the salad for all she was worth while she waited for them to wear themselves out. It had always been this way. She'd make a bid for independence, they'd rail at her, telling her why it was a bad idea and forbidding her to do it—whatever *it* might be—they'd eventually calm down, and then she'd go ahead and do it anyway.

Their overprotectiveness was a sign of their love for her. She knew that. They'd had more of a hand in raising her than their parents. But there was no denying that they could get suffocating at times.

'Enough!'

The voice came from the French doors. *Ryan.* She glanced around to find him framed in the doorway—all broad and bristling and commanding. Her blood did a cha-cha-cha. She swallowed and waved him inside, hoping no one noticed how her hand shook. 'You're right on time.'

He strode up to her side. 'Leave Marianna be. The one thing she doesn't need is to be bullied by the pair of you.'

'Bullied?' Nico spluttered.

'Who are you to tell us what to do?' Angelo said in a deceptively soft voice.

Ryan turned his gaze on her eldest brother—a determined intense glare that made her heart beat harder. 'I'm the father of her unborn child, that's who. And I'm telling you now that she doesn't need all of this…high drama.'

Her brothers blinked and she had to bite back a laugh. Normally it was she who was accused of the high drama.

It was her turn to blink when he took her shoulders in his hands and propelled her around the kitchen bench into the nearest chair at the dining table. 'Oh, but I was tossing the salad!'

He glanced at the bowl and his lips twitched. 'Believe me, that salad is well and truly tossed.' But he brought the bowl over and set it on the table in front of her.

Angelo glanced into the bowl and grimaced. 'You trying to mangle it?'

She bit her lip. Perhaps she had been a little enthusiastic on the tossing front.

'It looks great,' Ryan assured her.

The fibber! But it made her feel better all the same.

Angelo shook himself up into 'protective big brother' mode. 'Are you supporting my sister in this crazy scheme of hers to move out of the family home?'

'I'm supporting Marianna's right to assert her independence, to live wherever she chooses and to build the home she wants to for her child.'

'And *your* child,' Nico said, bringing the steaks across to the table.

'And my child,' Ryan agreed, not waiting to be told where to sit, but planting himself firmly in the seat beside Marianna.

'Are you planning to marry?'

Ryan glared at both of her brothers. 'You want Marianna to marry a man she doesn't love?'

Both Angelo and Nico glanced away.

Her shoulders started to slump. Why wouldn't they believe she could take care of herself? Maybe if she didn't have such a dreadful dating track record…?

She shook herself upright again, took the platter of steaks and placed a portion on each of their plates. She then handed the bowl of salad to Ryan, as their guest, to serve himself first. He didn't, though. He served out the salad to her plate first, and then his own before passing the bowl across the table to Nico. He seized the basket of bread and held it out for her to select one of the warmed rolls.

Her brothers noted all of this through narrowed eyes. Marianna lifted her chin. 'Ryan is going to stay here for a bit while we sort out how we mean to arrange things.'

Nico's eyes narrowed even further. He glared at Ryan. 'Where precisely will you be staying?'

Marianna rounded on him. 'Don't speak to him like that! Ryan is my guest. For as long as he's in Monte Calanetti he'll be staying at the cottage with me.'

Her brothers' eyes flashed.

Ryan drew himself up to his full seated height. 'Marianna and I might have decided against marriage, but I have an enormous amount of respect for your sister. I...' He shrugged. 'I like her.'

She blinked. Really? But... He barely knew her.

Still, if he could claim to like her after she'd thrown a vase of flowers at his head, and sound as if he meant it, then...who knew? Maybe he did like her.

'We're friends.'

'Pshaw!' Angelo slashed a disgusted hand through the air. 'If Mari hadn't become pregnant you'd have never clapped eyes on her again. That's not my idea of friendship.'

'But she is pregnant. I *am* the father of her child. We're now a team.'

Marianna speared a piece of cucumber and brought it to her mouth. A team? That sounded nice. 'Please, guys, will you eat before your steaks get cold?'

The three men picked up their cutlery.

'Still,' Nico grumbled. 'This is a fine pickle the two of you have landed in.'

Ryan halted from slicing into his steak. 'This is not a pickle. Granted, Marianna's pregnancy wasn't planned, but she's having a baby. She's bringing a new life into the world. That is a cause for celebration and joy, *not* re-criminations.'

Her eyes filled as he repeated her sentiment from earlier in the day.

Ryan took her hand. 'Do you think your sister won't be a wonderful mother?'

'She'll be a fabulous mother, of course,' Nico said.

'Do you not think it'll be a joyous thing to have a nephew or niece?'

'Naturally, when Marianna's *bambino* arrives, it will be cause for great celebration.' Angelo rolled his shoulders and then a smile touched his lips. 'I am looking forward to teaching my nephew how to play catch.'

'No, no, Angelo, we will have to teach him how to kick a ball so he can go on to play for Fiorentina.'

She rolled her eyes at Nico's mention of his and Angelo's favourite football team.

'What will you teach him?' Angelo challenged.

'Cricket.' Ryan thrust out his jaw. 'I'm going to teach him how to play cricket like a champion.'

'Cricket! That's a stupid sport. I—'

'And what if my *bambino* is a girl?' Marianna said, breaking into the male posturing, but she too found herself gripped with the sudden excitement of having a child. Her brothers would make wonderful uncles. They'd dote on her child and if she weren't careful they'd spoil it rotten.

'A girl can play soccer,' Nico said.

'And cricket,' Ryan added.

'She might like a pony,' Angelo piped in.

Her jaw dropped. 'You wouldn't let *me* get a pony when I wanted one.'

'I was afraid you'd try and jump the first fence you came across and break your neck.' Angelo shook his head. 'Mari, it was hard enough keeping up with you when you were powered by your own steam. It would've been explosive to add anything additional to the mix.' His eyes danced for a moment. 'Besides, if you do have a daughter and if she does get a pony, it'll be your responsibility to keep up with her. Something you'll manage on your ear, no doubt.'

She found herself suddenly beaming. Nico laughed and it hit her then that Ryan had accomplished this. He'd made her brothers—and her—excited at the prospect of their new arrival. He'd channelled their fear and worry into this—a new focus on the positive.

Reaching beneath the table, she squeezed his hand in thanks. He gazed at her blankly and she realised that he hadn't a clue what he'd done. She released him again with a sigh.

'Okay, Paulo,' Angelo said grudgingly. 'You're at least saying the right things. Still, in my book actions speak louder than words. I'll be watching you.'

Marianna rolled her eyes. Ryan shrugged as if completely unaffected by the latent threat lacing her brother's words. He glanced across at Nico. 'Anything you'd like to add?'

Nico stared at him with his dark steady eyes. 'I will abide by Marianna's wishes. You can stay. But I don't trust you.'

Marianna's stomach screwed up tight then and started to churn. She didn't know if she could trust him or not either.

Ryan's mobile phone chose that moment to ring. He pulled it from his pocket and glanced at the display. 'I'm sorry, but I have to take this.'

But…but…he was supposed to be making a good impression on her brothers!

With barely a glance of apology, he rose and strode out to the terrace, phone pressed to his ear.

He was supposed to be learning how to be a good father!

Lone wolf. The words went round and round in her mind. Was this how the next month would go? Ryan claiming he was invested and committed to their child, but leaping into work mode every time his phone rang? Her brothers stared at her with hard eyes. 'Excuse me.' Pressing a hand to her mouth, she fled for the bathroom.

CHAPTER FIVE

FOR THE NEXT three days, Ryan kept himself busy alternating between conference calls and prepping the inside walls of the three-bedroom stone cottage that Marianna had her heart set on calling home. In her parents' time, apparently, it had been used as a guesthouse and before that it had been the head vintner's cottage. For the last few years, however, the cottage had stood empty.

Ryan had insisted on cleaning everything first—mopping and vacuuming—before Marianna moved in. She'd grumbled something about being more than capable of wielding a mop, but he'd ordered her off the premises. Cleaning seemed the least he could do, even if it had delayed her move for an additional day. He'd claimed the smallest of the three bedrooms as his for the next month.

As Marianna had spent what he assumed was a long day tending grapevines and whatever else it was that she did, Ryan cooked dinner.

She walked in, found him stir-frying vegetables, and folded her arms. 'Do you also think me incapable of cooking dinner?'

He thought women were supposed to like men who cooked and cleaned. Not that he wanted her to like him. At least, not like *that*. 'Of course not, but I don't expect you to do all the cooking while I'm here. I thought we could take it turn about. You can cook tomorrow night.'

She grumbled something in Italian that he was glad he didn't understand. Throwing herself down on the sofa, she rifled through the stack of magazines on the coffee table and settled back with one without another word.

He stared at the previously *neat* stack. He itched to

march over there to tidy them back up, but a glance at Marianna warned him to stay right where he was.

Dinner was a strained affair. 'Bad day at work?' he asked.

'I've had better.'

Something inside him tightened. Had her brothers been hassling her again? He opened his mouth, but the tired lines around her eyes had him closing it again. His hands clenched and unclenched in his lap. What he should do was wash the dishes and then retreat to his room to do some work. Work was something he could do—something he had a handle on and was good at. He glanced at Marianna, grimaced at the way her mouth drooped, and with a silent curse pulled his laptop towards him. 'I thought maybe you could choose the colours for the walls.' He clicked on the screen, bringing up a colour chart.

The entire cottage oozed quaint cosy charm. The main living-dining area was a single room—long and low— with the kitchen tucked in one corner, sectioned off from the rest of the room by a breakfast nook. The ceiling was low-beamed, which should've made the room dark, but a set of French doors off the dining area, opening to a small walled garden, flooded the room with light. The garden was completely overgrown, of course, but if a body had a mind to they could create a great herb garden out there.

'Colour charts?' Marianna perked up, pushing her plate aside. 'That sounds like fun.'

Colour charts fun? That was a new one, but he'd go with it if it put a bit of colour back into her cheeks. He removed their plates as unobtrusively as he could. Hesitating on his way back from the kitchen, he detoured past the coffee table and swooped down to straighten the stack of magazines before easing into the seat beside Marianna at the dining table again.

She moved the laptop so he could see it too. 'That one.'

She pointed to a particularly vivid yellow. 'I've always wanted a yellow kitchen.'

He glanced at the screen and then at her. Did she really want a yellow so intense it glowed neon? 'That one's really bright.'

'I know. Gorgeous, isn't it?'

'Um… I'm thinking it might be a tad brighter on your walls than you realise.'

'Or it could be perfect.'

He didn't doubt for a moment she'd hate the colour once it was on her walls, but a colour scheme wasn't worth arguing about—especially if she was feeling a bit testy and—his gaze dropped momentarily to her breasts—sore. He reefed his gaze back to the computer screen. He'd paint her walls pink and purple stripes if she wanted. Pulling in a breath, he reconciled himself to the fact he'd be repainting said wall at some stage in the future. 'Butter Ball, right.' He made a note.

He'd started to twig to the fact that there were two Mariannas. There was the sunny, sassy Marianna he partially recognised from his holiday in Thailand. And then there was 'crazy pregnant lady' Marianna. She swung between these extremes with no rhyme or reason—sunny one moment and all snark and growl the next.

It kept a man on his toes.

'You mentioned you wanted some sort of green in the living and dining areas.' He glanced around. At the moment they were a nice inoffensive cream. With a shake of his head, he clicked to bring up a green palette. Heaven only knew what hideous colour she'd sentence him to using next.

She leaned in closer to peer at the screen, drenching him in the scent of…frangipani? Whatever it was, it was sweet and flowery and so fresh it took all his strength not to lean over and breathe her in all the more deeply.

'It'll have a name like olive or sage or something,' she said. 'Hmm…that one.'

He forced his attention back to the screen. 'Sea foam,' he read. It was a lot better than he'd been expecting.

'Does *it* pass muster?'

He didn't like the martial light in her eye. *Deflect the snark.* 'It's perfect.'

She blinked. Her shoulders slumped and he had to fight the urge to give her a hug. 'How are your breasts?'

She stiffened and then shot away from him with a glare. '*I beg your pardon?* What have my breasts to do with *you*?'

Heat crept up his neck. 'I didn't mean it in a salacious, pervy kind of way. It's just…the other day you said they were sore and…and I was just hoping that…that it had settled down.'

'Why should you care?' she all but yelled at him, leaping up to pace around the table and then the length of the room. She flung out an arm. 'You're probably happy! I've inconvenienced you so I expect you're secretly pleased to see me suffer.'

He stood too. 'Then you'd be spectacularly wrong! I have absolutely no desire to see you suffer. Ideally, what I want is you happy and healthy.'

She stopped dead in the middle of the room and stared at him, her hands pressed together at her waist. Ryan pulled in a breath. 'It's obvious, though, that at the moment you're not happy.'

Where did that leave him and her?

Where did it leave the baby? If she were having second thoughts about keeping the child…

She swallowed. Her bottom lip wobbled for a fraction of a sentence. Her vulnerability tugged at him. 'If I'm the cause of that, if my living here in your cottage, and invading your space, is adding to your stress, then I can easily move into the village. It wouldn't be a big deal and—'

He broke off when she backed up to drop down onto the sofa, covered her face with her hands and burst into tears.

He brought his fist to his mouth. Hell! He hadn't meant to make her cry. He shifted his weight from one foot to the other before kicking himself into action and lurching over to the sofa to put an arm around her. 'I'm sorry, Mari. I didn't mean to upset you. I'm a clumsy oaf—no finesse.'

At his words she turned her face into his chest and sobbed harder. He wrapped both arms around her, smoothed a hand up and down her back in an attempt to soothe her. Protectiveness rose up through him and all but tried to crush him. He fought back an overwhelming sense of suffocation. At the moment he had to focus on making Marianna feel better. His discomfiture had no bearing on anything. Her health and the baby's health, they were what mattered.

Eventually her sobs eased. She rested against him and he could feel the exhaustion pounding through her. So far this week all his suggestions that she rest had been met with scorn, sarcasm and a flood of vindictive Italian. Now he kept his mouth firmly closed on the subject.

'I'm sorry,' she whispered.

She eased away from him and her pallor made him wince.

'I can't believe I said something so mean to you, Ryan. I didn't mean it. It was dreadfully unfair. I know you don't want to see me suffer.'

'It's okay. It doesn't matter.'

'It's *not* okay. And it *does* matter.' Her voice, though vehement, was pitched low. 'I don't know what's happening to me. I'm being so awful to everyone. Today at work when I was lifting a bag of supplies, Tobias came rushing over to take it from me.'

She was heavy lifting at work!

'I mean, I know he meant well, but I just let fly at him

in the most awful way. I apologised later, of course, but Tobias has worked for my family for twenty years. He deserves nothing from me except respect and courtesy. And now I'm going out of my way to be extra nice to him to try and make amends and…this is terrible to admit, but it's exhausting.'

He could imagine, but… *She was heavy lifting at work?*

'And then I come home here and you've been working on my lovely cottage and am I grateful? No, not a bit of it!' She stiffened and then swung to him. 'I mean, I *am* grateful. Truly I am. But how on earth are you to know that when I keep acting like a shrew?'

Her earnestness made him smile. 'I know you are.'

She shook her head, her wild curls fizzing up all around her. 'How can you possibly know that when all I do is yell and say cruel things? I'm so sorry, Ryan. Even as I'm saying them a part of me is utterly appalled, but I can't seem to make myself stop. I just…' She swallowed. 'I don't know what's wrong with me.'

'I do.'

She stared at him. She folded her arms. 'You do?'

He tried not to let her incredulity sting. 'It's not that there's anything wrong with you. It's just your body is being flooded with pregnancy hormones. What you're feeling is natural. I read about it on the Net.'

She straightened. 'I should be able to deal with hormones. I should be able to get the better of them and not let them rule me.'

'Why? When your breasts are feeling sore, can you magically wish that soreness away just by concentrating hard?'

'Well, of course not, but that's different.'

'It's exactly the same,' he countered. 'It's a physical symptom, just like morning sickness.' From what he could tell, pregnancy put a woman's body completely through the wringer. He wished he could share some of the load with her, or carry it completely, to spare her the upheaval it was causing.

'So…' She moistened her lips. 'It'll pass?'

'Yep.'

'When?'

Ah, that was a little more difficult to nail down. She groaned as if reading that answer in his face. 'What am I going to do? If I keep going on like this I'm not going to have any friends left.'

It was an exaggeration, but it probably felt like gospel truth to her. He aimed for light. 'I could lock you up here in the cottage until it passes.'

Her lips twitched. 'It's one solution,' she agreed. 'My brothers, though, might take issue with that approach.' A moment later she bit back a sigh that speared straight into his gut. 'I guess I'm just going to have to ride it out.'

He stood, lifted her feet so that she lay lengthwise on the sofa, and moved across to grab his laptop. 'There're a couple of things we can try.' He came back and crouched down next to the coffee table. 'Meditation is supposed to help.'

She rose up on her elbows. 'Meditation?'

He gestured for her to lie back down. 'I downloaded a couple of guided meditations in case you wanted to try one to see if you thought it might help.'

'Oh.' She lay back down. 'Okay.'

He clicked play and trickling water and birdcalls started to sound. He moved back towards the dining table.

'Ryan?'

He swung back.

'Thank you.'

'You're welcome.'

She shook her head. 'I mean for everything. For understanding and not holding my horridness against me. You're really lovely, you know that?'

His throat thickened.

'I don't want you to move into the village, okay? It's nice to have…a friend here.'

A low melodic voice from his computer instructed her to close her eyes and she did, not waiting for his reply. Which was just as well because he wasn't sure he could utter a single word if his life depended on it.

He moved to sit at the dining table and suddenly realised that with his laptop already in use, he had nothing to do—couldn't lose himself in work as he'd meant to do. Pursing his lips, he glanced around. He'd start the dishes except he didn't want the clattering to disturb her.

Biting back a sigh, he pulled a magazine towards him— some kind of interior decorating magazine that Marianna must've picked up at some point…and left lying around the place. Instead of focusing on the magazine, though, he found his attention returning again and again to the woman on the sofa. He clocked the exact moment she fell asleep. He tiptoed across to cover her with a throw blanket, before moving straight back to his seat at the table where he wouldn't be in danger of reaching out to trace a finger down the softness of her cheek.

No touching. She'd said it was nice having a friend. He had to work on being that friend. Just a friend.

She slept for an hour. He registered the exact moment she woke too. 'How are you feeling?' he asked when she turned her head in his direction.

She stretched her arms back behind her head. 'Good. Really good.'

She sat up and smiled and he knew he had sunny Marianna back for the moment. He gestured. 'I've been looking through your magazines at the pictures you have marked.'

She leapt up, grabbed a jug of water from the fridge and poured them both a glass before moving across to where he sat. She left the jug on the bench top. He forced himself to stay in his seat and to not go and put it back in the fridge.

'Do you like any of them?'

He dragged his gaze from the offending jug and nodded. She had great taste. If one discounted that awful yellow she'd chosen for the kitchen walls.

She moistened her lips, not meeting his eye. 'Did you look at the pictures of the nurseries?'

Those were the ones he was looking at now. He angled the magazine so she could see. Her eyes went soft. 'They're lovely, aren't they?'

His heart started to hammer in his chest. Never in a million years had he thought he'd be looking at pictures of nurseries. He ran a finger around the collar of his T-shirt. 'Have you decided what kind of style and colour scheme you want in there yet?'

'I can't make up my mind between a nice calm colour that'll aid sleep or something vibrant that'll stimulate the imagination. I've been researching articles on the topic.'

Her enthusiasm made him smile. 'You're putting a lot of thought into this.'

She pushed her hair behind her ears. 'It's important and...'

'And?'

'I want my—our—baby to be happy. I want to give it every possible advantage I can.'

He stared at her. How long would their baby's welfare be important to her, though?

'Do you have any thoughts?'

Her question pulled him back. 'Personally I'd go for a calm colour because that's what I'd like best. I don't know what a baby would prefer.' He frowned. 'You could go with a calm colour on the walls and brighten the room up with a striking decal and a colourful mobile and...and accessories, couldn't you?'

'Hmm…' she mused. 'The best of both worlds perhaps?'

It warmed something inside him that she took his suggestion seriously. Still… What did he know? He knew nothing about this parenthood caper. 'It seems to me one needs a lot of equipment for a baby.'

'Ooh, yes, I know.' She rubbed her hands together, her eyes dancing. 'Shopping for the baby is going to be so much fun.'

Shopping in his experience was a necessary evil, not fun. Speaking of which… 'Marianna, where will I find the closest hardware store?'

'Ah.' She nodded.

He didn't point out that *Ah* wasn't an answer. He wanted Sunny Marianna hanging around for as long as possible.

'What do you have planned for Saturday?' she asked.

That was the day after tomorrow. He considered his work schedule. He had two video-conferencing calls tomorrow plus a detailed report to write by the end of next week. Saturday he'd planned… He glanced back at Marianna and gestured to the cottage. 'I was hoping to be painting by then.'

'Have you ever been to Siena?'

He shook his head. If that was where the nearest hardware store was, then he hoped it wasn't too far away.

'It's only an hour away. Write up a list of things that we need and we'll make a day of it.'

'Right.' Shopping. Yay.

Her smile slowly dissolved. She stared at him, twisting her hands together for a bit and he hoped he hadn't let his lack of enthusiasm show. He found a smile. 'Sounds good.'

Her fingers moved to worry at the collar of her shirt. She half grimaced, half squinted at him. 'Ryan, do you want to be present at the birth?'

He froze. Um…

'There's an information evening about…stuff coming up soon.'

How on earth had they gone from shopping to the birth? 'What stuff?'

'Like birthing classes.'

He didn't know what to say.

'I'm going to need a birthing partner.'

It became suddenly hard to breathe. 'Are you asking me to be your birthing partner?' What kind of time commitment would that demand?

Her eyes narrowed. 'No. I'm asking you to attend an information evening so we'll have all the available facts and can then make an informed decision about birthing classes and who I might want present at the labour.'

He thought about it. It didn't seem like much to ask. 'Right.' He nodded.

Her hands went to her hips. 'Is that a yes or a no?'

'It's a—yes I'll attend the information evening. When is it?'

'This Monday. Six-thirty.'

He pulled out his phone and put it in his electronic diary. He slotted the phone back into his pocket. 'Got it.'

'The town centre is heritage-listed,' Marianna said, gesturing around the Piazza del Campo. This was the real reason she'd brought Ryan to Siena—to have him experience something spectacular in an effort to make up for all he'd had to put up with from her for the last few days. So much for her resolve to give him a homey, welcoming environment. She'd been acting like a temperamental diva. He'd been incredibly patient and *adult* in the face of it.

Not to mention controlled. She bit back a sigh. If only she could channel some of that control.

Now, though, she had the satisfaction of seeing his eyes widen as he completed a slow circle on the spot to take in the full beauty and splendour of the town square. 'It's amazing.'

'Would you like to see the *duomo*?' Siena Cathedral. 'It's a three-minute walk away.'

At his nod, she led him across the Piazza del Campo and down one of the shady avenues on the other side, detailing a little of the history of the city for him, before eventually leading him to the cathedral.

They gazed at the medieval façade for a long moment, neither saying a word. Eventually Marianna led him through one of the smaller side doors and had the satis-faction of hearing his swift intake of breath. White and greenish-black marble stripes alternated on the walls and columns, creating a magnificent backdrop for the cool and hushed interior. She watched him as he studied ev-erything with a concentrated interest that reminded her of the way he'd explored the underwater wonders of Thailand on their scuba-diving expeditions. It reminded her of the way he'd explored her body during those warm fragrant evenings afterwards.

Something inside her shifted.

Catching her breath, she tried to hitch it back into place. Over and over in her mind she silently recited: *Do not fall for him. Do not fall for him.*

She couldn't fall for Ryan. It had the potential to ruin everything. It had the potential to ruin her child's relation-ship with him and she couldn't risk that.

She lifted her chin. She *wouldn't* risk that. It'd be self-ish, wilful and wrong. What she could do, though, was give Ryan a taste of home and hearth, a sense of how fam-ily worked. That was what would be best for their baby.

She turned to look at him and snorted. Fall for him? Not likely. She could never fall for someone so controlled, someone so cold.

He wasn't like that in Thailand.

Maybe not, but that was an aberration, remember? 'What's wrong?'

She snapped to, to find him staring at her. She dredged up a smile, reminding herself she wanted today to be a treat for him. 'Nothing, it's just...' She glanced around the medieval church. 'I've been here many times, but it amazes me all over again each time I come back.'

The smile he sent her warmed her to her very toes. 'I can see why.'

They spent two and a half hours wandering around the city and exploring its sights, and Marianna did her best to be cordial and friendly...and nothing more. After a leisurely lunch, though, Ryan reverted to the colder, more distant version of himself. 'We do need to get supplies at some stage today.'

She bit back a sigh. 'There's a hardware store not too far from where we parked the car.'

'Have you chosen what colour you want for the nursery yet?' he asked when they walked into the store a little while later.

She shook her head. She hadn't settled on anything to do with the nursery. In fact, she found herself strangely reluctant to decorate said nursery with Ryan.

'What?' he said.

She realised she was staring at him. 'I...I'm wondering if I shouldn't leave it and wait until I've had my scan.' She glanced around and then headed down an aisle.

He followed hot on her heels. 'Scan?'

'Hmm... If I find out whether I'm having a boy or a girl maybe that will make it easier to personalise the room.'

He didn't say anything and when she turned to gaze up at him she couldn't read a single emotion in his face. It worried her, though she couldn't have said why.

'You mean to find out the gender of the baby?'

She couldn't work out if that was censure or curiosity

in his voice. 'I…I, uh, hadn't made a decision about that yet. There's no denying it'd make things like decorating and buying clothes easier.'

'You don't want it to be a surprise?'

She peered down her nose at him. 'Ryan, don't you think there's been enough of a surprise factor surrounding this pregnancy already?'

He laughed and it eased something inside her. 'Perhaps you're right.'

'If you don't want to know the sex of the baby, then I can keep it a secret.'

He cocked an eyebrow. 'You think that's going to work?'

A chill hand wrapped around her heart. Did he think he could read her so easily?

Her heart started to thump. Maybe he could. She had a tendency to wear her heart on her sleeve while he—he could be utterly inscrutable.

'If I'm doing the majority of the decorating, don't you think your choice of colour schemes is going to give the game away?'

The hand clutching her heart relaxed. 'I could decorate the nursery on my own.'

'You're pregnant. You should be taking it easy.'

She loved that excuse when it came to ducking out of the dishes, but… 'Slapping on a coat of paint can't be that hard.'

One broad shoulder lifted and a little thrill shot through her at its breadth, its latent strength…its utter maleness. Her mouth started to water. *No thrills!*

'But you may as well make use of me while you have me.'

With an abrupt movement, she turned and marched across to an aisle full of decorative decals. It would be unwise to forget that he was only here for a month. And that he hadn't promised her anything more than help decorating her house. She ground her teeth together. If she could just get her darn hormones under control…

She pulled in a breath and willed the tightness from her body. 'If you wish to remain in suspense as to our baby's sex we best go with something neutral.'

'I didn't say that I didn't want to know.'

She left off staring at teddy bear decals to swing around to him, planting her hands on her hips. 'Well, do you or don't you?'

'I, um…I don't know.'

Helpful. *Not*. She didn't say that out loud, though. She'd been doing her best to aim for pleasant and rational and she had no intention of failing now.

'I…I kind of feel you've sprung this on me. Not your fault,' he added hastily, as if he thought his admission would have her losing her temper and hurling something at him. 'Can I think about it?'

She shrugged. 'Sure.' She could hardly blame him for feeling all at sea. This was uncharted territory and she felt exactly the same way. She pulled out one of the rolls. 'This is nice, isn't it?'

He took it from her and frowned. 'You can't use this in a boy's room.'

'Why on earth not? It has teddy bears. Teddy bears aren't gender specific. And it's not pink.' It gleamed in the most beautiful shades of ochre and gold.

'It has unicorns.'

'And…?'

He put the roll back on the shelf. 'Believe me, unicorns are a girl thing.' He picked up a different decal displaying jungle animals. 'What about this?'

She pointed. 'The tiger looks a bit fierce. I don't want to give the baby nightmares.'

He put it back and she found she didn't want to talk about nurseries any more, though if pressed she couldn't have said why. She'd been so excited at the prospect yesterday, but...

Before he could reach for another roll she said, 'Can I spring something else on you?'

He halted and then very slowly turned to face her. 'What?'

'I'm having that scan next week. Would you like to come along?'

'I've a few meetings next week.' His face closed up. 'I may even need to spend a day back in Rome, but if I'm free I'll be more than happy to drive you anywhere you need to go.'

'That's not what I meant, Ryan. I have a car. I can drive myself. What I'm asking is if you'd like to be present during the scan.'

He took a step back. 'I don't think...' He looked as if he wanted to turn and flee, but he set himself as if readying for a blow. 'What do you need me to do? What would you like me to do?'

She had to swallow back the ache that rose in her throat. 'It doesn't matter.' But it did. It mattered a lot.

'Then I'll just hang out in the waiting room until you're done.'

He didn't want to see the first pictures of his child, didn't want to hear its heartbeat? She turned from him to run her fingers along the decals, but she didn't see them. 'Ryan, do you love this baby yet?'

She glanced around at his quick intake of breath. He regarded her as if trying to work out what she wanted to hear and she shook her head. 'Honesty, remember? We promised to be honest with each other.'

His shoulders slumped a fraction. A passer-by wouldn't have noticed, but Marianna did. 'It still doesn't feel real to me,' he finally admitted.

She already loved this baby with a fierce protectiveness that took her completely off guard.

'You do.'

His words weren't a question, but a statement. She nodded. 'I expect it's different for a woman. The baby is growing inside of me—it's affecting me physically. That makes it feel very real.' Her stomach constricted at his stricken expression. 'I've also had more time to get used to the idea than you have, Ryan. There was no right or wrong answer to my question.' Just as long as he loved their baby once it arrived. That was all she asked.

He would, wouldn't he? It wouldn't just be a duty?

She reached up to scratch between her shoulder blades. 'How about we shelve the nursery for another day and focus on the things we need for the rest of the cottage?'

'Right.' He nodded. But he was quiet the entire time they bought paint, brushes, drop sheets and all the other associated paraphernalia one needed for painting. Marianna kept glancing at him, but she couldn't read his mood. While his expression remained neutral, she sensed turmoil churning beneath the surface.

'What next?' he asked when they'd stowed their purchases in the car.

'Soft furnishings.'

She waited for him to make an excuse to go and do something else and arrange to meet up again in an hour. He didn't. He said, 'Lead the way.'

Wow. Okay.

He didn't huff out so much as a single exaggerated sigh while endlessly shifting and fidgeting either. He didn't overtly quell yawns meant to inform her of his boredom, as her brothers would've done. He simply stacked the items she chose into the trolley he pushed, giving his opinion when she asked for it.

He had good taste too.

They moved from bedding to cushions and tablecloths and finally to curtains. 'They're just not right!' she finally said, tossing a set of curtains back to the shelf.

'What are you looking for?'

'Kitchen curtains. You know, the ones with the bit at the top and then...' She made vague hand gestures.

'Café curtains?'

She stared at him. 'Um...'

He rifled through the selections. 'Like these?'

'That style yes, but the print is hideous.'

'What kind of material are you after?'

She marched over to the store's fabric section and pulled out a roll with a print of orange and lime daisies. 'This is perfect.' A sudden thought struck her. 'Ooh, I wonder if I could find somebody to make them for me? I—'

'I can.'

'And then I—' She stopped dead. She moistened her lips and glanced around at him. 'Did you just say...' no, she couldn't have heard him right '...that you could make me a pair of curtains?'

'That's right.'

'You can sew?'

He nodded.

'How? Why?'

'I had a grandmother who loved to sew.'

He shuffled his feet and glanced away. She did her best to remake her expression into one of friendly interest rather than outright shock. 'She taught you to sew?'

He rolled his shoulders, glancing back at her with hooded eyes. 'Her eyesight started to fail and so...I used to help her out.'

She reached behind to support herself against a shelf. Of course he would love their baby. How could she have doubted it? A man who took the time to help an elderly lady sew because that was what she loved to do…because he loved her…

She swallowed and blinked hard. 'You'd make curtains for me?'

'Sure I will.' He suddenly frowned. 'Do you have a sewing machine?'

'My grandmother's will be rattling around somewhere.'

He shrugged again. 'Then no problem.'

Her eyes filled. He backed up a step, rubbed a fist across his mouth. 'Uh, Marianna…you're not going to cry, are you?'

She fanned her eyes. 'Pregnancy hormones,' she whispered.

He moved in close and took her shoulders in his hands. 'Okay, remember the drill. Close your eyes and take a deep breath.' As he counted to six she pulled in a long, slow breath. 'Hold.' She held. 'Now let it out to the count of six.'

They repeated that three times. When they were finished and she'd opened her eyes, he stepped back, letting his hands drop to his sides. 'Better?'

'Yes, thank you.'

'It's the silliest things, isn't it, that set you off?'

'Uh-huh.'

He snorted. 'It's just a pair of curtains.'

Oh, no, it wasn't. She spun around and pretended to consider the other rolls of fabric arrayed in front of them. These weren't just curtains. They were proof of his commitment to their baby. That wasn't nothing. It was huge… and she had to remember moments like this when he turned all cold and distant and unreadable. He was here for the baby. And he was here for her.

Who was there for him?

She swung back to him. 'You've been incredibly patient with me, Ryan. You haven't hassled me once yet about keeping up my end of our bargain.'

'You haven't been feeling well. Plus you've been working hard on the estate. I've no desire to add to your stress
levels.'

He might be cool and controlled but he had a kind heart.
'I've done enough mooching and mood swinging.' From
here on in she meant to help him as much as he helped
her. 'I need to make another stop before we call it a day.'

'No problem.'

She couldn't help it. She reached up on tiptoe and kissed
him.

CHAPTER SIX

'YOU SAID YOU wanted to learn about babies, right?'

Ryan eased back from where he taped the kitchen windows, to find Marianna setting a pile of bags onto the dining table. His pulse rate kicked up a notch, though he couldn't explain why. 'That's right.' He *needed* to learn about babies if he had any hope of making a halfway decent father.

She sent him a smile that carried the same warmth as the lavender-scented air drifting in from the French doors. It reminded him of how she'd smiled at him yesterday when he'd told her he'd make those stupid curtains she wanted.

It reminded him of the way she'd *kissed* him yesterday.

And just like that his skin tightened and he had to fight the rush of blood through his body—a rush that urged him to recklessness. He ground his teeth against it. Recklessness would wreck everything.

Marianna hadn't kissed him as a come-on or an invitation. She'd reached up on tiptoe and had pressed her warm, laughing lips to his in a moment of gratitude and high spirits. It wasn't the kind of kiss that should rock a man's world. It wasn't the kind of kiss that should keep a man up all night.

And yet hunger, need and desire had been gnawing away at him with a cruel persistence ever since. And now Marianna stood there smiling at him, eyes dancing, bouncing as if she could barely contain the energy coursing through her petite frame, and it was all he could do to bite back a groan.

Her smile wavered and she bit her lip. 'You don't have

other plans do you? Earlier you said you didn't mean to start painting in here until tomorrow.'

He wanted the smile back on her face. 'No plans.' Today he was prepping the walls for painting…and then getting to work on that report. He set the roll of tape to the kitchen bench and moved straight over to the table. 'I don't want the paint fumes making you feel sick. I thought that if I paint while you're at work…'

'The worst of it will have passed?' She wrinkled her nose—her darn gorgeous nose.

Don't notice her nose. Don't notice her mouth. Don't notice anything below her neck!

He shoved his hands into the pockets of his jeans. 'I'll air the house as well as I can. I bought an extractor fan, so…' He held out crossed fingers before shoving his hand into his pocket again where it was firmly out of temptation's way.

'Have I said thank you yet?'

Dear God in heaven, he couldn't risk her kissing him again. 'You have.' To distract her from further displays of gratitude, he nodded towards the bags. 'What have you got there?'

'A lesson.'

He tried to pull his mind to the task in hand. *Pay attention.* He had to learn how to take care of a baby.

She reached into the nearest bag and, with a flourish, pulled out a…

He blinked and backed up a step. "Uh, Marianna, that's a doll.' He scratched the back of his neck and glared at her from beneath a lock of hair that had fallen forward on his forehead. He really should get it cut. 'Don't you think we're a little old to be playing with dolls?'

She stared at that lock of hair and for a tension-fraught moment he thought she meant to lean across and push it out of his eyes. Hastily, he ran a hand back through his hair himself. She blinked and then shook herself. He let out a breath, his heart thumping.

She, however, seemed completely oblivious to his state. She dangled the doll—a life-sized version from what he could make out—from its foot, and smirked at him. 'Ooh, is the big strong man frightened of the itty-bitty dolly?'

He scowled. 'Don't be ridiculous.'

A laugh bubbled out of her and she sashayed around the table still dangling that stupid doll by its foot. 'Is your super-duper masculinity threatened by a little dolly?'

He snaked a hand around her head and drew her face in close to his. 'Tread carefully, Marianna.'

Her curls, all silk and sass, tickled his hand. 'I'm holding on by a thread here. My so-called masculinity is telling me to throw caution to the wind. It's telling me to kiss you, to take you to my bed and make love with you until you can barely stand.' And then he told her in the most straightforward, vivid language at his command exactly what he craved to do.

Her eyes darkened until they were nearly black. Her lips parted and she stared at his mouth as if she were parched. The pulse in her throat pounded. If he touched his lips to that spot they'd both be lost.

He hauled in a breath. With a super-human effort he let her go. She made a tiny sound halfway between an out-breath and a whimper that arrowed straight to his groin. He closed his eyes and gritted his teeth. 'You told me that if I do that—here in your real world—that I will hurt you, break your heart. I don't want to do that.'

He cracked open his eyes to find her nodding and smoothing a hand across her chest. She gripped the doll by its leg as if it were a hammer. He reached out and plucked it from her. 'There's no need to hurt poor dolly, though, is there?'

He said it to make her smile. It didn't work. She moved

back around the other side of the table, her movements jerky and uncoordinated. It hurt him somehow. It hurt to think he'd caused her even momentarily to lose her natural grace and bounce. Her gaze darted to him and away again. 'I'm sorry. I didn't mean for that to come across as any kind of...teasing.'

'I know. It's just...I'm...' He was teetering. He bit back a curse. 'I shouldn't have said anything. I—'

'No, no! It's best that I know.'

Not if it made her feel awkward. He shoved his hands as deep into his pockets as he could. 'It will pass, you know?'

'Oh, I know.' She nodded vigorously. 'It always does.'

He frowned then, recalling her brothers' taunting, *Paulo*. 'That sounds like the voice of experience.'

Her head snapped up. 'So what if it is?'

He blinked, but he had to admit that she had a point.

'It's okay for you to feel that way, but not me? It's okay for you to have had a lot of lovers, but not for me?'

'Not what I meant,' he growled. 'But if you do have experience in this...area, maybe you can hand out a tip or two about how to make it pass quickly.'

'Oh.' Her shoulders sagged. She lifted her hands and let them drop. 'In the past I haven't always had what's considered a good...attention span where men are concerned. I meet a new guy and it's all exciting and fun for a couple of weeks and then...'

Curiosity inched through him. 'And then?'

She wrinkled that cute nose. 'I don't know. It becomes dull, a bit boring and tedious.'

'This happens to you a lot?'

She shrugged, not meeting his eye.

'Which is why your brothers came up with the Paulo moniker.'

Her chin lifted. 'I believe in true love, okay? I don't believe there's anything wrong with looking for it.' Her chin hitched up higher. 'And I don't believe one should settle for anything less.'

'So... When a guy doesn't come up to scratch you what—dump him?'

She glared at him. 'What am I supposed to do? String him along and let him think I'm in love with him?'

'Of course not! I just—'

'I'd hate for any man to do that to me.' She folded her arms. 'I don't believe anyone should settle for anything less than true love.'

He couldn't have found a woman more unlike him if he'd tried!

'So what if I have high expectations of the man I mean to spend the rest of my life with? I'm more than happy for him to have high expectations of me too.'

Right...wow. 'So, you're happy to kiss a lot of frogs in this search for your Prince Charming?'

'Just because a man isn't my Prince Charming doesn't make him a frog, Ryan.'

Right.

She glanced at him. 'Isn't it like that for you—things becoming a bit boring and tedious after a while?'

He shook his head. 'One-night stands, that's what I do. No promises, no complications...and no time for them to become boring.' At her raised eyebrow he shuffled his feet. 'And once in a blue moon I might indulge in a holiday fling. A week is a long-term commitment in my book.'

'I should be flattered,' she said, her lips twisting in a wry humour that had a grin tugging at the corners of his mouth. She pulled out a chair and plonked down on it. 'What a pair.'

Cautiously he eased into the chair opposite.

She brightened, turning to him. 'All you need to do is start boring me.'

'I've been trying that with the colour charts.'

Her face fell. 'But I don't find them boring.' She tapped a finger to her chin. 'I could try nagging you,' she offered.

His lips twitched. A laugh shot out of her. 'Are you calling me a nag?'

'I wouldn't dream of it.'

She slapped her hands to the table, her eyes dancing. 'You're a bore and I'm a nag!'

Laughter spilled from her then—contagious, infectious—and Ryan found his entire body suddenly convulsing with it, every muscle juddering, a rush of warmth shooting through him. Belly-deep roars of laughter blasted out of him and he was helpless to quieten them even when he developed a stitch in his side.

Marianna laughed just as hard, her legs bouncing up and down, her curls dancing and tears that she tried to stem with her palms pouring down her cheeks. Every time he started to get himself back under control, Marianna would let loose with another giggle or snort and they'd both set off shrieking again. It was a complete overreaction, but the release in tension was irresistible.

'What on earth...?' Nico slid into the room, breathing hard. 'It sounds as if someone is being murdered in here!'

An utterance that only made Marianna laugh harder. Ryan choked back another burst of mirth. 'I'm thinking if I told you that I'm a bore and Marianna is a nag, that you wouldn't get the joke.'

'You'd be right.' But Nico's face softened when he glanced at his sister. He said something to her in Italian. She slowly sobered, although she retained an obscenely wide smile, and nodded.

It was stupid to feel excluded, but he did.

Marianna shot upright and clapped her hands. 'Ryan, will the painting be finished in here—' she gestured around the living, dining and kitchen areas '—by Saturday?'

He shrugged. 'Sure.' That was nearly a week away.

'Nico, are you busy next Saturday night? I want to invite you and Angelo for dinner—a housewarming dinner in my new home.'

Nico's face darkened. 'Are you sure you wouldn't prefer to live up at the villa?'

'Positive.' She tossed her glorious head of hair. 'Now say you'll come to dinner.'

He stared at her for a moment longer and finally smiled. 'I'd be delighted to.' He glanced at Ryan. 'I'll bring the wine.'

Ryan had a feeling that was meant to be some kind of subtle set down, but before he could form a response Nico's gaze lit on the doll. His mouth hooked up. *'You're playing dolls with my sister?'*

He squirmed and ran a finger around the collar of his shirt.

'We're learning to change a diaper,' Marianna announced.

Ah, so that had been her plan.

She raced around the table and dragged her brother across to the doll. 'You're going to want to play with *mia topolino* when it is born, yes?'

'Naturally.'

'"Mia topolino"?' Ryan asked.

'My little mouse,' she translated for him and his gut clenched. She had a pet name for their baby?

She turned back to Nico. 'You're going to want to babysit, yes?'

'Of course.'

'Then you need to know how to change a diaper.'

'I can already do so.'

Ryan stared at the other man. He could?

Marianna, however, refused to take Nico at his word.

She shoved the doll at him and then reached into another bag and brandished a disposable nappy. Ryan had never seen one before. With a supreme lack of self-consciousness, Nico quickly and deftly placed said nappy on the baby...uh, doll. Ryan frowned. That didn't look too hard.

He caught the doll when Nico tossed it to him with a mocking, 'Your turn.'

His stomach screwed up tight, but he refused to back down from the challenge. How hard could it be? He held out a hand to Marianna like a doctor waiting for a scalpel. 'Nappy.' She blinked. 'Diaper,' he amended. 'We call them nappies in Australia.'

She passed one across to him. He stared at it, turned it over. Why didn't these things come with Front and Back labels? And instructions? Gingerly he rested the baby on the table. *Doll, not baby.*

Nico's hands rested on his hips. 'You need to keep a hand on the baby to make sure it doesn't roll off the table.'

Marianna shushed her brother. Ryan tried to keep hold of the doll with one hand while unfolding the nappy with the other. Nico snickered. Damn it! He was all thumbs.

Ryan blocked his audience out as he tried to decipher the puzzle in front of him. Slipping what he hoped was the rear of the nappy beneath the baby, he brought the front up, and secured the sticky tabs at the sides. There, that hadn't been too hard, and for a first attempt it didn't look too bad. He lifted the baby under the arms prepared to crow at his performance, but the nappy slid off and fell to the floor with a soft thud. Damn!

Nico snorted. 'And you call yourself a father?'

Marianna opened her mouth, her eyes flashing, but Ryan touched her arm and she closed it again. He glared at Nico. 'I call myself a father-to-be.' He tossed the doll back. 'Show me how you did it again.' He would master this!

Twenty minutes later Ryan finally lifted the doll and

this time his effort at least stayed in place. Discarded diapers littered the table and the floor. He shook the doll.

'You're not—'

Ryan held up a finger to the man opposite. 'I know you're not supposed to shake babies, but this is a doll, in case you hadn't noticed. I've already killed it multiple times by letting it roll off the table, smothering it beneath a sea of nappies, and it's probably concussed from where I accidentally cracked its head on the back of the chair.'

Thank heavens Marianna had the foresight to give him a doll to practise on.

'I know it's probably peed on me—' that discussion had proved particularly enlightening '—puked on me and probably bitten me, but...' he shook the doll again '...that nappy isn't going anywhere.'

He felt a ludicrous sense of achievement. He could change a nappy!

'Don't get too cocky. Wait until you have to change a dirty diaper. One that smells so bad it's like a kick in the gut and—'

'Enough, Nico,' Marianna said. 'My turn now.'

She took the doll, and, with her tongue caught between her teeth, repeated the process of putting the diaper on. Ryan moved in closer to check her handiwork. 'That looks pretty good.'

She shook her head and frowned. 'I did what you did. I didn't make it tight enough.' She slid several fingers between the diaper and the doll to prove her point. 'It's just... I don't want to cut the poor baby's circulation off.' She glanced across at her brother. 'Are you going to say something cutting about my prospective mothering abilities?'

Nico shuffled his feet and glowered at the floor. 'Of course not.'

A surge of affection swamped Ryan then. She'd just risked criticism and scorn from her brother to show solidarity with him. Nobody had done anything like that for him before, and he was fairly certain he didn't deserve it now, but…to not feel cut off, adrift, alone. To feel connected and part of a team, it was… He rolled his shoulders. It was kind of nice.

Nico pointed a finger at Marianna. 'You've changed diapers before. You must have at harvest time. We have so many workers then. Many of them with children,' he added for Ryan's benefit.

'I did, but I was never particularly good at it and…well, people stopped asking me.' Her shoulders had started inching up towards her ears. In the next moment she tossed her head. 'I was really good at keeping the children entertained, cajoling them out of tears and bad tempers.'

For the first time it struck him that Marianna might be feeling as intimidated and overwhelmed as he did about their impending parenthood.

'And what's more, dearest brother of mine, if you mean to continue standing there criticising us, then be warned that I'll tell Ryan how you used to play Barbie dolls with me when I was a little girl.'

Nico backed up a step and pointed behind him. 'I'll, uh, leave you to it. I have work to do.' He turned and fled.

Ryan stared after him. Had he really played dolls with his little sister? He glanced at Marianna, who was having a second attempt at getting the nappy on, and then at the door again. The guy couldn't be all bad.

'Ryan?'

He turned to face her more fully. 'Yes?'

'I'm sorry about my brother.'

'No apology needed. And thank you.' He gestured to the table, the doll and the pile of nappies. 'This was a great idea. I'm going to have to start practising.' He was going to be the best damn nappy changer the Amatucci clan had ever seen.

* * *

Marianna watched Ryan put, oh, yet another diaper on the doll, his face a mask of determination, and something inside her softened. He was trying so hard. 'You're getting better,' she offered.

'We're going to run out of diapers soon.'

It was sweet too that he called them diapers now, probably for her benefit. 'We can get more.'

He glanced at her; his eyes danced for a moment, bringing out the deep blue in their depths that so intrigued her. 'I'll make a deal with you, Mari...'

The easy shortening of her name and the familiarity it implied made her break out in delicious gooseflesh. *It's a lie—an illusion.* She couldn't forget that. 'A deal?'

'I'll be the main diaper changer if you take on the role of dealing with Junior's tears and temper.'

'We'd need to be co-parenting together full-time for that kind of deal to work.' It was starting to hit her how difficult single parenthood was going to be. Sure, Ryan wanted to be involved, but they both knew the bulk of the baby's care would fall to her.

Unless Ryan moved to Monte Calanetti and they agreed to a fifty-fifty child custody arrangement. She bit her lip. She didn't like that thought. She wanted the baby with her full-time. She rolled her lip between her teeth. Okay, she was honest enough to admit that she might want the occasional night off, but nothing more. She didn't want the baby spending half its time away from her. She glanced at Ryan to find he'd gone deathly pale. What on earth...?

She went back over their conversation and then rolled her eyes. 'Get over yourself! I'm not angling for a marriage proposal. We decided against that, remember?'

He searched her face, and slowly his colour returned. He nodded and dragged a hand down his face.

'I haven't forgotten. You're commitment-shy and a lone wolf.'

'While you have a short attention span when it comes to men.'

She folded her arms and stared at him for a long moment. 'You're different from the other men I've known, though. This is different—us…we're different.' Why was that? 'But it doesn't mean I want to marry you.' She couldn't fool herself that it meant anything or that it would lead anywhere. 'I've never stayed friends with any of my previous lovers.' That probably had something to do with it.

'Me neither.'

'And I've certainly never had a baby with anyone before.'

He raised both hands. 'Nor I.'

'So obviously this is going to be different from any other experience we've had before, right?'

'Absolutely.'

She glanced at him but it wasn't relief that trickled through her. The itch she couldn't reach, the one right in the middle of her back between her shoulder blades, pricked with a renewed ferocity that made her grit her teeth. Her skin prickled, her stomach clenched, and a roaring hunger bellowed through her with so much ferocity it was all she could do not to scream. Sleeping with Ryan would sate that itch and need, soothe the burn and bite. Sleeping with Ryan would quieten the fears racing through her and—

'Don't look at me like that, Marianna!'

She started, the hunger in his eyes making her sway towards him, but he shook his head and took a step back. Instinct told her that if she continued to stare at him so boldly, so…lustfully, he'd seize her in his arms, kiss her and they probably wouldn't even make it to her bedroom.

She craved that like a drug. She craved it more than she'd ever craved anything. To fall into Ryan's arms and lose herself in a world of sensation and physical gratification, what a dream! But... What she felt for Ryan was different from what she'd felt for anyone. The intensity of it frightened her. She didn't want this man breaking her heart. That'd be a disaster. Through their child, they'd be tied to each other for the rest of their lives. It'd leave her no room to get over him.

She gripped the back of a chair and dragged her gaze from his. Pulling the chair out, she fell into it. 'I really, *really* can't wait for the time when you become boring. I...I have things to do.' With that she leapt up and strode away, and all the while her fickle heart urged her to turn back and throw herself into Ryan's arms, to throw caution to the wind.

Ryan pounced on his phone the moment it rang. 'Ryan White.'

'It's confirmed. Conti Industries are getting cold feet,' his assistant in Rome said without preamble. She knew his impatience with small talk and had learned long ago to get straight to the point. Time was money.

'Why?' Was someone conducting a smear campaign, attempting to discredit him?

'It appears the fact that you're not personally in Rome at the moment has them questioning your commitment.'

Damn it! He wheeled away, raking a hand back through his hair. He'd been afraid this would happen—that Conti Industries would develop cold feet. Why on earth had he promised to stay in Monte Calanetti for a whole month? He needed his head read!

He straightened, moving immediately into damage control. 'Can you arrange a meeting?'

'I already have.'

He let out a breath. 'That's the reason I pay you the big bucks.' Face-to-face with the Conti Industries' executive committee he'd be able to turn things around, prove their former faith in him wasn't a mistake.

'But it's this afternoon. You need to get down here *pronto*.'

Today!

'I tried making it for tomorrow, but they insisted. They're viewing this meeting as, quote, "a validation of your commitment to their project and your ability to deliver". They've left me in no doubt that agreeing to meet is an unprecedented demonstration of faith. I don't need to tell you what'll happen if you miss this meeting.'

He pressed his lips together. No, she didn't. If he weren't in Rome this afternoon, the whole deal would go down the gurgler. He thrust out his jaw. He wasn't letting that happen. Not without a fight.

'I'll be there,' he said, bringing the call to an abrupt end.

He glanced through his electronic diary as he hauled on a suit. The only thing he had slotted in was Marianna's information session this evening. He let out a breath. He'd be able to catch up on that another time. He slipped a tie around his collar and tied a perfect Windsor knot. He'd ring her later to let her know he couldn't make it.

As he drove away from the vineyard a short time later the rush of chasing the big deal sped through him, filling him with adrenaline and fire. He'd missed that cut-and-thrust this past week. This was the world where he belonged, not decorating nurseries. Drumming his fingers against the car's steering wheel, he wondered if he could cut his time at Marianna's vineyard a week or two short.

Marianna glanced at her watch and paced the length of her living room before whirling back. It was ten past six.

Where was Ryan? The information session at the clinic started in twenty minutes!

She'd reminded him about it this morning. He'd told her he hadn't forgotten, that it was in his diary, that he'd drive them. So where was he?

She glanced at her watch again. Eleven minutes past six. With a growl, she dialled his mobile number and pressed her phone to her ear. It went straight to voicemail. Brilliant. 'Where are you? The session starts in nineteen minutes! I can't wait any longer. I'll meet you at the clinic.'

Seizing her car keys, she stormed out and drove herself to the town's medical clinic. She'd just parked when her phone buzzed in her handbag. A text. From Ryan.

Something came up. In Rome. Won't be back till tomorrow. Sorry, couldn't be helped. Meeting very important. Will make next info session.

He couldn't even be bothered to ring her?

She stared at the screen. Blinking hard, she shoved the phone back into her bag. Right, well, she knew exactly where she and the baby stood in the list of Ryan's priorities—right at the very bottom.

How on earth did either one of them think this was going to work?

'Don't even think about it!'

Marianna spun around, clutching her chest, to find Ryan—with hands on his hips—silhouetted in the large cellar door. As he was backlit by the sun she couldn't see his face, but she had a fair inkling that he was glaring at her. She gestured to the barrel, her heart pounding. 'It's empty.'

He moved forward and effortlessly lifted it onto her trolley.

She swallowed and tried to smile. 'See? Not heavy.'

He stabbed a finger at her. 'You shouldn't be lifting anything. You should be looking after yourself.'

She batted his finger away. 'Stop being such a mother hen. I'm used to this kind of manual labour. It won't hurt the baby.'

'But why take the risk?' He gestured to the barrel. 'You must have staff here who can take care of these things for you?'

Of course they did, but she didn't want anyone thinking she couldn't do her job. She didn't want anyone thinking she was using her pregnancy as an excuse to slacken off. She wanted everyone to see how steady and professional she'd become since returning from Australia. She wanted everyone to see how she'd developed her potential, wanted them to say what a talent she was, what an asset for Vigneto Calanetti.

'I don't want to lose my fitness or my strength, Ryan. I'll need them for when I return to work after my maternity leave.'

He blinked.

'I'm going to need both for the labour too.' The information evening had brought that home to her with stunning—and awful—clarity. The information evening he *hadn't* attended so what right did he think he had ordering her around like this now?

He frowned. 'You're active—always on the go. I don't think you need to worry on that head.'

Ha! If he, Nico and Angelo had any say in the matter she wouldn't lift a finger for the next six and a half months. Well, at dinner on Saturday night she'd show her brothers how accomplished and capable she'd become. She'd wow them with her new house, a superb dinner and marvellous conversation. They'd realise she was a woman in charge of her own destiny—they'd stop worrying she'd screwed up her life and…and they'd all move forward from there.

'Are you worried about the labour?'

'Not a bit of it,' she lied. She straightened. 'How was your meeting in Rome?'

'Yes, I'm so sorry about that. It really couldn't be helped.'

Why wasn't he asking about the info session? She tried to keep the disapproving tone out of her voice. 'Did you come looking especially for me? Was there something you needed?'

'Just a break from painting for a bit.' He grimaced. 'The smell can become a little overwhelming.'

'I'm sorry. I didn't think about—'

'I'm enjoying it. Don't apologise. It's just…I found myself curious about what you do all day and—' he gestured around '—this place.'

So he was interested in her work, but not their baby. She had to remind herself that the idea of a baby was still very new to him, and that at least he was trying. And she couldn't wholly blame him—to her mind vineyards and wineries were fascinating.

He rolled his shoulders. 'I mean, you leave at the crack of dawn each day.'

She suddenly laughed. 'Ryan, I'm not leaving early to avoid you. I've always been a lark and I love checking the vines in the early morning when everything is fresh and drenched in dew. It means I can have the afternoons free if I want.' At his look she added, 'At the moment there's a certain amount of work that needs to be done, but it doesn't really matter when I do it.'

'The convenience of being your own boss.'

'Don't you believe it. Nico is the boss here. Don't let his easy-going mildness fool you. He has a killer work ethic.'

'Easy-going?' he choked. 'Mild?'

She laughed at his disbelief and led him out of the door and gestured to the row upon row of vines marching up the hill, all starting to flower. Those flowers might not be considered pretty, but she thought them beautiful. And if each of them were properly pollinated they'd become a glorious luscious grape. 'Beautiful, isn't it?'

He blew out a long breath and nodded.

'I can offer our child a good home, Ryan. A good life.'

'I know that.'

She hoped he did. 'Would you like a tour of our facilities here?'

'I'd love that.' He suddenly frowned. 'But only because I'm curious, not because I doubt you.'

She wasn't so convinced, but she showed him everything. She showed him what she looked for in a grape and what she was working towards. She took him to see the presses, the fermentation vats and the aging vessels. She even took him into the bottling room. She ended the tour at the cellar door where she had him try several of their more renowned wines.

'Things are relatively quiet at the moment, but at harvest time it becomes crazy here. In September, we eat, breathe and sleep grapes.' She glanced up at him. 'You should try and make it back then to experience it. It's frenetic but fun.'

'I'll see what I can do.' But he already knew he'd be tied up working the Conti contract. He glanced beyond her and nodded. 'Nico.'

She turned to find Nico with their new neighbour Louisa standing behind her. She straightened, hoping Nico didn't think she was skiving off. 'I was just showing Ryan around. Hello, Louisa.'

The other woman smiled and it somehow helped to ease the tension between the two men. 'I understand congratulations are in order,' the other woman said. 'News of your pregnancy has spread like wildfire through the village.'

She could barely contain her grin. *A baby!* 'Thank you.' Beside her, Ryan shifted and she came back to herself. 'Louisa, this is Ryan White. He's staying with me for a bit. Ryan, this is Louisa Harrison. She recently inherited the vineyard and glorious *palazzo* next door. Speaking of which, how are the renovations coming along?'

Louisa lifted a shoulder. 'No sooner did the architect arrive than it seemed the renovations to the chapel started. There are workers swarming all over the *palazzo*! The schedule is to have it completed by the end of July. But… it's such a big job.'

Marianna nodded. The *palazzo* was glorious and the family chapel absolutely exquisite, but it'd been neglected for a long time. It'd be wonderful to see it restored to its former glory.

'The architect is based in Rome and has a very good reputation,' Louisa continued. 'He used to holiday here as a child apparently. It seemed sensible to choose a firm that had connections to the area.'

'What's his name?' Marianna asked.

'Logan Cascini.'

'I remember him! He and Angelo were a similar age, I think. I'm sure they hung out together.'

Nico nodded. 'They did.'

'It'll be lovely to see him again. Is he married?' Was there a new woman in town who needed befriending? 'Any *bambinos*?' She bit back a smile. It wasn't as if she had babies on the brain or anything.

Louisa shook her head.

Beside her, Ryan shifted again and she glanced up at him, puzzled at the sudden tension that coursed through him. He glared at Nico. 'While you're here, perhaps you can talk some sense into your sister and tell her heavy lifting is off the agenda until after the baby is born.'

Oh, brilliant. She and Nico had already had words on this head.

Nico stiffened. 'Marianna?'

'I caught her lifting a barrel.'

She sent Ryan an exasperated glare. The big fat tale teller! 'It was an *empty* barrel.'

Nico let forth with a torrent of Italian curses that made her wince. Finally he stabbed a finger at her. 'Why can you not get this through your thick skull?'

She started to shrivel inside.

'No more lifting. One more time, Mari, and I'm firing you!'

Her jaw dropped. 'You can't!' This was her job, her work, her home!

'I can and I will!'

He would too. She battled the lump in her throat.

'No more lifting! You hear me?'

All she could manage was a nod. *Screw-up. Useless. Failure.* The accusations went around and around in her head. So much for proving her worth.

'Why have you not been keeping a better eye on her?' Nico shot at Ryan.

'Me? You're her employer!'

She closed her eyes. She opened them again when Louisa touched her arm. 'How have you been feeling? Have you had much morning sickness?'

She could've hugged her for changing the subject and bringing Ryan and Nico's finger-pointing to a halt. 'A little. And the morning part of that is a lie. It can happen at any time of the day.' She sucked her bottom lip into her mouth. 'I probably shouldn't have announced my pregnancy until after my scan.' What if something went wrong? Everybody would know and—

'But you were excited.'

Louisa smiled her understanding, and it helped Marianna to straighten and push her shoulders back. This incident might've been a backward step as far as Nico's view of her went, but she was going to be a mother, and she was determined to be a good one.

'Speaking of which,' Nico said, 'I believe you said your scan is tomorrow, yes?'

Ryan stiffened and then swung to her. 'Tomorrow?'

Nico's eyes narrowed and she could see his view of her maturity take another nosedive. *Damn it!*

She waved an airy hand in the air. 'Don't tell me you've forgotten? You did say you'd take me.'

To Ryan's credit, he adjusted swiftly and smoothly. 'Of course. Just as we planned.'

Damn it again! She hadn't wanted him to take her. What use would she have for a man who had no interest in hearing his baby's heartbeat?

CHAPTER SEVEN

MARIANNA THREW HERSELF down on a bench in the garden, slapping a palm to her forehead. 'Well done, you…doofus!' she muttered. To think she'd been making progress where Angelo and Nico were concerned, to think—

She leaned to the side until her head rested on the arm of the bench and did what she could to halt the flood of recriminations pounding through her. She tried the breathing technique that Ryan had taught her, but in this instance it didn't work. All it did was bring to mind the light in his eyes when he'd returned to the cottage to paint her walls. It'd told her that the subject of her scan—of her not telling him the actual date of said scan—would be the topic of conversation the moment she returned.

Yay. More talking. Which, of course, was why she was hiding out in the garden like a coward.

Very adult of you, Marianna.

Heat pricked the backs of her eyes and a lump swelled in her throat. What if they were right? What if she were making a hash of everything? She pressed a hand to her stomach. What if she made a mess of her baby's life?

'It's all a mess!'

For a moment she thought Nico's voice sounded in her own mind. When Louisa answered with, 'What do you mean?' Marianna realised that her brother and their neighbour passed close by on the other side of the hedge. The hedge's shade and its new spring growth shielded her from view. She shrank back against the bench, not wanting Nico to see her so upset.

'I don't trust this latest man of Marianna's.'

Marianna wanted to cover her ears. Ryan wasn't hers.

'Can I give you a word of advice, Nico?'

Her brother must've nodded because Louisa continued. 'You don't have to like Ryan, but if Marianna has decided that he's to be a part of her baby's life, then you're going to have to accept that. He's going to be a part of your niece or nephew's life for evermore—in effect, a part of your extended family. You don't have to like him, but if Marianna has asked that you respect her decision, then you're going to have to find a way to get along with him…for both Marianna and the baby's sake.'

'But—'

'No buts, Nico. You know, if you eased up on him for a bit, you might even find yourself liking Ryan.'

Her brother snorted. 'You think?'

'You never know.'

Marianna remained where she was, barely moving, until the voices drifted out of earshot. She hadn't meant to overhear. She hadn't meant to throw everyone into chaos with her baby news either. She forced herself off the bench and set off for the cottage.

The smell of paint hit her the moment she entered. She paused on the threshold, but her stomach remained calm and quiet and with a relieved breath she continued down the hallway to the living area.

She pulled to an immediate halt with a delighted, 'Oh!' Clutching her hands beneath her chin, she gazed around in wonder at the transformation a coat of deliciously tranquil 'sea foam'-coloured paint had created. Ryan must've worked his socks off!

She completed a slow circle. 'Oh, Ryan, it's perfect. Thank you.' She ached to lie on the sofa and revel in the calm, draw it into her soul.

'You weren't going to tell me that your appointment is tomorrow, were you?'

She bit back a sigh. The calm was only an illusion. In

the same way her and Ryan's *friendship* was an illusion. She turned towards the dining table where he sat. He rose and she wished herself back outside in her shady glen. 'Tea?' She stumbled into the kitchen and filled the kettle.

'Marianna?'

She didn't like the growl in his voice or the latent possessiveness rippling beneath it. 'No.' She turned and faced him, hands on her hips. 'You have that correct. I wasn't going to tell you about tomorrow's appointment.'

'Why not?'

She pulled two cups towards her and tossed teabags into them. 'Because you have no interest in being there.' Just as he'd had no interest in attending the information session.

'I said I would drive you.'

'And I told you I don't need a taxi service!'

His head reared back as if she'd slapped him. 'But... we're a team.'

Were they? Wasn't that just a polite fiction? 'If you don't want to be present at the scan, Ryan, then you're more use to me here fixing up the cottage.'

She spoke as baldly and bluntly as she could to remind herself that what they had here was a deal, an arrangement, and not a relationship.

He dragged a hand across his jaw, his eyes troubled. 'Then why the pretence in front of Nico?'

She pulled in a breath, held it to the count of three and let it out again. 'Because I don't want him to think badly of you...and I don't want him to think badly of me.'

'Why would he think badly of you? He worships the ground you walk on.'

She snorted and he frowned. She swung away to pour boiling water into their mugs. 'I'm his pesky little sister who's always getting into scrapes.'

'He adores you, Mari. He'd die for you.'

'I know.' He spoke nothing less than the truth.

'So would Angelo.'

That was the truth too. But sometimes she felt the weight of their love would suffocate her.

She started. 'Oh! I made you a chamomile tea. Should I—?'

'You should've asked me to make the tea! You've been on your feet all day.'

She nodded at the walls. 'And you haven't?' Not only was he painting her house, he was working on some new company report or other, taking endless calls on his mobile phone and making video calls on his laptop. If anyone were the slacker around here it'd be her.

He came around and took the mug from her. 'This will be fine, thank you.' When he gestured for her to take a seat on the sofa, she submitted. If they had to *talk*, then they might as well be comfortable while they did so.

'Look, I know you love your brothers.' He sat in the armchair opposite. 'I know you would die for them too.'

She would. In a heartbeat. She blinked, frowned. Did her love ever suffocate them?

'I understand it's important to you that I get along with them.'

He took a sip of his tea and grimaced.

She couldn't help grimacing too. In sympathy. 'You don't have to drink that, you know? Chamomile is an acquired taste.'

'You went to the trouble of making it, therefore I mean to drink it.'

What an enigma this man was proving to be. She slumped back. 'Getting on with my brothers isn't entirely in your control, Ryan. It's up to them too.'

His eyes had turned a stormy green that she was starting to recognise as a mixture of confusion and frustration. 'The fact you lied to Nico—'

'Lied is a bit harsh!'

'Well, let him believe I was included in tomorrow's appointment, then.'

Not that it'd worked. Nico had seen through her deception.

'Leads me to believe,' Ryan continued, 'that being present at this scan is something a *good* father would do.'

She leapt to her feet, setting her mug to the coffee table before she could spill it. 'Oh! You think?' How could this man be so clueless?

No, no, he couldn't be this clueless. It was just that whole stupid lone-wolf thing he had going and—

'Oh!' She stopped dead before racing across to the kitchen again. 'You made the kitchen curtains.' She ran her hands down the material. How had she not noticed them earlier? 'They're...*exactly* what I wanted.' They would look wonderful against the vibrant yellow of the walls once Ryan had painted in here—a nook of colour amidst the calm.

His voice came from behind her. 'You like them?'

She loved them. A lump blocked her throat and all she could do was nod. They were perfect. She glanced around the cottage at the new paint on the living and dining room walls, the kitchen primed and ready for its first coat of paint tomorrow, and at those darn curtains. Ryan was doing everything she asked of him without a murmur of complaint. He was doing everything he could to help her create the perfect home for their baby.

She moved across to the dining table and picked up the doll lying there—a doll sporting a perfect diaper and a ridiculous smile. She clutched the doll to her chest and swung to face him. 'Ryan, how can you not want to see the first pictures of our baby? How can you not want to hear its heartbeat?'

He dragged a hand across his jaw, not meeting her gaze. 'I have work to do.'

She dropped the doll back to the table. 'Work that's more important than your own child?'

Tension shot through him. With an oath, he started to pace. 'The truth?' he shot at her.

'The truth,' she demanded.

'Fine, then!' He swung back. 'Attending the ultrasound with you seems...'

'Seems what?' she pushed.

He skewered her to the spot with the ruthless light in his eyes. 'Too intimate.'

She rocked back on her heels, his words shocking her. 'It's not as intimate as the deed that's led us to this point in time.'

'True.' He nodded, his gaze not softening. 'But making love with you—our holiday fling...absolutely nothing out of character for me there.'

Except it'd lasted for a whole week rather than a single night. She left that observation unsaid.

'Attending an ultrasound with a woman...now that's utterly out of character. Can't see what use I'm going to be to you in that scenario, Marianna.'

Her chest cramped up so tight it became an effort to even breathe. Finally she managed a curt nod. 'If you want to become a halfway decent father, Ryan, you're going to have to get over this kind of squeamishness.'

His eyes bugged. 'Squeamishness?'

'Squeamishness about doing family things, feeling able to step up to the plate for another person, being relied upon.'

He swung away. 'I'm supposed to be in Rome tomorrow afternoon.'

'And just for the record, this isn't about you stepping up to the plate for me. It's not about you—' how had he put it? '—being of any use to me. This isn't about you and me.' There was no him and her. 'This is about you and the baby.'

His mouth thinned. 'This is all because I missed that damn info session, isn't it?'

"It's becoming obvious that your work is more important to you than our baby."

"Correction. That particular meeting was more important than attending an info session I can catch again at another time."

"And in the years to come a different important meeting will have you missing your child's second birthday, others will have you missing the school concert, a soccer grand final. You'll cancel promised outings and holidays because something important has come up at work. I want more than that for my child, Ryan. And you should too."

They stared at each other, both breathing hard. She swallowed and shrugged. 'The ultrasound is early—nine-thirty a.m.' He could attend the scan and still make an afternoon appointment in Rome. 'I'm driving myself. If you wish to attend, a flyer for the clinic with its address is on the fridge. I don't want to discuss this any more. I'm tired and I don't feel like fighting.' With that she walked back over to the sofa and picked up her chamomile tea.

He was quiet for a moment. 'I didn't mean to upset you.'

She waved that away.

He strode back and threw himself down into his chair. He leaned towards her suddenly, frowning. 'Are you worried about tomorrow's scan?'

She stared down into her tea. 'Of course not,' she lied.

But... What if she'd somehow hurt their baby? Her fingers tightened about her mug. For the best part of two months she hadn't even realised she was pregnant. She'd been drinking wine and coffee—not copious amounts, but still... She should've been taking special vitamins. If she'd planned this baby, she wouldn't have these worries. She'd have done everything right from the start.

She swallowed. She might be an irresponsible fool and

if the scan showed a problem tomorrow she'd have nobody to blame but herself. And now she wouldn't even have the comfort of Ryan's hand to cling to.

Marianna readied herself for the sensation of cold gel on her tummy when the technician's assistant tapped on the door and then popped her head around the curtain that screened Marianna. 'Sorry to disturb, but there's a Mr White out here who claims he's the baby's father.'

Marianna couldn't help it, her heart leapt.

'Shall I send him in?'

Marianna nodded. 'Yes, please.'

A moment later Ryan hovered awkwardly on the other side of the curtain, his face appearing in the gap. 'Sorry, I'm late.'

Marianna ached to hold her hand out to him, but she resisted the urge. She had no intention of making this all seem too *intimate*. 'I wasn't sure you'd make it.' She gestured to the equipment. 'Come on over and watch the show.'

He moved to stand beside her, but he didn't take her hand.

Marianna tried to ignore his warmth and scent, focusing on the monitor as the radiologist moved the sensor across her stomach and pointed out the baby's arms and legs, feet and fingers. She pronounced the baby to be in the best of health and Marianna let out the breath she'd been holding, her eyes still glued to the screen. *Thank you!*

Her heart started to pound, wonder filling her from the inside out, and she couldn't stop from reaching a hand towards the image on the monitor. She couldn't remember a more amazing moment in her life. Her baby!

Their baby.

She turned to Ryan and her heart stilled at the expression that spread across his face. She watched as his amazement turned to awe. He blinked hard several times, and a fist seized her heart. He swallowed and leaned towards the monitor...and she watched him fall in love with their baby.

That was the moment her chest cracked open. She felt as if she were falling and falling—as if there were no end in sight, no bottom to bring her up short—and then Ryan seized her hand, a breath whooshed out of her, and the world righted itself again.

He squeezed her hand, not taking his eyes from the screen. 'That's really something, isn't it?'

'Utterly amazing,' she breathed, not taking her eyes from his face.

But then he suddenly shot back, shaking his fingers free from hers, the colour leaching from him.

'Ryan?'

He glanced at his watch. 'I'm sorry, but if I don't get a move on I won't make my appointment this afternoon in Rome. I won't be back till tomorrow.'

With that he spun on his heel and left the room. Marianna turned back to the monitor and the image of her baby. Her temples started to throb.

Ryan stared around the chaos of the kitchen and grimaced. He rubbed the back of his head. 'What can I do?'

'Nothing!'

He glanced at his watch. Angelo and Nico weren't due to arrive for at least another hour, but...

The house was spick and span with not a single item out of place. Marianna had slaved over it all day. Ryan valued neatness and utility, but this was...*so* neat. Then again, maybe the kitchen made up for it. He turned to view it again and had to blink. The yellow on the walls was...bright.

He spun back to the rest of the room. It wasn't as if the neatness made things sterile, like a hotel room. Marianna's new scatter cushions and strategically draped throw rugs brightened the sofa, making it look like an inviting oasis to rest one's weary bones. But…

He shuffled his feet. 'Marianna—'

'No, no, don't talk to me! I have to concentrate. This recipe is complicated.'

He touched her arm. 'It's just your brothers. They won't care if you ring out for pizza.'

'Ring out?' Her mouth dropped open, her hair fizzing about her face in outrage.

He stared at that mouth and tension coiled up through him.

'I'm not ringing out! This dinner is going to be perfect!'

Why? Not because of him, he hoped. He didn't want her putting this kind of pressure on herself on his behalf.

He tapped a clenched fist against his mouth. It'd be pointless trying to reason with her when she was in this mood, though. Mind you, she'd been distant—wary—ever since he'd returned from Rome yesterday.

He winced anew when he recalled the way he'd bolted from the clinic during the ultrasound. The moment had been… He rubbed his nape. Well, it'd been perfect for a bit…before he'd started to feel as if he were drowning. Emotions he'd had no name for had pummelled him, trying to drag him under, and he'd needed to get away—needed time to breathe and pull himself back together.

It was all of those happy family vibes flying about the room. They'd tried to wrestle him into a straitjacket and put a noose around his neck. Worse still, for a moment he'd wanted to let them.

He didn't do happy families. He'd be the best father he could be to this child, but he wasn't marrying Marianna. He dragged a hand down his face. *That* would be a disaster.

He'd calmed down. Eventually. He had his head together again.

Now all he had to do was get through this evening.

He glanced at Marianna again. Her jerky movements and the way she muttered under her breath told him how much importance she'd placed on this meal. He made a mental note to do all he could to get along with her brothers tonight.

'There's nothing you can do. Go sit on the sofa and enjoy doing nothing for a change.'

He didn't. When she became absorbed again in some complicated manoeuvre involving flour, butter and potato, he slid in behind her and made a start on washing up the tower of dishes that was in danger of toppling over and burying her.

The scent of her earlier preparations—sautéed onion, garlic and bacon—rose up around him, making his mouth water. He managed to clear one entire sink of dishes without her yelling at him to get out from under her feet or accusing him once of being a neat freak. He even managed to dry and put them away, sliding out of her way whenever she spun around to seize another dish or wooden spoon or ingredient.

He was just starting on a second sink full of dishes— how could anyone use so many dishes to make one meal?— when a commotion sounded at the front door and Angelo and Nico marched in. Angelo carried an armful of flowers in one hand and a gift-wrapped vase under his arm. Nico bore a brightly wrapped gift. 'Happy housewarming!' they bellowed.

Marianna glared at them and pointed to the clock on the wall. 'You're early!'

'We couldn't wait to see you, *bella sorella*,' Angelo said, dropping an arm to her shoulders and easing her away from the stove and towards the living area. In one smooth movement Nico slid into her place and took over the cooking. 'Besides, we come bearing gifts.'

It was masterfully done and if he hadn't had wet hands Ryan would've applauded.

Marianna glanced at the flowers and clasped her hands beneath her chin. 'Oh! They're beautiful.'

Without a word, Ryan took the vase Angelo handed across the breakfast bar and filled it with water.

Marianna spun around to point a finger at Nico. 'I know exactly what the two of you are doing!'

Angelo took the now-filled vase and placed it on the coffee table. 'Should I just dump the flowers in?'

Marianna immediately swung back. 'No, you should not!' And set about arranging the flowers. 'But it doesn't change the fact that I know what the two of you are doing. You still don't think I can cook gnocchi.'

'You can't,' Nico said with a grin. 'And we knew it's what you'd try to make tonight.'

She shrugged. 'It's your favourite.' She straightened. 'And I'll have you know I've become very adept at the dish.'

'No, you haven't,' Angelo said with a grin. 'You're a brilliant tosser of salads, Mari, you make masterful pizzas, and your omelettes are to die for, but gnocchi isn't your thing. In the same way that Nico can't master a good sauterne.'

'Pah!' She waved that away. 'We don't grow the right grapes for sauterne.'

'And yet he keeps trying,' Angelo said with a teasing grin at his brother.

'Ooh, says you.' Marianna rolled her eyes. 'You keep telling me you have a green thumb, but who keeps killing my African violets?'

Ryan watched the three of them tease each other, boss each other, and a chasm of longing suddenly cracked open in his chest. He didn't understand it. He tried to shake it off. He told himself he was glad his child would have this family. And he was…but when Marianna eventually married *the man of her dreams* would their child feel an out-sider amidst all of this belonging? As he did.

'You've done a good job in here, Ryan,' Nico said in an undertone. 'How on earth did you make it into the kitchen without having something thrown at you?'

'Subterfuge…and a quick two-step shuffle to get out of her way whenever she was reaching for something.'

Her brothers obviously knew her well. And then it hit him. Nico had just called him Ryan, not Paulo. Did that mean Marianna's brothers had decided on a temporary ceasefire? He put the last dried dish away. 'Anything I can do?'

'Know anything about gnocchi?'

'Nope.'

'Know anything about wine?'

Ryan glanced at the bottle Nico had placed on the bench earlier. 'I know how to pour it.'

'Then pour away.'

He poured three glasses of wine and then filled a fourth with mineral water, three ice cubes and a slice of lime—the exact way Marianna liked it. When he took their drinks to them, though, Marianna pursed her lips, glanced over at Nico, and started to rise. Nico chose that moment to move out from behind the breakfast bar with his glass of wine and handed her the wrapped package, ensuring she remained ensconced on the sofa. 'It's not a housewarming present,' he warned. 'It's a…' He shrugged. 'Open and see.'

Ryan watched in interest, his breath catching in his chest when Marianna pulled forth the most exquisite teddy bear he'd ever seen. Her eyes filled with tears and she hugged it. 'Oh, Angelo and Nico, it's perfect. Just perfect!'

His heart thudded. Why hadn't he thought to buy a toy for their baby? Since the scan all he could think about was the baby—the tiny life growing inside Marianna. The moment he'd been able to make out the baby's image on the monitor a love so powerful and protective had surged through him that, even now, just thinking about it left him reeling. He craved to be the best father he could be. He didn't want this child to doubt for a single second that it was loved.

His hands clenched. Could he really bear to be away from Monte Calanetti once the baby was born? Could he really envisage spending months at a time away from his child?

Nico turned with a wry grin. 'Want to put a diaper on teddy to match the one on dolly?'

He forced a smile to lips that didn't want to work. 'You might be surprised to find yourself with serious competition in the diaper-changing stakes.'

As one, he and Nico turned to Angelo with raised eyebrows. The other man raised his hands. 'No way.'

Ryan took a sip of wine. 'Has Mari showed you the ultrasound pictures yet? Our baby is beautiful.'

Mari's mouth slackened as she turned those big brown eyes of hers to him. They filled and his chest cramped—*please don't cry,* he silently begged—and then they shone. 'Our baby is perfect!' She leapt up to seize the scan photos for her brothers to admire.

Ryan found it hard to believe, but he enjoyed the meal. He didn't doubt that the other two men were reserving their judgement for the time being, but they'd put their overt hostility to one side.

Why?

The answer became increasingly clear as the meal progressed. They adored Marianna and they wanted her to be happy. How could they not love her? She bossed them outrageously, she said deliberately preposterous things to make them laugh, she'd touch their arms in ways that spoke of silent communications he had no knowledge of, but he could see how both men blossomed under her attention, how they relished and treasured it.

In return, she looked up to them so much and loved them so hard that an ache started up deep inside him.

He gripped his cutlery until it bit into him. He wanted her to look up to him like that. He wanted to win her respect. He wanted...

Not love. Never that.

His heart throbbed. Would she love their baby with the same fierceness that she loved her brothers? If she did, then...then this baby didn't need him.

When the children of *another man* took up her heart and her time, though, would her love lose its strength?

A hard rock of resentment lodged in his gut.

If you don't like the idea, pal, marry her yourself.

He shot back in his seat. As if that'd work! Couples shouldn't marry just because they were expecting a baby. It made things ten times worse when they broke up. His parents were proof positive of that. No. He wouldn't be party to making Marianna resent their child more than she inevitably would.

He glanced up to find all eyes at the table on him. He straightened and cleared his throat. He had no idea what question had just been shot his way, but... 'There's something I've been meaning to raise.'

Marianna stared at him and her eyes suddenly narrowed. Nico gestured for him to continue.

'I understand that harvest time is pretty busy?'

Nico nodded. 'Flat out.'

Ryan glanced first at Marianna and then her brothers. 'Please tell me Marianna won't be working sixty-to eighty-hour weeks.'

'She'll be on maternity leave from August,' Angelo said. 'Nico and I have already discussed it.'

He let out a breath. Good.

'I beg your pardon?' Marianna's eyes flashed and she folded her arms. 'You haven't discussed this with me.'

He stared at her folded arms, at the way her fingers clenched and unclenched, recalled the way she'd flung that vase at him and reached out and took the bowl containing the remainder of the fruit salad they'd had for dessert, pretending to help himself to more before placing it out of her reach. Just to be on the safe side.

'I'll have you know that come harvest I'll still be more than capable of pulling my weight.'

'I need you to monitor the grapes until the end of July,' Nico said. 'But after that I take over.'

'But—'

'No buts.'

Ryan reached a hand towards her, but she ignored it. He soldiered on anyway. 'You're going to be in the last few weeks of your pregnancy. You're going to have a sore back and aching legs.' He wished he could bear those things for her.

'It doesn't make me incapable of doing my job.'

'No one is saying it is,' Angelo said.

She made a wild flourish in the air. 'You cannot exclude me from this!'

Nico seized her hand. 'We're not excluding you, but your health and your *bambino's* health is precious to us. You can sit in a chair in the shade and direct proceedings.'

'You mean I can sit and watch you all work while I put my feet up!'

'You'll still be a part of it.'

She pulled her hand free from Nico's. 'That's bunk and you know it.'

Ryan folded his arms. 'You're going to have to keep an eye on her.'

Nico met Ryan's gaze with a challenge in his own. 'You

could always come back for harvest and keep an eye on her yourself.'

It took an effort not to run a finger around the collar of his shirt. If things went to plan, he'd be neck deep in his assignment for Conti Industries. He might be able to get away for the odd day, but a week, let alone a whole month, would be out of the question. 'I'll see what I can do.' But he already knew he wouldn't be back for the harvest.

'Oh, and now they think I need a babysitter! Fabulous!"

Marianna stalked away to throw herself down on the sofa, where she glowered at them all. Ryan pushed his chair back a tad so he could still include her in the conversation. 'Marianna gave me a tour of the winery the other day.'

'And?' Angelo said.

'You two know what I do, right? That I get called in to turn ailing companies around?'

Nico glared. 'My vineyard is not ailing.'

From the corner of his eye he saw Marianna straighten and turn towards them. 'It's not,' Ryan agreed.

Nico's glare abated but Angelo's interest had been piqued. 'But?'

'You have bottling facilities that stand idle for much of the year. Did you know that further down the valley there's a brewery that specialises in boutique vinegars? It's an outfit that doesn't have its own bottling facilities. Currently they're sending their stock to Florence for bottling.'

'You're suggesting we could bottle their vinegar?'

Ryan shrugged.

Angelo pursed his lips and glanced at Nico. 'They'd be interested. It'd reduce their transportation costs. And it'd bring additional money into the vineyard with very little effort on our part.'

Nico tapped a finger to the table. 'It'd create more jobs too.'

Angelo and Nico started talking at each other in a rush.

Ryan glanced across at Marianna to find her frowning at him, consternation and something else he couldn't identify in the depths of her eyes.

She started when she realised he watched her. Seizing a magazine, she buried her nose in it. But he couldn't help noticing that she didn't turn a single page.

Ryan turned back to the other men. 'I figured it was worth mentioning.' If they were interested in expanding their operations here, it'd be a good place to start.

'How'd you know about this?' Angelo asked.

'It's my job to know.' Old habits died hard. 'I was called in a couple of years ago to overhaul a vineyard in the Barossa Valley. It's one of the things we did to improve their bottom line.'

'And did you save it?'

He shrugged. 'Of course.'

Nico and Angelo started talking ten to the dozen. Marianna came back to the table and joined the debate. Ryan sat back and watched, and hoped he'd proved himself in some small way, hoped he'd eased Marianna's mind and shown her that he and her brothers could get on.

CHAPTER EIGHT

MARIANNA GAVE UP all pretence of conviviality the moment her brothers' broad figures disappeared into the warm darkness of the spring night. Trudging back into the living room, she slumped onto the sofa and stared at the beautiful teddy bear they'd bought for their prospective niece or nephew.

Her eyes filled. Oh, how she loved them!

Ryan clattered about, taking their now-empty coffee cups and wine glasses into the kitchen. 'The evening seemed to go well, don't you think?'

A happy lilt she hadn't heard since Thailand threaded through his voice. She slumped further into the sofa. Of course he'd be happy. *He'd* had a chance to prove his worth and show off his expertise to her brothers.

He started to run hot water into the sink. 'Leave them.' She didn't shout, though it took an effort not to. Who'd have thought he'd have turned out to be such a neat freak? 'I'll do them in the morning.' At least washing dishes was something she *could* do.

Even though she didn't turn around, she sensed his hesitation before he turned the taps off. He moved across to the living area and she could feel him as he drew closer, as if some invisible cord attached her to him. All nonsense!

He picked up the teddy bear, tweaked its ear. 'I think perhaps your brothers are starting to see that I'm not the villain they first thought me.'

No, now they saw him as some kind of super-duper business guru.

He is a business guru.

She ignored that. She could practically see what her

brothers now thought. *Poor Ryan—Mari's latest victim who's headed for heartbreak because she's too erratic to settle down.*

She wasn't the one who couldn't settle down. Not that they'd see that. What they'd see was that she'd caught Ryan in her snares—the poor schmuck—and that he was paying a hefty price for it. And…and they'd *admire* him for making the best out of a bad situation.

Having a baby wasn't a bad situation!

'Marianna?'

She started. Had Ryan been talking to her this entire time? She hadn't heard a word of it beyond the fact her brothers didn't hate him any more. His eyes narrowed on her face. 'You didn't enjoy this evening.'

It was a statement, not a question, so she didn't feel the need to respond.

He eased down into the chair opposite, his frown deepening. 'But I thought you wanted me to get along with your brothers.'

She had. She did! But not at the expense of their opinion of her.

He leaned forward, his expression intent, and something in her chest turned over. She wasn't the one who couldn't settle down. She *ached* to settle down. Not necessarily with Ryan, but… She'd never planned to have a baby on her own. What she'd wanted was to fall in love, get married and then start a family. That sure as heck wasn't going to happen with Ryan. So now she was going to have a baby on her own and it scared her witless.

'This has nothing to do with pregnancy hormones, does it?'

How could he tell? How could he be so attuned to her and yet so far out of her reach?

'No,' she finally said, figuring some kind of response would eventually be expected.

'Do you want to tell me about it?'

She opened her mouth to say no, but the word refused to emerge. Did she want to talk about it? She blinked when she realised the answer to that question was a rather loud yes.

She moistened her lips and risked another glance into Ryan's face. She'd never spoken to anyone about this before. It seemed too...personal. Besides, all the people she could talk about it with knew Angelo and Nico too.

Ryan knows them now as well.

True, but he'd still be on her side.

Would he? She waved a hand in front of her face. This wasn't about sides. She fixed him with a glare. 'Do you want to know even if it's something you can't fix?'

His eyes didn't leave her face. 'Yes.'

'And if I tell you I don't want you to do anything to try and fix it, because I expect that would only make matters worse, and I don't think I could bear that.'

Slowly he nodded. 'Okay.'

'I meant for tonight to impress Angelo and Nico. I wanted them to recognise my maturity. I wanted to wow them with my graciousness as a hostess. I wanted to prove to them that I'm not an irresponsible idiot or a screw-up!' Her voice had started to rise and she forced it back down. 'But that's certainly not something I managed to accomplish this evening, is it?' She flung out an arm. 'They didn't even trust me to cook the meal properly!'

Ryan's jaw dropped and she leapt up to pace. 'And then you had to go and bring up the whole "Marianna can't work during harvest" thing and all that garbage.' She spun around to glare at him. 'Thank you very much for making me look even worse!'

He shot to his feet and the sheer beauty of his body beat at her. 'The harvest thing? That's because we're all concerned about you.'

She gave up trying to moderate her voice. 'Because none of you think I can look after myself!'

'It's not that at all!'

She folded her arms and kinked a disbelieving eyebrow.

'It's because—' he stabbed a finger at her '—we all want to...' He trailed off, shuffling his feet and looking mildly embarrassed. 'We all want to pamper you,' he mumbled.

It was her jaw that dropped this time. 'I beg your pardon?'

'You're the one who's doing all of the hard work where the baby is concerned. You're the one who has morning sickness, and has had to give up coffee and wine. You're the one who's growing the baby inside you, which probably means you'll get a sore back and sore legs. And then you're the one who's going to have to give birth.'

Ugh. Don't remind her.

'While we—' he slashed a hand through the air '—we're utterly useless! You should know by now that men hate feeling like that. So, while we can't do anything for the baby, we can do things for you—to try and make things easier and nicer for you.'

Ryan felt useless?

'I just...' He grimaced. 'It didn't occur to me that in the process we might be making you feel useless too.'

His explanation put a whole new complexion on the matter. How could she begrudge him—or her brothers—for wanting to help where they could with the baby? She moved a step closer and peered up into his face. 'So...you don't think I'm stupid or that I'm acting irresponsibly?'

'Of course not! I...'

She swung away. 'Of course there's a but.'

'All I was going to say is that I think, in your determination to prove to us all how capable you are, you could be in danger of overdoing it.'

He was talking about that incident with the barrel.

'I did hear you, though—your concern about losing your fitness.'

He had? She turned back.

'I've been trying to find a good time to raise the subject.'

Why? Because she was so touchy she was liable to fly off the handle without warning? She closed her eyes, conceding he might have a point there.

'So I picked up one of these for you.'

She opened her eyes to find him holding out a flyer towards her. She took it. Yoga classes. With an instructor who specialised in yoga for pregnant women. A lump lodged in her throat.

'I just thought you might...' More feet shuffling ensued. 'I mean, if you're not interested, if it's not your thing, then no problem.'

She swallowed the lump. 'No, it's great. I'd have never thought of it, but...it's perfect.'

He didn't smile. He continued to stare at her with a frown in his eyes. 'Mari, your brothers love you. They don't consider you a screw-up.'

Tension shot back through her. 'Those two statements are not mutually exclusive.' She speared the flyer to the fridge with a magnet, before grabbing a glass of water and downing it in one. 'I know my brothers love me.' *That* was why it was so important that she prove herself to them.

Weariness overtook her then. She turned to move back to the sofa, to collapse onto it—to put her feet up and close her eyes—but Ryan blocked her way, anger blazing from the cool depths of his eyes. She backed up a step. 'What?'

'If you believe your brothers think you a screw-up then you're a complete idiot!'

She blinked.

'They adore you!'

'Adoring someone, loving someone,' she found herself yelling back, 'has nothing to do with thinking them capable or adult or believing they're making good decisions about their life!' It didn't mean they thought she'd make a good mother.

'I don't know your brothers very well, but even I can see that's not what they think.'

'Oh, really?' She poked him in the chest. 'What makes you such an expert on the subject? They certainly thought my taking a year off to tour around Australia irresponsible.' Maybe it had been. It'd certainly been indulgent, but she'd needed to spread her wings or go mad. 'And you should've seen the looks on their faces when I told them I was expecting a baby. They definitely thought that an irresponsible mistake of *monumental* proportions.'

She slammed the glass she still held to the bench and pushed past Ryan's intriguing bulk and bristling maleness. His heat and his scent reached around her, making her feel too much, stoking her anger even more. 'So did you!'

'I was wrong! I want this baby. I love this baby!'

She fell onto the sofa, rubbing her temples. Ryan strode across and seized the teddy bear, shook it at her. 'And your brothers love this baby too.'

'You think I don't know that?' She pulled in a breath. 'But I'm not married. This baby wasn't planned.' That last was irresponsible. 'It doesn't mean they don't think I've made a mistake with my life.' And what if they were right? She touched a hand to her stomach. *I'm sorry,* mia topolino.

Ryan sat on the coffee table, knee to knee with her, crowding her. 'So what if they do?'

That was her cue to toss her head and say that it didn't matter, except she didn't have the heart for the lie. She lifted her chin. 'I love them. Their opinions matter to me.'

And what if they were right?

'In this day and age, being a single mother isn't scandalous.'

'I know that, but I live in a conservative part of the world.'

'Your brothers' shock is merely proof of their concern for you, their concern that you'd have no support with the baby—that you would have to do it alone.'

She did have to do it alone. Ryan wanted to be a part of the baby's life, but he didn't want to be part of a family. Ninety per cent of the baby's care would fall to her.

'For heaven's sake, Mari, they don't see you as incapable or a screw-up. Can't you see that? Haven't you worked it out yet? You're the glue that holds this family together.'

He stared at her with such seriousness her heart stopped for a beat. It kicked back in with renewed vigour a moment later. 'What on earth are you talking about?'

'Angelo and Nico obviously have their differences. They want different things from life.'

She snorted. He could say that again.

'Do you think they see each other as inadequate or incompetent?'

She stilled, suddenly seeing where he was going with this.

He leaned over and took her chin in his hand. 'The one thing they can bond over is you. Their love for you, their worry for you and their joy in you—that strengthens their bond and makes you a family.'

He paused. His index finger moved back and forth across her cheek and all Marianna wanted to do was lean into it and purr…to lean into him. An ache started up deep in the centre of her. An ache she knew from experience that Ryan could assuage.

He frowned, his attention elsewhere, and Marianna told herself she was glad he hadn't read her thoughts. 'I don't know what the deal with your parents is, but I've picked up enough to know that you act as a bridge between them and your brothers.'

That was true, but she could only acknowledge it dimly. Ryan continued to frown, but his gaze had caught on her lips and such a roaring hunger stretched through his eyes it made her breath catch and her lips part. His nostrils flared, time stilled. And then he reefed his hand away and shot back.

Not that there was really anywhere he could move back to—they still sat knee to knee. If she leaned forward, she could run a hand up his leg with seductive intent, a silent invitation that she was almost certain he wouldn't rebuff. Her thigh muscles squeezed in delight at the thought. Deep in the back of her mind, though, a caution sounded. She found herself hovering, caught between a course of action that felt as if it had the potential to change her life.

Sleeping with Ryan will not make him fall in love with you.

Of course it wouldn't. Yet she didn't move away.

'Tell me you've heard all that I've just said.'

She started at his voice.

'About your brothers,' he continued inexorably. 'That you can see they don't think of you as any kind of a failure. They may not agree with every decision you make about your life, just as you may not agree with every decision they make about theirs, but it doesn't mean any of you believe one of the others is a loser or a write-off. It doesn't mean that you don't respect each other.'

Her heart started to pound. 'You truly believe that?'

'I do.' He eased forward again, resting his elbows on his knees. 'Where is this coming from, Mari? Why haven't you spoken to Angelo or Nico about it?'

She glanced down at her hands. 'They've looked after me since I was a tiny thing. They've spoiled me rotten, indulged me and...I felt as if I'd disappointed them, that I hadn't honoured the faith they'd put in me.' She lifted one shoulder. 'I wanted to prove to them that I was up to the task—that I could do a really good job here at the vineyard *and* be a wonderful mother. But it seemed the harder I tried, the worse I came off. Working so hard suddenly became not looking after myself, or the baby. It seemed to me that everything I did was reinforcing their view of me being incompetent and needing to be looked after.'

'Crazy woman,' he murmured.

'And I didn't feel I should confide all of that in them. They've given me so much—they're the best brothers a girl could ever ask for—and it didn't seem fair to ask more from them, to ask them for assurances.'

'They'd have given them gladly.'

She swallowed. 'A part of me couldn't help feeling they were right.'

His jaw dropped.

She rubbed a hand across her chest. 'How could I take them to task for their reaction to my baby news when my own initial reaction wasn't much better? Oh, Ryan, joy and excitement weren't my first emotions when I found out I was pregnant. I was frightened…and angry with myself. I wanted it all to go away. I wanted the news to not be true. How dreadful is that?'

He reached out and took her hand 'It's not dreadful. It's human.'

She'd have said exactly the same thing to any one of her girlfriends who found themselves in a similar predicament. She knew that, but…

'Mari, you have to forgive yourself for that. And you have to forgive your brothers for their initial reaction too. And me.' He paused. 'You made a brave decision—an exciting decision—and I can't tell you how grateful I now am for that.'

She could tell he meant every word. And just like that a weight lifted from her.

'You should be proud of yourself.'

Proud?

'You're having a baby. It's exciting. It feels like a miracle.'

Her heart all but stopped. He was right!

She gave up trying to fight temptation then. She leaned forward, took his face in her hands and pressed her lips to his. He froze, but a surge of electricity passed between them, making her tingle all over. She eased back, her heart thumping. 'Thank you.'

He swallowed and nodded. The pulse at the base of his throat pounded and she could feel its rhythm reach right down into the depths of her. Her breath started to come in short sharp spurts. She'd never wanted a man or physical release with such intensity.

Ever.

Maybe it was a pregnancy-hormone thing?

Whatever it was, it was becoming increasingly clear that attempting to explain it, understand it, did nothing to ease its ferocity. She glanced at Ryan, and glanced away again biting her lip. They were both adults. They knew sex didn't mean forever. She tossed her head. If they chose to, they could give each other pleasure in the here and now.

Without giving herself time to think, Marianna slid forward to straddle Ryan's lap.

'What on—?'

Her fingers against his mouth halted his words. 'I want you, Ryan, and I know you want me. I don't really see the point in denying ourselves. Do you?'

She trailed her hand down his chest, relishing the firm feel of him beneath the cotton of his shirt. He slammed his hand over it, trapping it above the hard thudding of his heart. 'You said if I made love with you here in your real world, that I would break your heart.'

She lifted one shoulder and then let it drop. 'What do I know? Ten minutes ago I was convinced my brothers thought me an incompetent little fool. It appears I was wrong about that.'

For a moment the strength seemed to go out of him. She took advantage of the moment to slide her hands around his shoulders to caress the hair at his nape in a way that she knew drove him wild.

He reached up to remove her hands. 'Mari, I—'

She covered his mouth with her own—open mouth, hot, questing tongue, and a hunger she refused to temper. The taste of him, his heat, drove her wild. With a moan, she sank her teeth into his bottom lip and then laved it with her tongue. Ryan groaned, his hand at the back of her head drawing her closer. His mouth, his lips and his tongue controlled her effortlessly, taming her to his tempo and pace. He drank her in like a starving man and she could only respond with a silent, inarticulate plea that he not stop, that he give her what she needed.

She opened her thighs wider to slide more fully against him and he broke off the kiss to drag in a breath, his chest rising and falling as if he'd run a race.

'We can't do this,' he groaned.

'No?' Marianna peeled off her shirt and threw it to the floor. Her bra followed. She lifted his hands to her breasts, revelling in the way he swallowed, the way he stared at her as if she were the most beautiful woman in the world. 'I understand that you don't want to hurt me, and that's earned you a lot of brownie points, believe me. But at the moment I don't want you honourable. I want you naked and your hands on me, driving me to distraction.'

She moved against his hands. He sucked in a breath. 'Mari…'

She cupped his face, staring into his eyes. 'Just once I want to make love with the father of my child with joy at the knowledge of what we've created.'

He stilled. She swallowed. If he rejected her now she wasn't sure she could bear it. 'It seems to me,' she whispered, 'that would be a good thing to do.'

'Mari…'

She pressed a finger to his lips. 'No promises. I know that. Just pleasure…and joy. That's all I'm asking.'

She saw the moment he decided to stop fighting it and her heart soared. His eyes gleamed. 'Pleasure, huh?' He ran his hands down her sides, thumbs brushing her breasts and making her bite her lip. 'How much pleasure?'

'I'm greedy,' she whispered.

His hands cupped her buttocks, his fingers digging into her flesh through the thin cotton of her skirt.

She clutched his shoulders, swallowing back a whimper. 'I want a lot of pleasure.'

'A lot, huh?'

His fingers raked down her thighs with deliberate slowness…and with a latent promise of where they would go when he raked them back up again. Marianna started to tremble. Despite the weakness flooding her she managed to toss her head. 'As much as you have to give.'

His eyes darkened with wolfish hunger. 'Whatever the lady wants.' He eased forward to draw her nipple into his mouth and Marianna lost herself in the pleasure.

And the newfound joy that gripped her and seemed to bathe her entire being in sunlight.

The sound of Ryan's mobile phone ringing woke her. Through half-closed eyes, Marianna watched him reach for it, the long, lean line of his back making her mouth water.

He glanced back towards her and she smiled, sent him a little wave to let him know she was awake and that he didn't need to be extra quiet or leave the room. One side of his mouth kinked up, his eyes darkening as he took in her naked form beneath the sheet. She stretched cheekily, letting the sheet fall to her waist and his grin widened. It made her heart turn over and over. And over.

He finally punched a button on his phone and turned away to concentrate on his call.

A tumbling heart?

Very slowly Marianna sat up, a tight fist squeezing her chest as she continued to stare at Ryan. Her mouth went dry. She drew the sheet back over her. It took all her strength not to pull it right over her head. What on earth had she gone and done?

She didn't want to let this man go. *Ever.*

Her hands fisted. When had it happened? *How* had it happened? Why...?

She swallowed. What did any of that matter? What mattered was that she wanted Ryan to stay here with her forever and be a true partner. She wanted him to share in the day-to-day rearing of their child. She wanted to see him last thing at night and again first thing in the morning.

She *loved* Ryan.

He doesn't want that!

She bit down on her lip to stop from crying out, rubbing a hand across her chest to ease the ache there.

You should never have slept with him.

She waved that away with an impatient movement. Sex had nothing to do with it. Sex wasn't the reason she'd fallen in love with him. His determination to become a good father, his care and consideration of her, the effort he'd put into making a good impression on her brothers, the fact he wanted her to be happy—they were the reasons she'd fallen in love with him. She passed a hand across her eyes. It seemed for the last week she'd been doing her best to hide from that fact.

What good was hiding, though?

And yet, what good was facing the truth? He loved his work more than he'd ever love her.

'I'll be there as soon as I can!'

She snapped to at Ryan's words. 'What's wrong?' she demanded, pushing her own concerns aside at his grim expression and the greyness that hovered in the lines around his mouth.

'My mother has been taken ill. I need to return to Sydney as soon as I can.'

He had a mother?

She hadn't realised she'd said that out loud until he said, 'And a father. They divorced when I was young. They both have new families now.'

Which meant he had siblings. And yet…amidst this big family Ryan managed to be a lone wolf?

She surged out of bed, pulling on her dressing gown to race into the spare bedroom after him where he'd set about throwing clothes into his suitcase. She wanted to hold him, chase that haggard look from his face. 'What can I do?'

He stilled from hauling on a clean pair of suit trousers. He zipped them up and then moved to touch her face with one hand. 'I just want you to look after yourself and the baby.'

If he left now she'd have lost him forever. She'd never get the opportunity to win his love.

It could be for the best—a quick, clean break.

But…

Lone wolf.

If something terrible happened—if he received dreadful news or, heaven forbid, if his mother died—who would be there to comfort him, to offer him support and anything else he needed?

She moistened her lips, pulling the dressing gown about her all the more tightly. 'Can I come with you?'

* * *

Ryan froze at Marianna's request. He turned. 'Why would you want to do that?'

She pushed a strand of gloriously mussed hair behind her ears. 'I didn't know you had a family.'

He didn't. *They* were a family and *he* was an outsider. They were simply people he happened to be related to by blood.

So why is your heart pounding nineteen to the dozen at the thought of your mother lying in a hospital bed?

He pushed that thought away and focused on Marianna again. She swallowed. 'I'd like to meet them. They'll be a part of our baby's life and—'

'A small part,' he said. 'A *very* small part.'

She thrust out her chin and he found himself having to fight the urge to kiss her. 'You've met my family.'

'Not your parents.'

'But you will,' she promised. 'Just as soon as I can arrange it.'

How could she so easily make him feel part of something—like her family—when there was no place for him in it? It had to be an illusion.

'I don't mean to be gone long, Marianna. I need to be back in Rome in two weeks at the latest—' preferably sooner '—to settle the contract I've been working on.'

One of her shoulders lifted and then she surged forward to grip his hand. 'Ryan, we're friends, right?'

Were they? It was what he'd been striving for, but the word didn't seem right somehow.

Because you slept with her, you idiot.

He shook that off. He couldn't regret last night if he tried his hardest. He'd only regret it if it'd hurt Marianna.

He stared down into her eyes—their warmth and generosity caught at him. Her gaze held his, steadily. Neither pain nor regret reached out to squeeze his heart dry, only concern. Concern for him. He swallowed. Friendship might not be the right word, but it didn't mean he couldn't continue to strive for exactly that.

'Ryan, I'd like to be there for you if you receive bad news.'

It took an effort to lock his knees against the weakness that shook through him when he realised the kind of bad news she referred to. It didn't make sense. He was barely a part of his mother's life. Or his father's. Family made no sense to him at all.

But it made sense to Marianna. That might come in handy. She might be able to help him to navigate the tricky waters ahead.

She attempted a smile. 'I might even be able to make myself useful.'

He wanted her to come with him. The thought shocked him.

It didn't mean anything. It *couldn't* mean anything.

He pulled in a breath. He supposed he'd have to tell them all at some point that he was going to become a father. That would be easier with Marianna by his side.

Finally he nodded. 'Okay, but I want to be on the first available flight out of Rome for Sydney.'

She raced back towards her bedroom. 'I'll be ready!'

CHAPTER NINE

'TELL ME ABOUT your family.'

Ryan fought a grimace as he shifted on his seat—a generous business class seat that would recline full length when he wanted to sleep. Sleep was the furthest thing from his mind at the moment, though. He wished planes had on-board gyms. 'What do you want to know?'

'Do both of your parents live in Sydney?'

In stark contrast to him, Marianna looked cool and comfortable and *very* delectable. He tried to tamp down on the ache that rose up through him. 'Yes.'

She stared as if waiting for more. He lifted a hand. 'What?'

'Sydney is a big city, Ryan.'

Right. 'They live in the eastern suburbs. In adjoining suburbs, would you believe? It's where they grew up.'

She pursed her lips and he waited for her next question with a kind of fatalistic resignation. He supposed it'd help pass the time.

'You said they divorced when you were young. How old were you?'

'Four.'

'And...and did they share custody?'

Her questions started to make sense. He shook his head. 'I went to live with my maternal grandmother.'

She smiled and he couldn't explain why, but it bathed him in warmth. It made him very glad to have her sitting beside him. 'The grandmother who taught you to make curtains?'

'The very one.'

'Where were your parents? What were they doing?'

'They went their separate ways to "find" themselves.' He couldn't stop himself from making mocking inverted commas in the air.

She turned more fully in her seat to face him, crossing her legs in the process, and her skirt rode up higher on her thigh. He stared at the perfectly respectable amount of flesh on display, remembering how he'd run his hands up her thighs last night...and how he'd followed with his mouth. He wished he could do that right now—lose himself in the pleasure of being in her arms, give himself over to the generous delights of her body.

'That makes them sound very young. How old were they?'

He pulled himself back. He had to stop thinking about making love with Marianna. It couldn't happen again. Already it was starting to feel too concentrated, too...intimate. Like an affair. He didn't do affairs. He did one-night stands. He did ships passing in the night. He did short-term dalliances. Somehow, from the wreck of his and Marianna's entanglement, he had to fashion a friendship that would endure the coming years.

Boring.

He stiffened. It was the responsible route. The *essential* route. And like everything else he'd turned his hand to, if he worked at it hard enough he would achieve it.

'Ryan?'

He shook himself, dragged a hand down his face. 'They were eighteen when they had me.'

'Eighteen?' Her eyes widened. 'I'm twenty-four and most days I don't feel ready for parenthood. But eighteen? Just...wow.'

He'd started to realise that parenthood frightened her as much as it frightened him. It was why he had to remain close and keep things pleasant between them. When motherhood and the responsibility of raising a child overwhelmed Marianna, when it lost its gloss, he'd be there to take over.

'How long did you live with your grandmother?'

'Until I was nineteen.'

Her jaw dropped. She shuffled a little closer, drenching him with her sweet scent. 'You never lived with your parents again?'

He stared at the back of the seat in front of him. 'I visited with them.' But he'd never fitted in. It had always been a relief to return home to his grandmother. He'd only kept up the visits because his grandmother had insisted. For her he'd have done anything.

'So, you and your parents, you're not what one would call…close?'

'Not close at all.'

'But…'

He turned and met her gaze.

'You've dropped everything to go to your mother.'

'That's not a mystery.' He turned back to the front. 'I'm the one with the money, and money talks. I can make things happen.'

'Like?'

'Get in the best doctors, fly in the top specialists, fast-track test results—that kind of thing.' He'd do that—make sure everything was in place for his mother—and then he'd hightail it back to Italy to wrap up the Conti contract.

Marianna blinked and then frowned. 'That's terrible!'

It took an effort of will to stop his lips from twisting. 'It's the way the world works.'

She was silent for a moment. 'I meant it's terrible that's the way you feel, that that's the role you see for yourself in your family.'

Maybe he should've taken the time to pretty it all up for her, except she'd see it all for herself soon enough.

'You have siblings?'

Tiredness washed through him. 'Yes.' He didn't give her the time to ask how many. 'My father is onto marriage number three. He has a daughter to wife number two and two boys with wife number three. My mother has one of each with her second husband. The eldest of them is twenty-two—my mother's daughter who has a toddler of her own. The youngest is my father's son who is thirteen.'

'Wow. Where do you spend Christmas?'

'*Not* in Australia.'

She nodded, but the sadness in her eyes pierced him, making his chest throb. 'Why don't you get some sleep?' he suggested. She must be bone-tired. 'You didn't get a whole lot of rest last night.'

The sudden wicked grin she flashed him kicked up his pulse, making his blood pump faster. 'I wish I was getting next to no sleep tonight for exactly the same reason.'

So did he. Except… *No affairs.* He knew she'd said no promises, but… 'Do we need to talk about last night?' Did they need to double-check that they were still on the same page?

She smiled a smile so slow and seductive he had to bite back a groan. 'We can if you like,' she all but purred. 'There was a manoeuvre of yours that I particularly relished. It was when you—'

He pressed a finger to her lips, his heart pounding so hard the sound of it filled his ears. 'Stop it!' But a laugh shot out of him at the same time. 'You're incorrigible. Give me some peace, woman, and go to sleep.'

'On one condition.'

'Anything!'

'Kiss me first.'

Her eyes darkened with an unmistakable challenge. He leaned towards her. 'Do you think I won't?'

She leaned in closer still. 'I'm very much hoping you will.'

He seized her lips in a fierce kiss, not questioning the hunger that roared through him. He didn't gather her close. He didn't even cup her face. She didn't reach out a hand to touch him either, but a kiss he'd thought would be all fire and sass changed when her lips parted and softened and moved beneath his with a warmth and a relish that shifted something inside him. He went to move away, but her lips followed and he found himself unable to stop; he surged forward again to plunder and explore that softness and warmth, to pull it into himself. The kiss went on and on…and on, as if she had an endless supply of something he desperately needed.

Eventually they drew apart. 'Mmm…yum.' Her tongue ran across her bottom lip as if savouring the taste of him there.

He had no words. All he could do was stare at her. She reclined her seat. She reached out a hand to his knee; her touch… He couldn't find the right word for it—comforting, reassuring? 'Put your seat back and keep me company.'

He covered her with a blanket first and then did as she bid.

'Close your eyes,' she murmured, not even opening hers to see if he obeyed.

After a moment, he did. He could feel sleep coming to claim him and suddenly realised that Marianna's kiss had stolen some of the sting from his soul. He had no idea what it meant. He breathed air into lungs that didn't feel quite so cramped and drifted off to sleep, promising himself he'd work it out later.

He slept for three hours. Not just dozed, but slept. He woke and stretched, feeling strangely refreshed. He checked his phone, but there weren't any messages.

Half an hour later, Marianna stirred. 'Sleep well?' he asked when she opened her eyes.

'Perfectly,' she declared, sitting up. 'You?'

He nodded.

She sent him a grin that made his blood sizzle. 'Wanna kiss me again in a little while when I'm ready for another snooze?'

He laughed, but shook his head—trying to ignore the ache that surged through him. 'We can't keep doing that.'

She reached for the bottle of water the stewardess had left for her. 'I expect you're right, but I mean to enjoy it while it lasts.'

How long would it last? More to the point, how long did he want it to last? Could they maybe make love one more time without Marianna's heart becoming entangled? Twice more? He'd give up a lot to have another week like they had in Thailand.

But not at the expense of screwing up friendship and fatherhood.

His seat suddenly felt as hard and unyielding as a boulder. He excused himself and bolted to the rest room to dash cold water onto his face, to stare at himself in the mirror and order himself to keep his hands and lips to himself.

When he couldn't remain in there any longer without exciting comment, he forced himself back to his seat. 'Why don't you tell me about your parents?' he suggested, hoping conversation would keep his raging hormones in check. 'It seems that you and your brothers have different opinions on the subject.'

She nodded. 'Mamma and Papà have a very…tempestuous relationship. They're both very passionate people.'

Sounded like a recipe for disaster to him.

'When we were growing up there were a lot of…um… rather loud discussions.'

'Fights.'

She wrinkled her nose. 'A bit of shouting…a bit of door-slamming.'

He recalled the way she'd thrown that vase at him.

Uh-huh, utter nightmare. He thanked the stewardess when she brought him the drink he'd requested.

'They divorced once. And then they remarried.'

He choked on his drink. 'But…why?'

She lifted one slim shoulder. 'It's the same now. They're currently in America, but their relationship is as fiery as it ever was. They're forever threatening to leave each other, storming out for a few days before coming back. On again off again.' She gave a low laugh. 'They can't live without each other. It's wildly romantic.'

He stared at her. 'Romantic? Are you serious? It sounds like a nightmare.'

She leaned back, her gaze narrowing. 'Maybe it's a male thing. You seem to have jumped to the same conclusion as Angelo and Nico.'

They were obviously men of sense. 'You say they can't live without each other. Seems to me they can't live *with* each other.'

She shook her head. He tried not to let her dancing curls distract him. 'The intensity of their love drives them to distraction. So, yes, I think that romantic. Boredom is death to a relationship and while you can say a lot of things about my parents the one thing you can't accuse them of is being bored…or boring.'

Was that the kind of relationship she wanted? Did she mean to marry a man and raise Ryan's child in a battle-ground? 'Boredom?' he spat. 'I'd take it over never being able to relax or wind down. What on earth is wrong with contentment?'

Her face wrinkled up as if she'd just sucked on a lemon. 'Oh, yay, that sounds like fun.'

'The way your parents act, it's immature. Sounds as if neither one of them has the ability to compromise and I don't see what's particularly loving or romantic about that.'

She glared at him. 'I'm starting to think you wouldn't know love if it jumped up and bit you on the nose. You avoid love and connection as if it's some kind of plague, so you'll have to excuse me if I don't take you as an expert on the topic.'

She had a point, but... 'You'd really prefer to have the kind of screaming match that leaves you shaken and in tears than...than smiles and easiness and happiness?'

'It's not an either-or situation.' She folded her arms. 'Besides, I hear that make-up sex is the best.'

'Is it all about sex with you?'

'Oh, excuse me while I roll my eyes out loud! I like sex.' She thrust out her chin. 'And I have no intention of apologising for that.'

'You'd have that kind of crazy, outrageous relationship even if it made the people around you miserable?'

'My parents' relationship didn't make *me* miserable.'

'I expect that's because Angelo and Nico shielded you from the worst of it. It certainly made them miserable. What if it makes our child miserable?'

Her eyes flashed. 'Oh, no, you don't! You are not going to control me or my future romantic liaisons by means of some kind of twisted maternal guilt you feel you have the right to impose on me. I will marry whomever I choose, Ryan, and it will have nothing to do with you.' With that she grabbed a magazine and promptly set about ignoring him.

He had absolutely no right to tell her who she should or shouldn't marry but...

Why couldn't she just remain single?

With a groan, he dragged both hands back through his hair. Why on earth hadn't he simply forgone the small talk and kissed her again?

Marianna stood the moment Ryan returned to the waiting room, twisting her hands together and searching his face.

All they'd known prior to arriving at the hospital was that Stacey, Ryan's mother, had snapped a tendon in her calf playing squash and that a blood clot had formed at the site of the injury. The doctors were doing everything they could to dissolve the clot, but so far it hadn't responded. If the clot—or any part of it—moved and made its way to her heart or brain…

Marianna suppressed a shudder, and made a vow to never play squash again. 'How is she?'

Ryan didn't answer. His pallor squeezed her heart. She reached out and wrapped her arm through his. 'The doctors are doing everything they can.'

He nodded and swallowed and her heart bled for him. He might not be close to his family, but he loved his mother. That much was evident.

'She'd like to see you.'

She eased away to stare up into his face. 'Me?'

'The doctor said that's fine, but she's only allowed one visitor at a time and she's not to get excited or upset.'

No excitement and no upsetting the woman. Right. She pressed a hand to her stomach. 'Did you tell her about the baby?'

He nodded. 'That's why she wants to meet you.'

She moistened her lips. 'In my experience, news about a baby definitely falls under the heading of exciting.' And depending on the situation and the person being told, fraught with the possibility of distress and worry.

'She's fine with it.' He pushed her towards the door of his mother's room. 'Go and introduce yourself and then we can get the hell out of here.'

She didn't remonstrate with him. For pity's sake, she'd done enough of that on the plane! Not a smart move when trying to make oneself an attractive long-term romantic prospect. But behind his impatience and assumed insensitivity she recognised his fear. She wished she could do something to allay it.

He frowned. 'You don't want to meet her?'

She shook herself. 'I do, yes, very much.' She straightened her shirt and smoothed down her skirt, wishing she'd had an opportunity to at least shower before meeting Ryan's mother. Ryan collapsed onto a chair and rested back, his eyes closed. He must be exhausted. As soon as she'd visited a little with Stacey she'd get him to a hotel somewhere where he could rest up.

Pulling in a breath, she padded down the hallway and tapped on Stacey's door before entering. 'Mrs White, um, sorry...Mrs Pickering?'

'You must be Marianna. Do come in and, please, call me Stacey.'

Ryan had Stacey's colouring, and her eyes. For some reason it put Marianna at ease. 'It's lovely to meet you.' She took the hand Stacey held out to her, pressed it warmly, before taking a seat at the side of the bed. 'I've been ordered to not wear you out.'

Stacey sighed. 'It seems a whole lot of fuss and bother for nothing.'

That sounded like Ryan too. Marianna glanced down her nose and lifted an eyebrow.

Stacey laughed. 'I know, I know. It's not nothing, but the fact of the matter is I'm not even in that much pain and all of this sitting around is driving me mad.'

She sounded *a lot* like Ryan.

'You're having a baby.'

Straight to the heart of the matter. 'Yes.'

'That's lovely news.' The other woman nodded. 'A baby... That's exactly what Ryan needs.'

Marianna didn't know what to say.

'You care about my son?'

She didn't bother dissembling. Stacey was Ryan's mother and her baby's grandmother. 'Yes, I do.'

Their eyes met and held. They both knew that her *caring* about Ryan could end in heartbreak.

'I made a grave mistake when I separated from my then husband and left Ryan with his grandmother. She loved Ryan to bits, but I only ever meant to leave him with her for a couple of weeks.'

Marianna opened her mouth to ask why she hadn't gone back for him—how had two weeks turned into fifteen years—but she closed it again.

'My heart was broken,' Stacey continued, 'and it took me a long time to recover.'

Marianna could understand that, but she still wouldn't have given up her child.

Stacey met Marianna's gaze. 'I was crippled with self-doubt and a lack of confidence. I felt I'd made a mess of everything. I'd hurt Ryan's father. I'd disappointed my mother. I thought I must be a bad person and I convinced myself that I'd ruin Ryan's life. That is the single biggest regret I have.'

Marianna understood self-doubt all too well, and Stacey would've been even younger than Marianna was now. She reached out and touched Stacey's arm. 'You were young. It was all such a long time ago. It's in the past—'

'No, it's not.' Her gaze didn't drop. 'It's there between us every time I see him. He's not trusted me since. He's never forgiven me.'

Her heart burned for the both of them. But… What did Stacey want her to do—to reconcile Ryan with his past? She could try, but—

'I'm telling you this to help you understand my son a little better, Marianna. Since his grandmother died I'm not sure he's trusted anyone, but I think he might trust you. At least a little.'

She hoped he did.

'Maybe you'll be able to find it in your heart to make allowances for him when he doesn't act as emotionally invested as you'd like.'

Therein lay the rub. She wanted—needed—Ryan's wholehearted involvement, his complete commitment. She wasn't a masochist. She couldn't settle for anything less.

Ryan liked everyone to see him as cool and controlled, but she knew the passion that lurked beneath the impassive veneer. She lifted her chin. She and Ryan, they didn't have to end in heartbreak. She could win his love yet. The first step, though, would be to reconcile him with his family. It wouldn't be easy, of course. But it couldn't be impossible, could it?

'I still don't see why we have to stay at Rebecca's,' Ryan muttered.

'Because she asked us,' Marianna returned.

He opened his mouth.

'And because she's going to be our child's aunt. It's natural she should want to get to know me, and I'd like to get to know her.'

Yesterday, Marianna had walked out of Stacey's hospital room to find a large portion of Ryan's family in the waiting room—his stepfather, as well as his sister, her husband and their little girl. When Rebecca, Ryan's sister, had invited them to stay with her, Marianna had jumped at the invitation.

'What if I don't want these people to be part of my child's life?'

'Lulu, honey, don't put that in your mouth.' Marianna jumped up from her seat on the park bench to take the stick from the toddler's hand and to wipe her mouth, before distracting her with a bright red toy truck, helping her to push it through the sand.

She'd dragged Ryan out to the little park across the road from Rebecca's house on the pretext of taking his niece, Lulu, for a little outing.

In reality, though, she'd just wanted to get Ryan out of the house before he exploded—to give them all a bit of a breather. She took her seat on the bench again. 'I like your sister.'

'So that settles it, does it? I hate to point this out to you, but you might find it difficult to become best buds with my sister when she lives here and you live in Monte Calanetti.'

She swung to him, loathing the tone he'd assumed. 'And I hate to point out that it's not Rebecca's fault that your parents separated and left you with your grandmother.'

His eyes turned to chips of ice. 'Very mature.'

'My point exactly! Rebecca is making every effort to forge a relationship with you and you're freezing her out. Why?'

He dragged a hand down his face and she suddenly wished she'd spat those home truths out with a little more kindness. 'I have never felt a part of these people's lives.'

'I know,' she whispered. 'Life gets messy and people don't always know the right way to deal with things. But you're an adult now, Ryan. You can choose to become a part of this family.'

He stared at her. His lips twisted in mockery, but she recognised pain in the hidden depths of his eyes. 'What's the point?'

She couldn't speak for a moment. She turned away to check on Lulu. 'Belonging is its own reward,' she finally managed.

He shook his head. 'Lone wolf.'

'Family is a gift you can give our baby.' Couldn't he see that? 'The more people who love it, the better.'

'You mean the more people there will then be in the world with the potential to hurt it, let it down…betray it.'

She shot to her feet. He could *not* be serious. She started to shake. 'I will not let you turn our child into an emotional cripple…into an emotional coward.'

He turned those cold eyes to her. 'And I won't let you turn it into an emotion junkie.'

That was what he thought of her? She turned away to check again on Lulu, who was perfectly content crawling in the sand with her toy truck. Marianna pulled in a breath and closed her eyes. This wasn't about her. It was about Ryan. She could tell how much he hated being here—in Australia, at Rebecca's—but…

He'd organised a top specialist for his mother at his own expense. Rebecca had told her that her husband owed his job in a top-flying computer graphics company to Ryan's machinations. Rebecca owed her university education to him. They admired him, respected him, and looked up to him. He looked out for them—made sure they had everything they needed—yet he continued to hold himself aloof from them.

He might not want to acknowledge it, but he loved this family that he kept at arm's length.

She sat again. 'Rebecca loves you.'

He stiffened.

'And treating her the way you do…' She used his earlier words against him. 'It hurts her, lets her down, betrays her.'

He stood, his eyes wild. 'That's not true!'

'Yes, it is. Now sit back down and don't frighten the baby.'

He sat. His hands clenched. 'I don't mean to hurt anyone.'

The coldness had melted from him. It took all her strength not to take him in her arms. 'Rebecca would never hurt our child,' she said instead. 'She'd love it, protect it, support it.'

Lulu came over and pulled herself upright using Ryan's

trouser leg. She grinned up at him, slapping her hand to his knee in time to her garbled, 'Ga, ga, ga!'

'I, uh…' He glanced at Marianna, who kept her mouth firmly shut. He glanced back at the toddler, lifted a shoulder. 'Ga, ga, ga?' he said back.

Lulu chortled as if he were the funniest man alive. Just for a moment he grinned and it reached right down inside her. This man deserved to be surrounded by a big, loving family.

Lulu wobbled and then fell down onto her diaper-clad bottom. Her face crumpled and she started to cry.

His hands fluttered. 'Uh, what do I do?'

Was he talking about Lulu or Rebecca? Either way, the advice would be almost the same. 'You pick her up and cuddle her. Cuddles make most things better.'

Gingerly he picked Lulu up, sat her on his knee and patted her back, jiggling his knee up and down. She gave him a watery smile and Marianna's chest cramped as she watched him melt. She crossed her fingers and silently ordered Lulu to keep working her magic.

CHAPTER TEN

MARIANNA GLANCED UP from slicing salad vegetables when Ryan strode into the kitchen.

'Hey, Ryan,' Rebecca said from her spot by the grill where she turned marinated chicken breasts.

Ryan stole a cherry tomato from the salad bowl. 'Is there anything I can do?'

Marianna would've smacked his hand except she sensed the effort it took him to appear casual and relaxed.

'Not much to do,' his sister said. 'I think we have it all under control.'

He reached into the salad bowl again, and this time she slapped the back of his hand with the flat of her knife. 'Ow!'

'You can stop eating all the salad, for one thing.'

His gaze speared to hers. He visibly relaxed at her smile. He turned back to Rebecca. 'I kind of figured there'd be nothing useful I could do in here so I went out and bought this.'

He handed her a bottle of wine. Her eyes widened when she saw the label. 'Ooh, you really shouldn't have, but… nice!'

He shoved his hands in his pockets. 'I thought you deserved a treat after everything you've done—dealing with Mum, putting us up.'

Rebecca's chin came up. 'We're family, Ryan.'

He took the bottle of wine from her and poured out two glasses. He handed her one. He raised his own. 'Yes, we are.' Her eyes widened, a smile trembled on her lips, and then she touched her glass to his.

After his first sip, he set his glass down and poured

Marianna a big glass of mineral water, complete with lemon slice and ice. With his hands on her shoulders, he shepherded her around the kitchen bench and into a chair at the kitchen table, before taking over the slicing of a cucumber.

Marianna didn't make a single peep about not feeling useful. Instead, she held her breath as she watched Ryan begin to forge a relationship with his sister.

He glanced around. 'Where's my...ahem...where's Lulu?'

Rebecca laughed. 'Your niece is having a much-needed nap. And you are *not* disturbing her.'

'Wouldn't dream of it.'

'She has you wrapped around her little finger.'

'Can't deny that I've taken to the little tyke.' He paused, pursed his lips. 'You know, Lulu's going to be less than three years older than her yet-to-be-born cousin. They could—you know—' he lifted a shoulder '—become great mates.'

Rebecca stilled and Marianna saw her blink hard. She wanted to jump up and down, cheer, dance around the kitchen.

Rebecca simply nodded. 'Wouldn't that be great?'

Ryan focused doubly hard on slicing a red capsicum, and nodded.

A moment later his mobile rang. He fished it out, listened intently, murmured a few words and then shoved it back into his pocket. 'That was the hospital. The clot has started to dissolve and if all goes as the specialist hopes, Mum will be released in a couple of days.'

Rebecca clapped a hand to her chest and closed her eyes. 'Thank heaven.'

Ryan let out a long, slow breath and then lifted his glass. 'To the prognosis being correct.'

They drank. When he set his glass down, Ryan rolled

his shoulders. 'Do you think you could keep an eye out for a suitable property for me?'

Marianna stilled with her glass of mineral water halted halfway to her mouth. Had she just heard him right?

'Sure.' Rebecca—a real estate agent—nodded. 'What kind of property did you have in mind?'

Marianna's heart started to thud. Did Ryan mean to give up his anonymous hotel rooms for a real home?

'Here in Sydney?' Rebecca asked.

Ryan nodded.

'Preferred suburbs?'

Marianna waited for him to request some swish apartment overlooking Sydney harbour.

He threw the freshly cut capsicum into the salad bowl. 'The eastern suburbs are fine by me.'

'Apartment? Villa? Town house?' Rebecca shot each option at him.

'I want a house,' he said. 'With a yard.'

Marianna choked and had to thump her chest to get herself back under control.

He glanced at her. 'A child needs a yard, right? A place to run around and play?'

She nodded.

He frowned. 'You won't mind me bringing the baby to visit?'

She suspected she kind of would, but… 'Of course not.' She wanted their baby to know his family. 'You might have to wait until he or she is weaned first, though.'

'You could come too.'

If she had her way, that was exactly what would happen—the three of them coming here as a family. She dabbed her napkin to her mouth. When Ryan decided to do something—like become an involved father or build bridges with his sister—he certainly did it with gusto. If possible, it only made her love him more.

* * *

'Are you planning on going to the hospital today?' Marianna asked Ryan the next morning.

He didn't glance up from his newspaper. 'I don't think so.'

She bit her tongue to stop from asking, *Why not?*

They'd slept late—probably due to jet lag—and currently had the house to themselves. Rebecca's note had said she'd gone up to the hospital. Marianna took a sip of her decaffeinated coffee. Setting her mug back to the table, she ran her finger around its rim. 'Your grandmother lived close to here?'

'On the other side of the main street.' One shoulder lifted. 'Probably a ten-or fifteen-minute walk from here.'

'A walk would be nice. So would a big fat piece of cake.'

He glanced up. 'You want to see where my grandmother lived?'

'I want to see where *you* lived.'

'Why?'

She wanted each and every insight into him that she could get. She wanted to understand why he'd exiled himself from his family. She wanted every weapon she could lay her hands on to make sure he didn't exile himself from her.

Or their baby.

No. Their baby already had his heart.

But she didn't. Not yet.

And she couldn't simply blurt out, *I've fallen deeply and completely in love with you and I want to understand you so that I can work out how to make you fall in love with me.*

She imagined the look on his face if she did, and it almost made her laugh.

And then she imagined the fallout from such an admission and she wanted to throw up.

Ryan's frown deepened. 'You looked for a moment as if you might laugh and now you look as if you want to cry.'

Oops. 'Pregnancy hormones.'

'Breathing exercises,' he ordered.

She feigned doing breathing exercises until she had herself back under control. 'I'd like to see where you grew up. You've seen my world and now I'd like to see yours.' A sudden thought occurred to her. 'But if you'd rather not revisit your past then that's okay too.' She didn't mean to raise demons for him. 'I just…' She wrinkled her nose. 'It's probably a bit selfish of me, but knowing all this stuff— your life here in Australia—it'll make it easier for me when our child does come out here for visits.'

His face softened. 'You're frightened by how much you'll miss it?'

She nodded.

'Me too. I mean, how much I'll miss it when I'm away with work.'

Did that mean…? 'Are you planning on buying a home in Monte Calanetti too?'

He nodded and it occurred to her that she could use this baby as leverage, to convince him that marriage would be the best thing, but… She didn't want him to marry her for any other reason than that he couldn't live without her.

'You could come on the visits to Australia too if you wanted, Mari. You'd be very welcome. My family adores you.'

It was his adoration she craved, not his family's—as much as she liked them. 'You forget that I have a job.'

'I'll pay you so much child support you'll never have to work again.'

'You forget that I like my job.'

He stared at her for a long moment. With a curse he seized their mugs and took them to the sink. 'Don't worry.

I haven't forgotten that you don't want me cramping your style.'

A thrill shot through her at his scowl. If the thought of her with another man made him look like that, then… She left the thought unfinished, but in her lap she crossed her fingers. 'So, are you going to show me your grandmother's house or not?'

'I expect if I want any peace I'll have to,' he grumbled.

'And buy me a piece of cake on the way home?'

He battled a smile. 'And what do I get in return?'

She didn't bother hiding her grin. 'Peace.'

'Deal!'

This time he laughed and it lifted her heart. She could make him laugh. She could drive him wild in bed. She'd helped him make peace with his sister. *And* she was going to have his baby. Surely it was just a matter of time before he fell in love with her?

She crossed her fingers harder.

Ryan pulled to a halt and gestured to the simple brick bungalow. 'There it is.' The house he'd grown up in. He watched a myriad expressions cross Marianna's face. It was easier looking at her than looking at the house and experiencing the gut-wrenching loss of his grandmother all over again.

Avid curiosity transformed into a genuine smile. 'It's tiny!'

He glanced up and down the street. 'Once upon a time this entire suburb was composed of these two-bedroom miners' cottages.' Most had long since been knocked down, replaced with large, sprawling, modern homes.

'It's charming! It looks like a proper home…just like my cottage.'

He glanced back and waited for pain to hit him. It did, but it didn't crush him. He let out a careful breath.

Marianna swung to him. 'Don't you agree?'

She was right. Gran's house did remind him of her cottage.

'Was the garden this tidy when you were growing up?'

'Keeping this garden tidy was how I earned my pocket money.' That and stacking shelves at the local supermarket.

A teasing smile lit her lips and it tugged at his heart. 'So…were you a tearaway? A handful? Did you turn your grandmother's hair prematurely grey?'

He pressed his lips together as the old regrets rose up to bite him. 'Definitely a handful.' She didn't look at him, too interested in the house and garden, and he was glad for it. 'I was…rebellious.'

A laugh tinkled out of her. 'Surely not.'

He wanted to close his eyes, but he set his shoulders instead. Marianna ought to know the truth. 'As a teenager I fell in with a bad crowd. I was expelled from school.'

She spun around. Her mouth opened and closed, but no sound came out. He didn't blame her. 'My grandmother was a saint.'

'Expelled?'

He nodded.

'From school?'

'That's right.'

'But look at you now!' She suddenly seemed to realise that her shock might be making him uncomfortable. She tutored her face to something he figured she hoped was more polite. 'You, uh…certainly turned your life around.'

Not soon enough for his grandmother to have seen it.

She glanced back at the house and swallowed. 'I wish I could've met her.'

He hesitated for a moment before pulling his wallet from his pocket and removing a photo. Silently he handed it across to her.

She stared at it for a long moment, ran a finger across the face. 'You have her smile.'

He did?

She smiled at the photo before handing it back. 'I hope our baby has that smile.'

He hoped their child had Marianna's love of life, her exuberance, and her generosity.

He blinked, his head rearing back. Where had that come from? He put the photo away. Those things were all well and good as long as the child also had his logical thinking and the ability to read a situation quickly and accurately.

'Your grandmother helped you find your way again?'

Heaviness settled across his chest. 'In a manner of speaking. When she died, I realised I hadn't honoured her enough in life.'

She pressed a hand to her chest, her eyes filling. 'Oh!'

After a couple of moments she slid her arm through his and rested her head against his shoulder. It wasn't a sexy move but a companionable one and it immediately made him feel a little less alone.

'So you decided to honour her memory?'

He nodded.

'That was a good thing to do,' she whispered. 'I think she'd be proud of you.'

He hoped so. 'She always claimed I had a quick mind that I shouldn't waste.'

She eased away from him. 'I meant I think she'd be pleased with the way you're accepting your responsibilities as a prospective father.'

He swallowed.

'And with the way you're building a relationship with Rebecca.'

That would definitely have eased her heart. 'I…' He shrugged and then glanced at her helplessly. 'That thing you said yesterday about my distance hurting Rebecca, I…'

He dragged a hand back through his hair, that heaviness settling all the more firmly over him. He stared at the front door of his grandmother's old house and wished with everything he had that he could walk in there and talk with her one last time.

'You didn't know you were hurting her. It wasn't something you were doing on purpose.'

'But now that I do know I can't just...' He turned to face her fully. 'I can't ignore it. I can't keep hurting her.'

She reached up to touch his cheek. 'You're a good man, you know that?'

She made him feel like a good man. Rebecca's smile yesterday when they'd clinked wine glasses had made him feel like a good man too. Mari's hand against his cheek, her softness, made his heart start to pound, alerted all of his senses until they were dredged with the scent of her. It took all of his strength not to turn his mouth and press a kiss into the palm of her hand.

Kissing her would not be a good thing to do.

It'd be glorious.

He tried to shut that thought off.

She kept her hand there a beat and a half longer than she should've and it near killed him to resist her silent invitation. When she moved back a step, though, he had to grind back a groan of frustration.

'Thank you.'

He moistened suddenly dry lips. 'For what?'

'For showing me this.' She gestured to the house. 'For giving me a little insight into your background.'

She stared at him as if he were... As if he were a hero! His stomach lurched. He was no hero. And the last thing he needed was Marianna getting starry-eyed. *You should never have slept with her.* For the rest of their lives they'd be inextricably linked through their child. It only seemed right they should know each other, but... An ache stretched behind his eyes. He had to bring a halt to this right now. 'Friends, right?'

Her smile slipped a little and it was like a knife sliding in between his ribs.

He soldiered on. 'This sharing of confidences, it's what friends do, isn't it?' He hoped to God he wasn't leading her on.

She pursed her lips and then straightened with a nod. 'I've shared things with you I've never told another living soul.'

It made him feel privileged, honoured. It made him feel insanely suffocated too.

Lines of strain fanned around her mouth. He'd caused those. He took her arm, his chest burning. 'It must be time for that cake.' Cake would buck her up. She'd eventually realise that this—that friendship—would be for the best.

They found a funky bustling café on the main street and ordered tea and cake. When the waitress brought their order over, Marianna glanced at Ryan from beneath her lashes before fiddling with her teaspoon. 'You really don't mean to visit your mother today?'

Her too casual tone had him immediately on guard. 'Why is that so hard for you to believe?'

Her shoulder lifted. 'It's just that you've flown all this way...'

He'd done what he'd come here to do. His mother was recovering. As far as he was concerned, the sooner they left now, the better.

She stirred two packets of sugar into her tea, not meeting his eye. 'You never asked me what your mother and I spoke about that first day.'

He pulled his tea towards him. 'Is it relevant to anything?'

She sent him an exasperated glare.

He sipped his tea. He tried to get comfortable on his

chair. In the end he gave up. 'Fine! What did you and Stacey talk about?'

'You.'

He blinked. Not the baby?

'She told me the biggest regret of her life was leaving you with your grandmother.'

A ball of lead settled in the pit of Ryan's stomach. He moistened suddenly dry lips. He'd been doing everything he could to avoid being alone with his mother. He set his mug down with more force than necessary. 'No doubt she was just making excuses.'

'Oh, it wasn't anything like that.'

He suddenly frowned. 'If she made you feel uncomfortable, I'm very sorry.'

Her head shot up. 'It was nothing like that!'

A breath eased out of him. Good.

'I mean, I'm sure your mother likes me and everything, but, frankly, I doubt what I think of her matters to her one jot.'

He raised his hands, at a loss. 'So…'

'It was my opinion of you that mattered to her. She wanted to defend those…lone-wolf tendencies of yours.'

She'd what!

'And your opinion—what you think of her—that's what really mattered to her.'

He stared at her, unable to utter a word. If what Marianna said was true, and she had no reason to lie, then… then that meant Stacey cared for him. *That* was what Marianna was saying, whether she realised it or not. His breath jammed in his chest. On one level he knew Stacey must, but it had never been the kind of caring he'd been able to rely on, to trust in or to give himself over to.

For pity's sake, he didn't need the same family ties that Marianna did! He'd spent a lifetime guarding his privacy, his…isolation. He sat back. 'You want me to go and see her, don't you?' He glared. 'You want me to give her the opportunity to tell me what she told you?'

Marianna seemed impervious to his glare. She forked a piece of cake into her mouth and shrugged. 'What would it hurt?' she finally said.

What would it hurt? It'd... He suddenly frowned. What would it hurt?

'You want to bring our child to Australia to visit, yes?'

'Yes.'

'You'll be introducing our child to Stacey, yes?'

'Yes.'

'Don't you think the...tension between the two of you could be...awkward for our child?'

A tiny part of his heart clenched. 'You'd prefer it if I didn't let Stacey see our child?'

She huffed out a sigh and shook her head. 'No, Ryan, that's *not* what I'm saying.'

His heart started to thump, the blood thundering through his body. It hit him then that if he wanted to be the best father he could be, then making peace with his family would be necessary. He couldn't project his own issues with his mother onto his child. That would be patently unfair and potentially harmful to the child. He wanted to protect his son or daughter, help it grow up healthy in body and mind, not turn it into a neurotic mess.

Nausea surged through him. How did one go about fixing a relationship like his and Stacey's?

He glanced at the woman opposite. She'd tell him to listen to what Stacey had to say. She'd tell him to listen with an open heart. He passed a hand across his face. How did one unlock something that had been sealed shut for so long? It was a crazy idea. It—

Do it for the baby.

He stilled. If he wanted to do better than his parents had, he wouldn't run away when the going got tough. He pushed his shoulders back. It was time to man up and face his demons. It was time to lay them to rest.

'Fine.'

Marianna glanced up from her cake. 'Fine what?'

'I'll go and see Stacey.' Though, he had no idea what on earth he was going to say to her.

'You will?' she breathed.

There it was again, that look in her eye. He should never have brought her with him to Australia. *What had he been thinking?* He hadn't been thinking…at least, not with his head. He leaned towards her. 'Mari, even if I do patch up every rift between me and my family, that doesn't change things between us.'

She blinked.

He tried to choose his words carefully. 'It won't make me a family man. I'm never going to be the kind of man who can make you happy. You understand that, don't you?'

She tossed her head. 'Of course.'

His heart shrivelled to the size of a pea. He knew her too well, could see through her deceptions. She didn't believe him. She thought she could change him. She thought he'd offer her love, marriage, the works. If he didn't offer her those things would she keep his child from him?

A noose tightened about his throat, squeezing the air from his body. Marrying for the sake of their child would be a mistake—one that would destroy all of them. Anger slashed through him then. He should never have slept with her! And why couldn't she have kept her word? She'd sworn, *No promises!*

He shot to his feet. 'I'm going.'

'What, now?'

She started to rise too, but he shook his head. 'Stay and finish your cake.' He didn't give her time to reply, but turned on his heel and strode away.

* * *

Ryan tapped on the door to his mother's room, surprised to find her alone.

'You just missed Rebecca and Lulu,' she told him.

A stuffed cat with ludicrously long skinny legs had fallen behind the chair and he picked it up and stared at it, rather than at Stacey.

'Oh, dear.' Stacey sat up a little straighter in bed. 'You better take that home with you when you leave. It's Lulu's favourite. She'll be beside herself if she can't find Kitty Cat.'

That was why it looked familiar. He nodded. 'Right.'

'Colin should be along any minute. He promised to bring me a custard tart for afternoon tea.'

What was it with women and cake?

'Should I text and tell him to pick one up for you too?'

He shook his head and then realised he had barely said a word since walking into her room. 'No, thank you.' Eating custard tarts with his mother and her husband didn't fill him with a huge amount of enthusiasm. 'I…uh…how are you feeling?'

'Very well, thank you. The doctors are very happy with my progress.'

'That's good news.'

'The man you called in—the specialist—is a real wizard apparently. The rest of the staff have been whispering what an honour it is to see him in action.'

'Excellent.'

They glanced at each other and then quickly away again. An awkward silence descended. Ryan moved to stare out of the window.

'How is your Marianna doing?'

It wasn't so much the words as the tone that had an imaginary rope tightening around his neck and coiling down his body, binding him with suffocating tightness. He made an impatient movement to try and dispel the sense of constriction. 'She's not *my* Marianna.' And he wasn't *her* Ryan. The sooner everyone understood that, the better.

'Oh.'

He grimaced, wondering if he'd been too forceful.

'She's a lovely young woman.'

'She is.' But how on earth had he let her talk him into coming to see Stacey like this? 'We walked around to Gran's house this morning.'

'Ah.'

Ah? What the hell was that supposed to mean?

'Marianna encouraged you to come and see me today, didn't she?'

He halted his pacing to glance around at her. 'I don't think it was such a good idea.' He started for the door. 'I don't see the point in raking over the past.'

'Sit down, Ryan.'

His mother's voice held a note of command that made him falter. He turned and folded his arms, the stupid Kitty Cat still dangling from his hand.

'Please.'

He stared at the stuffed toy. He thought about Marianna. He knew how disappointed she'd be if he left now. He didn't want to disappoint her. At least, not on that head. He sat down.

'I want to tell you what I told Marianna when I first met her.'

He pulled in a breath. 'Which was?'

'That the biggest regret of my life was leaving you with your grandmother.'

He couldn't look at her, afraid his face would betray his disbelief and bitterness.

From the corner of his eye he saw her lean towards him. 'Will you listen? I mean *really* listen?'

With an effort he unclenched his hands from around the stuffed toy. 'Sure.'

She didn't speak for a long moment, but still he refused to look at her.

'It's hard to know where to start precisely, but we may as well start with the breakdown of my marriage to your father. You see, I thought it all my fault.'

That made him glance up and he tried not to wince at her pallor or the way she pleated and unpleated the bed sheet. 'Are you're sure you're up to this? Maybe we should wait until you've been sent home with a clean bill of health.'

'No!' She gave a short laugh. 'I'm under no illusion that I'll ever get another shot at this.'

He could just walk out, but Marianna's face rose in his mind. He cast another quick glance in his mother's direction. Walking out now might cause her more distress. He forced himself to remain in his seat and nod. 'Fine.'

'Ryan, I only meant to leave you with your grandmother for a couple of weeks. I needed to find a new place to live.'

'But Andrew—' his father '—had gone. There was no need for you to move out of the house as well.'

'I couldn't afford the rent on my own.'

'He would've had to pay you child maintenance. That would've helped.'

'I...I refused it.'

His head rocked back.

'As I said, I blamed myself for our split and it didn't seem right to me at the time to take his money.'

'You thought *that* in my best interests?'

'I thought that if I could just get a job...find a cheap place to rent, that I could make things perfect for us and...' She lifted a hand and then let it drop again. 'Getting a job proved harder than I expected. Eventually I managed to find one in the kitchen of a cruise ship, but it meant being away for months on end.'

Ryan folded his arms. 'You were gone for three years!'

'I know,' she whispered. 'I'm sorry. I saved every dollar I could and came home to make a life with you and—'

He leapt up to pace the room again. 'Let's not pretty it up. You met Colin on that cruise liner, got pregnant, and came back here to start a family with him.' *With Colin not with Ryan.*

'But you were part of our plans. We wanted you to live with us. It's just…when I came back it was as if you hated me.'

'I was seven years old. I barely knew you!'

'I cried for a week.'

'Poor you.'

She flinched and he knew he should feel ashamed of himself, but all he felt was a deep, abiding anger. 'From memory I don't recall you expending a whole lot of energy in an effort to win me over.'

'You brought all of my hidden insecurities to the surface,' she whispered. 'I told myself I deserved your anger and resentment. I didn't want to wreck things with Colin… and I had a new baby. I had to consider them. You were happy with your grandmother. It seemed best to leave you with her for a bit longer.'

A bit longer, though, had become forever.

He spun around and glared. 'Never once did you put my needs first.'

She paled. 'I didn't mean it to happen that way. I was crippled by guilt, a lack of confidence and low self-esteem. I never realised, though, that you would be the one to pay the price for those things.'

His lips twisted. In other words things had got tough and she hadn't been able to deal with them. But something in her face caught at him, tugged at some part of him that still wanted to believe in her.

Idiot!

He tried to smother the confusion that converged on him with anger.

'You're never going to forgive me, are you?'

'It's not about forgiveness.' His voice sounded cold even to his own ears. 'It's about trust. I don't trust you to ever put me and mine first. I don't trust you to ever have my back.'

She pressed both hands to her chest, her eyes filling. 'Heavens, your father and I really did a job on you, didn't we?'

'You taught me at a very young age how the world works. It's a lesson I haven't forgotten.'

'Son, please…'

He resented her use of the word.

'Tell me that you at least trust Marianna, that you don't keep her at arm's length.'

He gave a harsh bark of laughter. He wanted to trust Marianna. He couldn't deny it, but nor could he trust the impulse. An ache rose up through him—an ache for all of those things he could never have, all of those things Marianna wanted from him that he was unable to give. *Impossible!* The best way to deal with such delusions, the smartest, most logical course of action, was to deliver them a swift mortal blow.

He whirled back to Stacey. 'Trust? What you taught me, *Mother*, was the frailties and weaknesses of women. I'm ready for that. When motherhood and the responsibility of raising a child become too much for Marianna, I'll be there for my child. *I* won't abandon it.'

A gasp in the doorway had him spinning around. Marianna stood there pale and shaking, her eyes dark and bruised. Without another word, she turned on her heel and spun away.

CHAPTER ELEVEN

THE EXPRESSION IN Marianna's eyes pushed all thought from Ryan's mind. He surged forward and caught her wrist, bringing her to a halt. 'Wait, Mari—'

She swung back, her eyes savage. 'Don't call me that!'

He swallowed back a howl. 'You have to let me explain.'

'Explain? No explanation is necessary! You made yourself perfectly clear, and I have to say it was most enlightening to find what you really think of me and our current situation.'

It hit him then how badly he'd hurt her and it felt as if he'd thrust a knife deep into his own heart. He let her go and staggered back a step, wondering what on earth was happening to him, searching his mind for a way to make things right—to stop her from looking at him as if he were a monster.

'To think I thought... And all this time you've been thinking I would *abandon* our child?'

The jagged edges of her laugh sliced into him. Marianna might be impulsive, passionate and headstrong, but she was also full of love and loyalty. He need look no further than her relationships with her brothers for proof of that. The truth that had been growing inside him, the truth he'd been hiding from, slammed into him now, bowing his shoulders and making him fall back a step. She would never abandon her child. *Never.*

What right did he have to thrust his worst-case scenario onto her? How could he have been so stupid? So...*blind*?

His chest cramped. He'd held on to that mistaken belief as an excuse to justify remaining close to her. Because he'd wanted to be close to her.

She reached out and stabbed a finger to his chest. 'Stay away from me,' she rasped, her eyes bright with unshed tears. 'I will let you know when the baby is born, but you can't ask anything else of me.'

She wheeled away from him, making for the door. *He couldn't let her go!* He started after her, not sure what he could say but unable to bear losing sight of her. Rebecca, holding Lulu, stepped in front of him, bringing him up short. He couldn't thrust her aside, not when she was holding the baby. He made to go around her, but she laid a hand on his chest. 'You can't go after her when you look like that. You can't go after her without a plan.'

He lurched over to the chair and fell into it. A plan? He'd need a miracle!

'So it's true.' His mother's words broke into the darkness surrounding him. 'You're in love with her.'

He lifted his head and looked at her. In love with Marianna? Yes. The knowledge should surprise him more than it did. 'What do I do?' The words broke from him.

She didn't flinch from his gaze. 'We play to your strengths.' He could hardly believe she was still talking to him after all he'd just flung at her.

'You're a logical man. What does Marianna want?'

'Passion, an undying love, to never be bored.' The words left him without hesitation.

'Can you give her those things?'

He recalled the way her brothers had taunted him with their stupid Paulo joke. The fact, though, was there was a thread of truth running beneath that. What if, a month down the track, Marianna dumped him?

Darkness speared into him. For a moment it hurt to even breathe.

No! He shoved his shoulders back. He wouldn't give her the opportunity to get bored. He wouldn't let their life and relationship become dull. He loved her—heart and soul—

and if she'd just give him the chance he'd give her all the passion and intensity that her generous heart yearned for. He set his mouth—he'd make it his life's work.

He met his mother's gaze. 'I can give her those things.'

'You'll need to give a hundred per cent of yourself. Everything,' she warned.

Fine.

'I'm talking about your *time* here, Ryan.'

He frowned—what was she talking about?

'You're going to need to focus all your efforts on Marianna if you want to win her back.'

It hit him then—the Conti contract! If he signed on the dotted line, they'd need him on board from the week after next. He'd be working sixty-hour weeks for at least a month.

He swore. He scratched a hand through his hair. If he managed to smooth things over in the coming week with Marianna, maybe she'd let him off the hook for the following month and—

Fat chance! She'd demand all of him. Damn it! Why did she have to be so demanding? Why so unreasonable?

Suck it up, buddy. After the way you just acted, Marianna deserves to have any demand met, deserves proof of your sincerity.

Acid burned his throat. Panic rolled through him. What if he didn't succeed in smoothing things over?

What if she never forgave him?

He shot to his feet, paced the length of the room before flinging himself back into the chair. If she never forgave him he'd have lost both her and the Conti contract. Where was the sense in that?

He couldn't throw away all of that hard work. He couldn't just dismiss months' worth of nail-biting preparation. This was the contract that would set him up long term, would guarantee his livelihood for the rest of his working life and cement him as one of the business's leading lights. The Conti contract would prove once and for all that his grandmother's faith in him had been justified! He *couldn't* walk away.

Darkness descended over him, swallowing him whole. A moment later a single light pierced the darkness, making him lift his head. But what if he did win Marianna's forgiveness? What if she did agree to marry him, build a family with him…to love him? A yearning stronger than anything he'd ever experienced gripped him now. Wasn't winning Marianna's love worth any risk?

His heart pounded so hard he thought he'd crack a rib. No contract meant anything without Marianna and his child by his side. The knowledge filtered through him, scaring him senseless, but he refused to turn away from it. There'd be no point to any of his success—small or large— if he couldn't share it with Marianna and their child. He lifted his head. 'For Marianna, I'll make the time.'

Marianna stumbled into her cottage, clicking on all the lights in an attempt to push back the darkness, but it didn't work—not when the darkness was inside her. Forty hours of travel clung to her like a haze of grit. All she wanted to do was shower and fall into bed. The exhaustion, though, was worth not having had to clap eyes on Ryan again.

She halted in the doorway to her bedroom—the bed unmade, the sheets dishevelled from her and Ryan's lovemaking.

She dropped her bags and with a growl she pulled the sheets from the bed, resisting the urge to bury her face in them to see if they still carried a trace of Ryan's scent. She dumped them straight into the washing machine, set it going and then, leaving her clothes where they fell, she pushed herself under the stinging hot spray of the shower, doing what she could to rub the effects of travel and heartbreak from her body. She succeeded with the former, but it gave her little comfort.

Like a robot she dressed, remade the bed and forced herself to eat scrambled eggs. She didn't think she'd ever feel hungry again, but she had to keep eating for the baby's sake.

In the next moment she shot to her feet, the utter tidiness of the room setting her teeth on edge. With a growl, she pushed over the stack of magazines on the coffee table so they fell in an untidy sprawl. She messed up the cushions on the sofa, threw a dishtowel across the back of a dining chair—haphazardly. She didn't push her chair in at the table, and she slammed her plate and cutlery on the sink, but didn't wash them. She shoved the tea, coffee and sugar canisters on the kitchen bench out of perfect alignment.

None of it made her feel any better.

A tap on the door accompanied with a 'Marianna?' pulled her up short.

Nico. She swallowed. 'Come on through,' she called out.

He sauntered into the room. 'I saw the lights on and thought you must be home. You should've let us know to expect you. I'd have collected you from the airport.'

He pulled up short and took her in at a single glance. He'd always managed to do that, but she lifted her chin. She didn't want to talk about it.

'Alone?' he finally ventured.

She moved to fill the kettle. 'Yes.'

He was silent for a moment. 'How's Ryan's mother?'

'Out of danger and recovering beautifully.' She'd ring Stacey tomorrow to double-check that the scene in her hospital room hadn't had any detrimental effects on her recovery. And to assure her that she wouldn't prevent any of them from seeing the baby once it was born.

'That's good news.'

'It is.'

He paused again. 'How are you?'

She met his gaze and his expression gentled. 'Oh, Mari.'

She couldn't keep it together then. She walked into his arms and burst into tears, her heart shredding afresh with every sob. *Why couldn't Ryan love her?*

She refused to let the words fall from her lips, though, and she did what she could to pull herself together. She moved away, scrubbing the tears from her cheeks. 'I'm sorry. I'm tired.'

'You have nothing to apologise for.'

Was that true?

'I take it we shouldn't expect Ryan any time soon?'

Her brother deserved some form of explanation. 'I told him I'd let him know when the baby was born.'

Nico's eyes darkened in concern.

'It's okay.' She could see he didn't believe her and she didn't blame him. It wasn't okay, but there was nothing she could do about it. She just had to get on with it the best she could. 'We…we just messed up, that's all. And I find that I can't be…friends with him.'

He swore softly in Italian.

She managed a smile. 'It's okay, Nico. I'm a big girl. I will never denigrate him to my child. When we meet I will be polite and calm. That's what will be best for my darling *topolino*.'

He took her hand. 'But what's best for you?'

She could never tell him and Angelo all that had passed between her and Ryan. They'd have to find a way to be polite to him too. She didn't want to make that more difficult for them than it had to be. 'The baby has to come first. That's what matters to me.'

He swore again and his grip on her hand tightened. 'He's broken your heart!'

She moistened her lips and dredged up another smile.

'Some would say it's no less than I deserve for that trail of Paulos I've left in my wake.'

'I wouldn't agree.'

'I know that,' she whispered back, managing a genuine smile this time. Ryan might be a complete and utter idiot, but he had eased her fears about her brothers.

Time to change the subject. 'Where's Angelo?'

'Out with Kayla.'

'Naturally.'

They grinned at each other. 'We've missed you, Mari.'

She gave him a quick hug. 'I've missed you too.'

She made tea and they settled on the sofa. 'Now catch me up on all the news.'

Ryan turned the hire car in at the gates of Vigneto Cala-netti and made his way down the long drive. He'd been away less than three weeks, but he swore the grapevines were lusher and greener. The sky was blue and the day was warm, and inside his chest his heart pounded like a jackhammer.

Would she see him?

Please, God, let her spare him ten minutes. Please give him at least ten minutes to make his mark, to try and win her love.

He parked the hire car out at the front of Nico's villa. He wanted to race straight across to Marianna's cottage, but instinct warned him to check in with her brothers first. He wanted to do things right—by the book. He didn't want to make things worse for Marianna than he already had.

He recalled the last look she'd sent him, filled with pain and utter betrayal, and his gut clenched. *Please, God, let her be okay. Please let her and the baby be in good health.*

He knocked on the villa's wide-open door and tried to control the pounding of his heart. If Marianna should appear now...

He stared down the hallway, willing it to happen. A figure did appear. A male figure. It was what he'd expected, but he had to lock his knees against the disappointment. 'Nico,' he said in greeting as the other man strode down the hallway.

'Ryan.'

They stared at each other for a long moment. Nico bit back a sigh. 'She's not going to want to see you.'

'I can't say as though I blame her. I messed up.' Ryan pulled in a breath. 'I messed up badly. I won't retaliate if you want to take a swing at me.' He wouldn't even block the blow.

'I'm not going to hit you, but…whatever it is you want to say, can't you put it in an email?'

He moistened suddenly dry lips. 'I want to ask her to marry me.'

'For the sake of the baby?'

He shook his head. 'Not for the baby.'

'I see.'

Ryan suspected he did.

'I suppose I better take you to her.'

Ryan followed him through the house, out the French doors and across the terrace towards the outbuildings. 'You think I need an escort? I have no intention of harming a single hair on Mari's head.'

'I realise that, but my loyalty lies with my sister.' He cast a sidelong glance at Ryan. 'My one consolation is that you look in even worse shape than she does.'

Ryan seized Nico by the shoulders and dragged him to a halt, fear cramping his chest. 'She isn't well?' he croaked.

'Physically she's fine. She's taking very good care of her health.'

He released Nico, dragged a hand down his face and then continued to plant one foot in front of the other, his blood pounding a furious tempo through his body. 'That's…that's something.'

'It is.'

They walked through the shadowed cool of the vineyard's cellar door, skirting a group of tourists wine tasting, and out the back to where the great barrels of wine were stored, and then beyond that to the fermentation vats. That was when he saw her. He pulled up short and drank her in like a starving man.

In the soft light her hair fizzed about her face. He watched her direct a team of three workers to move barrels from one location to another and she then checked the gauges on the nearest vat. Her slim, vigorous form so familiar to him it made his arms ache with the need to hold her.

And then she turned and saw him. She froze. Her every muscle tightened and a bitter taste rose in his mouth. He did that to her. He made her tense and unhappy.

He thought she'd simply turn around and walk away. After several fraught moments, however, she lifted her chin and moved towards them. But her body that had once moved with such freedom and grace was now held tight and rigid. He had to bite back a protest. *How could he have done that to her?*

'I don't want you here, Ryan. Please go.'

Her pallor and the dark circles beneath her eyes beat at him. 'I can't say that I blame you.' He stared down at his hands and then back at her. 'I came to apologise. What I said—'

'Pah!' She slashed a hand through the air.

He tried to take her hand, but she snapped back a step, her eyes flashing.

He swallowed and nodded. 'What I said…I was wrong. I know you will love our child with your whole heart. I know you will never abandon it. And just because that's what I experienced in my family...' He shook his head. 'I had no right tarring you with the same brush. It was an excuse I was hiding behind. It let me justify to myself the amount of time I was spending with you. It helped me keep my distance. I...I didn't realise I'd been lying to myself, though, until you walked out of Mum's hospital room.'

She folded her arms and glanced away, tapped a foot. 'How is your mother?'

'Excellent. She sends her love. So does Rebecca.'

She finally glanced back. 'I accept your apology, Ryan, but I'm afraid you and I are never going to be friends.'

'I don't want to be friends.'

She paled and eased back another step. 'I'm glad we have that sorted.' Spinning on her heel, she stalked away.

'Damn it, Marianna!' Had she wilfully misunderstood him? 'I want a whole lot more than friendship,' he hollered to her back. 'I want it all—love, marriage, babies...a family.' He punctuated each word with a stab in the air, but she didn't turn around. *With you!'*

She didn't so much as falter. He shook off Nico's restraining hand and set off after her, muttering a curse under his breath. He waited, though, until she'd reached her stone cottage before catching her up.

She wheeled on him. 'Get out of my house!'

'I'll leave once you hear me out.'

'I've heard enough!'

'You've only heard what you want to hear!'

'Mari?' Nico stood in the doorway, one eyebrow raised.

Ryan planted his feet all the more solidly. No one was kicking him off the premises until he'd done what he'd come here to do.

Marianna's eyes flashed as if she'd read that intention in his face. She glanced at her watch. 'If his car is still here in ten minutes, come back with Angelo.'

With a nod, Nico left.

She was going to give him ten minutes?

He couldn't speak for a moment. He had to fight the urge to haul her into his arms and kiss her. If he did any such thing he'd deserve to be thrown out.

She remained where she stood, bathed in the sunlight that poured in at the kitchen windows, tapping her foot. She glanced at her watch as if counting down every second of his allotted ten minutes.

He missed her smile and her teasing. He even missed her untidiness and her temper. He'd rather she threw something at him than this *nothingness*.

'Since you left,' he started, 'I've been in a misery of guilt, a misery of mortification at my stupidity, and a misery of loss.'

'Good.' She lifted her chin. 'Why should you be exempt? I've been miserable on my baby's behalf that its father is such a jerk.'

His head throbbed. What was he doing here other than making a fool of himself? He should turn around and leave. She loathed him and he couldn't blame her. She was going to laugh at him; throw his love back in his face.

It's no less than you deserve.

He pulled in a breath and steeled himself. 'I love you, Mari.' He had to say what he'd come here to say.

Her eyes narrowed. 'I told you not to call me that.'

He ground his teeth together, unclenched them to say, 'I love you, *Marianna*.'

She moved in to peer up into his face. 'Piffle.' She stalked past him to the dining table, but she didn't sit.

'I want to marry you.'

She turned at that and laughed. He rocked back, her expression running him through like a sword. He locked his knees. 'You think it funny?'

'Absolutely hilarious!' But her flashing eyes and fingers that curved into claws told a different story. 'You've lost whatever advantage you think you had. You believe I'm going to withhold your child from you and this is your way to try and claw back all you've lost. I'm sorry, Ryan, but it's not going to work.'

The last puff of hope eased out of him in a single breath.

'You needn't worry, though.' She tossed her hair. 'I'm not going to stop you from seeing our child, but the visitation arrangements will be on my terms.'

He moistened his lips. 'This isn't about the baby, Mari.'

She turned away with a shrug, not even bothering to correct him—as if it no longer mattered to her what he called her. She glanced at her watch.

This couldn't be it! Where would he find that strength to walk away from her?

Think! How could he win her heart? *What is it she wants?*

He pulled up short. Passion, an undying love, and to never be bored—those were the things Marianna wanted. *Could* he give them to her?

He pulled in a breath and channelled his inner thespian. 'You want to know what I've been doing for the last two weeks?' He roared the words and she started and turned around, her eyes wide.

He stalked over to where she stood and stabbed a finger at her. 'I've been working on my relationships with my family so I'd have something of worth to offer you! And you want to laugh in my face and act as if it's nothing when it's been one of the most difficult and…and frightening things I've ever done?'

She moistened her lips and edged away. 'I didn't intend to belittle your…um, efforts. I'm… I'm sure they've been very admirable.'

'My efforts!' He threw both hands in the air and then paced the length of the room. He prayed to God he wasn't frightening her. He hated yelling at her, but if that was what she needed as proof of his love, then he'd do it.

He swung back to find her biting her thumbnail and staring at him, a frown in her eyes.

'If I'm correct it's not my efforts being disparaged but my intentions!'

He glared at her as hard as he could. She pulled her hand away from her mouth and straightened. 'You come in here and say outlandish things and expect me to believe you?'

'Saying *I love you* is not outlandish!' How could he make her see that? His gaze landed on the vase her brothers had given her. He grabbed it and lifted it above his head. 'I can't live without you, Mari! How can I get that through your thick skull?'

Marianna's bottom lip started to wobble, though she did her best to stop it. 'You're…you're going to throw a vase at me?'

He stared at her, and then rolled his shoulder. 'Of course not.' He lowered the vase, grimaced. 'I was going to throw it on the floor as evidence of my…high emotion.'

She couldn't drag her gaze from him. It hurt her to look at him, but she had a feeling it'd hurt more to look away.

I can't live without you!

She swallowed. 'Please don't break the vase. I…it has sentimental value.' Whenever she looked at it, it reminded her of her and Ryan's dinner with her brothers here in this cottage, and the conversation she and Ryan had had afterwards…how kind he'd been…and gentle.

She much preferred that Ryan to the shouting, angry man who'd just raged at her. It occurred to her now that his calm and his control had given her a safe harbour—that was what she wanted, not a stormy sea.

Ryan set the vase back on the table just as her brothers

burst into the room—their bodies tense, fists clenched and eyes blazing. Had they heard him yelling at her?

Angelo seemed to grow in size. 'Nobody speaks to our sister like that!'

They moved towards Ryan with unmistakable intent. 'No!' she screeched. Ryan's time might be up, but... She did the only thing she could think of. She ran across the room and hurled herself into Ryan's arms. He caught her easily, as if she weighed nothing. He held her as if she were precious.

Her heart pounded and it was all she could do not to melt against him. 'Turn me around,' she murmured in his ear.

He turned so that she could face her brothers. They glared at her, hands on hips. 'Go away,' she ordered.

They didn't move.

She tightened her hold on Ryan's neck, loving the feel of all his hardness and strength pressed against her. 'I have things under control here.'

Nico raised an eyebrow. Angelo snorted.

She widened her eyes, made them big and pleading. 'Please?' she whispered.

Muttering, they left.

Two beats passed. Marianna swallowed. 'You can put me down now.'

'Do I have to?'

'Yes.'

The minute he set her feet back on the ground, she moved away from him—put the table between them. The flare of his nostrils told her that her caution hurt him. She didn't want to hurt him. She loved him with every fibre of her being, but she couldn't accept anything less than his whole heart in return.

The silence stretched, pulling her nerves taut. She wiped damp palms down her trousers. 'You have to understand that I find your declaration a little unbelievable.'

'Why?'

'Lone wolf,' she whispered.

He adjusted his stance. 'That was a lie I told myself to make me feel better. It doesn't matter what happens today, I'm never going to be a lone wolf again. That all changed when I thought I'd lost you.'

He strode around the table and to her utter amazement dropped to his knees in front of her. He seized her hands and held them to his lips, and then his brow. Her heart hammered so hard she thought it'd pound a path right out of her chest.

'I'm nothing without you, Mari.'

And there it was, the thrill she couldn't suppress whenever he said her name.

'What I feel for you is so encompassing, so overwhelming it makes the thought of living without you unbearable. It's why I'd been resisting it so long and why I fought against it so fiercely. But it's no use fighting it any more or hiding from the truth. Marianna, you make me want to be a better man.'

He glanced up at her and what she saw in his face pierced her to the very marrow.

'Knowing you has brought untold treasures to my life—a baby.'

She nodded. He would cherish their child.

'You've shown me the way back to my family.'

Had he really reconciled with his mother? What about his father and the rest of his siblings?

'You've given me a vision of what my life could be like.'

He hauled himself upright, kissed the tips of her fingers before releasing her hands and stepping back. 'I understand your hesitation. I understand that you might see me as a poor bet.' He glanced at his watch and his chest heaved. 'I've taken up enough of your time. I should give you the space to consider all that I've said.'

He turned to leave and it was the hunch in his shoulders, the way they drooped in utter defeat that did it—that blasted away the last of her doubts. She pressed a hand to her heart, her pulse leaping every which way. 'You really do love me.'

He swung back, hope alive in his face. She could feel her face crumple. 'But you yelled at me.'

And then she burst into tears.

Ryan swooped across and pulled her into his arms, holding her as if he never meant to let her go. 'I only yelled at you to prove that I really do love you, to prove I could give you the passion that you said you've always wanted.'

She eased back, scrubbed a hand across her face. 'I hated it! I'm an idiot forever thinking that's what I wanted.'

He swiped his thumbs across her cheeks. 'You're not an idiot.'

'I love you,' she whispered.

He nodded gravely. '*That* might make you an idiot.'

'Are you going to break my heart?'

He shook his head. 'I'm going to take the very best care of your heart. I'm going to do everything within my power to make you happy.' The tension in his shoulders eased a fraction. 'I'm going to be very relieved if not yelling at you is on that list, though.' He smoothed his hands down the sides of her face. 'I hated yelling at you. I'm sorry it upset you.'

She wound her arms around his neck. 'Then I'm not an idiot. I'm the luckiest woman in the world.'

Her smile started up in the centre of her and reached out to every extremity. 'You really love me?' It wasn't that she didn't believe him. She just wanted to hear him say it again.

'I really love you.' His grin was all the assurance she needed.

'I really love you too,' she said, just in case he needed to hear it again as well.

'Will you marry me?'

A lump promptly lodged in her throat, momentarily robbing her of the ability to speak.

'I meant to go down on one knee and propose properly.'

She swallowed the lump. 'Don't you dare let go of me yet.'

'That's what I was hoping you'd say.'

This tough loner of a man had really trusted his heart and happiness to her? She touched his face in wonder. He let out a ragged breath. Plastered as closely as she was to him, she could feel how tightly he held himself in check. 'That…and yes,' he rasped.

She came back to herself with a start, the uncertainty in his eyes catching at her. 'Yes.'

He blinked.

'Yes, I will marry you. Yes, I will keep your heart safe. Yes, we'll build a wonderful family together, and grow old together and be generous with our love to all who want and need it.'

'You mean that?'

She reached up on tiptoe to cup his face. 'I love you, Ryan. How could you possibly think I would want anything else?'

'Can I kiss you now?' he groaned.

'In just a moment.'

He groaned louder.

'I want you to tell me how you reconciled with your mother…and father?' He nodded at the question in her voice. 'How did that all come about? I mean, you were so angry with them.'

He lifted her in his arms and strode across to the sofa with her, settling her in his lap as if she belonged there, as if he had no intention of letting her go anywhere else for a very long time. It sent another delicious thrill racing

through her. She pressed a kiss to his cheek. 'I'm not saying you weren't entitled to your anger.'

'But it was time to let it go.'

She let out a breath she hadn't realised she'd been holding.

'And I discovered that forgiveness is an act of hope.'

Her heart soared. 'Oh, Ryan, I'm so glad.'

'I'd made such a terrible mistake with you and the
thought of not winning your forgiveness was a torment.
The thought I might be putting my parents through a similar torment shook some sense into me.' He met her gaze.
'I couldn't live with that thought.'

Of course he couldn't. He had a heart that was too big
and generous for that.

'When you left I was beside myself.'

He would've been. She could see that now.

'And they all rallied around me, so worried for me. It
made me realise that they do all care for me.'

'They do.'

He touched her cheek. 'I'd have never realised if it
wasn't for you.'

She ran her hands across his shoulders and down his
arms, revelling in the sculpted strength of him. 'We're
good for each other, Ryan. I've heard of people finding
their soul mates, I knew that kind of love existed. I knew
it couldn't be wrong to hold out for it.'

'My soul mate,' he said as if testing the idea on his
tongue.

'Your rationality balances out my flights of fancy.'

'Your sense of fun balances out my seriousness.'

'Your control balances out my, uh…lack of restraint.'

He ran a finger down the V made by the collar of her
shirt, making her shiver. 'I promise never to yell at you
again.'

'But…' She lifted one shoulder. 'What if I'm testing

your patience beyond endurance, being stubborn and head-strong?'

He pressed a kiss to the tender spot behind her ear. 'I'll find a different way to get your attention.'

She arched against him. 'Mmm, I like the sound of that. I promise never to throw another vase at you.'

He eased back, a smile in his eyes. 'I don't know. That kind of thing keeps a man on his toes.' His eyes darkened. 'Mind you, I'll be doing my very best to not provoke you into throwing vases.'

'Ryan?'

'Yes?'

'You can kiss me now.'

His grin became teasing, wolfish, and a thrill shot through her. His mouth descended towards hers. He stopped millimetres short. 'Do you have to go back to work this afternoon?'

Her breath hitched. 'Not unless I want to.'

'You're really not going to want to,' he promised.

She tilted her chin, a smile building in the depths of her. 'Prove it.'

So he did.

* * * * *

LET'S TALK

Romance

For exclusive extracts, competitions
and special offers, find us online:

f facebook.com/millsandboon

⊙ @millsandboonuk

𝕐 @millsandboon

Or get in touch on 0844 844 1351*

For all the latest titles coming soon, visit
millsandboon.co.uk/nextmonth

2